A Text Book Of

ENVIRONMENTAL BIOLOGY AND TOXICOLOGY

T.Y.B.Sc. Zoology, ZY-334 : Paper IV, Semester III
As Per New Revised Syllabus with Effect from June 2016-17

Dr. Kishore R. Pawar
M.Sc., Ph.D.
Former Principal,
Karmveer Abasaheb Alias,
N.M. Sonawane Arts, Science and Commerce
College, Satana. District - NASHIK.

Dr. Ashok E. Desai
M.Sc., Ph.D.
Associate Professor,
P.G. Department of Zoology,
KTHM College, NASHIK.

NIRALI
PRAKASHAN
ADVANCEMENT OF KNOWLEDGE

N1822

Environmental Biology and Toxicology (T.Y.B.Sc. Zoology)   ISBN 978-93-51647-81-2

Second Edition : June 2017

©   : Authors

Published By :   Polyplate

NIRALI PRAKASHAN

Abhyudaya Pragati, 1312, Shivaji Nagar,
Off J.M. Road, PUNE – 411005
Tel - (020) 25512336/37/39, Fax - (020) 25511379
Email : niralipune@pragationline.com

☞ DISTRIBUTION CENTRES

PUNE

Nirali Prakashan : 119, Budhwar Peth, Jogeshwari Mandir Lane, Pune 411002, Maharashtra
Tel : (020) 2445 2044, 66022708, Fax : (020) 2445 1538
Email : bookorder@pragationline.com, niralilocal@pragationline.com

Nirali Prakashan : S. No. 28/27, Dhyari, Near Pari Company, Pune 411041
Tel : (020) 24690204 Fax : (020) 24690316
Email : dhyari@pragationline.com, bookorder@pragationline.com

MUMBAI

Nirali Prakashan : 385, S.V.P. Road, Rasdhara Co-op. Hsg. Society Ltd.,
Girgaum, Mumbai 400004, Maharashtra
Tel : (022) 2385 6339 / 2386 9976, Fax : (022) 2386 9976
Email : niralimumbai@pragationline.com

☞ DISTRIBUTION BRANCHES

JALGAON

Nirali Prakashan : 34, V. V. Golani Market, Navi Peth, Jalgaon 425001,
Maharashtra, Tel : (0257) 222 0395, Mob : 94234 91860

KOLHAPUR

Nirali Prakashan : New Mahadvar Road, Kedar Plaza, 1st Floor Opp. IDBI Bank
Kolhapur 416 012, Maharashtra. Mob : 9850046155

NAGPUR

Pratibha Book Distributors : Above Maratha Mandir, Shop No. 3, First Floor,
Rani Jhanshi Square, Sitabuldi, Nagpur 440012, Maharashtra
Tel : (0712) 254 7129

DELHI

Nirali Prakashan : 4593/21, Basement, Aggarwal Lane 15, Ansari Road, Daryaganj
Near Times of India Building, New Delhi 110002
Mob : 08505972553

BENGALURU

Pragati Book House : House No. 1, Sanjeevappa Lane, Avenue Road Cross,
Opp. Rice Church, Bengaluru – 560002.
Tel : (080) 64513344, 64513355,Mob : 9880582331, 9845021552
Email:bharatsavla@yahoo.com

CHENNAI

Pragati Books : 9/1, Montieth Road, Behind Taas Mahal, Egmore,
Chennai 600008 Tamil Nadu, Tel : (044) 6518 3535,
Mob : 94440 01782 / 98450 21552 / 98805 82331,
Email : bharatsavla@yahoo.com

niralipune@pragationline.com | www.pragationline.com
Also find us on 🅕 www.facebook.com/niralibooks

Preface ...

It is a matter of great pleasure to present this book **"Environmental Biology and Toxicology"** which has been written in accordance with the new syllabus to be implemented from June 2016-17 of the Third Year B.Sc. of Zoology.

The new syllabus covers the topics like Environmental Biology, Ecosystem, Environmental Pollution, Environment and Development, Natural Resources and Conservation, Wildlife Management, Toxicants and Toxicity and Toxicants of Public Health and Hazards. These various topics are described in an easy, clear, comprehensive and systematic manner.

The text book has been presented in simple and lucid language. Several illustrative figures have been included in each chapter which will help the students to grasp the ideas quickly and easily. We are deeply indebted to the authors and publishers whose book we referred while preparing this book.

We wish to express our appreciation to Mr. Dineshbhai Furia, Mr. Jignesh Furia and entire staff of Nirali Prakashan for bringing out this book in time.

We would greatly appreciate constructive criticism and suggestions from our colleagues and students.

July 2016

Prin. Dr. Kishore R. Pawar
Prof. Dr. Ashok E. Desai

Syllabus ...

Total Lectures: 48

1. Environmental Biology   (02)

Introduction - Definition, Basic Concepts and Scope

2. The Ecosystem   (08)

2.1   Definition, Abiotic and Biotic Components and their Interrelationship

2.2   Energy Flow in Ecosystem and flow Models

2.3   Major Ecosystems: (a) Natural Ecosystem e.g. Fresh Water, Forest, (b) Artificial Ecosystem. e.g. Cropland

2.4   Food Chain in Ecosystem and Food Web

2.5   Ecological Pyramids

3. Environmental Pollution   (12)

3.1   Definition and Types of Pollution

3.2   Pollutants, Types of Pollutants (Metallic, Gaseous, Acids, Alkalis, Biocides)

3.3   **Air Pollution:** Definition, Sources of Air Pollution and their Effects

3.4   Air Pollution and its Relevance with the following:

    3.4.1   Acid Rain

    3.4.2   Greenhouse Effect

    3.4.3   Ozone Layer Depletion

3.5   **Water Pollution:** Definition, Sources of Water Pollution and their Effects on Ecosystem

    I.   Sewage

    II.   Industrial Wastes

    III. Agricultural Wastes

3.6   **Land/Soil Pollution:** Definition, Sources of Land/Soil Pollution and their Effects

3.7   **Noise Pollution:** Definition, Sources of Noise Pollution and their Effects and Control Measures.

4. Environment and Development (05)

4.1 Bioindicators and Environmental Monitoring

4.2 Environmental Challenges in Land Degradation, Population Explosion, Urbanisation and Industrialisation

5. Natural Resources and Conservation (05)

5.1 Renewable and Non-renewable Resources

5.2 Soil Conservation

5.3 Forest Conservation

5.4 Energy Source: Conventional and Non-conventional

6. Wildlife Management (05)

6.1 Definition, Causes of Wildlife Depletion

6.2 Importance of Wildlife Management in India

6.3 Endangered Species, Vulnerable Species, Rare Species and Threatened Species

6.4 Wildlife Conservation

7. Toxicants and Toxicity (07)

7.1 Definition of Toxicology, Scope and Branches

7.2 Types of Toxicants

7.3 Factors influencing Toxicity (pH, Temperature, Reproductive Status, Age, Physiological State

7.4 Dose, LD_{50}, LC_{50}

8. Toxicants of Public Health and Hazards (04)

Pesticides, Heavy Metals, Fertilizers, Food Additives and Radioactive Substances.

***

Contents ...

***

Chapter **1** ...

Environmental Biology

Contents ...

1.1 Aim and Scope of Ecology

1.1.1 Introduction

Ecology is one of the important branches of science which is also called as Environmental Biology. This is one of the young branches which is connected with the organisms and their environment. The name ECOLOGY is derived from two Greek words i.e. *Oikos* = House and *Logos* = Study. Therefore, the studies of inter-relationships of organisms with their physical and biotic environment can be called as Ecology.

E. P. Odum (1963) defined Ecology as structure and function of nature.

Earnst Haeckel (1866) defined Ecology as a branch of science which deals with the total relationships of organisms to both their organic and inorganic environment.

All organisms live in environment. The structure, growth, reproduction etc. of an organism are controlled by the environmental factors like Soil, Temperature, Water, Nutrients in the soil etc. Along with these factors the organisms themselves interact with each other. Structure and numbers of organic community of a given area depends upon environmental and biotic factors which are present in that area.

In the early days, ecologists used to separate study of ecology into plant ecology and animal ecology just like biology. However, modern ecologists feel that as the environments which govern the life of plants and the animals is the same. Both the branches of ecology i.e. animal ecology and plant ecology must be unified and studied as a whole.

Broadly, ecology can be divided into: (i) Autecology and (ii) Synecology. Autecology is a branch of ecology in which we study an individual species or its population in relation to its biotic (living) and abiotic (non-living) environment. In this branch, one will study a species of organism or its population throughout its life, its interactions with the environment and among themselves. For example: In a forest, if we study the population of a rat or rat species, its increase in number, food taken by it, its relation to plants and other animals living in that locality, its birth rate, death rate and their interactions within their own population it is autecological study.

Synecology is a branch of ecology which deals with the structure, number, development, distribution and interactions of organic community of a locality with the environment and amongst themselves as a whole. For the synecological study, the autecological knowledge of individual species is necessary. Thus, autecological studies are necessary to understand the synecology of a given community. If we study the different plants and animals living in a forest and their interrelationships with the environment and among themselves called a synecology of forest.

Based on level of organisation, kinds of environment and taxonomic position, ecology can be subdivided into many branches. Some of the important divisions are as given below:

(1) **Habitat Ecology:** Study of different habitats of biosphere (life supporting zone) is called as habitat ecology e.g. Marine ecology, Freshwater ecology, Forest ecology, Cropland ecology, Grassland ecology, Desert ecology etc.

(2) **Population Ecology or Demecology:** Study of populations of different species of a ecosystem concerning their birth rate, death rate and the different factors affecting their growth in size and number called as population ecology.

(3) **Ecosystem Ecology:** Deals with analysis of ecosystem in relation to structure and function, the interrelationships of components of ecosystem. The reciprocal relationships of living and non-living components of ecosystem are studied in detail in this branch.

(4) **Conservation Ecology:** On the planet earth, the different raw material like coal, water, oil, minerals etc. which are required for the welfare of man are limited. They must be properly used, if they are misused future or man's life will be in danger. To avoid the difficulties for the future generations we have to plan the utilization of the resources properly. In this branch of ecology, we study the proper management methods of natural resources like land, water, forest, sea, oil, minerals etc. for the benefit of the human beings.

(5) **Production Ecology:** This branch deals with the gross or net production of different ecosystems, like freshwater ecosystem, marine (sea) ecosystem, agriculture, horticulture and proper methods of management of these ecosystems so that maximum production can be achieved by human-being.

(6) **Radiation Ecology:** In this branch, we study the effects of radiation and radioactive substances on organisms and environment. In recent years, man is establishing a number of nuclear reactors to get more and more energy for his factories etc. This is leading to side effects and accumulation of dangerous radioacitve waste in large proportions. If this is not properly managed the existence of human race will be in

danger. Radiation ecology studies help us to understand the problems and possible remedies for the same.

(7)   Paleoecology: With the help of fossil studies (Palaentological) we can have idea about the nature and structure of the organisms living in the geological past. In this branch of ecology, we study about the different forms living in different times in the past and the environment prevailing at that time. We also study how these life forms and the environment changed from time to time due to some specific factors. This knowledge help us as a guide to the future changes which we may try to bring in nature to suit the betterment of human life.

(8)   Gene Ecology or Ecological Genetics: In nature, we find that particular species of a genera are having capacity to survive and other fail to live and become extinct. This has been found to be due to the presence of particular genes present in these surviving species. At the same time we find that some species have a sort of genetic plasticity more than the other species. This helps them in struggle for existence. In gene ecology, we study the relationship of genes and their adaptability in nature.

(9)   Space Ecology: This is one of the most modern and latest branches, of ecology. Man is trying to reach to other planets which are located far away from earth. For this he has to travel millions of kilometres for a number of days. In this branch of ecology, construction and usage of partial or complete regenerating systems in space ships and effects of space travel on the organisms are studied.

(10)   Taxonomic Ecology: This branch of ecology is connected with different taxonomic groups. This branch can be subdivided into many branches viz. Plant ecology, Animal ecology, Microbial ecology, Vertebrate ecology etc.

(11)   Human Ecology: This branch deals with mainly the relationship between man and his environment.

1.1.2 Scope and Significance of Ecology

Ecology is a complex branch of biology which is related to almost all branches of science. Ecologist uses the knowledge of Chemistry, Physics, Botany, Zoology, Microbiology, Mathematics, Statistics, Morphology, Anatomy, Taxonomy, Cytology, Genetics, Physiology, Biochemistry etc. He also requires the knowledge of usage of Radioactive isotopes, spectrometer, calorimeters, pH-meters, computers etc. to understand the ecological problems.

An Ecologist must have a knowledge of uses of pesticides, detergents, sewage disposal, power dams, urban development, atomic radiations etc. to understand the ecological problems.

In recent days, man for his own needs started changing the natural communities thinking that it will result in giving better life for human beings. Expecting major benefits man changed the environment, but this many times created more problems than it solve. Thus, unplanned (with half knowledge) changes brought about by man resulted in Ecological Boomerangs or Ecological Backlashes. Few examples will make it clear that how the ecological boomerangs resulted due to the unplanned interference of man in nature.

(1) In our own country the thick forest were cut down to meet the needs of agriculture, timber, fuel, food for cattle etc. Thus, the clearing of forests increase the agricultural land to increase the food needed for our ever increasing population. But this deforestation resulted in constant floods of major rivers and soil erosion in the low areas. Thus, every year country is losing property worth of some crores and human lives due to the floods.

(2) Industrial expansion in almost all countries with a view to benefit the population has resulted in many problems like air and water pollution, increase in the urban population formation of slum areas causing social unrest and health problems.

If we study closely the civilized man's actions which are aimed for benefit of man have resulted in creating problems which he can not solve. So it is essential for every country and man to think and study closely the ecological aspects of the natural communities before trying to change the natural systems. Unless we are sure about the after effects and results we must not play with the natural ecosystems if not the existence of man itself may be in danger.

Points to Remember

- Ecology is also called environmental biology.
- Odum defined ecology as a structure and function of nature.
- Soil, water, temperature, light etc. are environmental factors.
- Autecology and synecology are two branches of ecology.
- There are many branches of ecology such as habitat ecology, population ecology, production ecology, paleoecology, space ecology, human ecology etc.
- Ecology is related to botany, zoology, chemistry, microbiology, statistics, mathematics.

Questions

1. Define the term ecology. Describe the different branches of ecology.
2. Add note on scope and significance of ecology.

Chapter 2...

The Ecosystem

Contents ...

2.1 Introduction

The term ecosystem was first coined by A. G. Tansley in 1935. The term is derived from two words namely *eco* and *system*. Eco refers to environment and system refers to an interacting, inter-dependent complex. Tansley defined ecosystem as *"the system resulting from the integration of all the living and non-living factors of the environment."* An ecosystem is a basic functional ecological unit. It consists of living organisms called biotic factors and non-living substances or abiotic factors. Ecosystem is an interacting system where biotic and abiotic factors interact to produce an exchange of materials between the living and non-living factors. Thus, structural and functional system of communities and their environment is called *ecosystem*.

The central theme of ecosystem concept is that at any place where an organism lives, there is continuous interaction between the living and non-living components. i.e. between the plants, animals and their environment. They continuously produce and exchange materials. This means, that these are mechanisms for continuous absorption of materials by organisms for the purpose of production of organic materials and their conversion back into inorganic form, much of which is then released back into the environment.

2.2 Structure of Ecosystem

Any ecosystem is formed of two components namely abiotic and biotic components.

2.2.1 Abiotic or Non-living Components

These are non-living factors of the environment. Abiotic factors include inorganic substances such as P, S, C, N, H etc. Water, soil, air, light, temperature, minerals, climate, pressure etc. are the important abiotic factors. For the survival of the biotic factors, abiotic factors are essential.

Abiotic or non-living factors are essential for the survival of living organisms. They are:
(1) Water (2) Light (3) Temperature (4) Gases (5) Humidity and (6) Soil.

(1) Water

Water is essential for life and without water life is impossible. The water available to plants and animals is due to rainfall. It occupies 71% of the earth surface in the form of fresh water, marine water and estuarine water. The water circulating between atmosphere and earth surface is called hydrologic cycle. The water is in the form of liquid, solid and vapour state. Water of the earth's surface reaches to atmosphere by evaporation and transpiration. Water plays an important role in the ecosystem which affects the distribution, growth and activities of organisms in it. The amount of rainfall and evaporation and their ratio determines the types of vegetation growing in an ecosystem. Depending on the availability of water, plants are called hydrophytes, xerophytes or mesophytes. Xerophytes grow in regions of water scarcity. The animals living in these conditions are called **desert animals**. Hydrophytic plants occur in water and the animals that live in water are called **aquatic animals**. According to the habitat, the plants and animals show certain morphological modifications. For example, xerophytes grow in conditions of very dry air, high temperature, strong winds, high transpiration rate and high rate of evaporation. Hence, xerophytic trees show very deep and long roots to absorb water. Plants may be succulents or with spines, reduced leaves and leaves bearing thick cuticle. The desert animals absorb water by skin spines. e.g. Lizard. Certain animals like camel can store large quantity of water in the stomach. The desert animals are nocturnal and burrow deep into the soil, during the day to escape the excessive heat and dryness. Desert animals move faster than other land animals.

(2) Humidity

The amount of water vapour or moisture in the air is called *humidity*. Humidity is of two types, namely, relative humidity and absolute humidity. The relative humidity is the ratio of the actual amount of water vapour in the air to the amount that can be held in the air, at a particular temperature and pressure. Absolute humidity is defined as the amount of water vapour or moisture present in the air.

Humidity plays an important role, as it affects the life of plants and animals indirectly. In warm and humid regions, birds and mammals tend to be darker in colour than those inhabiting in the cold and dry regions. As the air warms up, the relative humidity drops because warm air can hold more moisture than cool air. Generally, relative humidity is low during day time and high at night.

Both excessive and deficient moisture can be harmful to organisms. Low relative humidity increases the loss of water in plants through transpiration. Hence, during winter, they shed leaves. Some plants as orchids, lichens, mosses, etc. make direct use of atmospheric moisture. In fungi and other microbes, it plays an important role in germination of spores and subsequent stages in life cycle.

Humidity is greatly influenced by the intensity of solar radiation, temperature, altitude, wind, exposure, cover and water status of soil. Relative humidity is measured by an instrument called the psychrometer or by paper strip hygrometer, or thermo-hydrograph.

(3) Temperature

Temperature is a physicochemical, ecological abiotic factor. Temperature can be defined as *the intensity aspect of heat*. It is in the form of energy called thermal energy. Temperature is measured in Fahrenheit (°F) or Centigrade (°C). The biosphere obtains its thermal energy mainly from the sun in the form of solar radiation. Temperature affects all forms of life. It influences the various stages of life activities, such as growth, metabolism, reproduction, movement, distribution, behaviour, death, etc. Temperature is a variable factor. It varies from place to place and from time to time. During the day, temperature is high and at night, the temperature is low. Temperature is high at sea-level and low at high altitudes. It is high at the equator and low in the polar regions. Temperature is more in terrestrial habitat and low in the aquatic habitat.

Within a limited range of temperature, the rate of biochemical reactions doubles with every 10°C rise in temperature. This is known as Van't Hoff's rule. The temperature exerts profound influence on the physiological activities of organisms. Organisms differ in their tolerance limit to extreme temperatures. Most organisms perform their activities in a temperature range of 4 to 45°C.

Temperature affects plants and animals in various ways, which are as follows:

(1) **Effects on metabolism:** All metabolic activities are influenced by temperature. All chemical reactions, enzyme mediated chemical processes in organisms are controlled by temperature. It affects the rates of transpiration, photosynthesis in plants and respiration rates and other metabolic processes in plants as well as animals.

(2) Temperature also influences reproduction in animals and flowering in plants. In animals the temperature influences maturation of gonads or sex cells and their liberation.

(3) Temperature influences growth and development of all living organisms. Extremely high and very low temperatures both have adverse effects on the growth of organisms. In animals, temperature affects growth as well as development e.g. In blow fly, incubation period decreases with increase in temperature.

Temperature also influences crossing over in *Drosophila*, sex ratio in Rotifers and Daphnids.

Temperature also affects the colouration in some insects, birds and mammals. The animals living in warm and humid climate bear darker pigment than animals inhabiting cool and dry climate. Temperature also affects morphology of animals. Birds and mammals attain greater body size in cold regions than in warm areas. Cold blooded animals are smaller in cold regions. The tail, snout, ears and legs of mammals are relatively shorter in colder parts than in warmer areas. Desert and arctic fox show difference in the size of ears. Temperature is also responsible for the distribution of animals.

(4) Light

Light is the most important and indispensible abiotic factor without which life can not exist. All plants depend on light for their energy and all animals depend on plants and hence, without light life is impossible. Sunlight is the ultimate source of energy for the biological world. Light is a narrow band of visible radiant energy comprising wavelengths of 390 to 760 nm. If visible light is passed through a prism, it gives a spectrum of seven different colours. Light is a form of radiant energy. Ultra-violet radiation has damaging properties but most of it is absorbed by the ozone, which forms distinct layers in the stratosphere.

Chlorophyll is the dominant light absorbing pigment found in green plants. By the process of photosynthesis, it converts light or photon energy into chemical energy. Variation in the duration of light exposures also affects plant growth. Photo-period influences stem elongation, flowering, fruit growth and other physiological processes of plants and animals. Depending on the length of day required for the induction of flowering, plants are classified as short day plants, long day plants (more than 14 to 16 hours day length) and day neutral plants, which bloom regardless of the photo-period.

Light is not only responsible for photosynthesis, but it also plays an important role in transpiration and stomatal functioning. Photo-period also affects the structure of vegetative organs, growth, germination, pigmentation, nutrition requirement and even susceptibility to parasites. Light affects chlorophyll production and distribution of plants.

Light also has far reaching effects on animals, by affecting their activities like pigmentation, reproduction, development, growth, locomotion and migration. Light, particularly UV light induces gene mutations. Protective colourations, colour changes are also influenced by light. Cave dwelling animals lack eyes as no light penetrates these regions. Some animals like owls or loris can see even in dim light at night. Light affects the developmental process in many fish and in silk moth. A strong correlation exists between the reproductive cycles of some marine animals and the lunar cycle.

Light affects locomotion in animals and has an effect on the eye size of marine animals. Marine animals living at a depth of 500-3000 metres have much larger eyes than those inhabiting surface waters.

Biological production of light occurs in some bacteria, fungi and animals. Light production in animals is result of a chemiluminescent reactions.

Atmospheric Gases

Up to a height of about 300 km, above the earth's surface, there is present some sort of a thick gaseous mantle. The gaseous mantle consists of different gases in different proportions. Of these gases nitrogen, oxygen and carbon dioxide are major components. Argon, neon, helium, krypton, xenon, hydrogen, methane, ozone are other gases in very minute proportions.

Table 2.1: Relative proportions of various gases in atmosphere

Gases	% (By volume)	Gases	% (By volume)
1. Nitrogen	78.08	7. Crypton	0.00011
2. Oxygen	20.94	8. Xenon	0.00009
3. Argon	0.9340	9. Hydrogen	0.00006
4. Carbon dioxide	0.0318	10. Methane	0.0002
5. Neon	0.0018	11. Nitrous oxide	0.00005
6. Helium	0.00052	12. Ozone	0.000004

Oxygen

A supply of free O_2 is necessary for most forms of life. Aerobic organisms require it for obtaining energy through oxidative processes. Air contains about 21% oxygen and water usually contains about 4 to 10 ml oxygen per litre. In air, O_2 is abundantly available except at higher altitudes. Therefore, in high altitudes, (mountains) the respiratory activity of animals is increased significantly. Mammals react strongly to this change, when partial pressure of O_2 falls below 50% of its value at sea level. Because of their high O_2 requirement, they cannot remain at high altitudes for long time, if the partial pressure of O_2 is 45% below than present at sea level, it acts like a stress factor at high altitudes. Water contains dissolved oxygen, which does not combine chemically with water itself. Animals living in water use this O_2 for aquatic respiration and metabolic activities. The aquatic animals develop different adaptations, such as skin, gills, for respiration. Some have special respiratory pigments which help the animals to get O_2 at very low partial pressure.

Carbon Dioxide

Air contains 0.03% of CO_2 which is essential for photosynthetic activity. CO_2 forms carbonic acid when mixed with water and therefore, the amount of CO_2 present in water determines its pH. The pH of water determines the distribution of organisms. Sea water contains 3.5% salt and usually 47 ml CO_2 per litre. The concentration of CO_2 in water may also influence the orientation, movement and respiratory activity of organisms. At higher concentrations of CO_2, the rate of respiratory movement in some molluscs and arthropods increases. An increase in CO_2 content in the blood of animals usually causes decrease in O_2 carrying capacity of haemoglobin. Fishes are sensitive to CO_2 concentration in water. They usually choose streams containing a lower amount of CO_2, given an option.

Soil

Soil is also called edaphic factor in which structure, formation and characteristics of different soils are studied. It acts as a suitable substratum for plants and animals. It is a bridge between inorganic and organic materials. The study of soil is called **pedology** or **soil science**.

Soil is a complex physical biological system providing support, water, nutrient and O_2 for the plants. It is made up of mineral matter (40%), organic matter (humus) (10%), soil water

(25%), soil air (25%) and biological system. The soil contains top soil, which may be of different colours depending upon the types of humus and mineral materials. The top soil is followed by subsoil, which contains the roots of most plants, humus and minerals.

Soil is formed from the parent rock material (bed rock) by the process of physical, chemical and biological weathering. Physical weathering caused by various climatic factors, such as light, temperature, water, wind, etc. Chemical weathering involves the breaking down of complex compounds by the carbonic acid in water and by acidic substances derived from the decomposition process of organic matter in soil. Hydrolysis, hydration, oxidation and reduction are chemical processes which bring about the changes. These are irreversible changes occuring in rock constituents. Biological weathering involves the decomposition process by which organic materials are broken down and leads to humification and mineralisation. The organisms produce acid substances which help in the weathering of rock fragments. Humus is formed and it mixes with clay, sand and slit to form soil.

Soil Profile

Soil is formed of many horizontal layers arranged one below the other. This is called *soil profile*. The layers are called horizons. Soil is formed by five main horizons. They are O, A, B, C and R horizons.

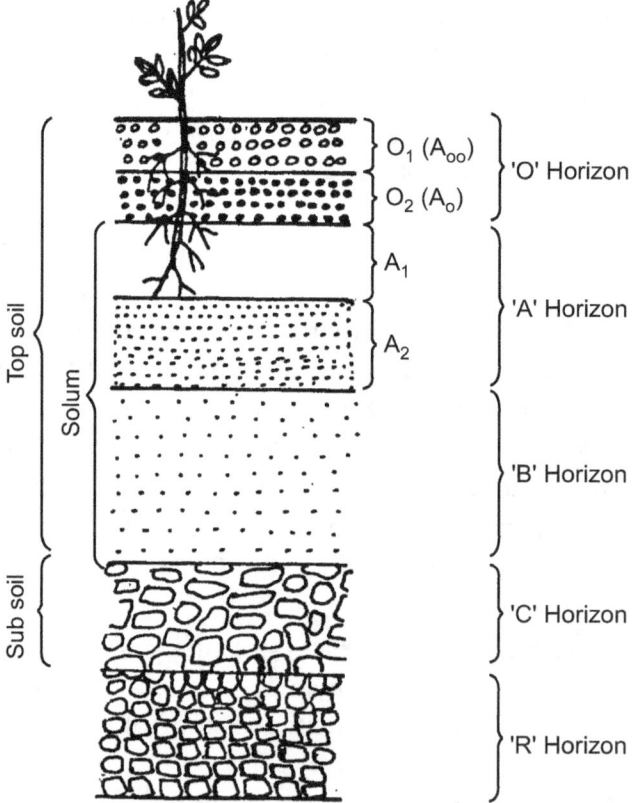

Fig. 2.1: Hypothetical diagram of the Soil Profile Indicating the Principal Horizons

'O' horizon: It is the top soil, very rich in organic matter content, dark in colour and of light texture marked by intense biological activity. Life is abundant in this horizon. It is again divided into two parts: O_1 and O_2. O_1 horizon is the upper layer formed of fresh fallen dead leaves, twigs, barks, flowers, fruits and animal excreta. O_2 horizon contains humus.

'A' horizon: It is the zone of alluviation or leaching. In this layer, humus mixes with mineral particles. It is divided into A_1, A_2 and A_3.

'B' horizon: This horizon forms the sub-soil and contains iron and aluminium compounds with clay and humus. It is again divided into three sub-horizons, B_1, B_2, B_3. B_1 is transitional layer between A and B. The B_2 layer shows maximum accumulation of silicate, clay, mineral, iron and organic matter.

'C' horizon: This is mineral horizon containing incompletely weathered large masses of rocks. It consists of $CaCO_3$ and $CaSO_4$. Long roots of big plants reach this horizon.

'R' horizon: This is the parent, unweathered bedrock, upon which there is collected water.

Soil is classified on the basis of mode of formation. Residual and transported soils are of two main types. Transported soil is classified as Colluvial (by gravity), Alluvial (by running waters), Glacial (ice) and Eolian (by wind).

Soil contains various components that shows its physical properties such as texture, mineral matter, soil porosity, soil air, soil water, soil organisms, etc. Soil contains particles of different sizes that determine the water holding capacity of soil. Aeration and water holding capacity determines vegetation that can grow. Soil contains sand, clay and silt in definite proportions. It also contains mineral nutrients important for plant metabolism and growth. Soil also contains micro and macro elements, which play an important role in development, metabolic functions and an enzymatic action.

Plants absorb water containing organic nutrients and minerals from the soil through their roots. The amount of soil water available to plants depend upon the type and properties of the soil. The source of soil water is rain.

Chemical Properties

Soil solutes are partly organic and partly inorganic compounds, usually soluble in water. Sources of these solutes are organic matter, parent rocks and chemical reactions that occur around soil roots. The substances are usually in the form of bicarbonates, nitrates, nitrites, chlorides and sulphates of sodium, potassium, calcium, iron, aluminium and boron. Highly alkaline or saline soils are also devoid of vegetation and are highly unproductive.

Soil Organisms

Soil organisms include microorganisms, such as bacteria, actinomycetes, fungi, algae, and soil animals, such as protozoa, helminth worms, nematodes, annelids, collembola, mites, insects and their larval forms, pupae, archnids, and other arthropoda, gastropods, etc. Some mammals and birds use the soil for various purposes. They also play an important role in determining the physical and chemical properties of soil, soil fertility and so on. Earthworms and termites play a significant role in soil formation. Many animals show burrowing or fossorial adaptations which shows certain modifications in their body and organs.

Soil is an important factor for life; hence its conservation is also equally important for survival of animals and plants.

Need for Public Awareness

Man has the capacity to change the environment more than any other organism on this planet. Human needs and greeds have disturbed the ecological balance. Human are radially depleting and degrading our ecological systems including air, water and land.

Although there are several laws for conversation and prevention of pollution. It cannot be implemented unless the society is aware of the risks of living in a deteriorating environment. Adequate knowledge to fully analyse the environmental problems and take appropriate actions. The society must make uses of reformative measures to improve the quality of our environment. The UN conference on Human Environment held in Stockholm from 5th-6th June, 1972, was a major breakthrough in creating awareness. The World Environment Day is observed every year on June 5th with a view of creating awareness among the masses and bringing environmental issues to the forefront of planning and development. The controversy over the Silent Valley hydel project to save "one of the last vestiges" of tropical rain forest, the "Chipko-Movement" in Himalayas (Almora Hills) and the Appiko movement (Karnataka) in India indicate people's awareness.

Environmental problems need attention and the change necessary to solve them. To fail to change is to deny the responsibility we have for one another and for those who come after us. It is therefore essential to generate public awareness about the consequences of environmental degradation.

2.2.2 Biotic or Living Components

Biotic components of environment are plants, animals including human beings and microbes.

Plants: The green plants, certain bacteria and algae can synthesise their own food with the help of chlorophyll in presence of sunlight. They are called *autotrophs* or *producers*.

Animals: Animals cannot produce their food but depend on plants and other organisms to obtain their food. These are called *heterotrophs* or *consumers*. Animals which feed on green plants are called primary consumers or *herbivores* e.g. deer, cow, giraffe. Organisms which consume a herbivore are called *secondary consumers* e.g. lion, frog. The organisms which consume secondary consumers are called *tertiary consumers* e.g. eagle. Organisms which consume both plants and animals are called omnivores e.g. bear.

Microbes: They are also called *decomposers*, because they are responsible for decomposition of dead organic matter. E.g. Fungi and bacteria.

The biotic factors include living organisms of the ecosystem.

They are classified into two types:

(i) Autotrophs: Organisms, basically green plants, certain bacteria and algae that can synthesise their own food in the presence of sunlight are called autotrophs or producers. These organisms contain chlorophyll with which they can prepare their own food material. They do not depend on others for food.

(ii) Heterotrophs: All other organisms that do not make their own food but depend on other organisms to obtain their energy for survival are called heterotrophs or consumers.

Among consumers some animals such as insects, cow, rabbit, deer, goat etc. which can eat green plants are called *primary consumers* or *herbivores*. Organisms which eat herbivore, like a frog that eats grasshopper are called *secondary consumers*. Organisms which eat these secondary consumers are called *tertiary consumers*. While the primary consumers are herbivores, the secondary and tertiary consumers are carnivores. Animals like lions and vultures which are not killed or eaten by other animals are *top carnivores*.

Heterotrophs are classified into two types i.e. macro-consumers and micro-consumers or decomposers.

Fig. 2.2: Grassland Ecosystem

Decomposers

Certain fungi and bacteria which are responsible for the decomposition are called *decomposers* or *reducers*. The role of the decomposers is very special and important. Certain decomposers are also called *scavengers*. They are saprotrophs and they breakdown complex compounds of dead or living protoplasm and release water, CO_2, phosphates and a number of organic compounds which are largely the metabolic by-products and release them in the environment, making them available again to autotrophs.

Consequently, an ecosystem is considered as a basic unit, where complex natural community obtain their food from plants through one, two, three or four steps and accordingly, these steps are known as the first, second, third, and fourth *trophic levels* or food levels such as:

(1) Green plants (producers), Trophic level I
(2) Herbivores (primary consumers), Trophic level II
(3) Carnivores (secondary consumers), Trophic level III
(4) Top carnivores (Tertiary consumers), Trophic level IV.

The amount of living material in different trophic levels or in a component population is known as *standing crop*. This term is applicable to both plants as well as animals. The standing crop may be expressed in terms of:

(i) Number of organisms per unit area or
(ii) Biomass i.e. organism mass in unit area, which can be measured as living weight, dry weight, ash free dry weight or carbon weights or calories.

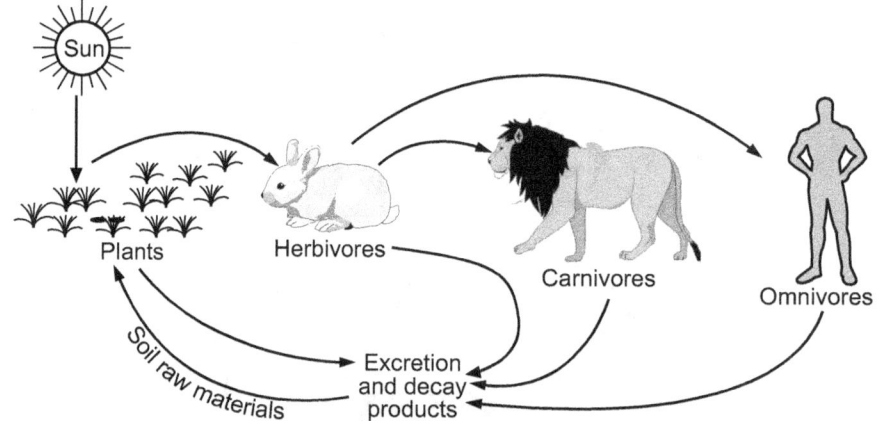

Fig. 2.3: Generated Scheme of Nutritional Relationships among Different Biotic Components of an Ecosystem

Different Types of Ecosystems

There are two major types of ecosystems; the aquatic and terrestrial.

Terrestrial ecosystem consists of:

(i) Forest ecosystem (ii) Grassland ecosystem (iii) Desert ecosystem.

Aquatic ecosystems are further distinguished as:

(i) Freshwater ecosystems which may be *lotic* (running water as spring, stream, or river) or *lentic* (standing water as lake, pond, pools, puddles, ditch, swamp etc.)

(ii) Marine ecosystem includes deep bodies as an ocean or shallow ones as a sea.

(iii)   Estuarine ecosystem is a transitional ecosystem between freshwater and marine ecosystem.

Sometimes ecosystems are broadly classified into two types namely:

(i) Natural ecosystems and

(ii) Artificial ecosystems (man engineered ecosystems).

Natural ecosystem includes terrestrial and aquatic ecosystems; and artificial ecosystem includes crop lands like maize, wheat, rice fields etc. where man tries to control the biotic community as well as physico-chemical environment. Another type is a space ecosystem.

Pond Ecosystem

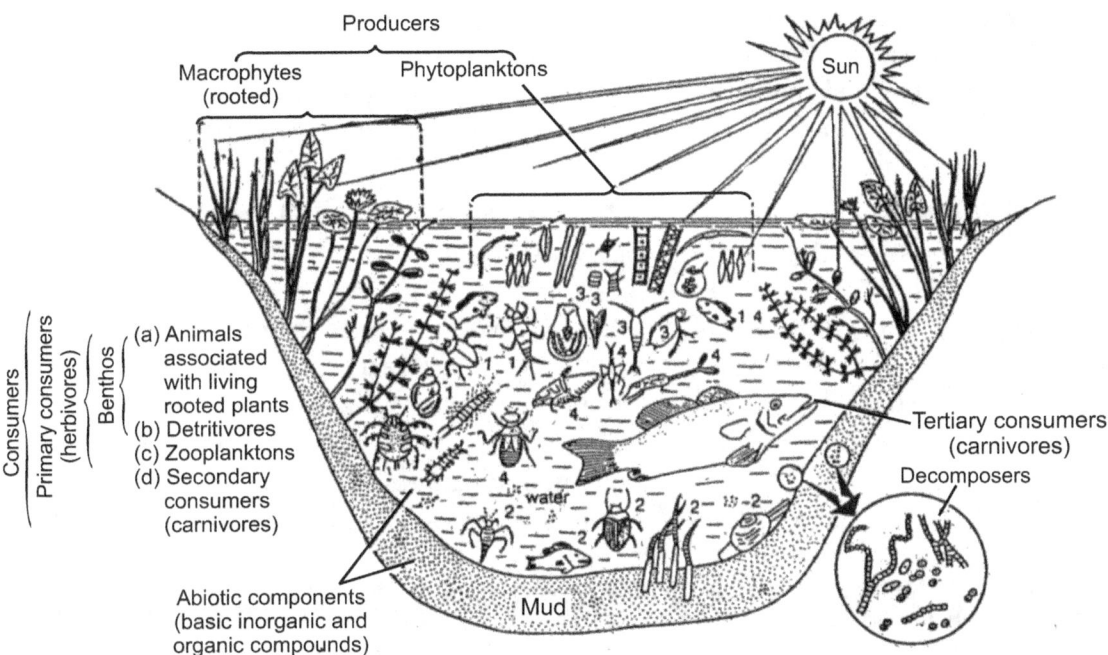

Fig. 2.4: Diagram of the Pond Ecosystem, Showing its Basic Structural Units the Abiotic (Inorganic and Organic Compounds) and Biotic (Producers, Consumers and Decomposers) Components

A pond as a whole serves a good example of a freshwater ecosystem. A pond is a self sufficient and a self regulating system. It consists of both living (plants and animals) components as well as non-living components such as light, temperature and water in which nutrients, O_2, other gases and organic matter are dissolved.

Biotic Components

(1) Producers: The green plants and some photosynthetic bacteria are autotrophs. They fix the radiant solar energy and produce carbohydrates by the process of photosynthesis.

Producers are of two types:

(i) Macrophytes: These are rooted, larger plants which are partly or completely submerged, floating and emergent hydrophytes. The common plants are *Typha, Nymphaea, Chara, Hydrilla, Vallisneria, Utricularia, Eichhornia, Spirodela, Lemna.*

(ii) Phytoplankton: These are small minute, floating or suspended lower plants. They are filamentous algae as *Zygnema, Ulothrix, Spirogyra, Diatoms, Volvox, Anabaena, Spirulina.*

(2) Consumers: These are animals and heterotrophs which depend for their nutrition on producers. Most of the consumers are herbivores which feed on plant material, whereas insects, fish, frog, etc. are carnivores as they feed on herbivores. Some organisms which feed on both plants and animals are called omnivores.

(i) Herbivores: They directly feed on living plants. They may live at the bottom called *benthos.* e.g. insect larvae, beetles, mites, molluscs, crustaceans etc. Zooplanktons which are small, microscopic forms that live on the surface of water include rotifers, protozoans (*Euglena, Coleps*), Crustaceans (*Cyclops*). Herbivores are also called primary consumers.

(ii) Carnivores: These may feed on herbivores e.g. insects, fish, water beetles. They are also called secondary consumers. Those that feed on secondary consumers are called tertiary consumers. e.g. larger fish, frog, duck, aquatic birds.

(3) Decomposers: These are also called microconsumers as they feed on dead organic matter. They bring about the decomposition of complex dead organic matter of plants and animals. They are chiefly bacteria, actinomycetes and fungi.

Abiotic Components: In pond, the several non-living or abiotic factors that are present are water, temperature (heat), light, pH, inorganic compounds such as CO_2, O_2, calcium, nitrogen, phosphates, amino acids, humic acid etc. These constituents are essential for the survival of living factors.

2.3 Forest Ecosystems

Forests are natural plant communities with dominance of phanerogams or phanerophytes and occupy nearly 40% of the land. In India, the forest occupies roughly 19-20% of the total land area. Indian forests are of 11 types and are classified on the basis of physiography, physiognomy, floristics, habitat etc.

Components of Forest Ecosystem

Abiotic Components: They are inorganic and organic substances found in the soil and atmosphere. The climate (temperature, light, rainfall etc.) and soil minerals are the abiotic components. Apart from minerals the occurrence of litter is characteristic feature of majority of forests.

Biotic Components

Producers: These are plants, which grow around the world. They trap solar energy and produce food by photosynthesis. They grow in diverse habitat, for example, in the tropical moist deciduous forests the dominant trees species are *Tectona grandis, Butea frondosa, Shorea robusta and Largestroemia parviflora* and in temperate coniferous forests and temperate deciduous forests, the dominant trees and species are *Quercus, Acer, Betula, Thuja, Picea, Abies, Pinus, Cedrus, Juniperus, Rhododentron* etc.

Consumers

(a) **Primary Consumers:** These are herbivores which feed on tree leaves such as ants, flies, beetles, lealf-hoppers, bugs, spiders etc. and larger animals grazing on shoots or fruits of plants are elephants, neelgai, deer, moles, squirrels, shrews, flying foxes, mongoose etc.

(b) **Secondary Consumers:** These are carnivores and feed herbivores. For example: snakes, birds, lizards, foxes etc.

(c) **Tertiary consumers:** These are the top carnivores. For example, lion, tiger etc. They feed on carnivores of secondary consumer level.

Decomposers: There are wide variety of microorganisms like **Fungi** - *Aspergillus, Polyporus, Alteraria, Fusarium, Trichoderma* etc. **Bacteria** - *Bacillus, Pseudomonas, Clostridium, Actinomycetes, Streptomyces*. Rate of decomposition in tropical and subtropical forests is more rapid than in the temperate ones.

2.4 Artificial Ecosystems

Man is dominant animal on the earth. His activities modify natural ecosystems into manmade or artificial ecosystem. Man has cleared forest land and converted that land into agricultural land. Cropland is nothing but the artificial ecosystem. He cultivates crops as per his will. For example, sugarcane farm, Grape farm, Wheat crop, Bajara Crop or vegetable farm. Rose farm. Now he is using polyhouses for getting better yield. He protects his crop from herbivore pests.

Construction of dam and fish, prawns are developed in such artificial ecosystems. Besides, space crafts, and aquaria may be manmade ecosystems.

2.5 Characteristics of an Ecosystem

1. An ecosystem is an open system with a continuous, but variable influx and loss of materials and energy. The flow of energy and materials depend on the ecosystem structure.
2. It is the smallest unit of biosphere.
3. An ecosystem is an overall integration of all the organisms that interact with each other and their environment.
4. It is a basic, functional unit with no limits of boundaries.
5. It consists of biotic and abiotic components interacting with each other.
6. It is capable of energy transformation, circulation and accumulation.
7. An ecosystem is an overall integration of all the organisms that interact with each other and their environment.

The organisation of various species in the ecosystem, their abundance, reproduction and other strategies determine the functioning of an ecosystem. The organisms in an ecosystem are interconnected and interdependent through activities like predation, symbiosis, parasitisation etc. Study of the energy flow, food webs and ecological pyramids are essential for the complete understanding of an ecosystem.

2.6 Function of An Ecosystem

Plants use solar energy for their production of food. Very limited amount i.e. about 1/50 millionth of the total solar radiation reaches the earth's surface. The solar radiation travels through the space in the form of waves during which most of it is lost in the space. The solar energy which reaches the earth surface is largely of visible light (45%), infrared components (45%) and ultraviolet rays (10%). Plants mostly absorb red and blue light.

Thus, in ecological energetics we study the following aspects:

(1)   Amount of solar energy reaching an ecosystem.

(2)   Amount of solar energy used by green plants for the process of photosynthesis and

(3)   Path and amount of energy flow from producers to consumers.

About 34% of the sunlight reaching the earth's atmosphere is reflected back into its atmosphere. 10% is absorbed by ozone layer, water vapour and other atmospheric gases. The remaining amount of solar radiation i.e. around 56% reaches the earth's surface. A very small fraction, about 1-5% of solar energy is utilised by the plants for photosynthesis. The remaining energy is absorbed as heat by ground vegetation or water. In true sense, only about 0.02% solar energy is used by the plants for photosynthesis. Despite of this; the survival of living organisms depends on this small fraction in an ecosystem.

Energy Flow in an Ecosystem

The behaviour of energy in ecosystem is called energy flow. The flow of energy is unidirectional. In ecological energetics, we can study the following aspects:

(1) The efficiency of the producers in absorption and conversion of solar energy.

(2) Use of this chemical energy by the consumers.

(3) The total input of energy in the form of food and its efficiency of assimilation.

(4) The loss through respiration, heat excretion, etc. and

(5) The gross net production.

The principle of food chains and working of thermodynamics can be explained by energy flow diagram.

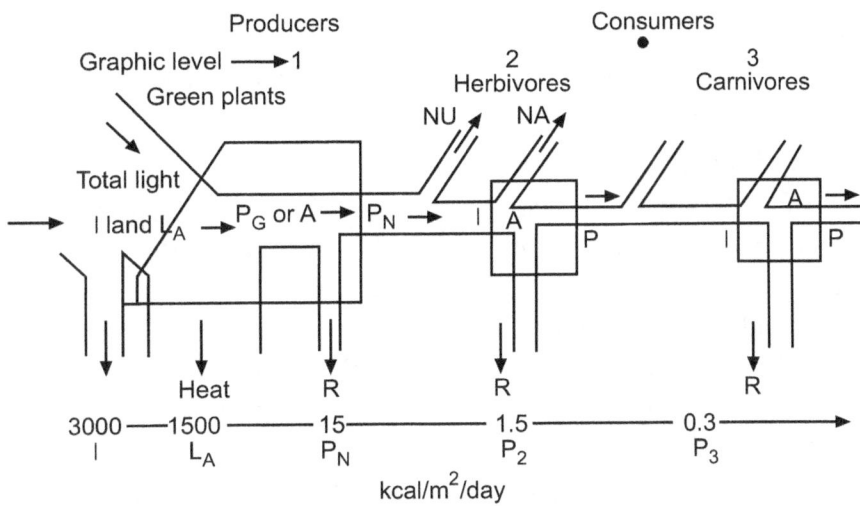

Fig. 2.5: Simplified Energy Flow Diagram Depicting Three Trophic Levels (Boxes Numbered 1, 2, 3) in a Linear Food Chain

I – Total energy input; L_A – light absorbed by plant cover; P_G – gross primary production; **A** – total assimilation; P_N – net primary production; **P** – secondary (consumer) production; N_U – energy not used (stored or exported); N_A – energy not assimilated by consumers (egested); **R** – respiration, Bottom line in the diagram shows the order of the magnitude of energy losses expected at major transfer points, starting with a solar input of 3,000 kcal per square metre per day.   (E.P. Odum, 1963)

The transfer of energy from one trophic level to another trophic level is called energy flow. The flow of energy in an ecosystem is unidirectional, i.e. it flows from the producer level to the consumer level and never in the reverse direction. Hence, energy can be used only once in the ecosystem.

The figure represents a very simplified energy flow model of free trophic levels, from which it becomes evident that the energy flow is greatly reduced at each successive trophic level from producers to herbivores and then to carnivores.

Thus, during each transfer of energy from one level to another level, major part of energy is lost as heat or in any other form.

In Fig. 2.5, the boxes represent the trophic levels and the pipes depict the energy flow in and out of each level. Energy inflows balance outflows as required by the first law of thermodynamics and energy transfer is accompanied by dispersion of energy into unavailable heat i.e. respiration as required by the second law.

Thus, as shown in Fig. 2.5, about 3000 kcal of total light falls on the green plants, of this approximately 50% i.e. 1500 kcal is absorbed, of which only 1 per cent (15 kcal) is converted at first trophic level. Thus, the net primary production is merely 15 kcal. Secondary productivity (P_2 and P_3 in diagram) tends to be about 10 per cent at successive consumer trophic levels i.e. herbivores and the carnivores although efficiency may be sometimes higher as 20%, at the carnivore level as shown (or P_3 = 0.3 kcal) in the diagram.

Models of Energy Flow

For explaining mode of energy flow in various types of ecosystems, ecologists have suggested the following models:

1. Single-channel Energy Flow Models

(a) Lindeman's Model: This model was proposed by Lindeman (1942). As shown in Fig. 2.6 out of total incoming solar radiation (118,872 gm cal/cm^2/yr), 118,761 gm/cal/cm^2/yr remain unutilized. Thus, gross production (net production + respiration) by autotrophs is 111 gm cal/cm^2/yr with an efficiency of energy capture of 0.10 per cent. It may also be noted that 21 per cent of this energy or 23 gm cal/cm^2/yr is consumed in metabolic reactions of autotrophs for their growth, development, maintenance and reproduction. It can be observed further that 15 gm cal/cm^2/yr are consumed by herbivores that graze or feed on autotrophs. This amounts to 17% of net autotroph production. Decomposition (3 gm cal/cm^2/yr) accounts for about 3.4% of production. The remainder of plant material, 70 gm cal/cm^2/yr or 79.5% of net producing is not utilized at all but becomes part of accumulating sediments of the total energy incorporated at the herbivores level (i.e. 15 gm cal/cm^2/yr) 30% or 4.5 gm cal/cm^2/yr is used in metabolic reactions. Thus, there is considerably more energy lost via. respiration by herbivores (30%) than by autotrophs (21%). Again there is considerable energy available for the carnivores, namely 10.5 gm cal/cm^2/yr or 70% of net production passes to carnivores.

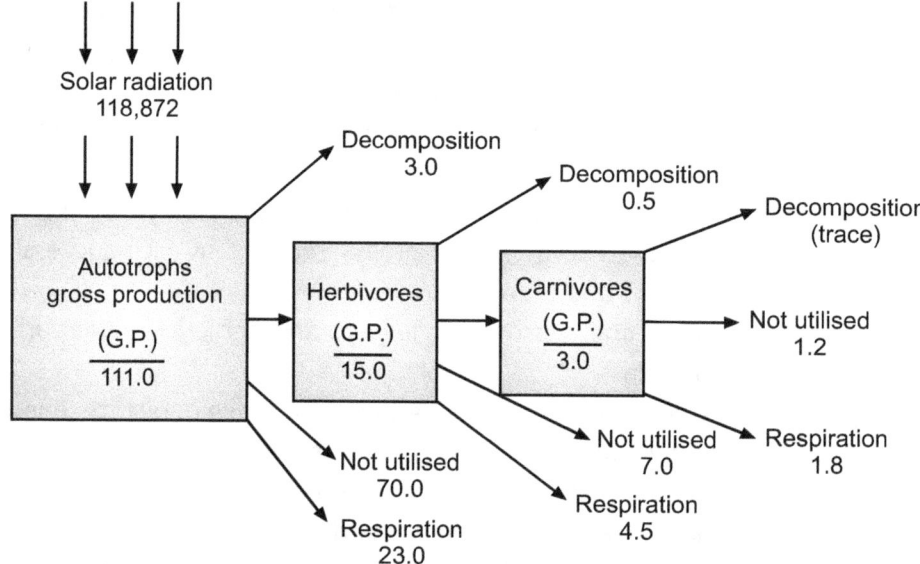

Fig. 2.6: Energy flow diagram for a lake (freshwater ecosystem) in a gm cal/cm^2/yr. (Lindeman's single-channel energy flow model

This is more efficient utilization of resources that occurs at autotroph-herbivore transfer level. At the carnivore level about 60% of the carnivore's energy intake is consumed in metabolic activity and the remainder becomes part of the not utilized sediments; only an insignificant amount is subject to decomposition yearly.

From this energy model two facts are clear:

1.   Energy flow is unidirectional. It moves through various trophic levels. System may collapse if the primary source the sun is cut-off.

2.   There is progressive decrease in energy level at each trophic level. The energy dissipated as heat in metabolic activities and measured here as respiration coupled with unutilized energy.

(b) Box and Pipe Energy Flow Model: It was suggested by **E. P. Odum (1953)**. It is simplified energy flow model of three trophic levels. In such single-channel energy flow model 'boxes' represent the trophic levels and the 'pipes' depict the energy flow in and out of each level. Energy inflows balance outflows as required by the first law of thermodynamics, and energy transfer is accompanied by dispersion of energy into unavailable heat (i.e. respiration) as required by second law.

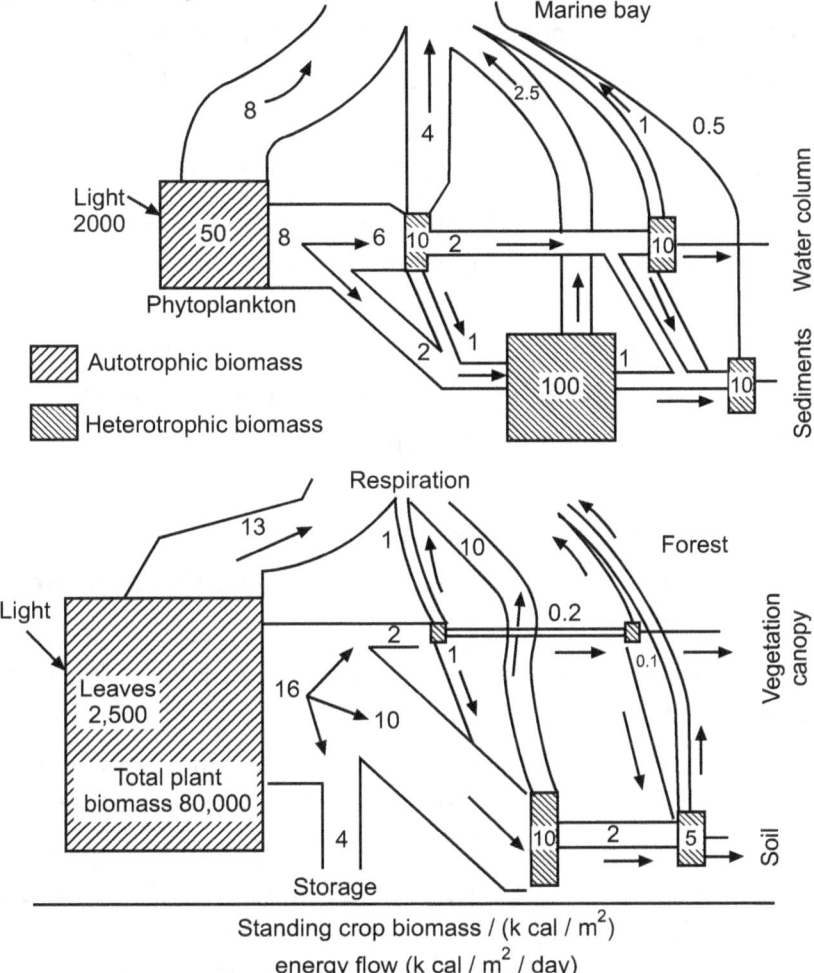

Standing crop biomass / (k cal / m^2)

energy flow (k cal / m^2 / day)

Fig. 2.7: A Y-shaped or two channel energy flow diagram that separates a grazing food chain (water column or vegetation canopy) from a detritus food chain (sediments and in soil). Estimates for standing crops (shaded boxes) and energy flows compare a hypothetical coastal marine ecosystem (upper diagram) with a hypothetical forest (lower diagram)

E. P. Odium (1983) gave generalized model of Y-shaped or two channel energy flow which is applicable to both terrestrial and aquatic ecosystem (Fig. 2.8).

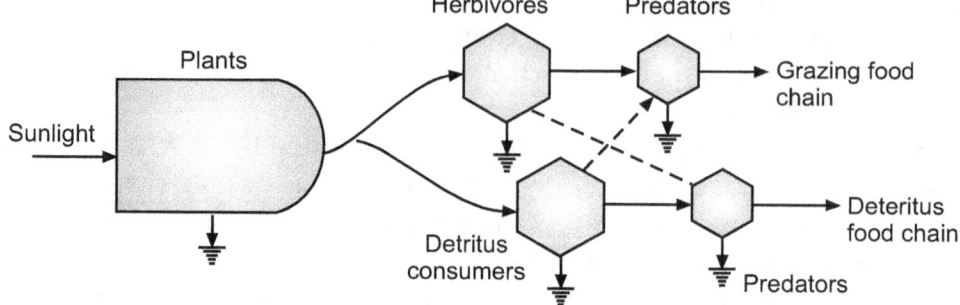

Fig. 2.8: Y-shaped energy flow model of Odum (1983)
showing linkage between grazing and detritus food chains

The Y-shaped model is more realistic practical working model than the single-channel model because

(i)   It conforms to the basic stratified structure of ecosystem.

(ii) It separates the grazing and detritus food chains (i.e. direct consumption of living plants and utilization of dead organic matter respectively) in both time and space and

(iii) That the microconsumers (bacteria, fungi) and macroconsumers (phagotrophic animals) differ greatly in size-metabolism relations in two models.

The important point in this model is that the two food chains are not isolated from each other.

2. Y-shaped or Two Channel Energy Flow Model

E. P. Odum (1962) depicted this model. He pointed out that there are two basic food chains in nature in any system.

1. The grazing food chain beginning with green plant base going to herbivores and then to carnivores and

2. The detritus food chain beginning with green dead organic matter acted by microbes, then passing to detritivores and their consumers (predators).

Fig. 2.9 shows two Y-shaped energy flow models. In each Y-shaped model, one arm represents the herbivore food chain and the other decomposer (detritus) food chain. The two arms differ fundamentally in the way in which they can influence primary producers. In each model the grazing and detritus food chains are sharply separated. The figure contrasts the biomass energy flow relationships in the sea and forest. In the marine bay, the energy flow via. the grazing food chain is shown to be larger than via. detritus pathways, whereas reverse is shown for the forest in which 90% or more of the net primary production is normally utilized in detritus food chain. Thus, in marine ecosystem the grazing food chain is the major pathway of energy flow whereas in the forest ecosystem the detritus food chain is more important.

In grazing food chain, herbivores feed on living plants and therefore, directly affect the plant populations. What they do not eat is available, after death, to the decomposers. As a result, decomposers are not able to directly influence the rate of supply of their food.

Odum's Universal Model:

E. P. Odum (1968) suggested a Y-shaped energy flow model (Fig. 2.9 which is applicable to any living components, whether a plant, animal, microorganism or individual, population or a trophic group. It is called universal model of energy flow.

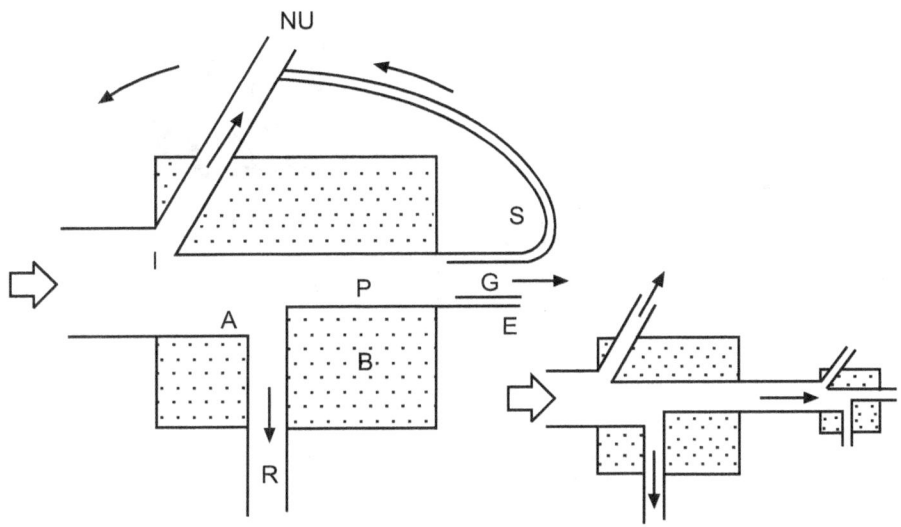

Fig. 2.9: Components of a universal model of energy flow. I = Input or ingested energy'
NU = Not Used; A = Assimilated energy; P = Production; R = Respiration;
B = Biomass; G = Growth; S = Stored energy; E = Excreted energy

In Fig. 2.9, the shaded box labeled 'B' represents the living structure or biomass of the component. The total energy input is indicated by 'I' which is light for autotrophs and organic food for heterotrophs. Such a model may depict food chain as already shown in other Y-shaped energy flow systems, or the bioenergetics of an entire ecosystem. This model can be used in two ways:

(i)   It can represent a species population in which case the appropriate energy inputs and links with other species would be shown as conventional species oriented food web diagram or

(ii) The model can represent discrete energy level in which case the biomass and energy channels represents all or parts of many populations supported by same energy sources.

2.7 Food Chain

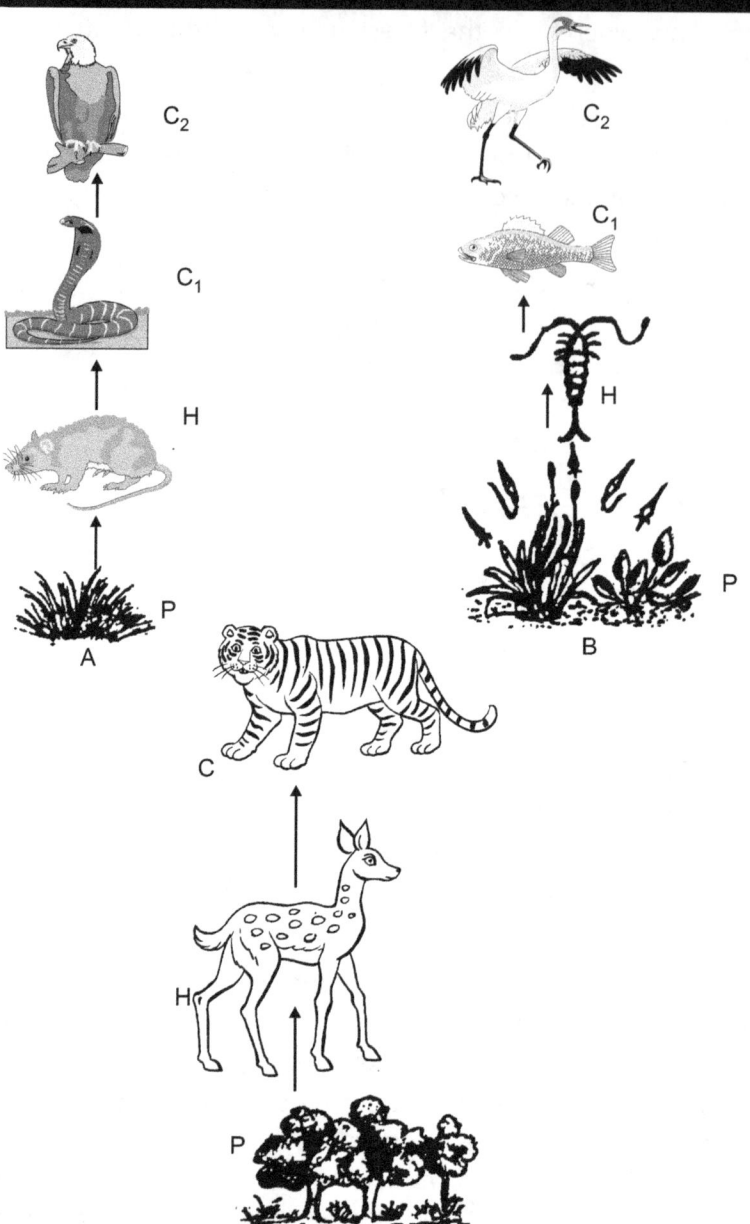

Fig. 2.10: Food Chain in Nature

A – food chain in a grassland; B – food chain in a pond; C – food chain in a forest. The base of the food chain is always formed by autotrophs (producers). The links are usually 3 to 5 and the arrangement is mainly, producer → herbivore → carnivore (P = producer, H = herbivore, C_1 = carnivore order - 1, C_2 = carnivore order - 2)

In an ecosystem, various living organisms such as plants and animals are arranged in a definite sequence according to their food habits. Plants are producers which are eaten by herbivores. The herbivores in turn are consumed by carnivores. This transfer of food energy from producers (plants) through a series of organisms (herbivores to carnivores to decomposers) with repeated eating and being eaten is known as the food chain.

Plants convert solar energy into chemical energy i.e. carbohydrates by the process of photosynthesis. The producers always remain in any ecosystem at the first trophic level or producer level. The food energy stored in the body of plants is utilised by herbivores or plant eaters which form the second trophic level called *primary consumers*. In an ecosystem, the herbivores are eaten by carnivores which constitute the third trophic level or *secondary consumers* level. These carnivores in turn may be eaten by other carnivores at the tertiary consumers level i.e. by *tertiary consumers*. In an ecosystem, there are a number of organisms which eat both plants as well as animals at the lower level in a food chain. Such animals are called as omnivores. Such organisms occupy more than one trophic level in the food chain.

For example, plants are eaten by insects, which are eaten by frogs, which in turn are eaten by fish, which are ultimately eaten by human beings. In this food chain, there are five trophic or feeding levels. Several factors are important in determining an animal's position in a food chain. Each species occupies a specific place and participates in the flow of energy in the ecosystem, from sunlight through photosynthesis into autotrophic producers, to the tissues of herbivores, the primary consumers, to the tissue of carnivores, the secondary consumers. The energy flow determines the number and biomass of organisms at each level in the ecosystem. Flow of energy is greatly reduced at each successive level of nutrition, because of the energy utilisation by the organisms and heat loss at each step in the transformation of energy. This largely accounts for the decrease in biomass at each successive level. Moreover, no predator is completely efficient at capturing its prey; some energy is lost in the hunt.

An animal may be a primary consumer in one chain, eating plants but a secondary or tertiary consumer in other chains, eating herbivorous animals or other carnivores.

Food chain in grassland ecosystem starts with

Grasses → Grasshoppers → Frogs → Snakes → Hawk.

In a pond ecosystem the food chain starts with

Phytoplanktons → Water fleas → Smaller fish → Bigger fish → Birds or Man.

In nature, three types of food chains have been distinguished.

(1) Grazing Food Chain

The consumers which start the food chain, utilising plants or plant parts as their food, constitute the grazing food chain. The food chain begins from green plants at the base and the primary consumer is herbivore.

For example: Grass → Grasshopper → Bird → Hawk.

(2) Parasitic Food Chain

It also begins from green plant base, and then moves to herbivores which for example, may be the host of a huge number of lice which live as ectoparasites. The parasitic food chain begins with a green plant which may support a large number of herbivores. These herbivorous animals support a large number of hyperparasites.

(3) Detritus Food Chain

This type of food chain goes from dead organic matter into micro-organisms and then to organisms feeding on detritus (detrivores) and their predators. Such ecosystems are thus less dependent on direct solar energy. These mainly depend on the influx of the organic matter produced in another system. For example, such type of food chain operates in the decomposing accumulated litter in a temperate forest. A good example of this food chain is based on mangrove leaves.

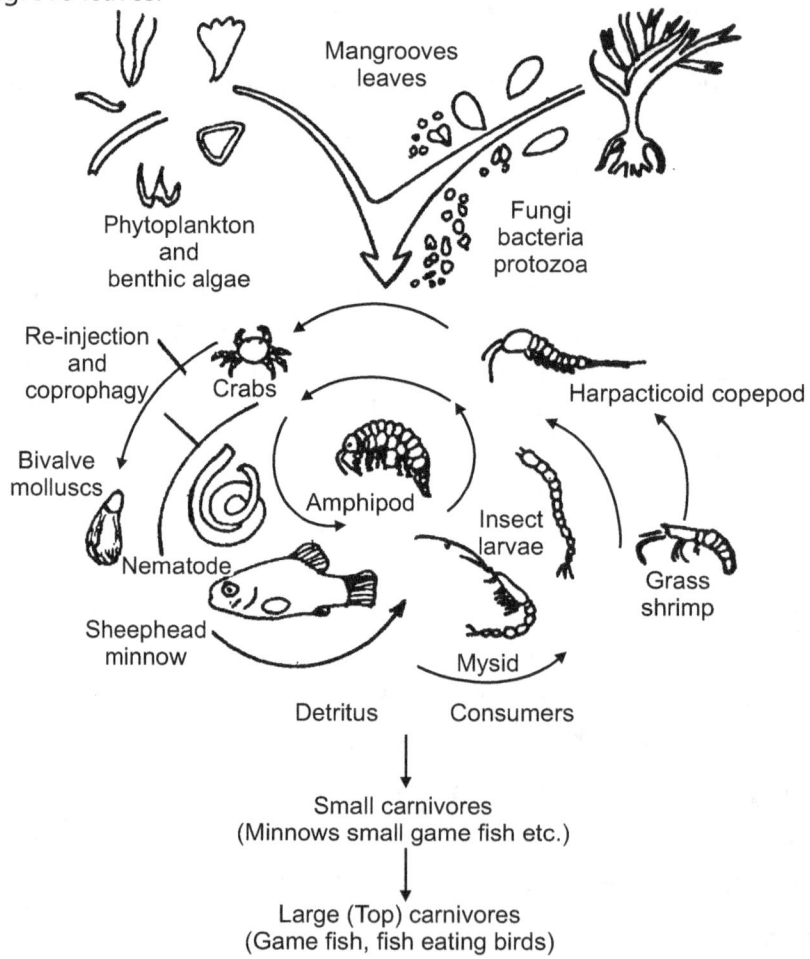

Fig. 2.11: Detritus food chain based on mangrooves leaves falling into shallow estuary waters. Leaf fragments acted on by the saprotrophs and colonised by algae are eaten and re-eaten (coprophagy) by a key group of small detritivores which in turn, provide the main food for game fish, herons, storks and ibis

Leaves fallen in shallow water → Saprotrophs (fungi, bacteria, protozoa etc.) → eaten and re-eaten by small organisms like crabs, copepods, insect larvae, grass shrimp, mysid, nematodes, bivalve molluscs → small carnivores → fish → birds (Top carnivores).

2.8 Food Web

Food chains in natural conditions never operate as isolated sequences, but in an ecosystem the various food chains are interconnected with each other forming some sort of interlocking pattern called **food web**. Simple food chains are very rare in nature, this is because each organism may obtain food from more than one trophic level. In other words, one organism forms food for more than one organism of the higher trophic level. For example, in a grazing food chain of grassland, in the absence of rabbit, grass may also be eaten by mouse. The mouse in turn may be eaten directly by hawk or snake first which is then eaten by a hawk.

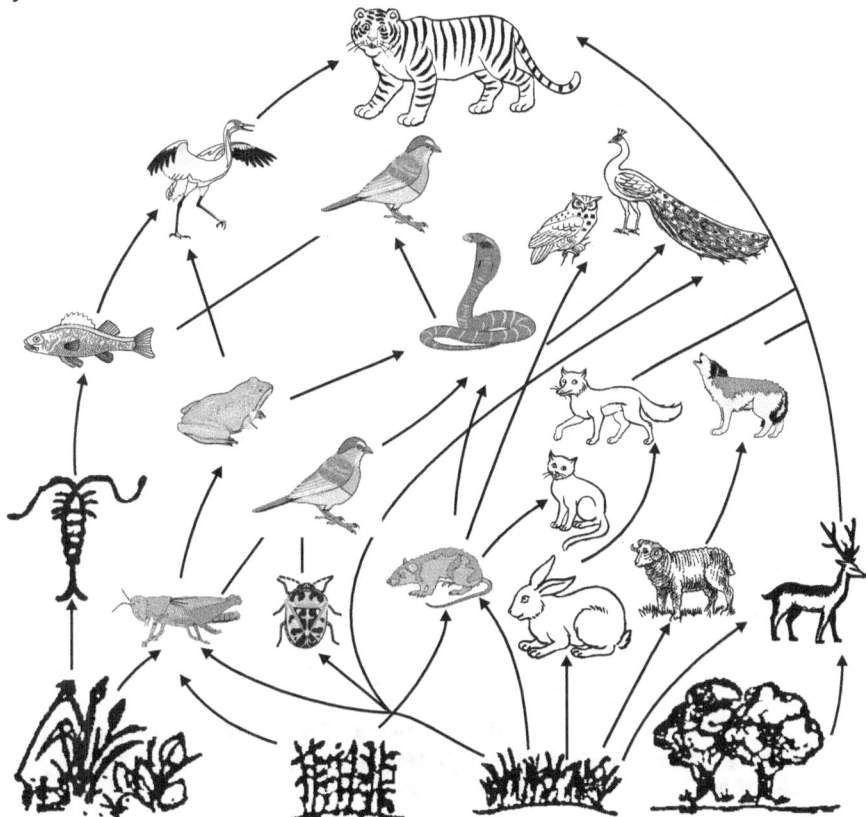

Fig. 2.12: A Food web shows the main Food Links and Interconnection of many Food Chains

An organism may form a food source for many other organisms thus forming a web.

The grass is eaten by grasshopper, rabbit and mouse. Grasshopper is eaten by lizard which is eaten by hawk. Rabbit is eaten by a hawk. Mouse is eaten by a snake which is eaten by hawk. In addition, hawk also directly eats grasshopper and mouse. Thus, there are fine linear food chains which are interconnected to form a food web.

(1) Grass → Grasshopper → Hawk

(2) Grass → Grasshopper → Lizard → Hawk

(3) Grass → Rabbit → Hawk

(4) Grass → Mouse → Hawk

(5) Grass → Mouse → Snake → Hawk

Food webs are very important in maintaining the stability of an ecosystem. For example, decrease in population of rabbit would naturally cause an increase in the population of alternative herbivore, the mouse. This may decrease the population of the consumer (carnivore) that prefers to eat rabbit. The alternatives or substitutes serve for maintenance of stability of the ecosystem. When one type of herbivore becomes extinct, the other types of herbivores increase in number and control vegetation. Similarly, when one type of herbivorous animals becomes extinct, the carnivore predating on this type may eat another type of herbivore. Thus, each species of any ecosystem is indeed kept under some sort of a natural check, so that the system may remain balanced. The complexity of any food web depends upon the diversity of organisms in the system.

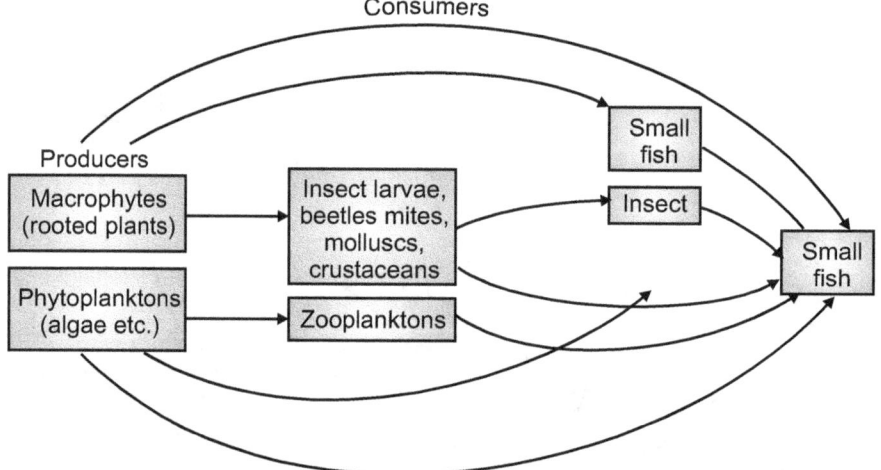

Fig. 2.13: Diagrammatic sketch showing the food web in a pond

2.9 Ecological Pyramids

The number, biomass and energy of organisms gradually decrease from the producer level to the consumer level. These few steps of tropic level can be expressed in a diagrammatic way and are referred to as **ecological pyramids**. Ecological pyramid is the graphic representation of the number, biomass, and energy of the successive trophic levels of an ecosystem. Charles Elton in 1927, first used and described the term ecological pyramid.

In the ecological pyramid, the producers form the base and the final consumer occupies the apex. The ecological pyramids are of three types:

(1) Pyramid of numbers

(2) Pyramid of biomass

(3) Pyramid of energy

(1) Pyramid of Numbers

They show the relationship between producers, herbivores and carnivores at successive trophic levels in terms of their number. The number of individuals at the trophic level decreases from the producer level to the consumer level. The number of producers in an ecosystem is very high. The number of herbivores is lesser than the producers.

Similarly, the number of carnivores is lesser than the herbivores. For example, in crop lands the producers or crops are more in numbers and the grasshoppers feeding on crop plants are lesser in number. The frogs feeding on grasshoppers are still lesser in number. The snakes feeding on frogs are still fewer in number. In a pond ecosystem, the number decreases in the following order:

Phytoplankton > Zooplankton > Fishes > Snakes

Thus, the pyramid is upright. In a forest ecosystem, however, the pyramid of numbers is somewhat different in shape. The producers are large sized trees which are lesser in number and form the base of the pyramid. The herbivores, fruit eating birds, elephants, deers, etc. are more in number than the producers. Then, there is a gradual decrease in the number of successive carnivores, thus making the pyramid upright again.

However, in a parasitic food chain, the pyramids are always inverted. This is due to the fact that a single plant may support the growth of many herbivores and each herbivore in turn may provide nutrition to several parasities which support many hyper-parasites. Thus, from the producers towards consumers, there is reverse position, i.e. the number of organisms gradually shows an increase making the pyramid inverted in shape.

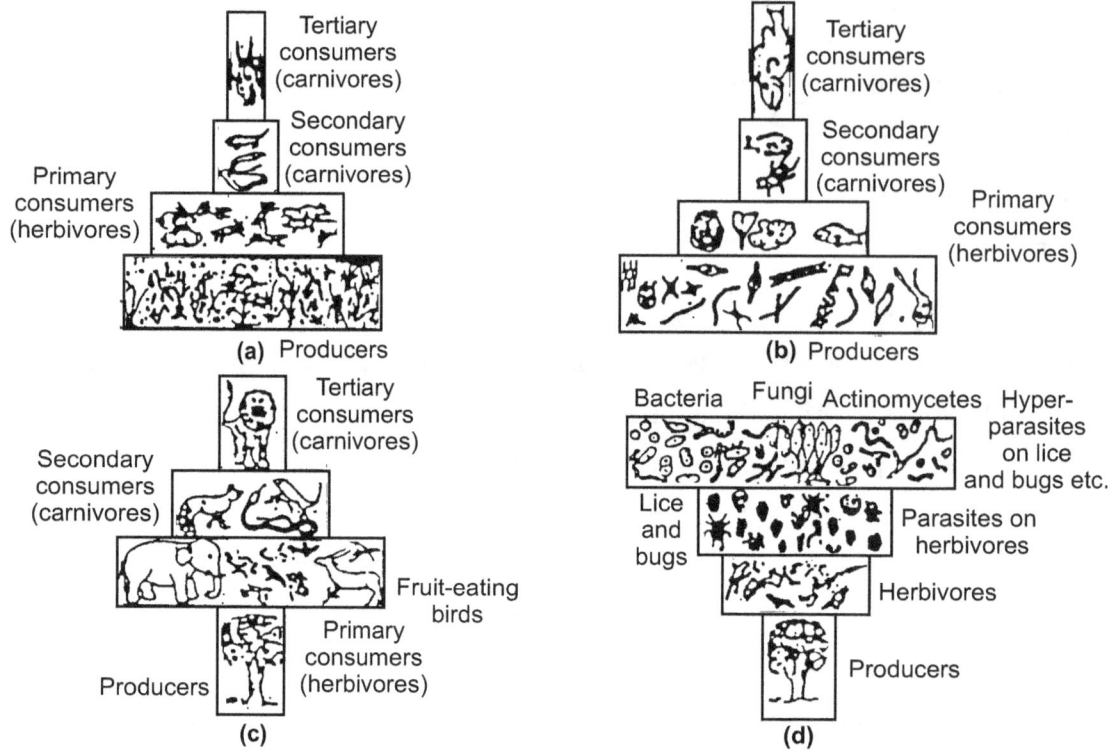

Fig. 2.14: Pyramid of numbers (individuals per unit area) in different kinds of ecosystem/food chains

(a) Grassland ecosystem, (b) Pond ecosystem, (c) Forest ecosystem, In (a) – (c) parasitic micro-organisms and soil animals are not included, (d) Parasitic food chain.

Actually, the pyramids of numbers do not give a true picture of the food chain as they are not very functional. They do not indicate the relative effects of the 'geometric' 'food chain' and size factors of the organisms. They generally vary with different communities with different types of food chains in the same environment. It becomes sometimes very difficult to represent the whole community on the same numerical scale (for example; forest).

(2) Pyramid of Biomass

Biomass refers to the total weight of living matter per unit area.

Therefore, the pyramid of biomass is to weigh individuals in each trophic level instead of counting them. This would give us a pyramid of biomass i.e. the total weight of all organisms at a given level. In an ecosystem, the biomass decreases from the producer level to the consumer level. For most ecosystems on land, the pyramid of biomass has a large base of primary producers with a small trophic level perched on the top. In grassland and forest, there is generally a gradual decrease in biomass of organisms at successive levels from the producers to the top carnivores. Thus, pyramids are upright. However, in a pond or aquatic ecosystem as the producers are small organisms, their biomass is least, this value gradually shows an increase towards the apex of the pyramid, thus pyramid becomes inverted in shape.

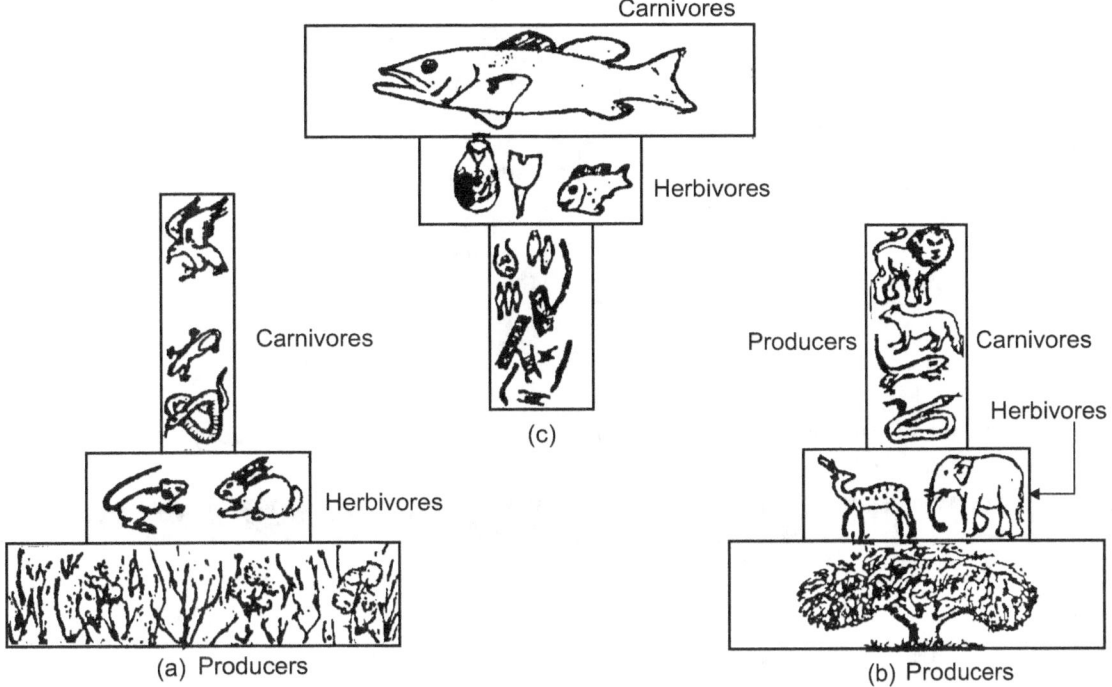

Fig. 2.15: Pyramids of Biomass (gm dry wt. per unit area) in different Kinds of Ecosystems (a) Grassland, (b) Forest, (c) Pond

(3) Pyramid of Energy

Of the three types of ecological pyramids, the pyramid of energy is the most informative and gives the best picture of the overall nature of the ecosystem. The energy in an ecosystem flows from the producer level to the consumer level. At each trophic level 80 to 90% of energy is lost. Hence, the amount of energy decreases from the producer level to the consumer level. This can be represented by the pyramid of energy.

An energy pyramid more accurately reflects the laws of thermodynamics; hence the pyramid is always upright, with a large energy base at the bottom. A pyramid of energy must be based on the determination of the actual intake of energy of an individual, how much is utilised during metabolism, how much remains in the waste products and how much is stored in the body tissues.

The energy inputs and outputs are calculated so that energy flow can be expressed per unit of land or water per unit time. For example, an ecosystem receives 1000 calories of light energy in a given day. Most of the energy is not absorbed; some is reflected back to space. Of the energy absorbed, only a small portion is utilised by green plants, out of which the plant uses some part of the energy for respiration, growth and repair. Of the 1000 calories, therefore only 100 calories are stored as energy rich materials. Now suppose an animal, say a deer, eats the plant containing 100 calories of food energy. The deer uses some of it for its own metabolism and stores only 10 calories as food energy. A lion that eats the deer gets an even smaller amount of energy. Thus, usable energy decreases from sunlight to producer to herbivore to carnivore. Therefore, energy pyramid will always be upright.

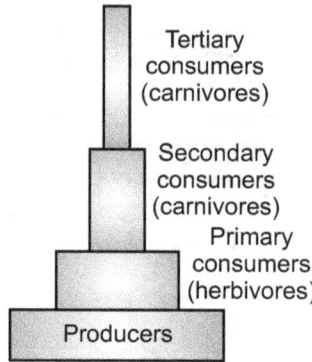

Fig. 2.16: Pyramid of Energy

(kcal per unit area within unit time, season or years in any ecosystem)

Points to Remember

- Ecosystem is integration of living and non-living factors of environment.
- Ecosystem is formed by living or abiotic factors and biotic or non-living factors.
- Water, light, temperature, gases and humidity are abiotic factors.
- Autotrophs, heterotrophs and decomposers are the biotic factors.
- Ecosystems are of two types: Terrestrial and aquatic.
- Energy flows through ecosystem.
- There is food chain in ecosystem.
- When various food chains are interconnected called food web.
- Ecological pyramids are of three types.

Questions

1. Define ecosystem. Give an account of biotic and abiotic components of ecosystem.
2. Give an account of function of ecosystem and energy flow in it.
3. Describe the structure and function of ecosystem.
4. What is food chain and food web. Describe both in detail.
5. Describe different types of ecosystems.
6. Write short notes on:
   (a) Food chain
   (b) Food web
   (c) Ecological pyramid
   (d) Grazing food chain
   (e) Forest ecosystem
   (f) Pond ecosystem
   (g) Energy flow in ecosystem
   (h) Biotic components of ecosystem
   (i) Single channel energy flow model
   (j) Characteristics of ecosystem

✷✷✷

Chapter **3**...

Environmental Pollution

Contents ...

3.1 Introduction

In the prehistoric period, primitive man was largely dependant on his physical strength for gathering food from nature mainly by hunting. Then he discovered fire, which was used for cooking the food. Most of man's activities were in harmony with nature. The industrial revolution brought tremendous change in human life. But, it also marked, the start of man's increasing interference with nature. Population increased, villages multiplied and became towns, cities and nations. The demand for food for the ever increasing population had increased. Man cleared forests and introduced many chemicals into the environment to increase agricultural production. These hazardous chemicals used for the control of crop pests have created environmental problems which man did not face before. The rapid industrialisation and urbanisation have also created several problems in the environment. Industrial growth has definitely resulted into increased production and progress in different sectors.

India today is one of the first 10 industrialised countries of the world. Every year in our country, big industrial projects are set up which have again created the serious problem of environmental pollution. The emission of dust and toxic gases, discharge of effluents has polluted our atmosphere, aquatic as well as soil habitats. Man is continuously exploiting natural resources instead of conserving them for future generations. Serious degradation and depletion have been caused through overuse, misuse and mismanagement of resources to meet the human needs and to satisfy the increasing greed. Indefinite exploitation of nature by man has disturbed the delicate ecological balance between the living and non-living components of the biosphere.

Pollution may be defined as '*an undesirable change in the physical, chemical or biological characteristics of air, water and soil that harmfully affect human life or create a potential health hazard of any living organism*'. Pollution is thus, direct or indirect change in a component of the biosphere i.e. harmful to living components and in particular undesirable for man, adversely affecting the overall quality of life. Not only in India, but in developed western world also pollution is a scare-word. Pollution is a man made problem, mainly of prosperous countries. The heavily industrialised countries dump hazardous waste materials in developing countries. Thus, pollution is infact exported to developing countries.

3.2 Types of Pollution

Various types of pollution are classified in different ways. Depending on the type of environment being polluted, the pollution may be recognised as, air pollution, water pollution, soil pollution and sound pollution.

(1) Air Pollution: Air is precious and life cannot sustain on earth without it. Air is present in the atmosphere and it is composed of oxygen, carbon dioxide, nitrogen, argon, methane, hydrogen, neon, helium, methane, krypton and water vapour. Thus, atmosphere is an envelope of gases divided into different layers and forms an insulating blanket around the earth, without which there will be no life. An alteration of composition of the atmosphere by introduction of potentially harmful substances like gases and particulate matter causes air pollution. About 100 million tonnes of pollutants are poured into the atmosphere every year and this amount is increasing every year. Aeroplanes release a large amount of burnt and unburnt fuel and gases into the air. A huge amount of smoke comes out of factory chimneys or household cooking, when the fuel used is coal, wood, sawdust, or dry cow dung. The automobile exhausts also cause air pollution in big cities like Kolkata, Delhi, Mumbai, Chennai and Bengaluru. Pesticides used for the control of insect pests also cause air pollution. Thermal power plants release fly ash, soot and SO_2 in the air. Fertiliser plants, textile industries, smelters, steel plant, oil refineries, chemical plants, and decomposition of organic waste and garbage pollute the air. The secondary pollutants, such as acid rain, Peroxy Acetyl Nitrate (PAN), photochemicals and smog are dangerous pollutants of air. The air pollutants cause various ill effects on animals and plants too. The detailed account of the air pollution is given later in this chapter.

(2) Water Pollution: Water is an important natural resource essential for the survival of life. *The addition of any substance to water or changing of water's physical and chemical* *characteristics in any way which interferes with its use for legitimate purposes is called water pollution.* Water pollution adversely changes the quality of water. It disturbs or destroys the balance of ecosystems and causes hazards to public health. Water becomes polluted due to the discharge of inorganic or organic substances or biological agents. Water pollution occurs when sewage and domestic waste water, industrial wastes, suspended solids, heavy metals, cyanide, oil, agricultural chemicals, fertilisers, pesticides, thermal and radioactive wastes are discharged into water bodies like rivers, lakes, oceans, etc. The oceanic water pollution takes place due to navigational discharges of oil, grease and petroleum products, detergents, sewage and garbage, including radioactive waste. Polluted water is unfit for drinking purpose, irrigation and recreational use. Several diseases are caused by the use of polluted waters, such as cholera, typhoid, dysentery, etc. A detailed account of the water pollution has been described later in this chapter.

(3) Soil Pollution: Soil is a very important resource, as it is the substrate on which plants grow. In recent times, the pollution of soil in rural, urban and industrial areas has become a serious problem. There are various sources of soil pollution. For the control of weeds in the fields $CuSO_4$, sodium chlorate and arsenic compounds are used. These toxic substances are harmful to the beneficial organisms of the soil and are dangerous to wildlife and man. The crop pests are controlled by fungicides, nematicides, insecticides, pesticides, herbicides, which are incorporated into the soil and then into the food chain. The persistent organochlorine pesticides like DDT, BHC, Aldrin and Dieldrin are highly poisonous to humans and wildlife as they kill non-target organisms like earthworms, symbiotic bacteria and algae. The human excreta, sewage water, industrial effluents also pollute the soil. Salination of soil is another important aspect of soil pollution. The soil pollutants and the control of soil pollution are discussed later.

3.3 Pollutants

Any substance which causes pollution is called a *pollutant*. A pollutant may thus, include any chemical or geochemical (dust, sediment, grit, etc.) substance, a biotic component or its product, or physical factor (heat) that is released intentionally by man into the environment in such a concentration that may have adverse harmful or unpleasant effects. Thus, *pollutant can be defined as any solid, liquid or gaseous substance present in such a concentration, which may be harmful or injurious to the environment.* There is large variety of pollutants released from different sources. Industries, thermal power plants, fertilisers and pesticide plants, automobile exhausts, smelters, mining, domestic waste waters, garbage, solid wastes, nuclear weapons testing, radioactive wastes are the sources of different pollutants.

Following are the important air, water and soil pollutants

1. **Particulate matter:** Soot, fly ash, smoke, dust, grit, etc.
2. **Gases:** SO_2, NO, NO_2, CO, CO_2, H_2S.
3. **Acid droplets:** H_2SO_4, HNO_3, etc.
4. **Fluorides.**
5. **Halogens:** Chlorine, Bromine, Iodine.
6. **Heavy metals:** Hg, Cd, Pb, Zn, Ni, Cr.
7. **Agrochemicals:** Biocides like pesticides, insecticides, herbicides, fungicides, nematicides, weedicides, bactericides, and Fertiliser like superphosphate, urea.
8. **Organic substances:** Benzene, benzopyrenes.

9. **Photochemical oxidants:** These are secondary pollutants like photochemical smog, ozone, peroxy acetyl nitrate (PAN), peroxy benzoyl nitrate (PBN), aldehydes.

10. **Solid wastes:** Rubber, plastic, glass, paper, etc.

11. **Radioactive waste.**

12. **Noise.**

Biodegradable and Non-biodegradable

Basically, pollutants are of two types, namely biodegradable and non-biodegradable pollutants.

3.2.1 Biodegradable Pollutants

These are the pollutants which can be easily decomposed under natural conditions by micro-organisms. These substances do not persist in the environment for longer period. But they are converted into simpler forms from their complex form. For example, agricultural wastes and garbage. During the process of decomposition or degradation, some living micro-organisms utilise them as food substrate and sewage containing animal and human excreta which can be digested and converted into simple organic material by micro-organisms. They convert the sewage into methane, CO_2 and H_2O. A variety of biodegradable pollutants, such as pollutants from tannery, food processing industries, garbage, etc. are converted or oxidised into simpler forms, but there is high biological oxygen demand.

During the process of biodegradation, more and more oxygen present in the polluted water is utilised by the micro-organisms hence, there is depletion of oxygen level in the water.

3.2.2 Non-biodegradable Pollutants

This class of pollutants, remains unchanged for a very long period of time in the environment. These are not easily degradable by organisms hence; they are called *non-biodegradable* or *persistent pollutants*. These are the materials and poisonous substances like aluminium cans, mercuric salts, long chain phenolics, DDT, etc. that do not degrade or degrade only very slowly in nature. Rubber, plastic, synthetic fibres, solid waste are the pollutants which are not degradable in the environment. The pesticides like DDT, BHC, aldrine, endrine are organo-chlorine pesticides, which are highly toxic. They last long in the environment and hence, create problems. These are hazardous mainly due to their concentration in the food chain. They have high stability, low vapour pressure and very low solubility in water, but have substantial solubility in oils and fats. These chemicals enter in the body of animals through food chain. For example, the concentration of DDT in fresh water is about 0.00001 ppm. It tends to become more concentrated from one trophic level to another tropic level due to the process of bioaccumulation. DDT affects calcium metabolism in birds and also affects reproduction. Even these chemicals are found in considerable amounts in human fat tissues.

The industrial effluents contain mercury, lead, nickel, cadmium which pollute underground water. Consumption of such water leads to bioaccumulation of these toxic heavy metals. They are not metabolised in the body and are stored in fat tissues. These chemicals increase in concentration in the human tissues through food chain and process is called *biological magnification*. Radioactive substances also show biomagnifications. Cadmium has a very long biological half-life and hence, it tends to accumulate in the human body. The chronic effects are kidney and liver damage and even death.

3.4 Air Pollution

The environment, which supports life and sustains various human activities, is widely known as the biosphere. The biosphere is a shallow layer compared to the total size of the earth and extends to about 20 km from the bottom of the ocean to the highest point in atmosphere at which life can survive without man-made protective devices. The atmosphere, which makes up the largest fraction of the biosphere, is a dynamic system that continuously absorbs a wide range of solids, liquids and gases from both natural and man made sources. These substances travel through air in the atmosphere, disperse, and react with one another and with other substances both physically and chemically. Most of these constituents, eventually find their way into a depository, such as the ocean, or to a receptor such as man. Some substances, such as helium escape from the biosphere. Others, such as carbon dioxide, may enter the atmosphere faster than they enter a reservoir and thus, gradually accumulate in the air.

Normal composition of clean, dry atmospheric air is as follows:

Gases	Per cent (by volume)
1. Nitrogen	78.09
2. Oxygen	20.94
3. Argon	0.934
4. Carbon dioxide	0.031
5. Methane	0.0002
6. Hydrogen	0.00005
7. Other gases	Minute

The mixture of CO_2, helium, argon, krypton, nitrous oxide and xenon form about 0.97% and as well as very small amounts of some other organic and inorganic gases whose amount in the atmosphere vary with time and place. A variety of contaminants or pollutants is continuously added in the atmosphere through both natural and man made processes. After addition of these substances they interact with the environment and cause toxicity, diseases, aesthetic distress, deterioration of property, damage to plants and animals, physiological effects and environmental decay. The pollutants are natural as well as man made. The natural pollutants, such as hydrocarbons and sulphur oxides in atmosphere and radiations cause air pollution but the severity is less whereas the artificial pollutants i.e. those produced by human actions are more significant because their adverse effects of pollution are most severe. Thus, the primary cause of pollution is action of people and as population increases, the problem of pollution also increases proportionately. The problem of air pollution was not acute in past because there was no human encroachment on nature. However, in the age of science and technology, there is heavy industrialisation and the ever expanding world population is responsible for the world wide problem of air pollution.

Air pollution is basically the presence of foreign substances in air.

This is the simplest definition of air pollution but there are also some specific definitions given below:

"Air pollution may be defined as any atmospheric condition in which certain substances are present in such concentrations that they can produce undesirable effects on man and his environment. These substances include gases (sulphur oxides, nitrogen oxides, carbon-monoxide, hydrocarbons), particulate matter (smoke, dust, fumes, aerosols), radioactive materials and many others."

– C.S. Rao

"Air pollution is the excessive concentration of foreign matter in the air which adversely affects the well being of the individual or causes damage to property".

– American Medical Association

"Air pollution means the presence in the outdoor atmosphere of one or more contaminants, such as dust, fumes, gas, mist, odour smoke or vapour in quantities, with characteristics and of durations such as to be injurious to human, plant or animal life or to property or which unreasonably interfere with comfortable enjoyment of life and property.

– Engineers Joint Council (U.S.A.)

"Air pollution is nothing but the excessive concentration of foreign matter in the ambient atmosphere, generally resulting from the activity of man, present for sufficient time and under circumstances which interfere significantly with the comfort, health, or welfare of persons or with full use or enjoyment of property".

– Indian Standards Institution

There are several factors responsible for the air pollution, such as rapid industrialisation and urbanisation, tremendous increase in number and excessive use of automobiles, use of pesticides and insecticides in agriculture, mining and smelting and so on. Therefore, some critics called air pollution as the 'gift of the industrialisation' or 'the price of industrialisation'. Air pollution caused by automobiles has been described as 'the disease of wealth'. Further, the severity of the problem of air pollution varies from place to place. For example, air pollution in Tokyo or Los Angeles is not the same as that in Kolkata or Mumbai.

Air pollution can cause several problems, such as diseases, death, and reduced visibility bring about vast economic losses and contribute to the general deterioration of our both cities and country side. It can cause intangible losses to our historical monuments, such as the 'Taj Mahal' which is believed to be badly affected by air pollution. The acid rain is another evil of the air pollution, which has destroyed many lakes in Canada and made the water unfit for the survival of aquatic life. Acid rain has also reduced forest growth and destroyed thousands of hectares of forest areas and caused damage to crop plants. It results due to large scale industrial activities in technologically advanced countries like U.S.A., U.K. and other European countries. The problem of acid rain is common in Scandinavia.

Air pollution is also responsible for destruction of basic ecology, large scale deforestation, imbalance in oxygen concentration in atmosphere and also affects the weather and rain patterns.

The industrial activity, particularly in thermal power stations, cement plants, oil refineries, chemical industries, metallurgical industries, steel plants, fertiliser factories, cause major problems of air pollution.

Air pollution problems are felt more acutely by the elderly people and people with chest and respiratory diseases. Tragic instances of death have been reported due to air pollution episodes, such as the London disaster of 1952 and the Bhopal gas tragedy of 1984.

It is, therefore, a matter of great importance that engineers, scientists, factory owners, common public should take care that they do not contribute to atmospheric pollution. In addition, they must apply their ingenuity and problem solving abilities to minimise air pollution, and restoring the natural environment.

3.4.1 Sources, Classification and Properties of Pollutants

The variety of pollutants or air contaminants are continuously emitted into the atmosphere by natural and anthropogenic or man made sources and is so diverse that it is difficult to classify air pollutants properly. Some authors classify air pollutants as follows:

1. Natural pollutants e.g. Natural fog, pollen, bacteria and their spores and products of volcanic eruption.
2. Aerosols or particulate matter e.g. dust, smoke, mists, fog and fumes.
3. Gases and vapours e.g. Sulphur, Nitrogen, Oxygen and Halogen compounds, Organic and Radioactive compounds.

Table 3.1: Different Air Pollutant and Vapours

Sr. No.	Group	Examples
1.	Sulphur compounds	SO_2, SO_3, H_2S, mercaptans
2.	Nitrogen compounds	NO, NO_2, NH_3
3.	Oxygen compounds	O_3, CO, CO_2
4.	Halogen compounds	HF, HCl
5.	Organic compounds	Aldehydes, hydrocarbons
6.	Radioactive compounds	Radioactive gases

There are some other contaminants which are formed from the above pollutants, as they undergo chemical reactions and enter the atmosphere. As a result, the end products formed are more harmful and toxic than the original or parent pollutants. For example, smog also known as photochemical smog is formed by reaction of unsaturated hydrocarbons with nitrogen dioxide in sunlight. This is also called as secondary pollutant. However, pollutants are usually divided into two categories, such as

(I) Primary pollutants and

(II) Secondary pollutants

(I) Primary Pollutants: The pollutants which are emitted directly from the sources are called *primary pollutants*. There are several typical pollutants, which are included in this category:

(i) Particulate matter, such as ash, smoke, dust, fumes, mist and spray.

(ii) Inorganic gases such as Sulphur dioxide (SO_2), Hydrogen sulphide (H_2S), Nitric oxide (NO), Ammonia (NH_3), Carbon monoxide (CO), Carbon dioxide (CO_2), Hydrogen fluoride (HF), Olefinic and aromatic hydrocarbons and radioactive compounds.

Although, a large number of primary pollutants are emitted into the atmosphere, only a few pollutants are present in sufficient concentrations to be of immediate concern. There are five major types of primary pollutants, which are responsible for causing the air pollution and serious hazards to animal and plant life. They are particulate matter, oxides of sulphur, oxides of nitrogen, carbon monoxide and hydrocarbons. Carbon dioxide is generally not considered as an air pollutant but because of its increased influence on global climatic patterns it is now of great concern. Global warming is a serious consequence of the ever increasing concentration of CO_2 in the atmosphere. The radioactive pollutants are of specialised nature and they are important air pollutants.

(II) Secondary Pollutants: The secondary pollutants are those that are formed in the atmosphere by chemical interactions among primary pollutants and normal atmospheric constituents. In this category, pollutants such as Sulphur trioxide (SO_3), Nitrogen dioxide (NO_2), Peroxy acetyl nitrate (PAN), Ozone, Aldehydes, Ketones and various sulphate and nitrate salts are included. Secondary pollutants are formed from chemical and photochemical reactions in the atmosphere. The secondary pollutants are more dangerous than the primary pollutants. The formation of secondary pollutants is a complex process in which several reaction mechanisms and various steps are involved. The process is influenced by many factors such as concentration of reactants, the amount of moisture present in the atmosphere, degree of photoactivation, meteorological forces and local topography.

Concentration of pollutants: Concentration of pollutants is often expressed by fractions. A concentration of one part per million (1 ppm), corresponds to one part pollutant per one million parts of the gas, liquid or solid mixture in which the pollutant occurs. In a gas mixture, the reference is generally to ppm by volume; in liquids and solids, the reference is generally to ppm by weight. More recently, it has become customary to express gaseous pollutants and particulate matter in the atmosphere in mass density units of micrograms per cubic metre ($\mu g/m^3$), and in this case, it is necessary to specify temperature (usually 0 to 25°C) and pressure (usually 1 atmosphere) at which the concentration is expressed. **Table 3.2** lists some common fractional concentrations. At first glance, a concentration of ppm seems ridiculously small and negligible. Nevertheless, concentrations of pollutants at levels of 1 ppm or less can have serious adverse effects. For example, 0.2 ppm average SO_2 level in the atmosphere has been shown to lead to an increase in the human mortality rate. 0.02 ppm peroxy benzoyl nitrate, a constituent of photochemical smog can cause severe eye irritation in humans. 0.001 ppm hydrogen fluoride (HF) gas in atmosphere can injure certain sensitive plants.

Table 3.2: Fractional Concentration

Symbol	Definition	Fraction
ppm	parts per million	10^{-6}
pphm	parts per hundred million	10^{-8}
ppb	parts per billion	10^{-9}
ppt	parts per trillion	10^{-12}

Natural Pollutants: These pollutants are released naturally in the atmosphere. Among them are biological agents such as pollen grains, bacteria and spores of fungi. Pollen grains are important as some people are allergic to them. Pollen grains are the male gametophytes of gymnosperms and angiosperms and they are discharged into the atmosphere from weeds, grasses and trees. Wind pollination causes the dispersal of millions of pollen grains which are between 5 μ to 100 μ (micron) in size. The microscopic fungal spores which are discharged into the atmosphere are also considered as air contaminants. The pollen grains and fungal spores act as allergens of the skin and the respiratory tract. From the point of view of pollution, air borne pollutants are significant because of the allergic responses such as asthma, hay fever, bronchitis and dermatitis; they elicit in susceptible individuals. A variety of pathogenic bacteria is present in the air which again causes various diseases in the individuals.

How pollen grains or air borne pollutants are responsible for allergy and asthma was investigated in Bengaluru. The garden city of Bengaluru is famous for its fine climate, but many people here are known to suffer from asthma. The cases of bronchial asthma are particularly high in this city. The people who had never shown the tendencies earlier, have, on coming to Bengaluru had attacks of asthma. Furthermore, those who had only mild attacks elsewhere experienced severe ones here. It has also been recorded that the percentage of people/patients who reported relief when they left Bengaluru is as high as 37.6%.

The Asthma Research Society of Bengaluru had taken a systematic investigation of pollen grains and fungal spores content of the atmosphere in Bengaluru for 2 years i.e. from July 1976 to July 1978. The study revealed that there were 75 types of identified pollen grains and 120 types of fungal spores. The samples were collected from 10 different sampling stations around Bengaluru. It was found that the pollen grains were present all the year around in the city atmosphere and all the identified pollen types were attributed to local plants. The study showed highest number of pollen grains of *Parthenium* (41%) followed by grass pollen (29%) and the *Cassia* species (11.8%).

Particulate Matter: Solid and liquid aerosols suspended in the atmosphere are referred to as particulate matter. Thus, the particulate matter is nothing but the atmospheric substances that are not gases. They can be suspended liquid droplets or solid particles or mixture of the two. They are also called by the name *aerosols*. An aerosol can also be defined as a colloidal system in which the dispersion medium is a gas and the dispersed phase is solid or liquid such as dust, smoke or mist. The term aerosol is used when the dispersed phase is suspended in air. After it has settled either by virtue of its weight, by agglomeration or by impact on a solid or liquid surface, the term no longer applies. Thus, particulate matter is an air pollutant only when it is an aerosol. These arise either from condensation processes or from dispersion processes, for example, erosion, grinding and spraying. Although, smoke is popularly used to denote mixtures of particulate matter, fumes, gases, and mists, it actually refers to solid (or solid and liquid) condensation aerosols. Dust refers to solid dispersion aerosols and mist to liquid aerosols.

Aerosols differ widely in terms of particle size, particle density and their importance as pollutants. Particulate matter or aerosol can be composed of inert or extremely reactive materials. Their diameter generally ranges from 0.01 µ or less up to about 100 µ. The inert materials do not react readily with the environment nor do they exhibit any morphological changes as a result of combustion or any other process, whereas the reactive materials could be further oxidised or may react chemically with the environment.

Following are the various aerosols:

Dust: Dust is made up of solid particles of the size ranging from 1 to 100 µ. These particles are larger than those found in colloids and capable of temporary suspension in air or other gases. These are formed by natural disintegration of rock and soil or by the mechanical process of grinding, and spraying of organic and inorganic materials. They have large settling velocities and are removed from air by gravity, electrostatic forces and other inertial processes. The fine dust particles act as centres of catalysis for many of the chemical reactions taking place in the atmosphere. Generally, the particles are over 20 µ in diameter, although some are smaller. Thermal power station chimneys discharge fly ash particles and their size varies from 3 to 80 µ. Fly ash particles from cement factory have a diameter ranging from 10 - 150 µ and foundry dust from 1 - 200 µ. The major bulk of the dust particles settle to the ground, but the fine particles having diameter of 5 µ or less tend to form stable suspensions.

Smoke: Smoke consists of very fine particles of size ranging from 0.01 µ to 1 µ produced by incomplete combustion. These fine smoke particles can be liquid or solid. Smoke particles consist predominantly of carbon particles and other combustible materials. Generally, the size of smoke particles is less than 1 µ. For example, coal smoke particle size is from 0.2 to 0.01 µ and oil smoke particle size is from 0.03 to 1.0 µ. Smoke may have different colours depending on the nature of the material.

Fumes: These are solid particles of the size ranging from 0.1 to 1 µ. Fumes are formed by condensation from the gaseous state, generally after volatilisation of melted substances, and often accompanied by a chemical reaction, such as oxidation. Fumes are normally released from chemical or metallurgical processes.

Table 3.3: Sources of Atmospheric Dust

Sources	Examples
1. **Combustion**	(i) Fuel burning (coal, wood, fuel, oil)
	(ii) Incineration (house and municipal garbage).
	(iii) Others (open fires, forest fires, tobacco smoking).
2. **Materials handling and processing**	(i) Crushing and grinding (ores, stones, cement, rocks and chemicals)
	(ii) Loading and unloading (sand, gravel, coal, ores, lime, cement)
	(iii) Mixing and packing (chemicals, fertilisers)
	(iv) Food processing (flour, corn starch, grains)
	(v) Cutting and forming (saw mills, wall board, plastics)
	(vi) Metallurgical (foundries, smelters)
	(vii) Industrial (paper, textiles manufacture)
3. **Earth moving operations**	(i) Construction (road, buildings, dams, site clearance)
	(ii) Mining (blasting)
	(iii) Agriculture (soil filling, ploughing, land preparation)
4. **Miscellaneous**	(i) Winds
	(ii) House cleaning
	(iii) Mud road cleaning
	(iv) Crop spraying (dust, powder)
	(v) Poultry feeding
	(vi) Engine exhaust

Mist: It is made up of liquid droplets generally smaller than 10 μ which are formed by condensation in the atmosphere or are released from industrial operations. In meteorology, it means a light dispersion of minute water droplets suspended in the atmosphere. Natural mist particles formed from water vapour in the atmosphere are rather large ranging from 40 to 500 μ in size.

Fog: Fog is nothing but visible aerosols in which the dispersed phase is liquid. It is usually formed by condensation. In meteorology, it refers to dispersion of water ice in the atmosphere near the earth's surface reducing visibility to less than 1/2 km. In natural fog, the size of the particles ranges from 1 to 40 μ.

The chemical composition of the particulate pollutants varies over a wide range. The composition dependents on the origin of the particulate matter. Particles from soils and minerals primarily contain calcium, aluminium and silicon compounds. Smoke from combustion of coal, oil, wood and solid waste contains mainly organic compounds. Insecticide dusts and certain fumes released from chemical plants also contain organic and inorganic compounds. Hydrocarbons themselves can coalesce into aerosol droplets that form one kind of particulate matter. The most harmful components of incomplete combustion are generally grouped as Particulate Polycyclic Organic Matter (PPOM). These materials are derivatives of benzo α-pyrene, a potent carcinogen. Of all the different types of aerosols or particulate matter in the atmosphere, the presence of trace elements, such as lead, cadmium, nickel and mercury may constitute the greatest health hazard. They are highly toxic and occur in combined forms, such as oxides, hydroxides, sulphates and nitrates.

Effects of Particulate Matter

The particulate matter discharged in the atmosphere creates variety of problems in the environment and also for plants and animals. Following are some of the problems:

1. The particulate matter can scatter and absorb the sunlight, thus, reducing visibility.

2. The particulate matter in the atmosphere is believed to have the effect of cooling the earth. Thus, it may affect the global climate.

3. Dust on snow and ice reduces reflection, increases absorption and can promote melting.

4. Particles also reduce visibility by attenuating the light from objects and illuminating the air, thus, reducing the contrast between the objects and their background. Reduced visibility is aesthetically undesirable and dangerous for aircraft and motor vehicles.

5. The particulate matter has many effects on materials, such as corrosion of metals when air is humid, erosion and soiling of buildings, sculpture and painted surfaces and soiling of clothing and draperies. Many buildings in London are blackened due to centuries of soot.

6. A new problem produced by particulate matter is its corrosion and damage of electronic equipment, especially through chemical or mechanical action on electrical contacts. This problem is created because of particles which settle out of the air.

7. The particulate matter can cause toxic effects on animals and humans and they are of three types

(i)   Intrinsic toxicity due to chemical or physical properties.

(ii) Interference with clearance mechanisms in the respiratory tract.

(iii) Toxicity due to adsorbed toxic substance.

The fine particles are more harmful because they reach the lungs more easily and remain in the lung. The toxic particles are smaller and carcinogenic. Polynuclear aromatic hydrocarbons are always smaller in size.

(1) **Chronic bronchitis:** In this illness, the bronchial tubes are permanently damaged, leading to the failure of the cilia, over production of mucous and consequently a chronic cough to remove the mucous.

(2) **Bronchial asthma:** Foreign matter leads to an allergic reaction of the bronchial membranes, which swell and cause wheezing and shortness of breath.

(3) **Emphysema:** The branchioles (the smaller branches of the bronchial tubes) constrict, causing the lung air sacs (alveoli) to over inflate and burst, this results in fewer blood capillaries, which means less oxygen transfer into the blood and chronic shortness of breath.

(4) **Lung cancer:** Large numbers of toxic particles have been discovered in polluted urban atmospheres including metal dusts, asbestos, and aromatic hydrocarbons, such as the carcinogen 3, 4-benzopyrene. Their concentration is very small but they may play a role in the higher cancer rates that occur in urban areas as compared to rural areas.

Gases and Vapours

Following are the gases which are air pollutants:

1. Sulphur dioxide or oxides of sulphur
2. Hydrogen sulphide
3. Nitrogen dioxide or oxides of nitrogen
4. Carbon monoxide
5. Carbon dioxide
6. Chlorine and hydrogen chloride
7. Ozone
8. Aldehydes
9. Organic vapours
10. Radioactive gases
11. Hydrocarbons

Sulphur Dioxide (SO_2)

The most important sulphur oxide emitted by pollution sources is sulphur dioxide (SO_2), although some sulphur trioxide (SO_3) is also generally produced, but its percentage is always less than SO_2. The main source of sulphur dioxide is the combustion of fuels, especially coal. Thermal power stations are the main sources of SO_2 gas, where thousands of tonnes of coal are burnt. Concentration of SO_2 gas in the atmosphere depends upon the sulphur content of the fuel (coal or liquid fuel) used for heating and power generation. The sulphur content of fuels varies from less than 1% for good quality anthracite to over 4% for bituminous coal. Indian coal contains high amount of sulphur. In recent years in USA, there has been progressive decrease in the average atmospheric concentrations of SO_2 of several cities because of increased use of coal with low sulphur content. In certain places, there is a ban on use of high sulphur content coal. Another source of SO_2 in the atmosphere is petroleum and refineries. The petroleum oxide products contains less than 1% sulphur, a few contains upto 5%. Refining processes tend to concentrate sulphur compounds in the heavier fractions. Fuel gases also contain sulphur, but, in small quantities.

The major source of SO_2 emission are burning of fossil fuels (coal) in thermal power plants, smelting industries (smelting sulphur containing metal ores) and other processes such as manufacture of sulphuric acid and fertilisers. These account for about 75% of the total SO_2 emission. Remaining 25% emission is from petroleum refineries, fuel gases and automobiles.

It is estimated that sulphur oxides from human activities introduce 66 million metric tonnes of sulphur or 132 million metric tonnes of SO_2 into atmosphere annually, largely from coal and petroleum combustion. It is believed that about 10^9 million tonnes of SO_2 are added each year into the global environment.

In our country, SO_2 emission is on the increase over the years due to a corresponding increase in coal consumption in the country. There is increasing demand of coal for different thermal power stations for generation of the electricity, thus the production of SO_2 is also increasing every year.

The open burning of refuse, municipal incinerators, sulphuric acid plants, paper manufacturing plants also contribute some amount of SO_2 to the atmosphere.

SO_2 is a colourless, non-flammable gas that has an arid taste at concentrations less than 1 ppm of air and which has a pungent, irritating odour at concentrations above about 3 ppm. It is moderately soluble in water (11.3 gm/100 ml) forming weakly acidic sulphurous acid (H_2SO_3). SO_2 is oxidised slowly in clean air to sulphur trioxide (SO_3). In a polluted atmosphere, SO_2 reacts photochemically or catalytically with other pollutants or normal atmospheric constituents to form sulphur trioxide, sulphuric acid (H_2SO_4) and salts of sulphuric acid. In presence of moisture, the SO_3 becomes H_2SO_4 or a sulphate salt, both of which are dangerous to health.

SO_3 is generally emitted along with SO_2, at about 1-5 per cent of the SO_2 concentration. SO_3 rapidly combines with moisture in the atmosphere to form H_2SO_4 which has a low dew point. Both SO_2 and SO_3 are relatively quickly washed out of the atmosphere by rain and settle out as aerosols. This is the reason why SO_2 mass in clean dry air is so small as compared to annual emissions from anthropogenic sources.

Table 3.4: Comparison of the Amount of Anthropogenic Pollutants with the Amount Naturally Present in Dry, Clean air

Pollutants	Amount (millions of tonnes)	
	Anthropogenic (per year)	Dry, Clean Air
Particulate matter	269	–
SO_2	132	2
NO_2	48	8
CO	400	500

Effects of SO_2

(1) The SO_2 and H_2SO_4 are both capable of irritating the respiratory system of animals and humans. The pathological lung damage or mortality are caused in higher concentrations, but lower concentrations also produce adverse health effects. It is absorbed in the moist passage of upper respiratory tract, leading to swelling and stimulated mucous secretion. Exposure to 1 ppm level of SO_2 causes a constriction of air passage and causes significant brancho-constriction in asthmatics at even low concentration. In London, a rise in the daily death rate of 20% or more has been detected for SO_2 concentrations of 0.5 ppm lasting for a full day. Mean concentrations of 0.2 ppm has led to increased mortality in

Rotterdam, and levels of 0.1 ppm are believed to be responsible for the same results. Increased mortality is always accompanied by increased morbidity (illness), SO_2 levels below 0.25 ppm are also associated with increased mobility. The elderly and patients with heart or lung diseases suffer severely.

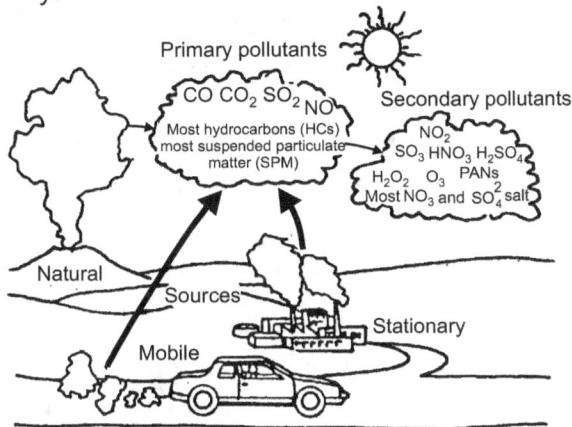

Fig. 3.1: Primary and Secondary Air Pollutants

(2) SO_2 causes intense irritation of eyes.

(3) SO_2 is oxidised to SO_3 in presence of water vapour or water and forms sulphurous and sulphuric acid respectively. SO_3 is a very strong irritant, much stronger than SO_2, causing severe bronchospasms at relatively low levels of concentration. H_2SO_4 is a stronger irritant (4-20 times) than SO_2.

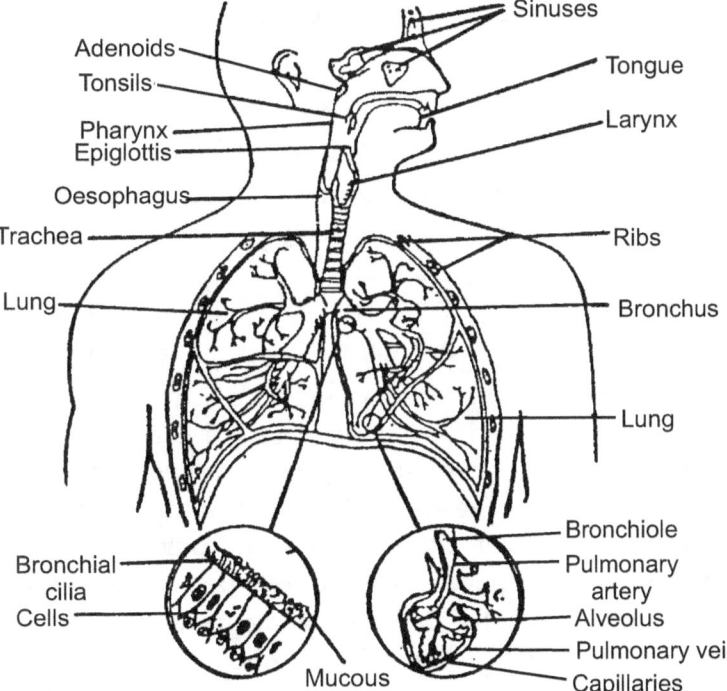

Fig. 3.2: The Human Respiratory System

(4) SO_2 aggravates existing respiratory diseases in humans and contributes to their development. Even healthy individuals experience broncho-constriction when exposed for a few minutes to levels of 1.6 ppm. This condition is accompanied by shallow breathing and an increased respiratory rate. Acute irritant effects of gas are confined to the upper respiratory tract where more than 95% of inhaled SO_2 is absorbed. The chronic effects resulting from prolonged exposure to low concentrations include incidence of respiratory infection in children.

Table 3.5: Effects of SO_2 on Humans

Concentrations in ppm	Effects
0.2	Lowest concentration causing a human response
0.3	Threshold for taste recognition
0.5	Threshold for odour recognition
1.6	Threshold for inducing reversible broncho-constriction in healthy individuals
8 - 12	Immediate throat irritation
10	Eye irritation
20	Immediate coughing

(5) SO_2 has been found to adversely affect vegetation even at concentrations below 0.03 ppm. Plants are relatively more sensitive to SO_2 than are animals and man. Thus, threshold levels of SO_2 injury in plants are quite low as compared to animals and man.

Table 3.6: Concentration of SO_2 producing Threshold Injury

Category	SO_2 concentration in ppm	
	Short-term exposure for one hour daily	Long-term exposure for one hour daily
Plants	0.5 – 2.0	0.01 – 0.05
Animals	0.5 – 3.0	0.02 – 0.10
Man	1.0 – 4.0	0.05 – 0.20

High concentrations over short periods can produce acute leaf injury, such as necrotic (tissue-destroying), blotching of broad leaved plants and grasses or brownish discolouration in the tips of pine needles. Lower concentrations over longer periods (days or weeks) lead to chronic leaf injury, such as a gradual yellowing (chlorosis) because chlorophyll production is impeded. There is bleaching of leaf pigments due to conversion of chlorophyll - a to phaeophytin - a. Thus, SO_2 in air reduces the pH of leaf tissue of some trees, increasing the total sulphur content of leaves and tree bark. Experimentally, it is proved in case of wheat that exposure to 0.8 ppm of SO_2 with coal smoke for 2 hours daily for 60 days resulted in the reduction of root and shoot lengths, number of leaves per plant, biomass, productivity, number of grains per spike and in yield.

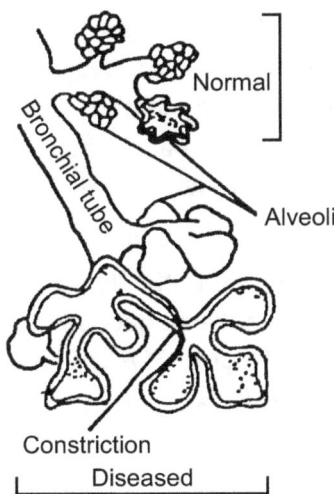

Fig. 3.3: Bronchitis-emphysema, a disease caused or aggravated by air pollution. In the normal lung, the bronchial tubes branch into millions of alveoli where transfer of oxygen to blood takes place. In a diseased lung, alveoli coalesce reducing the area for oxygen transfer. Also, bronchi are constricted reducing the rate at which are exchanged

(6) SO_2 affects stomatal pores, stomatal frequency and trichomes as well as chloroplast structure.

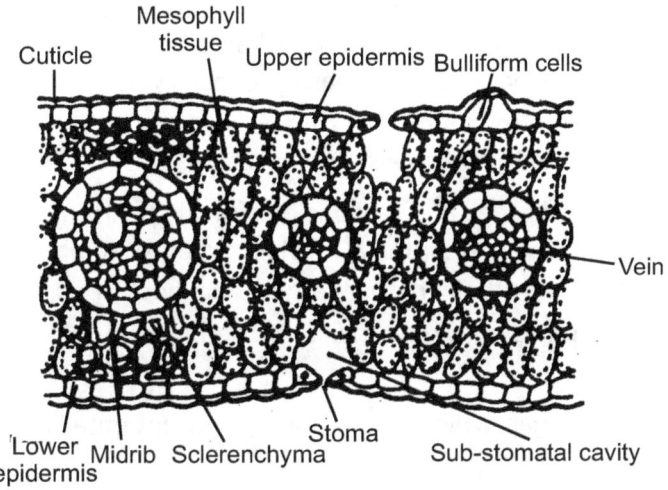

Fig. 3.4: Cross Section of a Common Leaf

(7) SO_2 itself may also be toxic to plants. H_2SO_4 aerosols are toxic to plants.

(8) SO_2, SO_3 can damage materials and property, through their conversion into the highly reactive H_2SO_4. Discolouration and physical deterioration are produced in building materials. H_2SO_4 mist in the atmosphere causes deterioration of structural materials such as marble, limestone, roofing slate, and mortar. Many priceless marble sculptures and buildings have suffered damage in the last 30 years because of increased SO_2 content in the atmosphere.

Atmospheres polluted by SO_2, particulate matter and humidity, accelerate the corrosion of most metals especially iron, steel and zinc. At levels of 0.09 - 1 ppm, SO_2 affects fabrics, leather and paint. SO_2 is readily absorbed by leather and causes its disintegration. Paper is also discoloured by SO_2 and becomes brittle and fragile. The drying time, brittleness, gloss and even colour of paints can also be affected.

(9)　A particular concern of SO_2 is acid rain. In certain regions, near industrial sources of air pollution (For example, Scandinavia and the North-eastern United States), the rain is much more acidic today than it was several decades ago, sometimes even as acidic as vinegar. This acid rain probably is due to both SO_2 and SO_3 and nitrogen oxides. It adversely affects agricultural crops, forests, human and human artifacts. Acid rain deteriorates the historic monuments.

Hydrogen Sulphide (H_2S)

This is a foul smelling gas. The chief sources of H_2S are decaying vegetation and animal matter, especially in aquatic habitats. It is emitted due to anaerobic biological decay processes on land, marshes and the oceans. Volcanoes and natural springs emit H_2S to some extent. Coal pits, sulphur springs and sewers also emit H_2S gas. One of the major sources of hydrogen sulphide is the kraft pulp industry, which uses a sulphide process for manufacturing paper. The other industrial sources of hydrogen sulphide are petroleum refineries, coke oven plants, viscose rayon plants and some chemical operations. About 30 million tonnes of H_2S is released every year by oceans and 60 to 80 million tonnes per year by land. Industries emit about 3 million tonnes every year. The chief industrial sources of H_2S are, users of sulphur containing fuels.

Other sulphur compounds that are responsible for air pollution, principally because of their strong odours are methyl mercaptan (CH_3SH), dimethyl sulphide (CH_3SCH_3), dimethyl disulphide (CH_3 SS CH_3) and their higher molecular homologs. The main sources of mercaptans are pulp mills, petroleum refineries and chemical manufacturing plants.

Effects of H_2S

1. It is a foul smelling gas which may destroy the appetite at 5 ppm level in some people.
2. At a low concentration, H_2S causes headache, nausea. At higher concentrations it may lead to coma and finally death.
3. Conjunctivitis and irritation of mucous membrane are caused at a concentration of 150 ppm.
4. Exposure at 500 ppm for 15–30 minutes may cause colic diarrhoea and bronchial pneumonia.
5. The gas can easily pass through the alveolar membrane of the lung and penetrate the blood stream. Death occurs due to respiratory failures.

Hydrogen Fluoride

In minute quantities, fluorocarbons are beneficial in helping prevention of tooth decay in man. However, higher levels of these compounds are toxic. This causes the problems of fluorosis in our country as well as in many other countries like France, U.S.A., Italy, Germany, Japan, China and some African countries.

The major sources of fluorides are the industries that manufacture phosphate fertilisers, the aluminium industry, brick plants, pottery and ceramics, ferro enamel works, fluorinated hydrocarbons, refrigerants, aerosol propellants, etc., fluorinated plastic, uranium and other metals. The pollutant is in gaseous or particulate state. Small amounts are also emitted from other metallurgical operations, such as zinc foundries and open-hearth steel furnaces. Burning coal also contributes to about 0.01% fluorine. On an average, fluoride level of air is 0.05 mg/m^3 of air but higher levels of 15.14 mg/m^3 have been reported from some Italian factories. Residents of this area, inhale about 0.3 mg of fluoride daily. In air, hydrogen fluoride is an important contaminant even at extremely low concentrations of 0.001-0.10 ppm by volume. These levels of hydrogen fluoride cause injuries to vegetation and animals. Fluorides enter plant leaves through stomata. In plants, it causes tip burn due to accumulation in leaves of conifers. Fluoride pollution in man and animals is mainly through water. In our country, it is a public health concern in states of Gujarat, Rajasthan, Punjab, Haryana, U.P., A.P. and Tamil Nadu.

Chlorine and Hydrogen Chloride

In the polluted atmosphere, chlorine is found as the element itself (chlorine), as hydrogen chloride, as chlorine containing organic compounds, such as perchloroethylene as an inorganic chloride. Some compounds are in gaseous form while some are found in particulate form.

The chief source of chlorine in the atmosphere is where it is manufactured or used as a material to produce other chemicals. Chlorine is used for purification of water in water purification plants, in sewage plants and in swimming pools. Sometimes, equipment failure or damage of chlorine container leads to leakage of chlorine into the atmosphere. Hydrogen chloride is used in numerous industrial chemical processes. It is easy to recover, so very little amount reaches the atmosphere.

Chlorine and its compounds are respiratory irritants, highly corrosive and cause damage to the vegetation.

Oxides of Nitrogen (NO$_X$)

Next to SO$_2$, nitrogen oxides are the second most abundant atmospheric contaminants in many cities. Even in unpolluted atmosphere, measurable amounts of different oxides of nitrogen, such as nitrous oxide (N$_2$O) or laughing gas, nitric oxide (NO) and nitrogen dioxide (NO$_2$) are found. These pollutants are emitted in to the atmosphere in significant quantities by human activities; of these nitric oxide (NO) is the main compound. It is formed by reaction of nitrogen (N_2) and oxygen (O_2) in the atmosphere at high temperatures (about 1100°C) i.e. during lightning discharges and the cooling occurs fast enough to prevent decomposition.

$$N_2 + XO_2 \rightleftharpoons 2 NO_X$$

Often, NO and NO_2 are analysed together in air and are referred to as NO_X or total oxides of nitrogen. It is a standard practice in the chemical industry to absorb and recover significant quantities of oxides of nitrogen. Actually, there are a total of seven oxides of nitrogen (N_2O, NO, NO_2, NO_3, N_2O_3, N_2O_4, N_2O_5) but only nitric oxide (NO) and nitrogen dioxide (NO_2) arise from human activities and are considered as harmful pollutants. NO is also produced by bacterial oxidation of ammonia (NH_3) in soil. The biological production of NO and N_2O amounts to about 1 billion metric tonnes annually and that combustion processes produce about 8 million metric tonnes of NO_X (expressed as NO_2) annually. These emissions are important parts of the environmental nitrogen cycle. The biological ammonia production of over 1 billion metric tonnes annually is also significant. NO combines with O_2 or even more readily with O_3 to form the more poisonous nitrogen dioxide (NO_2). NO_2 may react with water vapour in the atmosphere to form nitric acid (HNO_3). This acid combines with NH_3 to form ammonium nitrate.

Fossil fuel combustion is also another source of oxides of nitrogen. About 95% of the nitrogen oxide is emitted as NO and remaining 5% as NO_2. In urban areas, about 6% of oxides of nitrogen in atmosphere come from automobiles and 25% from electric generation and the rest from other sources. In metropolitan cities, vehicular exhaust is the most important source of nitrogen oxides. The concentration of NO and NO_2 in non-urban areas are only a few ppb, however these gases have a residence time in the atmosphere of only 3 or 4 days.

Human NO_X pollution is significant in urban areas because peak NO concentrations are often above 1 ppm and NO_2 levels occasionally exceed 0.5 ppm. These oxides play an important role in the production of photochemical smog.

(1) Nitrous oxide (N_2O): It is a colourless, odourless, non-toxic gas present in the natural atmosphere in relatively large concentrations (0.25 ppm). In atmosphere, maximum N_2O level is about 0.5 ppm. The major source of N_2O in the atmosphere is the biological activity of the soil and these are non-significant anthropogenic sources. This gas is generally not considered as air pollutant.

(2) Nitric oxide (NO): It is also a colourless and odourless gas produced largely by fuel combustion. The chief sources of this gas are the industries manufacturing nitric acid and other chemicals and the automobile exhausts. NO is oxidised to NO_2 in the polluted atmosphere through series of photochemical reactions. Thus, it is responsible for the formation of several secondary pollutants like peroxy acetyl nitrate (PAN), ozone, and carbonyl compounds in the presence of other organic compounds. There is little evidence of the direct role of this gas in causing a health hazard, at the levels found in urban air.

(3) Nitrogen dioxide (NO_2): NO_2 is a deep reddish brown pungent gas whose odour can be detected at concentrations of about 0.12 ppm. It has a irritating odour. This gas is the chief constituent of photochemical smog in metropolitan areas. Its importance in photochemical reactions is due to its strong absorption of ultraviolet radiation. Small concentrations of NO_2 have been detected in the lower stratosphere and they are probably produced by the oxidation of NO by ozone.

Concentrations of 100 ppm or more for a few minutes can be lethal to humans and animals and exposure to 5 ppm for a few minutes leads to adverse effects on the respiratory system. Exposure of monkeys to 15 to 50 ppm of NO_2 for 2 hours damaged their lungs, heart, liver, and kidneys and produced pulmonary changes similar to those occurring in human emphysema (inflammation). Long term exposures to 0.6 ppm have been related to an increase in acute respiratory disease in humans. It is thus, clear that NO_2 levels in polluted urban atmospheres are associated with adverse health effects.

NO_2 causes irritation of alveoli, leading to symptoms resembling emphysema upon prolonged exposure levels of about 1 ppm. Lung inflammation may be followed by edema and finally death. Smokers may readily develop lung diseases as cigarettes and cigars release 330-1500 ppm NO_2. The gas was responsible for 12 deaths in a fire at Cleveland's Crile Hospital on May 15, 1929, when X-ray film containing nitrocellulose accidently caught fire and produced NO_2.

NO_2 is highly injurious to plants. Their growth is suppressed when exposed to 0.3-0.5 ppm for 10-20 days. Sensitive plants show visible leaf injury when exposed to 8 ppm for 1 hour. Fuel combustion and nitric acid factories emit NO_2.

Carbon Monoxide (CO)

It constitutes the single largest pollutant in the urban areas. Carbon monoxide is colourless, odourless and tasteless gas against which humans have no protection. It originates from the incomplete combustion of carbonaceous materials. It has a boiling point of 192°C. It has a strong affinity towards the haemoglobin of the blood stream and is generally classified as a dangerous asphyxiant.

The chief source of CO in the atmosphere is combustion, especially due to automobile exhausts. However, except for motor vehicles and other internal combustion engines, very little CO is found in the gaseous emissions from properly adjusted, and operated installations. Although, certain industrial operations, such as electric and blast furnaces, petroleum refining operations, gas manufacturing plants, and coal mines are potential contributors of CO to the atmosphere, automobile exhausts are by far the most important sources.

Surprisingly, little is known about the sources and links of CO in the atmosphere, these matters are currently being actively studied. Human activities produce perhaps 250 million metric tonnes annually and some biological sources of CO exist, although not much is known about them. It has been found that the oceans are a natural source of CO, although they probably produce only 10 million metric tonnes annually and that much CO is present in rainwater. The exact average concentration of CO in the atmosphere is not well known. The values may be several times high or too small. The average residence time of CO in the atmosphere is short, probably a month or less. Moreover, the natural sources are far more significant than artificial sources.

CO can be oxidised to carbon dioxide (CO_2) but rate of oxidation is very slow. Mixtures of CO and O_2 exposed to sunlight for several years have remained almost unchanged. Since, residence time of CO in the atmosphere is only a few months, some removal process must exist. Perhaps, it might be absorbed and oxidised on surfaces, perhaps it is removed and utilised by plants or animals, or perhaps photochemical or catalytic processes are involved in its removal. Recent research indicates that soils are capable of removing large amount of CO from atmosphere, probably because of the activity of soil micro-organisms.

Effects of CO

The toxic effects of CO on human beings and animals arise from its reversible combination with haemoglobin (Hb) in the blood.

$$HbO_2 + CO \rightleftharpoons HbCO + O_2$$

Haemoglobin has a much greater affinity for CO than it does for O_2. When O_2 and CO are present in sufficient quantities to saturate the haemoglobin, the concentrations of HbO_2 (oxyhaemoglobin) and HbCO (carboxyhaemoglobin) are related by the Haldane equation.

$$\frac{[HbCO]}{[HbO_2]} = M\frac{P\,(CO)}{P\,(O_2)}$$

Where, P (CO) and P (O_2) are partial pressures (or volume concentrations) of the CO and O_2 gases. M is a constant that depends on the species, for humans M is about 200 to 300. Since, the ordinary air contains 21% of O_2, the ratio of HbCO to HbO_2 in man is approximately equal to 1/1000 of CO concentration expressed in ppm. It generally takes a few hours to reach this equilibrium, but the time is decreased by increased respiration rates.

The combination of haemoglobin with CO reduces the oxygen carrying capacity of the blood, so that less O_2 is available to the body cells. It also reduces dissociation of oxyhaemoglobin (HbO_2) into haemoglobin and O_2, so that anorexia (oxygen starvation) may result even though the blood is carrying several times as much O_2 as the body requires. CO also impairs cell functioning by blocking oxidation in other ways.

The affinity of CO for haemoglobin is 210 times greater than that of oxygen and as a result the amount of haemoglobin available for carrying oxygen for body tissue is considerably reduced. The body tissues are thus, deprived of their oxygen supply and death could result by asphyxiation (lack of oxygen). In addition, the presence of COHb in the blood, retards the dissociation of remaining oxyhaemoglobin, so the tissues are further deprived of oxygen.

The various concentrations of COHb in the blood causes various effects in healthy individuals and those suffering from the heart disease. The equilibrium level of COHb may be estimated for concentrations of CO below 100 ppm in the inhaled air by using approximate equation

$$\% \text{ COHb in blood} = 0.16 \text{ (ppm. CO)} + 0.5$$

Table 3.7: Health Effects of COHb Blood Levels

COHb blood level (%)	Effects on healthy individuals	Effects on heart patient
1 – 5	Blood flow to certain vital organs increases to compensate for reduction in O_2 carrying capacity of blood.	Patient may lack sufficient cardiac reserve to compensate.
5 – 9	Vital light threshold increased.	Patients with angina pectoris required less exertion to induce chest pain.
16 – 20	Laboured respiration during exertion, visual evoked response abnormal.	May be lethal for patients with severe cardio-vascular diseases.
20 – 30	Headache, nausea.	
30 – 40	Severe headache, nausea and vomiting, dizziness	
40 – 50	Slurring of speech, tendency to collapse.	
50 – 60	Convulsions, coma	
60 – 70	Fatal coma if not treated.	

Carbon monoxide levels in cities are usually between 10 and 40 ppm on an annual 8 hours basis and occasional short term concentrations may exceed 100 ppm. These levels can lead to COHb concentration in blood of approximately 2 to 8 per cent. A concentration up to 500 ppm in the air, when inhaled for 1 hour produces no observable symptoms but a similar exposure to 1000 ppm can be dangerous. Concentrations of 4000 ppm and above are fatal, usually within 1 hour. Increased COHb in the blood deprives O_2 supply to various vital organs, especially the brain. This leads to impairment of mental performance, visual ability and other functions. The chronic effect of CO may induce heart and respiratory disorders.

Table 3.8: CO Levels in Urban Areas

City	Maximum 1 hour CO values, ppm
London	50
Chicago	46
Los Angeles	43
New York	27
Kolkata	35

The most effective treatment for CO poisoning is to place the victim in a hyperbaric (high pressure) chamber with 2 to 2.5 atm. of O_2. This procedure speeds elimination of the CO and more importantly, it also corrects tissue anoxia by providing large amounts of dissolved O_2 in the blood plasma, thus permitting the body to bypass the haemoglobin mechanism. A non-smoker person breathing air containing no CO will have a background HbCO level of about 0.4% from biological CO production inside the body. A person who smokes a pack of cigarettes daily and inhales the smoke may have blood HbCO levels of 5% or more. Although these levels do lead to clinical symptoms, they have been associated with impairment of mental performance. Weekly average CO concentrations of around 10 ppm may produce increased mortality among hospitalised heart patients. High rates of heart disease in smokers may be due to the CO from cigarette smoke.

Ozone (O_3)

The origin of ozone in the air has not been clarified but it may be formed by combustion and sunlight. O_3 is also formed in the atmosphere through chemical reactions involving certain pollutants like SO_2, NO_2, aldehydes on absorption of ultraviolet radiations. There is the ozone layer in the stratosphere (above 16 km up to 50 km) which protects us from harmful UV radiations from sun. Thus, ozone layer acts as a protective shield for living organisms on the earth. Since, last few years there is depletion of this O_3 layer due to human activities which may have serious implications on life. On the other hand, the atmospheric ozone is now being regarded as potential danger to human health and crop growth. Thus, ozone plays dual role of destroyer as well as protector. It is necessary to study its biopotency from the viewpoint of human welfare.

Ozone as the Destroyer

In the troposphere (8 to 16 km from earth surface), temperature decreases with increasing altitude while in stratosphere (above 16 km up to 50 km), it increases with increasing altitude. This rise in temperature in stratosphere is caused by the ozone layer. The ozone shield has two important effects which are interrelated with each other. Firstly, ozone layer absorbs ultraviolet light from solar radiation and thus, protects all lives on the earth.

Second, by absorbing the UV radiation, the ozone layer heats the stratosphere, causing temperature inversion. This is very interesting phenomenon. It limits the vertical mixing of air pollutants, thereby causing the dispersal of pollutants over larger areas and near the earth's surface. It is the common experience that the dense clouds of pollutants usually hang over the atmosphere in highly industrialised areas causing several unpleasant and harmful effects. The pollutants spread horizontally relatively fast (than slow mixing vertically) reaching all longitudes of the world in about a week and all latitudes within months. Thus, this is an important global problem. Inspite of slow vertical mixing, some of the pollutants like chlorofluro carbons (CFCs) enter the stratosphere and remain there for years until they are converted to other products or transported back to the stratosphere. In the stratosphere, these (CFCs) pollutants unfortunately react with ozone and deplete it. The O_3 near earth's surface in troposphere creates pollution problems. Ozone and other oxidants, such as peroxy acetyl nitrate (PAN) and hydrogen peroxide are formed by photochemical reactions between hydrocarbons and NO_2. O_3 may also be formed by NO_2 under UV radiation effect. These pollutants are responsible for the formation of photochemical smog which is a secondary pollutant and will be discussed in detail later.

Effects of O_3

(1) Increased O_3 concentration near the earth's surface cause harmful effects on crops. The crop yields are reduced considerably.

(2) In plants, O_3 enters through the stomata and produces visible damage to leaves and thus, leads to decrease in yield and quality of plant products. The low concentration about 0.02 ppm also damages tomato, tobacco, bean and pine and other plants. It causes tip burns in pine seedlings. In USA, due to O_3 pollution, fruit and vegetable yields have reduced considerably. Every year there are crop losses worth billions of dollars.

(3) O_3 and other pollutants, such as SO_2 and NO_2 in combination cause crop losses over 50% in several European countries. There is tremendous decrease in the yield of potato, clover, spinach, alfa-alfa, bean and poplars.

(4) O_3 also causes destruction of fibres like cotton, nylon, polyster and dyes. The damage is more pronounced in presence of light and humidity. O_3 hardens rubber.

(5) At higher concentrations, O_3 is hazardous to human health.

Table 3.9: Effects of O_3 on Human Health

Concentration of O_3 in ppm	Effects observed
0.2	No ill effects
0.3	Nose and throat irritation
1.0 - 3.0	Extreme fatigue after 2 hours
9.0	Severe pulmonary edema

Ozone Depletion (Threat to O$_3$ layer): O$_3$ plays the vital role of protection from the harmful UV radiations from sun. O$_3$ acts as a protective shield. It also plays a major role in climatology and biology of the earth. It filters out all radiations below 3000 A°. It is intimately concerned with the life sustaining process. Any change or depletion in ozone layer would therefore, have catastrophic effects on the life on earth. Over the last few years, it has been observed that O$_3$ shield is thining out. Near the Antarctic region, the O$_3$ layer has two large holes due to which there is 5 to 10% rise in the skin cancer.

There are several reasons for depletion of O$_3$ layer. They are:

1. Some pollutants enter the stratosphere and they react with O$_3$ converting it into other pollutants. Thus, they deplete O$_3$.

2. The chlorofluorocarbon (CFCs), nitrogen oxides and hydrocarbons are the major pollutants responsible for O$_3$ depletion. CFCs are widely used as coolants in air conditioners and refrigerators, clearing solvents, aerosols, propellants and in foam insulation.

3. CFC is also used in fire extinguishing equipment. They escape as aerosols in the stratosphere.

4. The supersonic air-crafts flying at stratosphere heights cause major disturbances in O$_3$ levels.

5. Motor vehicles, jet engines, nitrogen fertilisers and other industrial activities are responsible for emission of CFCs, NO$_x$ by 14% at the current emission rate.

Effects

1. Depletion of O$_3$ would lead to serious temperature changes on the earth and consequent change to life support systems.

2. The O$_3$ depletion would lead to temperature changes and rainfall failure on earth.

3. Due to reduction of O$_3$, UV radiation reaching the earth increases, causing skin cancer in man and injures various parts of plants.

4. There are other harmful effects of O$_3$, such as cataracts, destruction of aquatic life, vegetation and loss of immunity.

5. O$_3$ depletion causes indirect effect such as green house effect, 20-50% reduction in growth, reduction in chlorophyll content and increase in harmful mutations. Increased UV radiation also impairs fish productivity.

For the protection of O$_3$, efforts are being made on global level.

In 1985, the first global conference of depletion of O$_3$ layer was held in Vienna (Australia). In the same year, British scientists discovered a hole as large as that of the United States in the O$_3$ layer at the South Pole. This was followed by Montreal Protocol in 1987, in which decision was taken to drastically reduce the use of CFCs. The European community also decided to cut production by 85%. In March 1989, conference on "Saving the O_3 layer" was jointly organised by British Government and the UNEP in London. The CFCs and other chemicals which depleted O_3 should be withdrawn and many countries signed the agreement.

Mumbai, Delhi and Kolkata are the three metropolitan cities in India which are responsible for producing O_3 on a large scale.

Another conference organised in Helsinki on May 1989, in which 80 nations agreed to have total ban on chemicals causing O_3 depletion by 2000.

In June 1989, two Japanese leading companies have claimed to have jointly developed an alternative to CFCs.

Hydrocarbons

Hydrocarbons are chemical compounds containing only carbon and hydrogen. There are open chain hydrocarbons which contain non-cyclic chains, sometimes straight, sometimes branched hydrocarbon. These are chains of carbon atoms to which hydrogen atoms are bonded. They may be saturated (parafinic), for example, methane and propane or they may be unsaturated (olefinic), for example, ethylene.

Methane

Benzene

Propane

Ethylene

Cyclic hydrocarbons: They contains rings of carbon atoms and they may be saturated or unsaturated. The unsaturated hydrocarbons derived from benzene are referred to as aromatic hydrocarbons.

The light hydrocarbons: They are gaseous at ordinary temperature. Methane occurs naturally and is the principal constituent of the fuel called natural gas. It is colourless and odourless. The odour of natural gas is due to sulphur compounds added. Ethylene and propane are also gases.

Heavier hydrocarbons: Those which occur naturally like petroleum are liquids. They are usually separated in petroleum refining processes into various liquid fuels and solvents, such as gasoline and kerosene. Some of these hydrocarbons are quite volatile. Very heavy hydrocarbons may be solids at ordinary temperatures.

The gaseous and volatile liquid hydrocarbons are air pollutants. The hydrocarbons with more than 12 carbon atoms are not present in the atmosphere in high concentrations, hence they are not considered as air pollutants.

Sources of hydrocarbons: Natural sources of hydrocarbons are largely biological. Annually, methane production amounts to well over 1 billion metric tonnes and that is mainly from anaerobic decay of organic matter. Some plants also produce volatile terpenes and isoprenes which are complicated cyclic hydrocarbons.

The hydrocarbons produced by humans is about 30 million metric tonnes annually in USA and it is probably about three times as much worldwide. Large amount of hydrocarbons which have higher molecular weight are responsible for the formation of photochemical smogs. Therefore, these non-methane hydrocarbons are important air pollutants.

Effects of Hydrocarbons

1. The pure hydrocarbons are harmful to plants. For example, ethylene inhibits plant growth, by interfering with the activities of plant hormones. 0.01 ppm ethylene also affects the plants.

2. Methane, when in concentration of 50% or more can be dangerous, because suffocation may result. A small concentration of methane may lead to explosions.

3. Aromatic compounds can be irritating to the mucous membranes at concentrations lower than 500 ppm and injury can result, but no adverse effects on health have been reported at levels below 25 ppm.

4. Hydrocarbons are responsible for the production of photochemical oxidants which cause eye irritation and other effects. Formaldehyde (HCHO), a partially oxidised form of methane has been found to produce physiological responses at concentrations of 0.06 ppm and eye irritation beginning about 0.01 to 1.0 ppm in different individuals.

5. Benzopyrene is the most potent cancer inducing pollutant.

3.4.2 Carbon Dioxide and Green House Effect

Carbon dioxide is actually not a pollutant. The amount of CO_2 formed due to animal respiration is utilised by the plants for the process of photosynthesis. But due to heavy industrialisation and heavy consumption of fossil fuels, vast amount of CO_2 is released in the atmosphere which may probably bring about drastic changes in the world climate in the next 50 years. Increasing global consumption of fossil fuels is steadily increasing the CO_2 level in the atmosphere, since the beginning of 20th century. It has been estimated that global consumption of fossil fuels like coal, petroleum, natural gas, etc. release about 9×10^9 tonnes of CO_2 per year.

The primary source of CO_2 is the burning of fossil fuels. The secondary source is the oxidation of carbon compounds in marshes and forests by natural degradation. Cement plants are also another important source of increase of CO_2 in the atmosphere.

The atmospheric CO_2 in natural carbon cycle is normally removed by two major sinks called plants and oceans. Plants absorb CO_2 during the process of photosynthesis and some of the CO_2 dissolves in oceanic water. Now this balance is disturbed as the production of CO_2 is more than the absorption of CO_2 by these two important sinks. Therefore, the CO_2 level in atmosphere is increasing day by day and it has become the threat to world climate.

The increased level of CO_2 in the atmosphere has an influence on the earth's climate. This is called the 'green house effect'. The CO_2 layer above the earth acts like the glass in a green house. CO_2 admits short wave radiation from the sun but absorbs the longer wave radiation from the earth. This causes heating of the earth. The green house effect has been recognised since the late 19th century. Recent calculations have predicted a rise about 1.9°C in surface temperature due to doubling of CO_2 concentration. Such an increase would have great effects on the climate.

If the CO_2 content of the atmosphere doubles, which may occur by the middle of the next century, it will result in increase in the present world temperature, by about 3.6°C. If there will be continuous rise in earth temperature all the glaciers will recede and the ice caps in the Antarctica and the Arctic will begin to melt. Consequently, the sea level will rise by a few metres, and most of the cities on the sea shore may be submerged.

The destruction of forests and of soil organic matter will reduce the volume of the biomass sink. These conditions will increase the CO_2 level in atmosphere.

The situation in India is alarming. There were dense forests in Gangetic plains, the Deccan, the Central Plateau and Rajasthan in the past. About 36% of the Indian continent was covered with forests but today it is reduced to 20%. Thus, deforestation and heavy consumption of fossil fuels are responsible for increasing deviation in the climate with decrease in rainfall.

In the climatology of larger urban areas, a similar situation exists. Decline of trees combined with heat sink effect of the buildings are increased many folds by the accumulation of CO_2 in the local atmosphere. Studies in the cities like Mumbai, Delhi and Kolkata have revealed that the heat island effect raises night temperatures by 4-6°C above open areas. There are some factors, which counteract the CO_2 effect. The warming of atmosphere will increase cloud cover and this will reduce the amount of incoming solar radiation. Agricultural and industrial operations as well as deforestation may generate large quantity of dust which in turn can reduce the effective radiation and thus, maintain the atmospheric temperature more or less at the same level.

To overcome this ecological crisis due to CO_2, community based forestry schemes should be undertaken. A good example of this is China, where people brought land under forest and this trend has increased from 5% in 1949 to 12.7% in 1978.

Photochemical Smog

Smog is a synchrony of two words *smoke* and *fog*. Smog can be of two types: Photochemical and coal induced.

Photochemical smog is a secondary pollutant which is produced in the air by interaction of two or more primary pollutants or by reaction with normal atmospheric constituents with or without photoactivation.

Photochemical smog is restricted to highly motorised areas in metropolitan cities e.g. Los Angeles. This kind of pollution occurs where inversion conditions prevail in the atmosphere. It is due to the action of sunlight on two pollutants - hydrocarbons and nitrogen oxides. The major sources of these two pollutants are the exhaust gases from automobiles. The main constituents of photochemical smog are peroxy acetyl nitrate (PAN), nitrogen oxides, hydrocarbons, CO and O_3. It reduces visibility, causes eye irritation damage to vegetation and cracking of rubber.

The coal induced smog is called fog and it is formed by the burning of coal. This fog covers the urban areas at night or on cold days when the temperature is below 10°C and when very calm meteorological conditions exist for example, London (December 1952). The main constituents of the fog are smoke, sulphur compounds and fly ash. Constant and prolonged exposure to smog results in a high mortality rate, especially among the aged and those suffer from chronic bronchitis, asthma, broncho-pneumonia and other lung or heart diseases.

The first major Los Angeles 'smog' to attract public concern occurred in 1943. In the next few years recurrences became more and more common. Early attention focused on injury to plants in the Los Angeles basin. The smog causes injury to the variety of plants, vegetable crops. Extensive studies were carried out and it was found that smog is formed by mixture of pollutants exposed to sunlight. Prof. A. J. Haagen Smith, proposed the theory of formation of smog which is generally acceptable as it is very comprehensive.

It has been found that at the time of photochemical smog formation, there is considerable increase in the amount of O_3 and oxidant material. The O_3 is not found in appreciable amounts at night, but only during day. It begins to form simultaneously through out the Los Angeles basin shortly after dawn. These facts clearly indicate that photochemical formation of O_3 oxidant from impurities, takes place due to action of sunlight.

Nitrogen oxides play an important role in this set of reactions. NO_2 is an efficient absorber of ultraviolet light energy. The NO_2 becomes highly energised molecule (NO_2^*) which then cause NO_2^* molecule to decompose or photolyse into nitric oxide (NO) and atomic oxygen (O).

$$NO_2 + \text{Ultraviolet light} \rightarrow NO_2^*$$

$$NO_2^* \rightarrow NO + O$$

The atomic oxygen (O) reacts quickly with molecular (O_2) oxygen to form O_3.

$$O + O_2 \rightarrow O_3$$

The atomic oxygen can react with molecular oxygen (in presence of a collisional molecule to conserve energy) to form O_3.

$$O + O_2 + M \rightarrow O_3 + M$$

The O_3 in turn can react with NO to form NO_2 and O_2 again, completing the atmospheric nitrogen dioxide photolytic cycle. The M represents a collisional molecule (a molecule whose only role in the reaction is to ensure compliance with the laws of conservation of energy and of momentum).

$$O_3 + NO \rightarrow NO_2 + O_2$$

In the above reactions, NO_2 behaves like a catalyst.

During night time, the NO and O_3 levels will be low and the NO_2 level will generally be a little higher. During the day, nitrogen oxides are being produced by automobiles and the concentrations of NO and NO_2 rise. The NO_2 photolyses rapidly to NO + O, which then leads to a rise in O_3 concentration.

In the presence of hydrocarbons (HC), a number of other reactions occur. Some of the atomic oxygen, ozone, and nitric oxide react with hydrocarbons to form a variety of products and intermediates with which even further reactions can probably take place. Some of the products formed are aldehydes like formaldehydes and acrolein, peroxides and peroxy acetyl nitrate (PAN).

$$O + HC \text{ (hydrocarbon)} \rightarrow HCO^*$$

HC refers to a hydrocarbon and an asterisk (*) is used to denote a free radical. R denotes an alkyl group, such as methyl ($CH_3 -$) or ethyl ($CH_3 CH_2-$).

$$HC O^* + O_2 \rightarrow HCO_3^*$$

$$HC O_3^* + Hc \rightarrow \text{Aldehyde (RCHO), ketones (R}_1, R_2 \text{ CO) and so on.}$$

$$HCO_3^* + NO \rightarrow HCO_2^* + NO_2$$

$$HCO_3^* + O_2 \rightarrow HCO_2^* + O_3$$

$$HCO_3^* + NO_2 \rightarrow \text{Peroxyacyl nitrates (RCOOONO}_2)$$

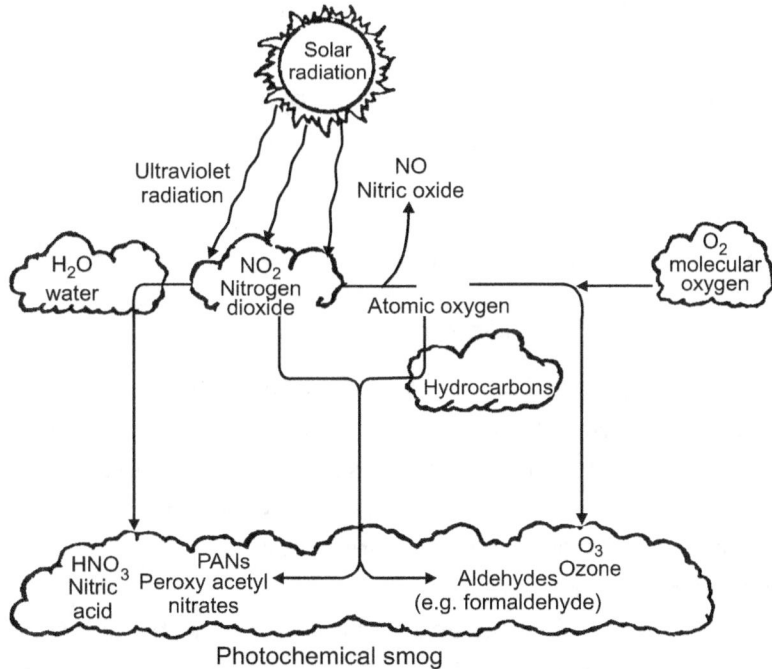

Fig. 3.5: Simplified Scheme of the Formation of Photochemical Smog

The partially oxidised hydrocarbons and free radicals react with NO to form more NO_2, upsetting the balance of O_3 consumption by NO. Consequently, the NO level decreases and NO_2 and O_3 levels rise, with the O_3 level peaking about midday.

Once O_3 is present in the atmosphere, other chemical reactions leading to other irritants occur; these include aldehyde, ketones and peroxy acetyl nitrate (PAN). These are all common eye irritants. Their chemical structures are given below.

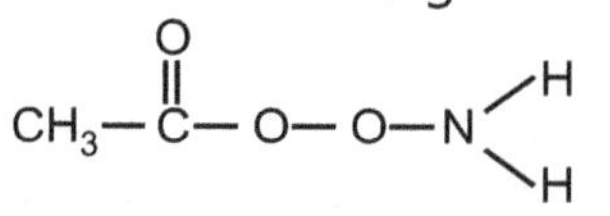

$$CH_3-\overset{\overset{\displaystyle O}{\|}}{C}-O-O-N\overset{\displaystyle H}{\underset{\displaystyle H}{\diagdown}}$$

Peroxy acetyl nitrate (PAN)

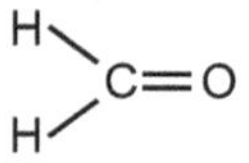

$$\overset{\displaystyle H}{\underset{\displaystyle H}{\diagup}}C=O$$

Formaldehyde

$$\overset{\displaystyle H}{\underset{\displaystyle H}{\diagup}}C=\overset{\overset{\displaystyle H}{|}}{C}-\overset{\overset{\displaystyle H}{|}}{C}=O$$

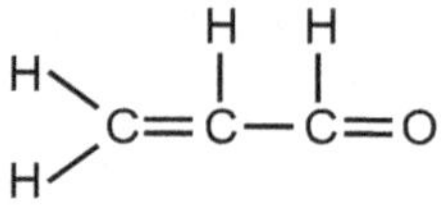

Acrolein

Fig. 3.6: Some Eye Irritants of Photochemical Smog

If NO is present in the air, following reactions can take place

$$NO + O_3 \rightarrow NO_2 + O_2$$

If O_3 is present in excess, then

$$2\ NO_2 + O_3 \rightarrow N_2O_5 + O_2$$

In presence of water vapour, the following reaction can take place

$$N_2O_5 + H_2O \rightarrow 2\ HNO_3$$

Thus, nitric acid may be formed.

Photochemical Reaction due to SO_2

O_3 may be formed in the atmosphere as a byproduct during the photochemical oxidation of SO_2 to H_2SO_4. The reaction takes place as follows:-

$$SO_2 + \text{Ultraviolet light} \rightarrow SO_2^*$$

$$SO_2^* + O_2 \rightarrow SO_4$$

$$SO_2^* + O_2 \rightarrow SO_3 + O_3$$

$$SO_3 + H_2O \rightarrow H_2SO_4 \text{ (Sulphuric acid)}$$

The photochemical reactions depend on light intensity, hydrocarbon reactivity, ratio of hydrocarbons to nitric oxide, presence of light absorbers and meteorological variables.

The oxidants of photochemical smog can be measured calorimetrically. PAN may be measured either by gas chromatography or infrared spectroscopy.

Effects of Photochemical Smog

The effects of photochemical smog on plants, materials and human beings have been studied in places like Los Angeles where this problem usually occurs. Additional information has also been obtained by stimulating photochemical smog in environmental chambers.

(1) Eye irritation: The oxidants of photochemical smog enter as part of inhaled air and alter, or interfere with the respiratory process and other processes. Serious outbreaks of smog occurred in Tokyo, New York, Rome, Sydney in 1970, causing spread of diseases like asthma and bronchitis in epidemic proportions. Tokyo-Yokohama asthma occurred in 1946, in some American soldiers and families living in smog affected areas of Yokohama, Japan. Another serious disease caused by smog is emphysema, a disease due to structural breakdown of alveoli of lungs. In this disease, the total surface area available for gaseous exchange is reduced and this causes severe breathlessness.

Among the photochemical products, the aromatics are the most potent pollutants. These are benzopyrene, peroxy acetyl nitrate (PAN) and peroxybenzoil nitrate (PBN). Benzopyrene is carcinogenic. PAN is potent eye irritant at about 1 ppm or less. PAN and O_3 both cause respiratory distress and toxic. Aldehydes as HCHO and olefin, acrolein irritate the skin, eyes and upper respiratory tract.

(2) Vegetation damage: The photochemical smog causes silvering and bronzing of the underside of leaves, followed by collapse of cells and necrosis. Growth of plants is also retarded. Olefins affect plants seriously. They wither the sepals of orchid flowers, retard the opening of carnation flowers and may cause dropping of their petals. They retard the growth of tomatoes. PAN blocks Hill's reaction in plants. It causes injury in spinach, beets, celery, tobacco, pepper lettuce, alfalfa, aster, primrose, etc. O_3 causes only tip burns.

(3) Visibility reduction: It is the most commonly observed effect of photochemical smog. The aerosol particles causing the photochemical smog contain compounds of carbon, oxygen, hydrogen, nitrogen, sulphur, and halides. The size of the particles is about 0.3 μ. The liquid phase is largely made up of organic matter.

(4) Cracking of rubber: It is because of O_3 constituent of photochemical smog. The economic effect of it in Los Angeles is the deterioration of the side walls of automobile tyres. To avoid this problem, antiozonant is being used. Moreover gaskets, hoses and wire insulation are also affected.

(5) Fading of dyes: Photochemical smog also affects the colour of dyes.

3.4.3 Effects of Air Pollution

Air pollution shows its effects on the following:

(i)　　Human health　　(ii)　Animals

(iii)　Plants　　　　　　(iv)　Materials and　　(v) Art treasures

Effects on Human Health

Air pollution is one of the greatest environmental evils. Unpolluted air, which we breathe, has life supporting properties but the polluted air has life damaging properties. Thus, the polluted air is dangerous and affects human health. There are several factors which are responsible for affecting human health

(i)　Nature of pollutants

(ii)　Concentration of pollutants in air

(iii)   Duration of human exposure

(iv)   Age group of the individual and

(v)   State of health of the individual.

Infants, children and aged individuals are generally more susceptible to pollutants. Those who suffer from chronic diseases of the lungs or heart are thought to be at great risk. Seasonal changes also affect human health. People are most susceptible during winter as pollution levels are highest during this season. Air pollutants come in contact with the exposed membranes and skin and may cause damage. The toxic gases, vapours, fumes, mist and dust may be absorbed by the exposed membranes and they cause irritation of the membranes of eyes, nose, throat, larynx trachea, bronchii and lungs. Air pollutants cause the following important health effects in humans:

(1)   Irritation of eyes.

(2)   Irritation of nose, throat and respiratory tract.

(3)   Certain odoriferous gases like H_2S, NH_3, mercaptans cause odour nuisance even at very low concentrations. This results in vomiting and nausea.

(4)   The constant exposure to polluted air causes increased mortality and morbidity.

(5)   Pollen grains, dust particles may initiate asthmatic attacks.

(6)   The high concentrations of SO_2, NO_2, particulate matter and photochemical smog are responsible for chronic pulmonary diseases like bronchitis and asthma.

(7)   Carbon monoxide combines with haemoglobin in the blood and consequently increases stress on those suffering from cardiovascular and pulmonary diseases.

(8)   Fluorosis is a disease of bone and caused due to hydrogen fluoride. It also causes mottling of teeth.

(9)   Carcinogenic agents like polycyclic aromatic hydrocarbons, nitrosamine, nickle, pesticides are responsible for cancer.

(10)   Dust particles cause respiratory diseases. Silicosis and asbestosis are the diseases caused by silica and asbestos dust.

(11)   The heavy metals like lead, cadmium, nickel, mercury are harmful to human health. Lead is neurotoxic, affects the circulatory system and causes behavioural disorders and even death.

(12)   Cadmium is responsible for cardiovascular disease and hypertension and kidney damage. Nickel causes respiratory disorders and lung cancer. Mercury causes nerve, brain and kidney damage.

(13)   Radioactive pollutants cause somatic and genetic damage. The genetic mutations due to DNA damage causes cancer and teratogenic effects.

Effects of Pollutants on Plants

It has been already known that the air pollutants have adverse effects on plants. The gaseous pollutants, particulate matter, pesticides, heavy metals, number of industrial chemicals are responsible for the destruction of vegetation. Following are the effects of air pollutants on plants.

The most obvious damage caused by air pollutants to vegetation occurs in the leaf structure. The leaf surface is covered by waxy coat called cuticle. Epidermis lies beneath cuticle. Its chief functions are the protection of the inner tissues from excessive moisture loss and the diffusion of CO_2 and O_2 to these internal tissues. There are a large number of openings on the leaf surface called stomata. Each stomata is protected by a pair of guard cells which control the opening and the closing of the stomata. Through stomata toxic gases diffuse into the leaf.

Pollutants cause necrosis, chlorosis and epinasty in plants.

Necrosis   :   Dead areas on a leaf structure are called necrosis.

Chlorosis   :   Chlorosis is the loss or reduction of chlorophyll and leads to the yellowing of the leaf. Chlorosis generally indicates a deficiency of some nutrient required by the plant.

Epinasty   :   Leaf epinasty is a downward curvature of the leaf due to higher rate of growth on the upper surface.

Abscission : The dropping of leaves is called abscission.

The plant injury may be acute or chronic. In acute injury, plants are exposed to relatively high concentrations of pollutants whereas in chronic injury, the plants are exposed to low levels of pollutants for longer period.

The pollutants enter the inner tissues through the stomata, where they destroy the chlorophyll and disrupt photosynthesis. This causes reduction in growth and death of the plants.

The particulate dust like cement deposited on the leaves causes plugging of stomata resulting in damage to the plants.

Prevention and Control of Air Pollution: Different techniques are used for controlling air pollution caused by 'gaseous pollutants' and that caused by 'particulate pollutants'.

Methods of controlling gaseous pollutants: The air pollution caused by gaseous pollutants like hydrocarbons, sulphur dioxide, ammonia, carbon monoxide, etc. can be controlled by using three different methods - Combustion, Absorption and Adsorption.

1. **Combustion:** This technique is applied when the pollutants are organic gases or vapours. The organic air pollutants are subjected to 'flame combustion or catalytic combustion' when they are converted to less harmful product carbon dioxide and a harmless product water.

2. **Absorption:** In this method, the polluted air containing gaseous pollutants is passed through a scrubber containing a suitable liquid absorbent. The liquid absorbs the harmful gaseous pollutants present in air.

3. **Adsorption:** In this method, the polluted air is passed through porous solid adsorbents kept in suitable containers. The gaseous pollutants are adsorbed at the surface of the porous solid and clean air passes through.

   Methods of controlling particulate emissions: The air pollution caused by particulate matter like dust, soot, ash, etc., can be controlled by using fabric filters, wet scrubbers, electrostatic precipitators and certain mechanical devices.

4. **Mechanical Devices:** It works on the basis of the following:

   Gravity: In this process, the particulate settle down by the action of gravitational force and get removed.

   Sudden change in the direction of air flow: It brings about separation of particles due to greater momentum.

5. **Fabric Filters:** The particulate matter is passed through a porous medium made of woven or filled fabrics.

   • The particulate present in the polluted air are filtered and gets collected in the fabric filters, while the gases are discharged.

   • The process of controlling air pollution by using fabric filters is called 'bag filtration'.

6. **Wet Scrubbers:** They are used to trap SO_2, NH_3 and metal fumes by passing the fumes through water.

7. **Electrostatic Precipitators:** When the polluted air containing particulate pollutants is passed through an electrostatic precipitator, it induces electric charge on the particles and then the aerosol particles get precipitated on the electrodes.

Some other methods of controlling Air Pollution:

1. Tall chimneys should be installed in factories.

2. Better designed equipment and smokeless fuels should be used in homes and industries.

3. Renewable and non-polluting sources of energy like solar energy, wind energy, etc., should be used.

4. Automobiles should be properly maintained and adhere to emission control standards.

5. More trees should be planted along roadsides and houses.

There are many factors which regulate the air pollution. It states that there should always be a distance between the industrial and residential area. The chimneys must be tall in size so that the emissions must be released higher up in the environment. The filters and precipitators must be used in the chimneys. The scrubber or spray collector must be used to remove the poisonous gases. The ash production must be reduced by the high temperature incinerators. The sulphur must be removed after the combustion. The non-combustive sources of energy are the nuclear power, geothermal power, solar, tidal and wind power. The gasoline must have antiknocking agents. The railway track must be electrified. The mining area must be rich in trees. The gas fuel must be used instead of the coal fuel. The emission control system must be present in the automobiles. The wastes must be removed and recycled in the industrial plants and refineries. The automobiles must be pollution free by making the fuel alcohol based and using the battery power. There are certain plants which have the ability to fix the carbon monoxide. These should be grown in the larger numbers. It includes the ficus and coleus. There are certain plants which have the ability to metabolize the nitrogen oxides and other pollutants. It includes the pinus and ribes.

3.5 Air Pollution and its Relevance

3.5.1 Acid Rain

On earth, rain is the main source of fresh water. But in the past few decades 'acid rain' is another environmental problem created by man. The rain water has become progressively acidic. The problem of acid rain is the result of massive air pollution – the gift of industrialisation. It is a global problem. Because of acid rainfall today more than 200 lakes in New York State are 'dead'. In Sweden nearly 5000 lakes are devoid of fish. About 4000 lakes in Canada are unable to support trout fish due to acidification of water and if this situation continues more than 48000 lakes in Canada will be without any life forms by the end of this century. It is reported that about 30% of West Germany's Black forests are dying a slow death due to acid rain. In India, acid rain has been reported in Mumbai and Pune. In China, rapid industrialisation growth and an increasing demand for fossil fuel coal in the 1990s has created threat to environment from acid rain. Nearly 40% of China's land area is now affected.

What is Acid Rain?

Rains containing acid-forming chemicals, chiefly pollutants that have been released into the atmosphere and combined with water vapour are called acid rains. Unpolluted rain water is slightly acidic because of the presence of CO_2 in the air. Its pH is generally 5.7.

$$CO_2 + H_2O \rightarrow H_2CO_3 \text{ (carbonic acid)}$$

Therefore, rainwater with pH values lower than 5.7 is called acid rain. In some parts of the world, rain water pH is recorded as low as 2.5. An acid gives a characteristic sour test to water. Acidity is measured on a pH scale, ranging from 0 to 14. Neutral solution, for example: distilled water has pH 7. From pH 7 up to 14, solutions are alkaline or basic. From pH 7 down to 0, indicates acidity. Thus, lower the pH, higher will be the acidity.

In many parts of Scandinavia, Western Europe, Canada, and the USA, rain has become increasingly acidic. Now the latest reports indicate that even the countries in Southern hemisphere like Brazil, Australia, Thailand, etc. are also suffering from acid rain. Measurements before forties did not show any problem of acid rain but now in Eastern North America rains having pH of 4.6 are common. This indicates that the acid rains are 10 times more acidic than the clean rain water.

Causes of Acid Rain

The problem of acid rain is man-made. Heavy urbanisation, industrialisation, thermal power plants, unlimited use of fossil fuel are the main causes of acid rain. Large quantities of sulphur dioxide (SO_2) and nitrogen dioxide (NO_2) are emitted in the atmosphere from the chimneys of industrial plants. They react with the moisture in the air to form sulphuric and nitric acids which fall as acid precipitation. Therefore, acid rain is nothing but the mixture of sulphuric and nitric acids. Currently, about 60-70% of the acidity is thought to be due to sulphuric acid and 30-40% is due to nitric acid.

SO_2 is oxidised slowly in clean air to sulphur trioxide i.e. SO_3. SO_3 is generally emitted along with SO_2 at about 1-5% of SO_2 concentration.

$$2\, SO_2 + O_2 \ \rightarrow\ 2\, SO_3 \text{ (Sulphur trioxide)}$$

$$SO_3 + H_2O \ \rightarrow\ H_2SO_4 \text{ (Sulphuric acid)}$$

From SO_2, SO_3 is formed for which certain atmospheric conditions like sunlight, temperature, humidity, hydrocarbons, particulates and nitrogen oxides, etc. are necessary. Besides the formation of sulphuric acid (H_2SO_4), sulphurous acid is also formed.

$$SO_2 + H_2O \ \rightarrow\ H_2SO_3 \text{ (Sulphurous acid)}$$

Burning of fossil fuels in thermal power station is a major contributor (60-70%) of SO_2 to the atmosphere. Sulphur dioxide content is also increased in the atmosphere due to smelting of sulphide ores, particularly of lead, zinc and copper.

Another causative agent of acid rain is oxides of nitrogen which are continuously poured in the atmosphere through automobile exhaust, power houses and smelters.

$$2\, NO + O_2 \ \rightarrow\ 2\, NO_2$$

$$4\, NO_2 + 2\, H_2O + O_2 \ \rightarrow\ 4\, HNO_3 \text{ (Nitric acid)}$$

Thus, when nitrogen dioxide mixes with water vapour, it is converted into nitric acid. Nitric acid and sulphuric acid are the two main constitutents of acid rain.

Effects of Acid Rain

The ecological consequences of acid rain are quite serious because these changes are irreversible.

Following are some of the ill effects of acid rain:

(1) Acid rain affects the aquatic animals and plant in streams and lakes. The high acidity results in the killing of fish, retarded growth and reproductive failure.

(2) Change in pH of water prevents hatching of fish eggs. There is large scale destruction of economically important fishes like salmon and trout.

(3) Acidity also kills useful bacteria and green algae in the aquatic system. Rate of decomposition is reduced and ultimately organic matter increases in lakes and streams causing water pollution. Sometimes aquatic system collapses.

(4) Acid rain affects vegetation and soil. The growth of trees is adversely affected by acid rain. Acid rain affects germination of seeds, leaf surface erosion, forests and greenery.

Soil is damaged by acid rain. Due to leaching out of important plant nutrients like potassium and toxic elements like zinc accumulates in the soil. Beneficial soil micro-organisms are adversely affected by acid rain. The earthworms which are friends of farmers are also affected due to acid rain because they cannot inhabit acidic soil.

(5) Acid rain is responsible for killing fauna and flora in rivers, lakes and streams. Thousands of lakes in Canada, U.S.A., are adversely affected and they have become dead. Scandinavian countries are also great sufferers due to acid rain. Their lakes have been sterilised and forests are badly affected.

(6) Acid rain can damage great historical monuments, statues, building and metals. Taj Mahal is one of the victims of acid rain. It is affected due to SO_2 pollution from nearby Mathura Oil Refinery. The pages of books also become brittle due to acid rain. In USA one library has lost books worth millions of dollars only because of acid rain problem.

(7) Acid rain also affects furniture, carpets, window frames, leather articles, marble, paints, etc.

(8) Acid rain also causes damage to common building materials such as limestone and marble.

(9) Acid rain can oxidise metals. Iron corrodes in presence of acid rain to form rust.

(10) Acid rain is highly hazardous to human beings and animals because SO_2 and H_2SO_4 are both capable of irritating the respiratory system. Respiratory diseases are caused due to acid rain.

(11) Plants also suffer from leaf injury, yellowing or necrosis because chlorophyll production is impeded due to acid rain.

3.5.2 Ozone Layer Depletion

Ozone is a highly reactive molecule that contains three oxygen atoms. Ozone molecules absorb UV light between 310 and 200 nm, following which ozone splits into a molecule of O_2 and an oxygen atom. The oxygen atom then joins up with an oxygen molecule to regenerate ozone. The ozone layer is a belt of naturally occurring ozone gas that is present 15 to 30 kilometres above the Earth and serves as a shield from the harmful ultraviolet B radiation emitted by the sun.

The ozone depletion process begins when CFCs and other ozone depleting substances (ODS) are emitted into the atmosphere. Strong UV light present in the stratosphere breaks apart the ODS molecule which releases halogen atoms like chlorine and bromine. It is these atoms that actually destroy ozone, not the intact ODS molecule. It is estimated that one chlorine atom can destroy over 100,000 ozone molecules before it is removed from the stratosphere.

Since, ozone filters out harmful UVB radiation, less ozone means higher UVB levels at the surface. The more the depletion, the larger the increase in incoming UVB. UVB has been linked to skin cancer, cataracts, damage to materials like plastics, and harm to certain crops and marine organisms. Although some UVB reaches the surface even without ozone depletion, its harmful effects will increase as a result of this problem.

The adverse effects of ozone depletion are as follows:

- Skin cancers, basal and squamous cell carcinomas, sunburns and premature aging of the skin.
- More cataracts, blindness and other eye diseases: UV radiation can damage several parts of the eye, including the lens, cornea, retina and conjunctiva.
- Weakening of the human immune system (immunosuppression): Too much UV radiation can suppress the human immune system, which may play a role in the development of skin cancer.
- Several of the world's major crops such as wheat, rice, barley, oats, corn, soybeans, peas, tomatoes, cucumbers, cauliflower, broccoli and carrots are particularly vulnerable to increased UV, resulting in reduced growth, photosynthesis and flowering.
- Plant growth, especially in seedlings, is harmed by more intense UV radiation.
- Planktons (tiny organisms in the surface layer of oceans) are threatened by increased UV radiation. Planktons is the first vital step in aquatic food chains.
- Decrease in planktons could disrupt the fresh and saltwater food chains, and lead to a species shift.
- Loss of biodiversity in our oceans, rivers and lakes could reduce fish yields for commercial and sport fisheries.
- In domestic animals, UV overexposure may cause eye and skin cancers. Species of marine animals in their developmental stage (e.g. young fish, shrimp larvae and crab larvae) have been threatened in recent years by the increased UV radiation under the Antarctic ozone hole.
- Wood, plastic, rubber, fabrics and many construction materials are degraded by UV radiation.

3.5.3 Green House Effect (Global Warming)

Development has resulted in indefinite exploitation of the natural resources. Thus, man has disturbed the ecological balance of the nature. Indiscriminate industrialisation and urbanisation all over the world have posed a great threat to the global environment. Deforestation is another serious problem which has disturbed the global carbon cycle because burning of biomass also increases the CO_2 in the atmosphere. Now-a-days, coal is used as a fuel in industries and domestic purposes which pump large quantities of CO_2 in the atmosphere. Green house gases like methane (CH_4), nitrous oxide (N_2O) and chloroflurocarbons (CFCs) are also increasing in the lower atmosphere. The main cause of global warming is the green house gases.

Therefore, global warming is nothing but an increase in earth's temperature due to the green house gases. These gases play a major role in the heat balance of the atmosphere due to their capacity to absorb long wave infrared radiations. There is an increased amount of green house gases in the atmosphere which affect the global climate and the phenomenon is called global climatic change or global warming. Global warming takes place due to green house effect. In very cold climate, glass houses are used for growing delicate and sensitive plants. These glass houses are also called green houses. In a green house, there is higher temperature inside than outside though the inner side receives less solar radiation. It is called green house effect. For this effect glass walls, high CO_2 content, higher water vapour content in the green house are responsible. The green house lets the short wave radiation pass through them but prevent the passage of long wave i.e. infrared radiations emitted by the earth's surface. This makes the inside of green house warmer than outside.

In the atmosphere, atmospheric gases act like a glass of a green house. The atmospheric gases play an important role of selective energy absorption. They allow short wavelength energy to pass through but absorb longer wavelength (infrared) radiation and reflect heat back to earth. In other words, the atmospheric gases are permeable to short wave solar radiations, but are strong absorbers of long wave radiations (heat) emitted from the surface of earth and hence very slowly earth's temperature is rising. These gases are called green house gases. The main contributor of green house effect is CO_2 gas and methane, CFCs are also potent green house gases but their concentration in atmosphere is very less as compared to CO_2. The mean annual temperature of earth is 15°C. In the absence of green house gases, the temperature of earth would have been – 20°C. Therefore, these gases play a vital role in keeping the earth warm. Therefore, all living organisms are able to survive in this normal temperature.

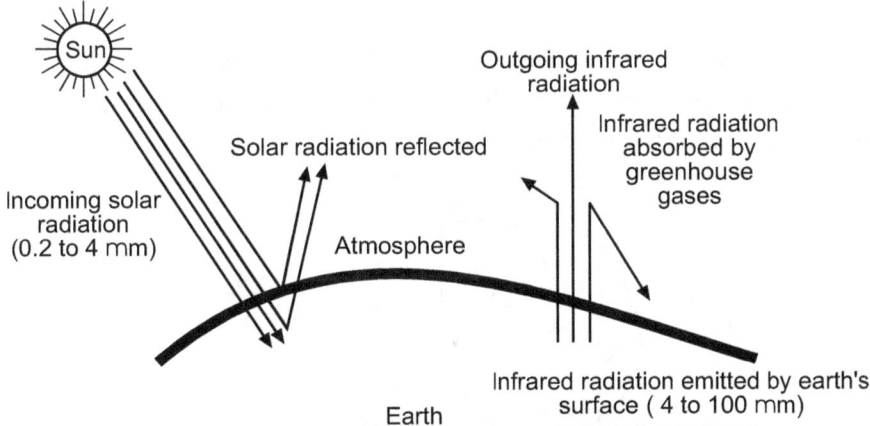

Fig. 3.7: Green House Effect: The atmosphere is permeable to incoming short wave radiations and it is impermeable to the long wave infrared radiation (heat) which are absorbed by green house gases and earth surface becomes warm

Due to heavy industrialisation there is a constant increase in the concentration of these green house gases in the atmosphere and hence they are responsible to maintain more and more infrared radiation, resulting in enhanced green house effect. This ultimately increases the global mean temperature resulting in global warming. The assessment of atmosphere green house gases is periodically made by the agency called Inter Governmental Panel on Climatic Change (IPCC). There is considerable increase in the concentration of green house gases since pre-industrial times.

1. Carbon dioxide (CO_2): It is abundantly present in the atmosphere and chiefly produced by burning of fuels like coal, wood, and natural gas. This green house gas is also released by plants and animals during the process of respiration. Its level increases from pre-industrial level of 280 ppm to 368 ppm (parts per-million) in 2000. This is because of burning of fossil fuel, deforestation and change in land use.

2. Methane (CH_2): It is produced by incomplete decomposition which is brought about by a group of bacteria called methanogens, under anaerobic conditions. It is also liberated from garbage dumps, swamps, flooded rice fields, and burning of biomass. Its concentration was 700 ppb (parts per billion) during pre-industrial times but it has now elevated to 1750 ppb in 2000.

3. Chloroflurocarbons (CFCs): These are synthetic gaseous compounds of carbon and halogens. These are non-toxic, non-flammable and highly stable compounds. The CFCs were synthesised during the 20th century, and extensively used as refrigerants, aerosol, propellants, insulators and fire extinguishers. They enter the atmosphere through air conditioners and refrigerators, or refrigeration units, evaporation of industrial solvents, production of plastic foams and propellants in aerosol spray cans. These gases can persist for 45 to 260 years or more in the atmosphere. Their concentration (CFC – 11, HFC – 23) is about 282 ppb (parts per billion) in recent times.

4. Nitrous oxide (N_2O): It is released due to burning of biomass, agriculture, industrial processes, burning of nitrogen rich fuels, live stock waste, breakdown of nitrogen rich fertilisers in the soil and nitrate containing ground water.

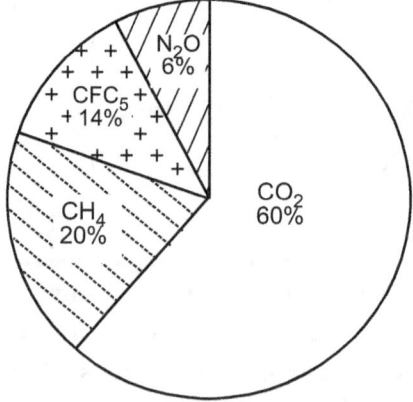

**Fig. 3.8: Distribution of different Green House Gases
in the Atmosphere responsible for Global Warming**

Effects of Global Warming

1. Effects of weather and climate: Due to greenhouse effect there is an increase of global mean temperature by 0.6°C in the 20th century. The average temperature of earth may increase by 1.4 to 5.8°C by year 2100 from 1990.

(1) There will be warming of the earth's surface i.e the lower atmosphere and cooling of stratosphere.

(2) Due to warming of atmosphere, the moisture carrying capacity of the atmosphere will also increase.

(3) Precipitation patterns will be changed. Precipitation will increase at higher latitudes but will decrease at lower latitudes. Some areas will become wetter and some areas dryer. Thus, frequency of extreme drought and floods will increase.

(4) Soil moisture regimes will be changed due to changes in the evaporation and precipitation.

(5) Wind direction and wind stress over the sea surface will be changed, which will alter ocean currents and cause change in nutrient mixing zones and productivity of oceans.

(6) Human diseases will increase in tropical and subtropical countries due to increase of vectors and waterborne pathogens.

2. Rise in sea level: If no efforts are made to control the emission of greenhouse gases, the ultimate consequence will be a rise in sea level. This will be the result of thermal expansion of ocean and melting of glaciers and ice caps of mountains. The sea level has been rising by 1-2 mm per year during the 20th century. It will rise 10 to 30 cm by the year 2030 and 30 to 100 cm by the end of the next century. A rise of even half a meter in sea level would affect human population. Many of world's important cities and coastal areas are likely to be hit by storms and floods. Shorelines will be submerged and wet lands will be affected and shore birds and fishes will become extinct. Thus, rise in sea level will have an adverse impact on human settlements, tourism, fisheries, agriculture, and water supplies and coastal ecosystems.

3. Effect of fauna and flora: Plants and animals are distributed in a particular area in a specific temperature range. Global warming will affect the patterns of the organisms. This may cause large scale loss of trees or animals because they are sensitive to the temperature stress. Many species may disappear as they may not cope up with temperature changes.

4. Impact on food production: Global warming may hamper food production. It may be reduced due to plant diseases pests and uncontrolled growth of weeds. In temperate regions, small rise in the temperature may also enhance the crop productivity. But if there is increase in temperature, crop productivity decreases. However, in tropical and subtropical regions, small rise in temperature will have adverse effect on crop productivity. It is estimated that the yield of rice in South East will decrease by 5% for each 1°C rise in temperature. Thus, there will be a decrease in world food production due to global warming.

3.6 Water Pollution

Water is a vital natural resource, which is essential for a variety of purposes to human beings as well as plants and animals. Its many uses include drinking and other domestic uses, industrial cooling, power generation, agriculture or irrigation, transportation and waste disposal. In many chemical industries, water is used as a reaction medium, a solvent, a scrubbing medium and a heat transfer agent. Water is a source of life for living organisms hence it cannot be replaced.

Most of our water bodies such as ponds, lakes, streams, rivers, sea, oceans have become polluted due to urbanisation, industrial growth and other man-made problems.

Water pollution is one of the most serious environmental problems. It occurs when water is contaminated by such substances as human and animal wastes, toxic industrial chemicals, agricultural residues, oil and heat. Most of our water bodies rivers, lakes, seas, oceans, estuaries and underground water sources like tube wells, bore wells are generally becoming polluted.

Thus, water pollution is defined as *"the addition of any substance to water, changing physical and chemical characteristics of water in any way which interferes with its use for legitimate purposes"*.

Generally, water is never pure in the chemical sense. It always contains impurities of various kinds, dissolved as well as suspended. These include dissolved gases like CO_2, H_2S, NH_3 and N_2, dissolved minerals Ca, Mg and Na salts, suspended matter clay, silt, sand and even microbes. The natural impurities in water are in very low concentrations which are derived from the atmosphere and soil. These impurities do not pollute water and the water is potable.

The polluted waters however are turbid, unpleasant, bad smelling, unfit for bathing and washing or other purposes. They are harmful and are sources of a number of diseases such as cholera, dysentery, typhoid, etc. Polluted water may look clean or dirty but contains germs, chemicals and other harmful toxic materials that can cause inconvenience, illness or death.

Types of Water Pollution

Classification of water pollution depends on the criterion used for categorisation of pollution. Based on the medium in which pollutants occur, types of water pollution may be distinguished as *freshwater pollution* and *marine pollution*.

Freshwater pollution can be categorised into pollution of *surface water* and pollution of *ground water*. When the pollutant enters a water body such as lake, pond or river, it is known as *surface water pollution*. If, however, the pollutant finds its way into an aquifer, along with percolation of water it deteriorates the quality of ground water and is called *ground water pollution*. The freshwater bodies have the very low salt content always less than 5 ppt. Marine water bodies have salt content of 35 ppt or above. Estuaries and brackish waters have salt content between 5 to 35 ppt. Thus, the pollution of oceans, seas, estuaries, salt marshes and other similar water bodies is known as *marine pollution* or *ocean pollution*.

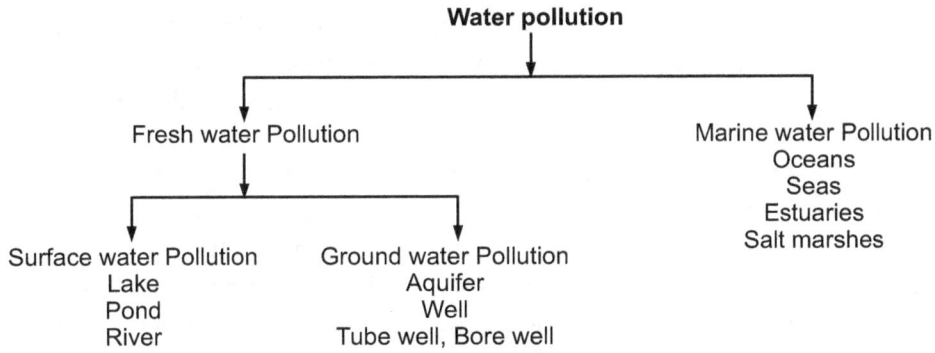

Fig. 3.9: Water Pollution

General Problems: The problem of water pollution due to discharge of domestic and industrial wastes into aquatic systems like rivers, ponds, lakes, seas, oceans and estuaries has already become a cause for serious concern in our country. Most of our rivers and freshwater streams which pass through or near the major cities, townships or other human dwellings are polluted by industrial wastes or effluents. All our major rivers are polluted either by industrial effluents or by sewage or domestic waste. Most of our holy rivers such as Ganga, Godavari, Yamuna resemble open sewers. The sewage, industrial effluents containing toxic chemicals and heavy metals are responsible for various diseases like enteric disorders, typhoid, cholera, dysentery, dysfunction of kidney, liver, reduction in haemoglobin and mental retardation. Fluoride causes knock-knee syndrome i.e. pain in the bones and joint and outward bending of legs from knees, mottling of teeth. Many heavy metals and pesticides are highly toxic and teratogenic. Consumption of fish contaminated by methyl mercury causes Minamata disease.

Water is polluted naturally as well as through human activities. For example, fluoride, a strong pollutant, which causes knock-knee disease occurs naturally in water bodies but it also results from industrial activities such as ceramic industries, phosphate fertiliser plants and aluminium factories.

Sources of Water Pollution

There are several water pollutants which contaminate water. Following are the chief sources of water pollution.

1.   Domestic waste water and sewage
2.   Industrial wastes (effluents)
3.   Agricultural wastes
4.   Physical pollutants (thermal and radioactive)

3.6.1 Domestic Waste Water and Sewage

It includes water borne wastes derived from household activities such as bathing, laundering, food processing and washing of utensils. Domestic waste contains garbage, soaps, detergents, waste food, paper cloth, used cosmetics, toiletries and human excreta. This waste water, which is known as sewage, is the largest primary source of water pollution. Most of our natural water bodies like rivers, ponds, lakes and streams are heavily polluted by sewage. There is uncontrolled dumping of wastes of rural areas, towns and cities into our ponds, lakes, streams, rivers and oceans. Most of our cities, towns and villages are located on the banks of rivers and they directly discharge their domestic wastewater into the river. Therefore, there is accumulation of sewage and other wastes in these bodies on a very large scale. Because of the heavy load of sewage, the natural water bodies have lost their self regulatory capability.

Domestic waste water and sewage are largely carbonaceous organic material that can be oxidised by microorganisms to CO_2 and water. The decomposition of these wastes by aerobic microbes decreases due to higher levels of pollution. The self-purifying ability of water is lost and such water becomes unfit for drinking and other domestic purpose. The decomposition of sewage and other oxygen demanding wastes is largely an aerobic process. When these wastes are accumulated on a large scale in water, the aerobic process increases its oxygen requirements. This is called 'Biological Oxygen Demand' (BOD).

Biological Oxygen Demand (BOD): *BOD is the amount of oxygen required for biological oxidation by microbes in any unit volume of water.* It is the common parameter used to measure the oxygen demand of waste. The test is done at 20°C for at least 5 days. In this test, the amount of dissolved oxygen required for oxidation over a five-day period is measured and the results are expressed in milligrams of oxygen per litre (mg/l). When the amount of sewage discharged is relatively minor, a river will not become badly polluted, because biological degradation will soon remove most of the wastes, however, strong sewage or other oxygen demanding wastes from industry or agriculture can lead to the depletion of the dissolved oxygen in the water. "Septic" conditions are said to be present when the dissolved oxygen level is very low. Aquatic organisms like fish and other life requires dissolved oxygen (DO) for survival and DO level should normally be at least 5 mg/l. Under aerobic conditions, when sufficient O_2 is present for degradation of organic materials, carbon is converted to CO_2, sulphur is converted to sulphate, phosphorous is converted to phosphate, and nitrogen is converted to ammonia and nitrates.

When DO is insufficient carbon gets converted into methane, nitrogen compounds gets converted into amines (whose odours typically make one think of rotten fish decaying in a stinking cesspool), sulphur compounds gets converted into hydrogen sulphide, (the rotten egg odour) and phosphorous compounds can have wormy odour. Under such anaerobic conditions, O_2 may be obtained from dissolved nitrate and sulphates.

Strong oxidising compounds (such as $KMnO_4$) can oxidise organic compounds that are not biologically degradable, and they are sometimes used to determine the Chemical Oxygen Demand (COD) of the water. COD values will be larger than BOD values.

The BOD values generally approximate the amount of oxidisable organic matter and is, therefore, used as a measure of degree of water pollution and waste level. Thus, mostly BOD value is proportional to the amount of organic waste present in water.

Thus, due to increased load of sewage and waste O_2 levels in the water are depleted which are reflected in terms of BOD values of water. The number of microbes like *Escherichia coli* (bacterium) also increases tremendously and they consume most of the O_2. The number of *E. coli* in unit volume of water is also taken as (index) a parameter of water pollution. BOD values are thus useful in evaluation of self purification capacity of a water body and for possible control measures of pollution.

Sewage and other oxygen demanding wastes are classified as water pollutants because their degradation leads to oxygen depletion which affects (and even kills) fish and other aquatic life; produce annoying odours, impair domestic and livestock water supplies by affecting taste, odour, and colours and they may lead to scum and solids that render water unfit for recreational use. They may also contain infectious agents.

Infectious Agents: Waste water from municipalities, sanatoriums, tanning and slaughtering plants and boats may be the source of bacteria or other microorganisms capable of producing diseases in men and animals, including livestock. Disease causing microorganisms are always present in sewage. There are several types of human infections but some of them such as cholera and typhoid are transmissible through water. These diseases are water-borne and water-borne epidemics still widely prevalent in some countries including India. There are many animal infections that are of public health importance because they are transmissible to humans either through water or by direct contact. Tetanus, bubonic plague, anthrax, rabies, bovine tuberculosis, cholera, typhoid, fever, bacillary dysentery, infectious hepatitis are spread by the ingestion of infected water and food.

The pathogens in water can be identified by many sophisticated techniques. These tests are too expensive and time consuming for routine pollution tests. The standard method used universally to check water quality is the determination of Most Probable Number (MPN) of coliform organisms in the water sample. Coliform bacteria like *E. coli* are normal inhabitants of human and animal intestines and the daily per capita excretion in human faeces may number from 125 to 400 billions. Treatment processes can reduce the number of these organisms. Although these organisms are not pathogens and they do not affect water environment in exactly the same manner as pathogens, their existence and density are proved to be a fairly reliable indicators of the adequacy of treatment for reduction in pathogens and. Various standards have been suggested for various uses of water but typical maximum levels for faecal coliform counts are about 2000/100 ml for general recreational use, 200/100 ml for primary contact use (swimming) and 1/100 ml for drinking water.

Thus, quantity of O_2 or DO along with BOD is indicated by the kind of organisms present in water. Inadequate DO leads decrease in fish population (4-5 mg/l DO makes fish rare) and further decrease in DO values may lead to increase in anaerobic bacteria.

Domestic waste contains soaps and detergents. Phosphates are the main ingredient of major detergents. Plant nutrients such as nitrogen and phosphorous can stimulate the growth of aquatic plants, which later decay to produce disagreeable odours and add to the BOD of the water. Phosphates and nitrates favour the luxuriant growth of algae which form algal blooms. The excessive algal growth also consumes most of the available O_2 from water body. This leads into decrease in O_2 level, which becomes detrimental to the growth of other organisms as it produces foul smell after decay. Some decomposing plants are known to produce toxins as strychnine that kills animals including cattle.

Eutrophication

Too high levels of nutrients in water may cause eutrophication. Eutrophication denotes the enrichment of a water body by input of organic waste containing nutrients, chiefly nitrates and phosphates. Sewage and domestic waste water contains these nutrients. The decomposition of organic matter makes the water rich in nutrients. Due to phosphates and nitrates, the water body becomes highly productive or eutrophic and the phenomenon is called *eutrophication.*

Many nutrients result from the natural disintegration of rocks and from mineralisation of organic matter. Natural eutrophication is a very slow process, taking often a period of over hundred years. Ponds, lakes and rivers during their early stages of formation are relatively barren and nutrient deficient. Thus, such water bodies support very poor aquatic life. When water bodies are not enriched with nutrients they are called oligotrophic and they have very small plant and animal populations and very clear blue water.

Artificial eutrophication, which results from human activities, is a dramatically fast process. This happens when domestic waste, agricultural residues (plant nutrients) land drainage and industrial wastes reach a water body. The problem of eutrophication arises due to nutrients released from organic wastes by the activity of aerobic bacteria in presence of O_2. The nutrients induce changes in the ecosystem balance and composition of aquatic life. Addition of nutrients stimulates luxuriant growth of algae in water. There is also shift in the algal flora and blue green algae begin to predominate. There start forming algal blooms, floating scums or blankets of algae. The algal blooms are not utilised by zooplanktons. The algal blooms compete with other aquatic plants for light to perform photosynthesis. Larger plants such as duck weed and water hyacinth also flourish in water. More of these plants grow as a result of additional nutrients. The water becomes turbid and greenish. As more plants grow, more also die and decay. Both these processes consume O_2 resulting in O_2 deficit. Nutrient and organic wastes added by people imbalance the cycle, as shown in the flow chart. Addition of nutrients at an increased rate increases the rate of growth of algae. As the algae die, they add to wastes. Bacteria use large amounts of O_2 to convert wastes into nutrients depleting, O_2 levels. Moreover, these blooms also release some toxic chemicals which kill fish, birds and other animals, thus water begins to stink. The water is poorly oxygenated with higher CO_2 levels, which kill fish and other aquatic animals. Such water body is said to be eutrophied. It smells offensively as BOD rises and its aesthetic value goes down. Eutrophication is thus a limiting factor in supply of clean water for drinking, fishing and navigation.

The excellent example of manmade eutrophication is Lake Erie in U.S.A. In 1965, more than 80 tonnes of phosphates were added daily in this lake. Each 400 gm of phosphates encourages 350 tonnes of algal slime. There were big mounds formed on the shore by algal growth which produced unpleasant odour, clogging of pipes and interfering with fishing and navigation.

Eutrophication usually has an adverse effect on fishing.

Flow chart showing the sequence of events which may result from eutrophication

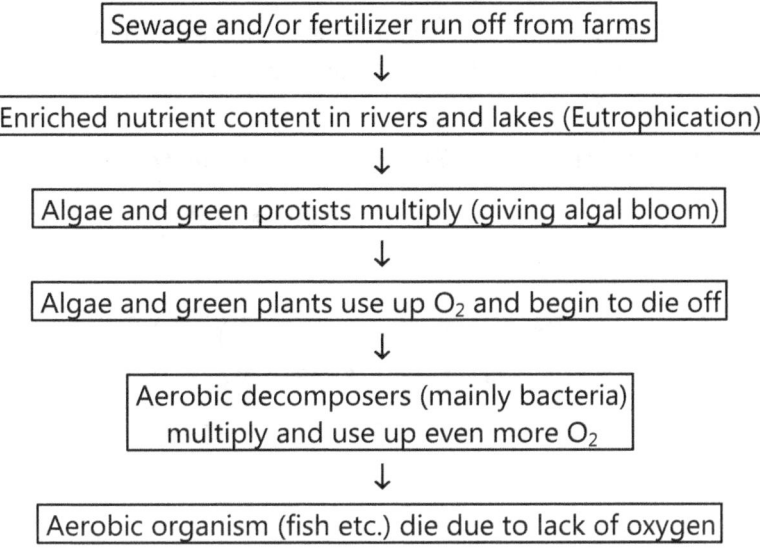

Eutrophication can be stopped or reversed by the following methods:

1. Sewage and domestic waste water must be treated before its discharge into a lake or river. This would reduce nutrient input.

2. Growth of aerobic decomposers must be stimulated in order to reduce the amount of nutrients solubilised in water. This would help disruption of algal food web.

3. Prevent the recycle of nutrients into the water through harvest and removal of algal blooms after their death and decomposition.

4. Use physical and chemical methods for the removal of dissolved nutrients from water. By precipitation, phosphates can be removed. Nitrogen can be removed by biological nitrification and denitrification or by air stripping of NH_3 from an alkalised waste water or by ion exchange, electro dialysis or reverse osmosis.

In a eutrophic lake or river many pathogens like bacteria, viruses, protozoa are present. These may result into spread of fatal water borne diseases, some of which may assume an epidemic state. These are viral hepatitis, polio (viral), cholera, typhoid, diarrhoea (bacterial), amoebiasis etc.

3.6.2 Industrial Wastes or Effluents

Most of the rivers and freshwater streams which flow near the major cities, townships or other human dwellings are polluted by industrial wastes called *effluents*. A wide variety of both inorganic and organic pollutants are present in the effluents of common industries such as paper and pulp industry, textile, sugar mills distilleries, breweries, tanneries, steel industries and mining operations and thermal power plants. The kinds of effluents generated by industries are also numerous. The paint and varnish industries produce aromatic long chained hydrocarbons, textile industries release various dyestuffs and metal salts which are used as mordants. The other industrial effluents contain many pollutants such as oils, greases, plastics, plasticizers, metallic wastes, phenols, acids, salts, dyes, cyanides, DDT etc. The metallic wastes such as, copper, zinc, arsenic, cadmium, lead, mercury, chromium, are also discharged from industries.

Table 3.10: Some Polluted Indian Rivers and their Major Sources of Pollution

Name of the River	Sources of Pollution
Bhadra (Karnataka)	Paper and Steel industries.
Cauvery (Tamil Nadu)	Tanneries, distilleries, paper and rayon mills.
Chambal (M.P.)	Rayon mills, caustic soda mills.
Damodar	Fertilisers, steel plants, coal washeries and power stations.
Ganga (at Kanpur)	Chemical metal and surgical instrument industries, tanneries, textile mills.
Godawari (A.P.)	Paper mills.
Gomati (Near Lucknow)	Paper and pulp mills.
Hooghly (Near Delhi)	Jute, paper pulp, chemical, paint, varnishes, metal, steel, vegetable oils, rayons, soap and polythene industries.
Jamuna (Near Delhi)	DDT factory, power station, Mathura refineries.
Kali (at Meerut)	Sugar mills, distilleries, paint, soap, rayon, silk, yarn, tin, glycerine industries.
Narmada (M.P.)	Paper mills.
Siwan (Bihar)	Paper, cement, sulphur and sugar mills.
Sone (U.P.)	Paper mills.
Suwap (Balrampur)	Sugar industries.

About 130 million litres of toxic effluents are discharged into the Periyar river every day by the industrial units in the greater Cochin area.

The holy river Yamuna has been converted into an open sewer. The various industries located in Delhi dump the toxic effluents in the river. The belt of about 48 km is highly polluted and Yamuna water near Delhi is not fit even for irrigation so there is no question of using the water for other purposes such as drinking, bathing, swimming etc. About 515000 kilo-litres of effluents are discharged in the river by 16 large and 500 odd medium industrial units. The effluents include sodium, salts, acids, phenols, cyanide, metals, DDT and dyes.

The Ganges is also in a similar state. Its worst stretch is in Kanpur and Varanasi. Effluents contain a variety of toxic organic and inorganic pollutants, and they are capable of killing living organisms in the water bodies.

Mine drainage is major source of increased acidity in natural waters. The main constituent is sulphuric acid. Acids cause corrosion of metals and concrete and can be fatal to fish. Alkalies discharged by industries such as textiles, paper industries, tanneries and coke-oven operation can also destroy aquatic life.

The sources of freshwater salinity are varied. They include industrial effluents, minerals, dissolved by water used in irrigation, salt brines from mines or oil wells, and ocean salts. Salts cause the 'hardness' of water. Hard water can cause scale formation in pipes, boilers, tubes and other industrial equipments. Chloride concentrations, if present in excess of 400 ppm, can be fatal to fresh water fish and other organisms.

The toxic properties of numerous inorganic compounds, particularly heavy metals have been known for years. The detection of these substances in natural waters in concentrations approaching toxic levels has created a great amount of concern. Most of these substances produce physiological poisoning by accumulating in the body tissues. Consequently, their increasing concentrations can build up in food chains. The metals of particular concern in industrial waste waters are mercury, lead, cadmium, chromium and silver.

Mercury Pollution

Mercury is an important water pollutant found in various industrial effluents such as those from manufacture of paint and paper, chlorine and caustic soda, fertilisers and pesticides. It is a potent hazardous substance and it is present in both inorganic and organic forms which are highly toxic. Inorganic mercury undergoes rapid methylation in aquatic environment by the anaerobic bacteria in bottom muds forming methyl mercury (CH_3Hg^+) which can be concentrated in living organisms and can lead to mercury poisoning. Mercury pollution affects the rate of photosynthesis of phytoplanktons. Methyl mercury gives off vapours and it was responsible for Minamata epidemic that caused several deaths in Japan and Sweden. The cause of deaths was due to the consumption of fish contaminated with mercury in the Minamata Bay of Kyushu in Japan during 1953-1961. The water of the bay was contaminated by mercury discharged in the bay from single chloride producing plant, using $HgCl_2$ as a catalyst. In Sweden, rivers have become polluted due to mercury released from paper and pulp industries and those manufacturing pesticides. Methyl mercury is persistent and accumulates in food chains. It accumulates in fatty tissues. In Minamata bay, the fishes that were heavily contaminated with mercury were consumed by the people. Effluents of industries making switches, batteries, thermometers, fluorescent light tubes and high intensity street light lamps also contain mercury. The symptoms of methyl mercury are malaise, numbness, visual disturbance, dysphasia, ataxia, mental deterioration, convulsions, and finally death.

Methyl mercury and inorganic mercury are potent teratogens causing deformities in the developing embryos of frog and fish. They affect the nervous system. The children suffer from mental retardation, cerebral palsy and convulsions. Mercury concentration in blood and brain of the foetus is about 20% higher than mother.

Mercury is also responsible for bringing about genetic defects causing chromosomal defects, interference with cell division, resulting in polyploidy or abnormal distribution of chromosomes. Moreover, mercury can inhibit oxygen producing activities of phytoplankton at very low levels as low as 0.001 mg/l.

In the 1960's, Sweden became concerned when it discovered that mercury poisoning had killed birds. Methyl mercury was used as fungicide to prevent seed spoilage. Certain bird populations declined sharply and many birds that remained alive were obviously ill and were suffering from cramps. These fungicides have caused severe cases of mercury poisoning elsewhere among humans. Methyl mercury led to over 6500 cases of intoxication and over 450 deaths. Methyl mercury poisoning in humans leads to severe damage to the nervous system, characterised by loss of sensation at the extremities of the limbs and areas near mouth, loss of coordination in gait, slurred speech, by diminution of vision, and by loss of hearing.

Lead Pollution

Lead may arise as a contaminant from various industrial and mining effluents. It is also the constituent of effluents arising from battery manufacture, printing, painting and dyeing. Lead is a natural constituent of air, water and the biosphere and human beings ingest a certain amount in food, water and air.

In some plastic pipes, lead is used as a stabiliser. The water becomes contaminated in these pipes. From rocks also it reaches to water. Once it reaches in water, lead enters the food chain.

Effects of Lead Pollution

1. Lead is highly toxic to plants and animals including man.

2. It affects children more severely than adults.

3. Lead poisoning causes variety of symptoms such as liver and kidney damage, reduction in haemoglobin formation, mental retardation and abnormality, infertility and pregnancy.

4. It causes gastrointestinal troubles, neuromuscular effects (lead palsy), central nervous system syndrome that may result into coma and death in industrial workers.

5. Lead poisoning causes constipation and abdominal pain.

6. Lead is a potent enzyme inhibitor because it is easily incorporated into enzyme structures especially with sulphidryl (–SH) groups. It also inhibits the synthesis of heme and utilisation of iron in the body.

7. Chronic exposure interferes with fertility and can cause female menstrual disturbances.

8. Lead poisoning causes brain damage, and symptoms are clumsiness, subtle changes in mental attitude, sluggishness, and poor memory, loss of concentration, restlessness and hyperirritability.

9. Lead compounds are also teratogenic and carcinogenic.

10. Lead is deposited in the bones.

11. Lead poisoning may cause nervousness, depression, apathy, lack of ambition, frequent colds and mild psychoneurosis.

Cadmium (Cd)

Cadmium is now recognised as an environment pollutant. It is a soft, silvery–white metal used in nickel – cadmium rechargeable batteries, in alloys, in electroplating, and as a plasticizer for polyvinyl plastics. Biologically, it is neither essential nor beneficial.

Cadmium is generated in waste streams from pigment works, textiles, electroplating, chemical plants, metal alloys and by dissolution from galvanized iron objects. It can get into food from metal cans and plated utensils. The permissible level for cadmium in drinking water supplies is 0.01 mg/l.

Effects of Cadmium

1. Cadmium accumulates in the body of aquatic animals like shell fish, aquatic plants which is lethal to both oysters and aquatic plants. It can retard growth of aquatic plants.

2. It can combine synergistically with other metals like copper and zinc which increases its toxicity.

3. It can lead to very rapid sterilisation of animals because of its toxicity to testes and sperm cells.

4. Cadmium and its compounds produce malignant tumours in rats but it is not certain that they are carcinogenic to humans.

5. Cadmium leads to high blood pressure in rats, rabbits, and dogs and it is probably associated with heart disease in humans.

6. Cadmium poisoning also damages the kidneys and liver and prevents the proper functioning of the enzymes.

7. Cadmium is responsible for causing 'itai–itai' disease or ouch–ouch disease. This disease occured in Japan after World War II and most commonly among post menopausal women who had delivered several children. The most characteristic feature of the disease was pain from pressure on the bones, especially the femur,

backbone and ribs. It led to bone deformation, which produced a waddling gait. After several years, victims would be unable to walk and their bones could be easily fractured, even by a fit of coughing. Within 20 years, over 100 deaths had been recorded and that was due to cadmium poisoning.

Chromium

This metal is found in two forms in effluents - hexavalent and trivalent. The hexavalent chromium is present in the effluents of plating operations, aluminium anodising, paint and dye operations and other industries. Trivalent chromium occurs in waste waters from textile dyeing, the ceramic, and glass industry and photography. The permissible limit in drinking water is 0.05 mg/l.

Effects of Chromium

1. It is toxic to aquatic plants and animals including humans.

2. It produces lung tumours.

In addition to above inorganic pollutants silver, zinc, arsenic, nickel, selenium antimony metals have been of concern.

The industrial waste water is generated by the following industries and products:

1. Food and kindred products: Wastes from food processing industry – meat and dairy products, beet sugar refining, brewing and distilling, canning and similar industries are troublesome and hazardous because they contain decomposable organic matter. They deplete O_2 content of water. The meat processing wastes (from cattle, hogs, poultry) come from stock yards, slaughter houses, packing plants and rendering plants contains blood, fats, proteins, feathers and other organic wastes. The dairy industry produces organic wastes high in protein, fat and lactose from milk and cheese processing. Breweries and distilleries produce organic solids containing nitrogen and fermented starches from grain processing and alcohol distilling.

Textile products: Textile mill wastes have high BOD and are quite alkaline, requiring neutralisation and other treatment. Wool fibres, sand, grease, burrs are the constituents of waste water discharged from these industries.

Paper and allied products: The wastes from paper and pulp mills contain complex mixture of chemicals used in kraft process. Stray wood chips, bits of bark, cellulose fibres and dissolved lignin (woody tissue carbohydrate). It also contains toxic compounds such as methyl mercaptan, paper and wood pulp preservatives, such as pentachlorophenol and sodium pentachlorophenate. Sulfite liquor is also toxic to fish and shellfish.

Chemical industries: The chemical plants manufacturing acids, bases, synthetic fabrics, pesticides, detergents and many organic and inorganic compounds. Acid wastes are produced from all chemical plants including DDT and rayon manufacturing because large amount of H_2SO_4 is used, phosphate industries produce waste containing phosphorous, fluorine, silica and suspended solids. Mercury waste is highly toxic.

Petroleum industry: Oil drilling wastes includes drilling muds, salt water brines, crude oil. Oil refineries and petrochemical plants produce variety of pollutants. These include hydrocarbons, acids, alkalies, cyanides, numerous sodium salts, phenolic compounds, inorganic and organic sulphur compounds, halogenated and nitrogenated hydrocarbons.

Mining: Coal mines lead to acid mine drainage containing H_2SO_4, coal, shale, clay, sand stone and other solids. Asbestos like particles, several toxic chemicals, are also found in waste waters.

Rubber and plastics: Wastes from rubber manufacturing units have a high BOD and a bad taste and odour. Synthetic rubber is produced from butadiene and styrene in a soap solution and hence these chemicals are present in the effluents. Plastic manufacturing units produce wastes containing hydrocarbons and other organic compounds and reagents.

Metal industries: Steel mills produce waste water from the coking of coal and they contain acid, cyanogen, phenol, ore, coke, limestone, alkali, oils, mill scale and fine suspended solids. Other metal industries waste contains chromium, lead, nickel, cadmium, zinc, copper, silver as well as alkaline cleaners, grease and oil.

Other industries: Leather, tannery waste contain solids, salts, sulphides, chromium, lime, detergents, organic solids found in laundry wastes. Radioactive waste is discharged from nuclear power plants and fuel processing plants and hospitals and research laboratories using radio isotopes. Soft drink bottling plants produce highly alkaline wastes with high BOD from washing of bottles.

3.6.3 Agricultural Wastes

Agricultural chemicals, notably pesticides and fertilisers are also important water pollutants. Their discharges reach the water bodies. In addition to the agrochemical farm, animal waste also contributes to water pollution. Let us consider these pollutants and their harmful effects on aquatic life including human beings.

Pesticides: Biocidal agricultural chemicals collectively called pesticides, include insecticides, fungicides, acaricides, nematicides, herbicides, rodenticides and molluscicides, have proved to be the most effective, dependable and economical tool in pest management on crops. These chemicals have been effective in controlling diseases and pests that affect crops, livestock and even humans. Crop yields have greatly increased and many millions of lives threatened by insect borne diseases are saved by the increased use of these chemicals. At present, more than 1000 pesticides are in common use, all over the world and more than a quarter of a million tonnes of insecticides alone are sold annually.

As compared to developed countries, use of pesticides in developing countries, is relatively low. However, now a days there is considerable increase in the use of these agrochemicals. The consumption of technical grade pesticides in India is about 90,000 tonnes per annum and at present more than 100 pesticides is available to the farmer in India and about 55 different types of pesticides are imported from developed countries.

The widely used pesticides are classified into three groups:

1. Organophosphate pesticides e.g. Sumithion, Malathion.

2. Organochlorine pesticides e.g. BHC, DDT, Aldrin, Endrin etc.

3. Carbamate pesticides e.g. Furadan.

Pesticides enter the aquatic environment by various ways and pollute the water. They reach water either by direct application or indirectly and unintentionally. The indirect sources include runoff from agricultural fields, spray drifts, rainwater, sewage and effluent from industries manufacturing pesticides or using them in their processes.

1.   Runoff from agricultural fields: The pesticides used on crops in the field may get washed by rainwater and reach river or lake through agricultural runoff. The water-soluble pesticides are transported in a dissolved state, while the insoluble ones, are bound to the particulate matter, which is carried by water. In one study, 0.07% of dieldrin applied to soil appeared in runoff water.

2.   Spray drift: Contamination of water may arise due to the fallout from accidental spray from large scale aerial spraying forests or agricultural fields. Major fall out occurs close to the site of application polluting nearby water bodies.

3.   Rain water: Pesticides lost into atmosphere in the vapour phase are generally adsorbed on to the dust particles and get dissolved in the atmospheric water. Such residues from the atmosphere, particularly the lower strata ultimately reach land or water along with the rain water.

4.   Sewage and industrial effluents: Pesticide manufacturing factories release large amounts of pesticides in their effluents. These are the most important sources of contamination of rivers, streams and estuaries. For example, DDT factory in Delhi discharge effluent in Najafgarh Nallah contain 5 ppm of DDT.

5.   Direct applications of pesticides to water: Pesticides are applied directly to water for various reasons. For example: (1) killing undesirable fish, (2) for the control of fish predators like lampreys and aquatic snail which carry various diseases, (3) for controlling black fly and mosquitoes, (4) for controlling aquatic weeds like water hyacinth herbicides are used. Such treatment results in a great deal of pollution.

Effects of Pesticides

Many persistent organochlorine pesticides remain for a longer period in aquatic environment. DDT, BHC residues are most common. They are hazardous to aquatic biota and they may accumulate in the body of aquatic organisms.

Pesticide residues in water may reach humans through drinking water or by consumption of contaminated fish. However, the concentrations in most cases are far below the harmful levels. The permissible levels of some common pesticides in drinking water are given in the table as follows.

Table 3.11: Permissible Limits for Pesticides in Drinking Water

Pesticide	Maximum limit mg/l
Aldrine	0.017
DDT	0.003
Dieldrin	0.042
Endrin	0.001
Heptachlor	0.018
Lindane	0.056
Methoxychlor	0.035
Organophosphate and carbonates	0.100
Toxaphene	0.005
Herbicides (e.g. 2, 4–D; 2, 4, 5–T; 2, 4 – 5 TP)	0.100

Hazards of Pesticides

1. **Toxicity:** Pesticides are highly toxic to fauna and flora of aquatic environment. They are toxic to fish e.g. DDT, Endrin. LC_{50} values are very low to fishes like blue gills and rainbow trout.

2. **Bioaccumulation:** The pesticides present in water get concentrated in the tissues of plants and animals. Chlorinated organic pesticides like DDT, dieldrin and aldrin are hazardous mainly due to their concentration in the food chain. They have high stability, low vapour pressure and very low solubility in water but are more soluble in oils and fats. For example, the concentration of DDT in freshwater is about 0.0001 ppm. It tends to become more concentrated from one trophic level to another due to the process of biological magnification.

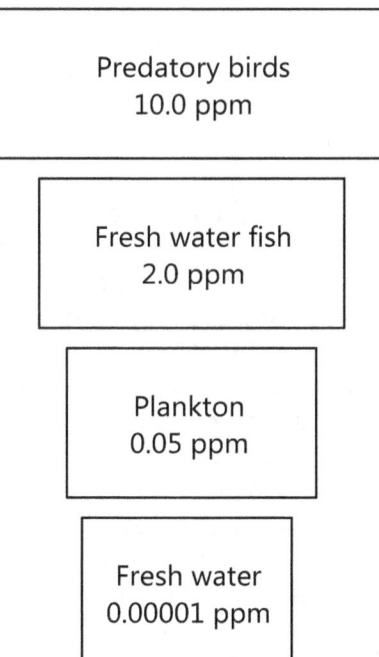

Fig. 3.10: Typical Food Chain Concentration of DDT

As a result of biomagnification fish and predatory birds are very susceptible to chlorinated hydrocarbons like DDT, Endrin, Dieldrin etc.

Effects of Pesticides

1. These pesticides impair calcium metabolism in birds which affects egg laying with thin egg shells and consequently reproductive failure.
2. Man is at the top of the food chain and pesticides accumulated in man results into cancer in humans and abortions in pregnant women.
3. Pesticides are mutagenic causing mutation in genes and chromosomes.
4. They are also teratogenic causing congenital malformations.
5. Pesticides like DDT, Aldrin, Heptachlor and Mirex are capable of producing tumours.
6. Pesticides also cause harmful effects on wildlife because they are often concentrated in food chains. The high levels of pesticides in birds and fish damage their health or reproductive abilities causing decline in their population.
7. Pesticides, particularly chlorinated hydrocarbons affect bird populations because they interfere with calcium metabolism through inhibition of the enzyme carbonic anhydrase. As a result, insufficient calcium is made available during the process of formation of egg shell and the egg shells are very thin.
8. Fish also exhibit acute responses to pesticides. The major fish kill occured due to pesticide spraying. Fish show hemorrhaging and death. The sublethal effects of pesticides on fish are behavioural changes, bone degeneration and vertebral damage.
9. Pesticides are also responsible for bringing about histopathological alterations in vital organs such as gills, skin, liver, digestive tract, kidney and reproductive organs in aquatic animals. Pesticides also show the depression in oxygen consumption in fish and prawns.
10. Pesticides are also found to be teratogenic in the embroys of fish and frog.

Artificial Fertilisers: Artificial fertilisers or plant nutrients are another important water pollutants. Nitrogen, phosphorous and potassium are essential elements, which are required by the plants and animals for maintaining their growth and metabolism. The small amounts of these nutrients are sufficient to maintain a balanced biological growth. Modern agriculture relies heavily on artificial or chemical fertilisers. The availability and low price of commercial fertilisers have led to rapid increase in their usage since World War II. Problem can arise from over use of the fertilisers, because they can be transported into ground water by leaching or into waterways by natural drainage and storm runoff. Nitrates are of special concern. They enter our wells and ponds making the water unfit for drinking but also causes diseases. When a person consumes such water, the nitrates are converted to nitrites by the microflora of intestine. These nitrites then combine with the haemoglobin of blood to form methaemoglobin which interferes with the O_2 carrying capacity of the blood. The disease produced is called methaemoglobinaemia in infants (or blue baby disease). This leads to various ailments as damage to respiratory and vascular system, blue colouration of skin and even cancer. The same process occurs in the stomach of ruminants, so livestock can also be affected by nitrate poisoning. Generally, a healthy person contains 0.8% of methaemoglobin, whereas in methaemoglobinaemia condition the level reaches upto 10% in the blood. When this level reaches upto 20% there occurs headache, giddiness and above 60% the patient experiences loss of consciousness, stiffness, ocular problems etc. At 80% death occurs.

Nitrate poisoning problem is common in Rajasthan because of hard and saline water. Several children have died due to nitrate poisoning. In Rajasthan, nitrite level in water is as high as 300 mg/l whereas the WHO has set the permissible limit at 45 mg/l. The nitrates can be further converted to amines and nitrosoamines in the human body leading to a possible cause of gastric cancer.

Plants nutrients also contribute to eutrophication. Addition of phosphates and nitrates to water leads to depletion of oxygen due to excessive algal growth. It leads to death of fish and aquatic organisms.

In addition to the above mentioned pollutants there are also some miscellaneous agricultural pollutants which pollute water. They are:

(i)   Animal disease agents, which are transmitted by air, water and soil.

(ii)   Dead animals and their disposal is another problem. Sometimes, dead animals are disposed in old wells, thereby leading to ground water pollution.

(iii)   Rural domestic waste waters are disposed off in the ground through the use of pit, privies, cess pools or septic tanks. These pollute well and ground water.

(iv)   Agro-industries such as sugar factories, food processing industries cause both air and water pollution.

(v)   Irrigation water can percolate down to ground water supplies and make them increasingly salty. Salinity is a worldwide concern and has been a problem for many millennia.

Ground Water Pollution

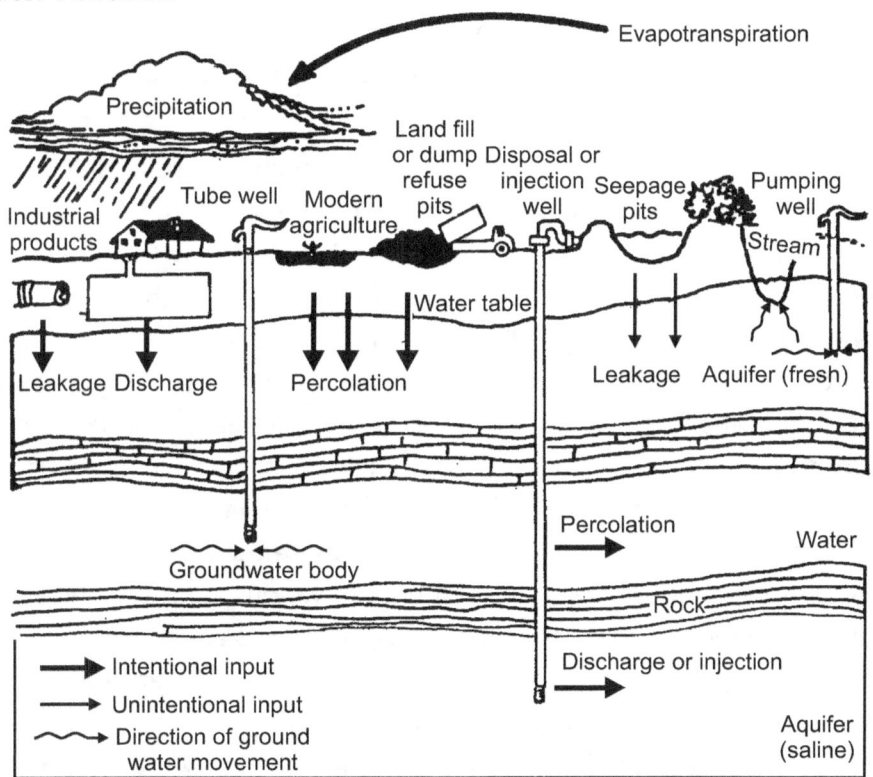

Fig. 3.11: Sources of Ground Water Contamination

The widespread practice of releasing raw sewage in shallow soakpits has caused pollution of ground water in many cities. Pollutants contained in seepage pits, refuse pits, septic tanks and barnyards may percolate through layers of earth and find their way into ground waters. Sometimes transport accidents may also lead to contamination of underground sources of waters. Some industrial products and process wastes may also cause pollution of ground water. In the industrial areas of Punjab and Haryana, for example, Ambala, Ludhiana and Sonepat where bicycles and woollen garments are manufactured significantly high concentration of nickel, iron, copper, chromium and cyanide have been detected in ground water samples.

Modernisation of agriculture has led to excessive use of nitrogenous fertilisers. These nitrates pollute underground water because of seepage of irrigation water into ground water recesses. Such water if used as drinking water cause serious health hazards and diseases like methaemoglobinameia or blue baby disease in rural areas. The nitrates, which are soluble in water, trickle down through layers of soil into deeper layers of earth and ultimately are added to the underground stores of water. In many villages and townships where ground water is the only source of drinking water this causes methaemoglobinaemia particularly in bottle-fed infants, because they are very sensitive to this pollutant. Therefore, removal of these soluble nitrates is an important task. It requires elaborate treatment procedures, such as chemical coagulation and filtration, carbon absorption, chemical oxidation, ion-exchange, electrodialysis and reverse osmosis. Any one or combination of methods can be used for removal of nitrates depending on availability of resources.

The indiscriminate release of toxic industrial wastes such as arsenic, lead, cadmium and mercury compounds and pesticides like polychlorinated biphenyls (PCB) may result in their trickling down to nature's underground water stores. This seriously threatens the quality of ground water supply, especially in areas where water table is high i.e. situated near the surface of the earth. Drinking of such polluted ground water may lead to bioaccumulation of these toxins in the body. These compounds are not metabolised in the body and are stored in the body usually in the fatty tissues. This phenomenon is called *bioaccumulation*. Human beings also consume the products obtained from various plants that thrive on polluted waters and store these toxic compounds in their biomass. Non-vegetarian diet such as fish, pork, and beef is also come from animals which store these pollutants in their biomass. Man here acts as a centre into whose body, pollutants from various kinds of sources pour in. The quantity of toxic substances is thus magnified. Thus, pollutants are concentrated into human tissues through biological sources. In the food chain, man is at the apex and toxic substances are increased in the body of man through biological food chain. This process is called as *Biological magnification*. During starvation when the body draws upon reserve food sources, these compounds are released into the blood stream producing toxic effects.

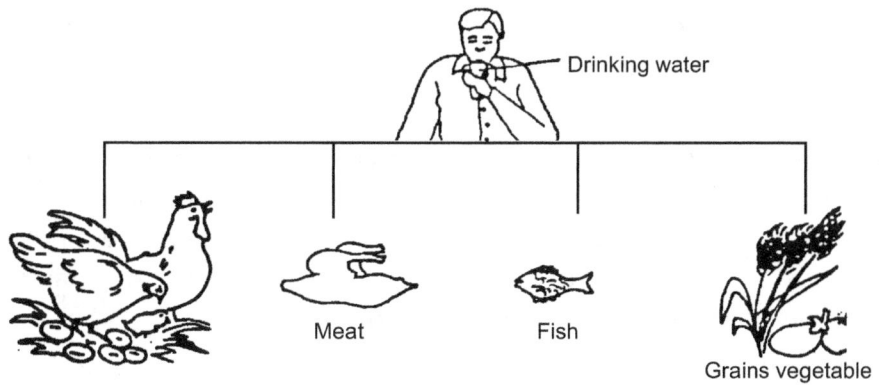

Fig. 3.12: Biological Magnification

Even in regions where water table is low, contamination of ground water may cause serious problems. For example, water pollution in Pali (Rajasthan) is an excellent example of ground water pollution. For nearly one lakh population of the city, underground water is the only source of drinking water. There are more than 450 textile units involved in designing, dyeing and bleaching of cloths. All these discharge effluents containing toxic substances. A study conducted by Rajasthan State Board for Prevention and Control of Water and Air Pollution concluded that with the onset of monsoon these toxic substances percolate down the earth, mix with underground water and contaminate it.

Ground water pollution is a serious problem in cities and villages. For instance trans-Yamuna areas of Delhi, Pali in Rajasthan face drinking water pollution problem at regular intervals. There had been epidemics of cholera hepatitis, dysentery and other diseases.

Marine Pollution

The oceans which cover about 71% of earth's surface are crucial for the maintenance of the environment for they contribute to the basic $O_2 - CO_2$ balance of the biosphere upon which human and animal life depend. About 70% of earth's oxygen is produced by ocean phytoplankton.

Water from the oceans evaporates and forms clouds which are carried away to hills and plains where they rain. Ocean is the major source of available water on earth. Any human intervention, addition of pollutants, exploitation of ocean resources such as pollutants from oil spoilage and nuclear testing are likely to bring about drastic imbalance in the global water cycle and this may change the pattern of the climate. Estuaries and coral reefs are the habitats of richest biological diversity.

On their way to sea, rivers receive huge amounts of sewage, garbage, agricultural discharge, biocides, including heavy metals. All these pollutants are eventually discharged into the sea. Besides these, discharges of oils and petroleum products and dumping of radionuclides waste into sea also cause marine pollution. Huge quantities of plastic are being added to seas and oceans. Large amounts of sewage and domestic wastes are directly dumped in the sea. Big cities like Mumbai, Chennai are situated near the sea. Communities located near the seashore, industries and agricultural farmers dispose 1,645 km³ of waste water into the sea.

Apart from the above sources, oil spills, industrial effluents and discharge of hot waters and mining of polymetallic nodules cause marine pollution. A spill in oil from petroleum tankers due to accidents or a deliberate discharge of oil waste brings about pollution. About 285 million gallons of oil are spilled each year into ocean mostly from transport tankers. Many small oil spills go unrecorded besides oil explorations.

Petrochemical refineries and waste from auto crankcases and petroleum industrial machinery contribute to oil pollution. On 24th March, 1989 Exxon, a 50 million gallons oil tanker leaked oil in Prince William sounds reef, near Alaska. Oil spillage assumes enormous dimensions when it is used as a war weapon. This is true of recent conflict in 1991 between Iraq and Allied coalition forces, in which millions of gallons of crude oil was pumped into the Gulf. Not to speak of the dangers faced by the flora and fauna of oceans, the water desalination plants of the adjoining countries were shut down, rest got contaminated. Especially Kuwait, Bahrain, and Saudi Arabia were immediately affected, where water scarcity is a real threat. Oil pollution causes damage to marine fauna and flora including algae, fish, birds and invertebrates. About 50,000 to 250,000 sea birds are killed every year by oil. The oil is soaked in feathers, displacing the air and thus interferes with buoyancy and maintenance of body temperature. Detergents used to clean up the spill are also harmful to marine life. Marine pollution affects the life of fish, clams and oysters by choking of gills by oil. Photosynthetic activity is inhibited by cutting off light. Inhibition of reproduction and genetic damage to endangered species of flora and fauna occur due to oil pollution.

Industrial chemicals which are dumped in sea cause Minamata disease in human beings by consumption of contaminated fish as in Japan.

Physical Pollutants

Thermal discharges and radioactive substances are the other physical pollutants of water.

1. Thermal discharges: Power plants and industry use large quantities of water for cooling purposes. Used coolant water is usually discharged directly into water bodies. This could result in increase in temperature of water bodies with deleterious effects on aquatic inhabitants. This is called *thermal pollution*. An increase in water temperature decreases the O_2 saturation percentage and lowers dissolved oxygen levels. This is because the hot water tends to form a separate layer above the cool water due to density differences between the two. The upper hot layer which itself holds less O_2 than the cooler layer below, prevents the replacement of oxygen in the cooler layer as it is denied contact with the atmosphere. The dissolved oxygen level falls rapidly due to normal biological functions in the lower layer and may lead to anaerobic conditions.

The thermal pollution adversely affects aquatic life. Some cold water fish like trout may die if the water temperature is above 25°C and their eggs will not hatch at temperatures above 14.5°C. An increase in temperature also increases the toxicity of some chemical pollutants.

Radioactive substances: Very little is known about the radiation damage to aquatic environment from wastes of uranium and thorium mining and refining from nuclear power plants and from industrial use of radioactive materials. The refining of uranium ore is an important source of radioactive waste producing radionuclides of radium, bismuth, etc. Radium is the most significant waste product and is considered to be a hazard in drinking water. Its permissible limit in drinking water should be not more than 3 picocurries per litre of radium^{226} and 10 picocurries per litre of Strontium^{90}. Certain marine organisms have the capacity for accumulating radionuclides from water.

This biomagnification results into objectionable radioactivity in living organisms. These radioactive substances can enter humans with food and water and get accumulated in blood and certain vital organs like bone, liver, thyroid gland and cause harmful effects like leukemia, bone cancer and mutagenic changes. At present radioactive wastes are sealed in containers and dumped into the ocean. If there is any damage or leakage from the containers, the nuclear waste could escape and enter the marine system.

3.7 Soil Pollution

The fundamental component of the life supporting system is the lithosphere. Land is the major constituent of the lithosphere and it is the source of many materials essential to man and other organisms. It forms about one-fifth of the earth's surface, covering about 13,393 million hectares. About 36.6% of the land area is occupied by human dwelling and factories, roads and railways, deserts and dunes, glaciers, polar ice marshes, rocks and mountains. About 30% of the total land mass is under forests, approximately 22% is occupied by meadows and pastures and only 11% is arable land.

The surface layer of the land is called soil. About four-fifths of the land area is covered by soil. Soil is one of the most important ecological factors. It is the natural resource, which supports life. Plants depend on soil for their nutrients, water supply and anchorage. Even for the free floating aquatic plants which require their nutrients to be dissolved into the water medium around them, soil or mud in aquatic environment is important as chief storage of all nutrients, which are made available to the water medium. It is also in soil that plant and animal materials decay and are released into the nutrient bank. Myriads of bacteria, fungi and several kinds of animals which are involved in the detritus pathway inhabit the soil. Each soil has its own distinctive flora and fauna such as bacteria, fungi, actinomycetes, algae, blue green algae, protozoans, rotifers, nematodes, earthworms, molluscs and arthropods. These soil organisms make the biological system of the soil complex. Among these organisms, some help in maintenance of soil fertility through nitrogen fixation and others are responsible for return of essential elements back to soil by decomposition of dead organic matter.

Soil is a mixture of mineral particles of different sizes derived from the weathering of rocks and humus consisting of organic matter. There are fine spaces or interstices between soil particles. These are filled up with air and water containing various dissolved substances. If the volume of water increases, as after rain or irrigation, the volume of air decreases. Also if the volume of water decreases due to evaporation or drainage the volume of air in the soil increases. Thus, soil is a complex system of solid, liquid and gaseous phases of different composition and texture. It is thus not merely a group of mineral particles. It has also a biological system of living organisms as well as gases and liquid components.

Types of Soil: The different types of soil vary in their physical and chemical properties. The type of soil is determined by the mineral composition of the parental rock and the size and relative proportion of different types of particles such as gravel, sand, silt and clay. Therefore, soil is classified into four types:

1. Sand soil   :   85% sand + 15% clay.

2. Loamy soil   :   70% sand + 30% clay.

3. Loam soil   :   50% sand + 50% clay.

4. Silt soil   :   90% sand + 10% clay.

Of the particular constituents clay and humus are the main determinants for the properties of soil. Sand and silt consist largely of quartz (SiO_2) and are chemically inert. Clay is chemically more active and has a high capacity to hold water and ions. Pure clay is not a suitable medium for plant growth, because it forms a solid impenetrable mass. However, when mixed with other constituents of the soil, the charges on the ions links the particles together to form aggregates or crumbs to produce granular soil. Soils devoid of clay particles are structureless, powdery and are incapable of holding water and nutrients.

Soil erosion, salination, water logging, and acidification and alkalination of soil brought by human actions are the great dangers to land resources.

The undesirable changes in soil which affects the life activities is called *Soil pollution.*

The study and control of soil pollution are important particularly in densely populated and developing countries. The process of soil formation is so slow that soil may be considered as a non-renewable resource.

There are many natural and synthetic materials, chemicals and toxic substances that can adversely affect the physical, chemical and biological properties of soil and seriously affect its productivity. Once the soil becomes infertile it is very difficult to convert it into fertile or productive soil.

3.7.1 Sources of Soil Pollution

Soil pollution is an extremely complicated process. It may be the direct effect of dumping and disposal of wastes, application of agrochemicals or the indirect result of air pollution i.e. secondary air pollutant such as acid rain.

Following are the important soil pollutants:

1. Pesticides
2. Fertilisers
3. Industrial wastes
4. Salts
5. Radio nuclides
6. Heavy metals
7. Asphalt, tin, iron, aluminium
8. Plastic, rubber
9. Discarded food, garbage, paper
10. Carcasses
11. Demolished buildings
12. Ashes
13. Crop residues
14. Manure (excretory products)
15. Broken glass pieces, bricks
16. Agro industries
17. Salinity of irrigation water.

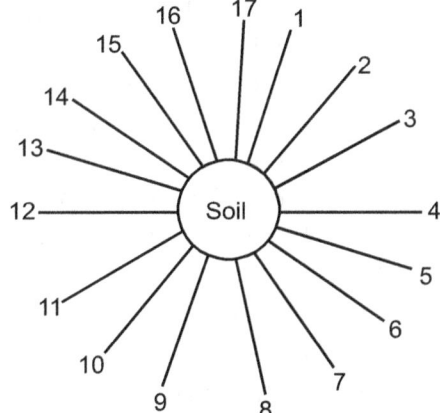

Fig. 3.13: Various Soil Pollutants

Pesticides: Pesticides are essential in agriculture and public health. Due to increased use of pesticides, food production has been increased many folds and many insect borne diseases are successfully controlled in human beings and live stock. However, indiscriminate use of pesticides has created serious problem of air, water and soil pollution. The chlorinated pesticides such as DDT (Dichloro-diphenyl-trichloro-ethane), dieldrin and aldrin, endrin are hazardous mainly due to their concentration in the food chain. They are persistent due to their high stability. DDT and many other pesticides used in the control of mosquitoes and agricultural pests, have become the more serious pollutants of water. Being long lasting under natural conditions, the pesticide goes on increasing in soil and water with successive applications. In soil, they kill the useful soil organisms like nitrogen fixing bacteria, algae and earthworms. Thus, they affect soil fertility. Such polluted soil becomes unproductive. In the food chain, dead earthworms and other organisms are eaten by birds which affect the reproductive ability of the birds. Due to the process of biomagnifications, these chemicals are concentrated from one trophic level to the another. Man is at the top of food chain thus ultimately these toxic chemicals finally find their way into the human body, where they are deposited into fat tissues. In the milk of Indian mothers there is high concentration of DDT and its metabolites. On fat break down, the pesticides are released into blood stream producing toxic effects. Many biocides are also absorbed by crop plants and they are deposited in the grains which ultimately enter the body of human beings. BHC, (Benzene Hexa Chloride), 2–4–D (2–4 Dichlorophenoxy acetic acid), 2, 4, 5-T (2, 4, 5-Trichloro-phenoxy acetic acid) are the common biocides, which pollute the soil.

Fertilisers: Fertilisers or plant nutrients both natural and artificial are essential for maintaining the growth of the plants. They should be applied in proper proportion. But to get more and more yield farmers use artificial or chemical fertilisers on a large scale, which creates adverse effects. Artificial fertilisers crowd out useful minerals naturally present in the top soil. The soil microbes such as bacteria, fungi, etc. present in top soil enrich the humus and help to produce nutrients to be taken up by the plants and later by animals. But fertiliser enriched soil cannot support microbial life and hence there is less humus and less nutrients and soil can become poor and eroded by wind and rain. Thus, the over use of chemical fertilisers make soil infertile. Chemical fertilisers are made up of only a few minerals. Thus, they impede the uptake of other minerals and imbalance the whole mineral pattern of plant body. Many crops today lack potassium due to excessive use of nitrogenous fertilisers. Nitrates, phosphates, potash, also affect the quality of food. Nitrate fertilisers increase the total crop yield but at the cost of protein. Excessive plant nutrients are harmful to soil organisms. Due to percolation, these chemicals find their way into well and underground water. They make the water unfit for drinking but cause diseases. Methaemoglobinaemia or blue baby disease is caused by water contaminated with nitrates.

Manure or Farm animal wastes: Over the centuries, farm animal wastes have been regarded by all people as an important soil fertiliser. Fields fertilised with manure generally show higher yields than those without manure and even when the manure treatment is over, the favourable influence persists for years. But it is observed that due to manuring yields have decreased by 50% in 10 years and by 40% after 30 years.

In U. S. today it is estimated that only $\frac{1}{3}$ of the value of farm manure is being realised.

The analysis of farm manure gives percent values about 0.5 (K), 0.1 (P) and 0.4 (K). The commercial fertilisers contain 20 to 30 times more these nutrients.

Another problem with farm manure is odour and water pollution in addition to public health problems arising from their role in transmitting diseases.

The excretory products of people and livestock and digested sewage sludge used as manure pollute the soil. In developing countries, the unhygienic practices of people and faulty sanitation aggravate soil pollution. There is a practice in some places where sewage water is directly supplied to the fields growing vegetable crops. However, the innumerable pathogens contained in these wastes contaminate the soils and vegetable crops and cause serious health hazards for man and domesticated animals. Therefore, vegetable fields should not be irrigated with such waste water.

Industrial Wastes: The composition of industrial wastages are highly variable. The content and proportion of industrial discharges depend on the nature of the industry and processing of waste water. Many a times these wastes are directly released on the soil, which pollute the soil and make unproductive. The mining waste contains chlorides, heavy metals, sulphuric acids, H_2S; Iron and Steel industries release sulphides, oxides of copper, chromium food processing industry, release highly putrescible organic matter and paper and pulp industry discharge organic acids, wood sugar cellulose etc. Sugar industries collect their spent wash and effluents in the lagoons which make soil acidic foul-smelling. Thermal power stations are a continuous source of fly ash, which ultimately settle on the soil. The fly ash contains particulate matter with different heavy metals like cadmium, mercury, lead, etc. When fly ash mixes with soil, the characteristics of soil change. It becomes contaminated and loses its fertility. This is a very common problem around the thermal power stations and there is a considerable decrease in the crop yields. The smelters also release the metallic dust which ultimately settle on the soil and it gets contaminated. These inorganic minerals affect soil fertility and retard the growth of crop plants.

Radionuclides: Radioactive pollution is a special form of pollution related to air, water and soil. Tests of nuclear arms release radioactive particles of Strontium 90, Cesium 137, Iodine 131, Uranium 235 in the atmosphere. These particles settle down to cause water and soil pollution. The radioactivity is transferred to soil particles. From soil, these particles enter the food chain affecting different forms of life including man. They cause somatic and genetic damage to the body.

Solid wastes and garbage: In large metropolitan cities, the problem of solid waste and garbage is always acute. Solid waste includes glass, glass containers as bottles, crockery, plastic containers, polythene, paper, and other packing materials that are used and then thrown away as garbage. The garbage contains discarded food, vegetable matter, kitchen refuse etc. The garbage piles up at public places and causes obstruction in daily life. The wastes from building material (during construction and demolition) sludge, dead animal skeletons etc. also contribute to solid waste. Many a times, city garbage and solid waste is deposited on the land away from city called garbage depot. Due to pathogen, soil is polluted and it becomes useless for cultivation. This garbage is mixed with soil which pollute the soil.

Dead animals: The disposal of dead animals is another problem. The dead bodies show decomposition and produce objectionable odours. Such dead bodies also pollute the soil.

Acid rain: Acid rain is the secondary but a very hazardous air pollutant. The oxides of sulphur and nitrogen are important gaseous pollutants of air. They are mainly produced by combustion of fossil fuels, smelters, power plants, automobile exhausts and domestic fires etc. They are released in the atmosphere and are oxidised into acid. Sulphuric acids and nitric acids are the two main acids which are formed when these gases mix with water vapour and precipitated on the soil. Acid rain create complex problems and their impacts are far reaching. They increase soil acidity, thus affecting the flora and fauna of the soil. Many bacteria and blue green algae are killed due to acidification, thus disturbing ecological balance. Acid rain kills forest cover. Acid rain causes acidification of lakes, and streams thus affecting aquatic life, affects crops productivity and human health.

Salination of soil: Increase in the concentration of soluble salts adversely affects the soil productivity and degrades the quality of land. Salts dissolved in irrigation water accumulate on the soil surface. This is aggravated by inadequate drainage especially in flood ravaged and well irrigated areas. Additional salt from the lower layers moves up by capillary action during summer season and are deposited as white crusts on the surface.

Intensive farming with poor drainage is causing serious salination damage in large areas of India. Total amount of saline land in our country is estimated at six million hectares. In Punjab alone annually 6000 to 8000 hectares of farm land is becoming unfit for agriculture. Nearly one-sixth of the arid and semi-arid lands of the world have high salinity.

Salinity has already impaired about one-fourth of the 12 million hectares of irrigated land in Western United States and has caused concern over another one fourth. The highly productive imperial valley of California uses the waters of the Colorado River water containing about 750 ppm dissolved salts. A farmer who uses 1-5 m of water during the irrigation season is applying about 11 metric tons of salts per hectare. Improperly drained fields produce a crop of 'Imperial Valley Snow' – a white crust of sodium sulphate.

Irrigation water can also percolate down to underground water supplies and make them increasingly salty. Salinity is a worldwide concern and has been a problem for many millennia.

3.7.2 Control of Soil Pollution

1. **Proper disposal of solid wastes:** Control of soil pollution is largely connected with solid waste disposal. Considerable time and money can be saved by constructing transfer stations at various points in a city for bulk transfer of refuse to discharge sites. Laying of pneumatic pipes for collecting and disposing wastes may be economical in the long run.

2. **Incineration of wastes:** Collection and burning of wastes practised in the developed countries is called incineration, however, it is an expensive operation. It leaves behind a lot of residue, and adds to air pollution. Pyrolysis, a process consisting of combustion in absence of oxygen is energy intensive and beyond the means of poorer countries.

3. **Recycling and recovery:** Recycling and recovery of materials appears to be a reasonable solution for reducing soil pollution. This would decrease the volume of the refuse and help in the conservation of material resources.

Materials such as paper, glass and some kinds of plastic can be recycled. Although the cost of recycling of paper and glass is high, it is worthwhile in terms of resource conservation. For example, recovery of one tonne of paper can save 17 trees. Recovery of metals from scrap has been considered as an economical option in several countries. In many countries including India, rubber and plastic which is commonly used is recycled in variety of ways. The material is again used as raw material for the production of plastic articles.

4.   Use of biofertilisers: Chemical fertilisers cause soil pollution when they are used on a large scale. To avoid this problem the better alternative to chemical fertilisers are biofertilisers and manures. These enrich the fauna and flora of soil, resulting in better crop yields.

5.   Biological control of pest: Indiscriminate use of pesticides for the control of crop pests and disease transmitting insects cause environmental pollution problem. Many insects and pests developed resistance for pesticides. Therefore, to avoid air, water and soil pollution due to pesticides, biological methods of pest control can be adopted, which can also reduce the use of pesticides and thereby minimise soil pollution.

6.   Legislation: Heavy penalties should be imposed on persons or industrialists who release the toxic wastes in the soil.

7.   Education: People should be made aware about the consequences of soil pollution by educating them with slide shows, video cassettes and T. V. programmes.

3.8 Noise Pollution

Noise is unwanted sound and it is also treated as a pollutant. In the modern times, man is also suffering from noise or man-made sounds from all sides. The super fast trains, their whistles, aeroplanes, trucks, buses and cars, pneumatic drill machines, sirens, radio and television all produce noise, the most dangerous pollutant of man's environment. Noise has become a permanent part of our day-to-day life, which we cannot avoid. This unwanted sound is continuously produced due to the development of machinery, industry and technology. Noise or sound has the ability to harm the body and mind of human beings. It is not only a cause of irritation or annoyance but responsible for constriction of blood vessels, increased flow of adrenaline and force the heart to work faster.

Noise (Latin *nausea*) is often defined as unwanted sound or unpleasant sound which causes discomfort. A better definition of noise is "*wrong sound in the wrong place at the wrong time*". Now-a-days man is living in an increasing noisy environment and hence the 20th century has been described as the "*Century of Noise*". Since, the noise pollution causes health hazards in man, it has become a very important stress factor.

3.8.1 Sound and Hearing

Sound is produced by the presence of mechanical waves in matter-gaseous, liquid or solid. These waves are longitudinal, i.e. the atoms and molecules transmitting the wave oscillate in the direction in which the wave is travelling. Sound waves in a material are characterised by alternate regions of compression and refraction of matter, as shown in the

Fig. 3.14 (a). The accompanying pressure wave is shown in Fig. 3.14 (b) varies sinusoidally along the wave at any instant in time, with regions of compression corresponding to regions in which the pressure exceeds atmospheric pressure, and regions of refraction corresponding to regions in which the pressure is less than atmospheric pressure The amplitude of the pressure wave is generally, denoted by P. The intensity of sound wave [Fig. 3.14 (c)] is a measure of the energy flow; it is the energy flowing each second through a unit area perpendicular to the direction of propagation of the wave and is measured in watts per square metre.

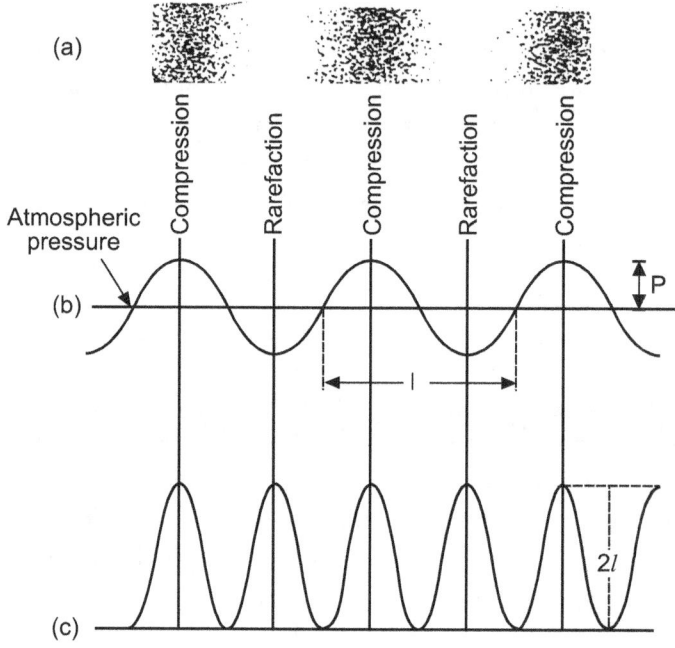

Fig. 3.14: Wave Nature of Sound

The human ear is capable of receiving sound waves and transmitting signals to the brain to create the sensation of hearing. The ear's response is not directly proportional to the intensity or the pressure of the sound wave, but is more nearly proportional to the logarithm of the intensity or the pressure; i.e. the ear subjectively judges the 'loudness' of two sounds by the ratio of the intensities or pressures of the sounds. Consequently, sounds are measured on a logarithmic scale, either by the intensity level or the sound pressure level.

The sound pressure level is most often used because it is easier to construct instruments to measure pressure than to construct those to measure intensity. These levels are expressed in decibels (dB).

The "Threshold of hearing" is the decibel level at which a sound can just barely be perceived. For a young person with good hearing, the maximum sensitivity occurs at a frequency of about 3000 Hz (Hertz). The ear is unable to perceive sounds of frequencies lower than about 20 Hz or higher than about 20,000 Hz.

3.8.2 Sources of Noise

There are many and varied sources of noise. These are automobiles, factories, industries, construction work, aircrafts, railways, rocket engines, sonic booms and the domestic noises from the radios, transistors, television, loud speakers, all adding to the quantum of noise in our daily life.

1.   Automobiles and motor vehicles: Motor vehicle noises are of concern to occupants of the vehicle as well as to those living or working near highways. These include trucks, taxis, cars, buses, scooters, motor cycles, trains etc. Every day, a large number of new motor vehicles is coming on the roads. Noise from motor vehicles account for much of the noise in metropolitan cities. The greater part of the noise, particularly when the vehicle is travelling at high speeds, arises from the rolling of the tires, both because of roughness of the road and the tread design. Heavily loaded trucks run with lower speeds and the engines make more noise. The pneumatic horns of the auto vehicles, which are too often used in non-emergency situations also add to the noise in the environment.

Loud noises are also produced by the steel wheels of trains moving on steel rails, especially at high speeds. The whistles of these railways on railway stations also add to noise pollution.

2.   Aircrafts: In the fast and modern life today, aircrafts play a crucial role in quick transport. But, at the same time they have also created the problem of noise pollution. For many years aircraft noises have been troublesome in the vicinity of airports and the existence of these noises represents a real cost to society one that has not been fairly assessed against the air transportation industry, just as numerous other pollution costs have not been assessed against polluters. The situation is being aggravated, by the continued growth of the airline industry. Areas near airports are subjected to noise from landing approaches, from takeoffs, and from the sideline noise of jet engines on the ground. Subjective annoyance increases with the increasing peak noise level and with the increasing number of aircrafts using the airport; a 'noise and number index' has been devised to measure the annoyance. Annoyance begins with noise levels in excess of 80 dB.

Most of the noise from jet aircraft comes from the jet engine. Part of the *'jet noise'* arises from turbulence, where the high velocity gas stream leaving the exhaust nozzle mixes with the outside air; this noise extends over broad frequency ranges and is generated outside the engine. The turbofan engine generates *'fan noise'* and this is propagated forward out of the air inlet and backward out of the fan ducts, it contains broad band noise from the flow of turbulent air through the fan, but it also contains some annoying discrete tones arising from the chopping of the blades.

Rocket engines used in the space programme, also produce noises that affect those near or on test sites; these noises tend to be very low in frequency.

3.   Factories or industries: There is rapid industrialisation every year. Large number of small scale and large scale industrial plants are established. Huge machinery, sirens of factories also contribute to noise in the environment.

4.   Domestic noises: On an average in every has a house radio, transistor, tape recorder, and television set. These devices also produce noise when they are played at high volume. In addition to these, there are different household appliances such as washing machines, vacuum cleaner, food mixers, pressure cookers, fans, air conditioners, coolers etc. which also add to the noise.

5.   Loud speakers: Loud speakers are the noise makers in community and religious functions and festivals. During elections, loud speakers are commonly used for canvassing. During Ganapati, and Navaratri festivals whole night loud speakers, hi-fi sound systems are used and the atmosphere becomes very noisy. Birth anniversaries of renowned personalities are commonly celebrated by the people, where loud speakers are used which produce a lot of noise. During Ganapati festival, Bhagawati jagran and Navratra, you cannot sleep the whole night due to noise.

6.   Construction activities: Construction noises also affect community, especially in large cities some construction or repairing is usually going on. Each year city like New York, 80,000 street repair jobs and 10,000 construction and demolition projects are handled. Very loud noises often 110 to 120 dB in the immediate vicinity are produced by pneumatic riveters and chippers, air compressors, hammers and other heavy equipments.

7.   Sonic booms: There is a new type of noise introduced in recent years called the sonic boom. This noise is produced by objects like supersonic air planes, travelling faster than the speed of sound, whose value in air at sea level is about 330 m/s (740 mi/hr.). Sonic booms or shock waves are produced constantly, not just when the object first reaches a speed greater than that of sound. A noticeable sonic boom is usually heard over a width of perhaps 80 to 130 km for supersonic planes flying at an altitude of about 20 km. The noise is harmful. Sonic booms cover area of 10 to 80 miles and when it hits the ground it damages windows pans and building structures. It also fastens rate of heart beat of the human foetus.

Properties of Noise

There are two basic properties of sound: (i) Loudness or intensity, and (ii) Frequency.

1.   Loudness or Intensity: Loudness or intensity depends upon the amplitude of the vibrations which initiated the noise. The loudness of noise is measured in decibels (dB). When we say that a sound is 60 dB, it means that 60 dB is more intense than the smallest distinguishable noise or the *'reference'* sound pressure which is understood to be 0.0002 microbar or dynes 1 cm^2. A dyne is $\frac{1}{1000,00^{th}}$ of atmospheric pressure. Normal conservation produces a noise of 60-65 dB; whispering, 20-30 dB, heavy street traffic, 60–80 dB; and boiler factories, about 120 dB. A daily exposure upto 85 dB is about the limit people can tolerate without substantial damage to their hearing.

It has been observed that the human ear responds in a non-uniform way to different sound pressure levels, that is, it responds not the real loudness of a sound, but to the perceived intensity. Acceptable noise levels are given in Table 3.12.

Table 3.12: Acceptable Noise levels (dB)

Residential	Bed room	25
	Living room	40
Commercial	Office	35 – 45
	Conference	40 – 45
	Restaurants	40 – 60
Industrial	Workshop	40 – 60
	Laboratory	40 – 50
Educational	Class room	30 – 40
	Library	35 – 45
	Wards	20 – 35

Table 3.13: Noise Produced by Different Objects in dB

Large rocket engine	160 – 180
Jet take off	150
Jet fly	100 – 110
Hydraulic press	130
Construction noise	110
Train whistle	110
Air craft	110 – 120
Heavy truck	90
Office with noisy machines	80
Pneumatic drill	110 – 120

The loudest sound a person can stand without much discomfort is about 80 dB. Sounds beyond 80 dB can be safely regarded as pollutant as it harms the hearing system. The WHO has recommended 45 dB as the safe noise level for a city. For international standards, a noise level upto 65 dB is considered tolerable. The metropolitan cities like Mumbai, Delhi, Kolkata and Chennai usually register more than 90 dB.

Loudness is also expressed in sones. One sone equals the loudness of 40 dB sound pressure at 1000 Hz.

2. Frequency: Frequency is defined as the number of vibrations per second. It is denoted as Hertz (Hz). One Hz is equal to one wave per second. The human ear can hear frequencies from about 20 to 20,000 Hz, but this range is reduced with age and other subjective factors. The range of vibrations below 20 Hz are infra-audible; and those above 20,000 Hz ultra-sonic. Many animals (e.g. dogs) can hear sounds inaudible to the human ear. Sometimes noise is expressed in psycho-acoustic terms – the phone. The phone is a psycho-acoustic index of loudness. It takes into consideration intensity and frequency.

Instruments of Noise Measurement

The main instruments used in the studies on noise are:

1. **The sound level meter:** It measures the intensity of sound in dB.

2. **The octave band frequency analyser:** It measures noise in octave bands. The resulting plot shows the *'Sound Spectrum'* and indicates the characteristics of the noise, whether it is mainly high pitched, low-pitched or of variable pitch.

3. **The audiometer:** This device measures the hearing ability of a person. The zero line at the top in the audiogram represents normal hearing. Noise induced hearing loss shows a characteristic dip in the curve at the 4000 Hz frequency.

3.8.3 Effects of Noise Pollution

The effects of noise exposure are of two types: Auditory and non-auditory.

1. Auditory Effect

These effects impair the hearing ability of the individual and these include auditory fatigue and deafness.

Auditory fatigue: It appears in the 90 dB region and is greatest at 4000 Hz. It may be associated with side effects such as whistling and buzzing in the ears.

Deafness: The most serious pathological effect is deafness or hearing loss. The victim is generally unaware of it in early stages. The hearing loss may be temporary or permanent. Temporary hearing loss results from a specific exposure to noise, disability disappears after a period of time upto 24 hours following the noise exposure. Temporary deafness occurs at 4,000 to 5,000 Hz. Repeated or continuous exposure to noise around 100 dB may result in a permanent hearing loss. This is common problem in the workers who are continuously exposed to the occupational noise. Prolonged exposure to noise is known to lead to a gradual deterioration of the inner ear and to subsequent deafness. These conditions are quite apart from the normal loss of hearing accompanying aging, which is referred to as *presbycusis*. This problem begins at higher frequencies, i.e. the threshold of hearing rises more at high frequencies than at low frequencies. The first indication of loss of hearing is difficult to distinguish the different frequencies of sound. As hearing loss continues, lower frequencies also become more and more difficult to hear.

Hearing loss problems are especially severe in certain industries; iron and steel manufacture, motor vehicle production, metal products, fabrication, printing and publishing, heavy construction, lumbering and wood products, mechanised farming and textile manufacturing. Constant occupational exposure to levels of 90 dB in the range of human hearing are dangerous, whereas levels of 80 dB are not. U.S. Environmental Protection Agency (EPA) has recommended a limit of 85 dB for an 8 hour working day. Compensation to workers for hearing loss have been increasing from year to year.

Due to continuous noise the inner ear damage may vary from minor changes in the hair cell endings to complete destruction of the organs of Corti. When this occurs as a result of occupation in industries, it is called *occupational hearing loss*. Exposure to noise above 160 dB may rupture the tympanic membrane and cause permanent loss of hearing.

2. Non-auditory Effects

There are several non-auditory effects of noise exposure. These are:

(a) Interference with speech: Noise interferes with speech communication. In every day life, the frequencies causing most disturbance to speech communication lies in the 300-500 Hz range. Such frequencies are commonly present in noise produced by road and air traffic. Conversations in the presence of noise requires louder talking. Noise of upto 60 dB does not interfere with speech, higher levels cause unintentional raising of voices, still higher; levels cause intentional raising of voices, levels of 80 to 85 dB make understanding barely possible by shouting and levels of 90 dB and over make understanding impossible.

(b) Work efficiency: Noise also produces inefficiencies in work, especially in tasks requiring a high degree of concentration – for example, classroom study, copy editing, proof reading and other activities requiring concentration. It has been experimentally proved that noise makes it harder to perform simple vigilance tasks, such as watching for the appearance of the successive odd digits presented in sequence on a screen. Reduction in noise has been found to increase work input.

(c) Annoyance: Annoyance is primarily a psychological response. It can interfere with relaxation and sleep of person. In general, annoyance seems to increase with the loudness of sound. Some persons are annoyed by certain noises. Many court cases in U. S. A. have been based on annoyance. Neurotic people are more sensitive to noise than balanced people.

(d) Physiological changes: Noise also produces physiological effects in the human body. A number of temporary physiological changes appear in human body as a direct result of noise exposure. There are:

(1) Vaso-constriction reflex in which the small blood vessels of body constrict and reduce the flow of blood. Vaso-constriction occurs even with short noises and persists for several minutes after cessation of the noise.

(2) A rise in blood pressure.

(3)   A rise in intracranial pressure.

(4)   An increase in heart-beat rate.

(5)   An increase in breathing rate.

(6)   An increase in sweating.

(7)   General symptoms such as giddiness, nausea and fatigue may also occur.

(8)   Noise is also said to cause visual disturbance.

(9)   Noise also causes narrowing of pupils, affecting colour perception and reduce night vision.

(10)   It also increases the incidences of peptic ulcers.

(11)   An increase in cholesterol level.

(12)   Cases of still births in mothers living near airports.

Control of Noise

Though noise cannot of course, be totally eliminated, it can be reduced. Following are the basic principles which can be adopted for the control of noise.

1.   Control of noise at source: This may be achieved by segregating the noisy machine, application of mufflers or other noise reducers to machines. Proper building construction can reduce noises from outside and inside the building. Many older houses are much quieter than newer houses because of their more massive construction, their large rooms, their heavy doors, and the use of heavy sound absorbing furnishings. Modern dwellings seem to be much noiser, as demonstrated by the frequent complaints by apartment residents. The reasons include, greater mechanization, such as noisy domestic appliances, noisy high pressure systems for heating, cooling and plumbing, poor acoustical design.

2.   Control of transmission: This may be achieved by building enclosures and covering the room walls with sound absorbing materials.

3.   Improvement of design: Noise from motor vehicles can be reduced by controlling the noise at the source by improving the design, construction and location of highways. Tire thread pattern is significant in noise production and automobile tire patterns are designed to avoid strongly tonal sounds. Much can be done to reduce engine and exhaust noises.

4.   Reduction of aircraft noise: This problem can be alleviated by operational procedures such as flying over unpopulated or sparsely populated areas wherever possible. Moreover, specific takeoff and landing procedures have been developed to reduce exposure to noise of persons near airport runways. In general, to reduce noise, it is desirable to increase altitude as early as possible after takeoff. Modification of engine and airframe design have also helped.

5.   Protection of exposed persons: Workers who are constantly exposed to noise louder than 85 dB should be protected. Workers must be regularly rotated from noisy areas to comparatively quite posts in factories. Workers should be provided simple dry cotton plugs, or rubber, plastic, or wax protection inserted into the ear. The earmuffs can be used. Periodical audiogram checkups and use of earplugs, earmuffs are also essential as situation demands.

6.   Legislation: Many states have adopted legislation providing for control which are applicable to a wide variety of sources. Workers have the right to claim compensation if they have suffered a loss of ability to understand speed.

7.   Education: No noise abatement programme can succeed without people's participation. Therefore, their education through all available media is needed to highlight the importance of noise as a community hazard.

Table 3.14: Important Health Hazards of Noise

Noise Intensity (dB)	Health Hazards
80	Annoyance
90	Hearing damage
95	Very annoying
110	Stimulation of reception in skin
120	Pain threshold
135	Nausea, vomiting dizziness
140	Pain in ear
150	Burning of skin
160	Rupture of tympanic membrane
180	Major permanent damage

Points to Remember

- Pollution is nothing but undesirable change in physical, chemical or biological characteristics of air, water and soil which are harmful to living organisms.
- Air, water, soil, noise and radioactive are the different types of pollution.
- Particulate matter, different toxic gases, heavy metals, pesticides, solid waste, noise and radioactive waste are the different types of pollutants.
- Biodegradable and non-biodegradable are two main types of pollutants.
- Secondary pollutants are formed in atmosphere by chemical reaction among the primary products.
- Pollen grains, bacteria, fungi are the natural pollutants.
- Solid and liquid aerosols suspended in the atmosphere are called particulate matter.
- Chronic bronchitis, bronchial asthma, emphysema, lung cancer are caused by particulate matter.
- Acid rain is formed by the combination of water vapour with SO_2, NO_2 and CO_2.
- Ozone gas acts as a protective shield for living organisms.
- CO_2 is responsible for green house effect.
- Peroxy acetyl nitrate (PAN) is formed by photochemical smog and it is eye irritant.
- Air pollution has effects on plants and animals.
- There are different methods adopted for control of air pollution such as combustion, absorption, adsorption, wet scrubbers, electrostatic precipitators.

- Acid rain is formed by combination of CO_2, SO_2, NO_2 gases with water vapour.
- Acid rain problem is man-made.
- SO_2 forms sulphuric acid and NO_2 forms nitric acid and CO_2 forms carbonic acid.
- Acid rain affects lakes and streams.
- Acid rain damage forest, vegetation, historical monuments.
- Ozone forms protective shield and filters out harmful ultra violet rays.
- Ozone causes several health problems.
- It is observed that ozone layer is thining.
- CO_2, NO_2, CH_4, CFCs, are responsible for global warming on green house effect.
- There are several effects of global warming.
- The gases which cause greenhouse effect are called greenhouse gases.
- The addition of any substance to water changing physical and chemical characteristics of water in any way which interferes with its use for legitimate purposes.
- Domestic waste water and sewage, effluents, agricultural wastes and physical pollutants are the source of water pollution.
- Several infectious agents are present in polluted water.
- Eutrophication denotes enrichment of water body by organic waste containing nutrients chiefly nitrates and phosphates.
- Industrial effluents pollute water.
- Mercury is highly toxic pollutant of water.
- Lead, cadmium, chromium are metal pollutants.
- Pesticides, fungicides and artificial fertilizers are agricultural pollutants.
- Some pesticides like DDT, Dieldrin, Aldrin are the pollutants which accumulate in the food chain called bioaccumulation.
- Pesticide cause adverse effects on animals.
- Ground water gets polluted by percolation of toxic pollutants.
- Marine pollution occurs due to discharge of sewage, garbage, agricultural discharge, effluent.
- Hot water and radioactive substance which are called physical pollutants are also responsible for water pollution.
- Soil is precious natural resource.
- Soil is classified into different types.
- There are many soil pollutants.
- Pesticides, fertilisers, animal waste, industrial wastes, radionuclides, garbage, acid rain are some of the important soil pollutants.
- Noise is unwanted sound called pollutant.
- There are several sources of noise like automobiles and motor vehicles, aircrafts, industries, domestic noise, construction activities and sonic booms.
- Loudness or intensity and frequency are the properties of sound.
- Sound level meter, octave band frequency analyzer and audiometer are the instruments of noise measurement.
- Noise pollution has auditory and non-auditory effects.
- Various measures can be used for control of noise.

Questions

1. What is meant by environmental pollution? Describe the various types of pollution and explain air pollution in detail.
2. What are pollutants? Explain types of pollutants with examples.
3. What is particulate matter? Describe different types of particulate matter and add a note on their effects.
4. Describe the gaseous pollutants with their ill effects on animals and plants.
5. What is ozone? Describe its role as a protector and destroyer. Add a note on its effects.
6. What is greenhouse effect?
7. What is photochemical smog? Describe its formation and effects.
8. Give an account of effects of air pollution on human health and plants.
9. What is acid rain? What are the effects of acid rain?
10. Give an account of ozone depletion and describe the adverse effects of ozone depletion.
11. What is global warming? Give an account of greenhouse gases responsible for global warming. Add a note on effects of global warming.
12. Define water pollution. Give an account of sources of water pollution.
13. Give an account of heavy metal pollution.
14. What is meant by agricultural wastes? How this waste is responsible for water pollution.
15. Describe ground water pollution.
16. What is soil? Describe the types of soil and give an account of soil pollutants.
17. Give an account of control measures of soil pollution.
18. What is noise pollution? Comment upon the various sources of noise pollution.
19. Give an account of effects of noise pollution.
20. What are the means for the control of noise.
21. Write short notes on:
    (i) Types of pollution
    (ii) Biodegradable and non-biodegradable of pollutants
    (iii) Sources, classification and properties of pollutants
    (iv) Primary and secondary pollutants
    (v) Natural pollutants
    (vi) Particulate matter
    (vii) Effects of particulate matter
    (viii) Sulphur dioxide
    (ix) Effects of SO_2
    (x) Carbon monoxide (CO) and its effects
    (xi) Ozone and its effects
    (xii) CO_2 and green house effects
    (xiii) Photochemical smog
    (xiv) Effects of photochemical smog

(xv)   Effects of air pollution on human

(xvi)   Effects of air pollution on plants

(xvii) Acid rain

(xviii) Effects of acid rain

(xix)   Ozone depletion

(xx)   Green house effect

(xxi)   Green house gases

(xxii) Effects of global warming

(xxiii) Artificial fertilisers

(xxiv) Effects of pesticides

(xxv)   Ground water pollution

(xxvi) Physical pollutants

(xxvii) Hazards of pesticides

(xxviii) Agricultural wastes

(xxix) Lead pollution

(xxx)   Mercury pollution

(xxxi) Cadmium pollution

(xxxii) Chromium pollution

(xxxiii) Industrial wastes

(xxxiv) Eutrophication

(xxxv) Infectious agents

(xxxvi) Biological oxygen demand

(xxxvii) Sources of water pollution

(xxxviii) Sewage pollution

(xxxix) Soil and soil types

(xl)   Soil pollutants

(xli)   Control measures of soil pollution

(xlii) Sources of noise

(xliii) Properties of noise

(xliv) Auditory effects of noise

(xlv)   Non-auditory effects of noise

(xlvi) Control measures of noise.

✳✳✳

Chapter 4...

Environment and Development

Contents ...

4.1 Bioindicators and Environmental Monitoring

Indication means pointing out. Biological indicators can be defined as the use of living organisms or plants or microorganisms as qualitative measures of the environmental status. Biological indication makes use of relatively easy, available and observable reactions of living matter as indicators. The living things that are used in the process of indication of environmental quality are also called bioindicators or biological indicator. Bearers of life such as macromolecules, organelles, cells, tissues, organs, organisms, population, community, ecosystem and biomes can all be used for bioindication.

Classification of Biological Indicators

They are classified into two main categories:

1. **Biological indicators:** They are also called ecological indicators, ecosensors or ecological indicator species.

2. **Biological accumulators:** They are also called chemical monitoring species or collector organisms.

Examples of Bioindications and Biological Indicators

Organisms, chiefly plant species, communities or even systems serve as a measure or index (indicator) of the environment. If plants serve as indicators, they are called plant indicators. Each response of plant is the effect of some factor or factor complex (interacting factors) acting as a cause and is, therefore, the indication of this factor. It is thus evident that every plant is a product of the conditions under which it grows and is, therefore, a measurement of environment. Dominant species in an area are most important indicators, as they receive the full impact of the habitat for over longer periods. Consequently, plant communities are more reliable indicators than individual plants. Plants are indicators of conditions, processes and uses of environment.

Further large plant species serve as better indicators than small species. Usually, steno or narrow species serve much better indicators than eury or broad species. Some of the evident cases where plants, animals and microbes serve as biological indicators of some characteristic types of environmental conditions are as follows:

1. **Indicators of potential productivity of land:** Forests serve as good indicators of productivity of land. For example, vegetative growth of trees such as species of *Quercus* is comparatively poor on low land or sterile sandy soil than the normal soil in which they grow under natural conditions. Plants as *Chrozophora, Heliotropium, polygonus* grow better in low lying lands.

2. **Indicators of agriculture:** Native vegetation of a particular region is the safe criterion of agricultural possibilities. Thus, plants growing under natural conditions provide more correct information on capabilities of land for the crop growth than those obtained through meterological data of soil.

3. **Indicators of climate:** Plant communities characteristic of a particular region provide information on the climate of that area. For instance, evergreen forests indicate high rainfall in winter as well as in summer; sclerphyllous vegetation indicates heavy rainfall in winter and low during summer; grassland indicates heavy rains during summer and low during winter. Xerophytic vegetation indicates a very low or no rainfall in the year.

4. **Indicators of soil type:** Many plant species are helpful in indicating the soil type.
   (i) *Grass Psoralea* indicates a sandy loam type of soil.
   (ii) *Andropogon grass* indicates the iron rich soil in the area.
   (iii) *Shorea, Cassia, Geranium* species indicates proper aeration of soil.
   (iv) *Grasses* indicates high lime content in the soil.
   (v) *Cpparis and Carissa* plants indicates intense soil erosion.
   (vi) *Zizyphus* is an indicator of soil formation.
   (vii) *Accacia glandulefera*: In Africa, it is used as indicator of ground water.

5. **Indicators of minerals:** Some plants grow in metalliferous soils. For example, pines and junipers grow in uranium rich soil.
   (i) *Viola calamines* grows only in soils rich in zinc in Belgium and England.
   (ii) *Stellaria setacea* grows in mercury rich soils in Spain.
   (iii) *Equisetum plebejum* grows in gold rich soil in India.
   (iv) *Silene cobalicola* indicates cobalt rich soil.
   (v) *Waltheria indica* indicates presence of copper, lead and zinc in the soil of India.

6. **Indicators of petroleum deposits:** Some animals as protozoan Fusilinds indicates petroleum deposits in the area.

7. **Indicators of fire:** Some plants such as *Agrostis epilobium, Pinum pyronema* dominate in areas destructed by fires.

8. **Indicators of grazing:** Horses, cattle prefer goats are grazers of non-grassy herbs and sheep are grazers of the pasture land. Annual weeds and short lived perennials as *Amaranthus, Chenopodium and Polygonum* etc. grow better in overgrazed area.

9. **Indicators of water conditions:** Burrowing many flies, indicates proper oxygen regimes in the water. Hydrilla, verticillata and ceratophyllum indicates hard water. *Atriplen sp. and Salsola sp.* indicate saline water.

10. **Indicators of pollution:** Plants as *Utricularia chara and Wolffia* grow in polluted waters. Water hyacyth grow in polluted water by sewage and industrial effluents.

    (i) **Escheria coli:** They are indicators of polluted water by sewage.

    (ii) **Algae:** Water gets colour, odour by algae. *Palmer* had made the list of 10 algae which are pollution indicators. These are *Oscillatoria* (blue green algae), *Euglena, Navicola, Clamydomonas* (Green algae), Chlorella, *Phormidium* (blue algae) etc.

    (iii) **Aquatic animals:** Sucker fish, guppy, mosquito fish, mosquito larva, chironomous larva are found in polluted waters. *Planorbis tubifex*, rat tail fly, sewage fly, rotifers are also pollution indicators.

Emigration and disappearance of certain fishes as *Catla catla, Labeo gonius, L. bata, L. rohita, Notopterus* etc. from the fresh water body indicate industrial pollution in water.

4.2 Land Degradation

Land Management: Land is the most precious resource which supports human population and other living beings on land. India is predominantly an agricultural country and nearly 44 per cent of land in India is used for agricultural purposes. Out of this land, 11-14 per cent is covered with forests and 4 per cent of land is used as pastures and grazing fields. The remaining 8 per cent is used for various other purposes such as housing, agroforestry, establishment of industries, development of roads and reservation, etc.

About 14 per cent of our land is barren i.e. it cannot be used for the cultivation of crops. Nearly $1/3^{rd}$ of the barren land has lost its productivity due to alkalinity or salinity of the soil and water logging. Soil erosion causes great harm to productivity of the soil, because in this process, the top soil which supports plant growth is washed away by water or swept away by wind. Depletion of the nutrient rich top soil affects plant growth and also results in desertification. The soil that is blown away blocks waterways, reducing the water carrying capacity of dams and rivers and adversely affects aquatic life. A large number of our industries also depend on agriculture. A survey of the present status of land in India has shown that most of our crop lands, woodlands and grasslands have already deteriorated owing to faulty agricultural practices. Soil erosion, deforestation, water logging, salination and urban enchroachment have considerably affected our productive lands.

The man to land ratio is very low in India. Due to high population pressure, the per capita available land in our country is only 0.48 hectares. We must learn to survive with this serious limitation. This requires understanding, planning and management of land.

Land Degradation: There are several factors responsible for land degradation. They are as follows:

1. **Soil pollution:** Soil pollution occurs due to dumping and disposal of wastes, application of agro-chemicals. The soil pollutants include pesticides, fertilisers, industrial wastes, salts, heavy metals, excretory products of people and livestock.

2. **Salination of soil:** Increase in the concentration of soluble salts adversely affects the soil productivity and degrades the quality of land. Salts dissolved in irrigation water accumulate on the soil surface. Additionally, salts from the lower layers move up by capillary action during summer season and are deposited as white crusts on the surface. Intensive farming with poor drainage is causing serious salination damage in large areas of India.

3. **Soil erosion:** Soil erosion occurs by water, wind, ocean waves and glaciers. Human activities such as felling of trees, over grazing, over cropping and improper tilling accelerate soil erosion.

4. **Shifting cultivation:** This consists of cutting down trees and setting them on fire and raising crops on the resulting ash. It is also called jhuming in north-eastern India. This is an unhealthy method of cultivation which degrades forest and disturbs soil stability.

5. **Desertification:** It results because of erosion of top soil, shifting of sand-dunes by wind and overgrazing in lands sparsely covered by grass.

Control of Land Degradation and Land Management: Land degradation can be controlled with the help of the following measures:

1. **Prevention and control of soil erosion:** It is attempted through restoring forest and grass cover to check erosion and floods. Construction of drainage system can prevent free, uncontrolled flow of water and control deep soil erosion. Formation of a broad wall of stone along coasts is also effective in controlling erosion by sea waves and currents.

In the mountain and hilly areas, planting of stems and branches of self propagating trees and shrubs, not only strengthens the slope of the terrace but also provides fuel, wood and fodder to the farmers. Alternation of beds of crops with strips of erosion resistant vegetation like grasses, shrubs, trees, maize, sugarcane, cotton, etc. brings about stabilisation of terraced fields on mountainous and hilly areas.

The most effective step in controlling erosion and mass movement, such as landslides in the hills, is the construction of a network of the drainage ditches, which are filled, with fragments of stones or bricks so that water flows out through them. Netting is another method to check the erosion, which holds the soil material together and adds nutrients.

2.   **Change in farming practices:** Shifting cultivation can be replaced by crop rotation, mixed cropping or developing plantation crops which would improve soil fertility and support large population.

3.   **Use of biofertilisers:** No doubt chemical fertilisers like urea, superphosphates, NPK mixtures are important for increasing yield, but their overuse causes the problem of soil pollution. Soil microflora is lost due to these chemicals. Therefore, cow dung, poultry excreta, compost manure and biofertilisers like algae, *Azotobacter* should be used to increase the fertility of soil. Use of pesticides for crop protection should be minimised to avoid soil pollution.

4.   **Rotation of crops:** Due to overuse, soil becomes deficient in the requisite nutrients and loses its fertility. Rotation of crops and vegetables, such as peas and beans, helps to remove the deficiency of nutrients. Plants such as peas add nitrogen to the soil and thus increase its binding property as well as productivity. The roots and off shoots of the crops are left in the field for a certain period of time to protect the soil from erosion.

5.   **Prevention of salinity:** Excessive irrigation causes complete saturation or water logging of the soil which consequently loses its productivity. As a result of over irrigation in some areas, salinity and alkalinity of the soil increases, making it sick. This kind of soil sickness can be controlled by sealing off all points of leakages from canals, reservoirs, tanks and ponds and by use of only required amount of water. Alkalinity and salinity of the soil can also be reduced by application of some chemicals like gypsum (a chalk like substance, from which plaster of paris is made), phosphogypsum (gypsum with phosphates), pyrites (sulphides of copper, iron, etc.) in addition to organic manures and fertilisers. Planting of salt resistant plants such as barley, millets, soya, cotton, spinach, date palm is another way of overcoming the problem of salination of the soil.

6.   **Use of mulching:** Shifting sand can be controlled by mulching (use of artificial protective covering) or covering the area with appropriate plant species and by growing trees as wind breaks.

7.   **Proper use of land:** The encroachment of fertile agricultural lands for non-agricultural purposes like construction of roads and buildings should be reduced to the minimum. Extreme care should be taken in selecting sites for development of industries, construction of dams and water reservoirs, etc. In locating sites for the development of urban centres, the need for housing, water supply, disposal of waste and garbage, etc. should be taken into consideration.

Essential Components of Land Management

1. Drawing up of a land capability map indicating soil productivity and ability to support various human activities in rural and urban areas. This kind of map is prepared with the help of photos and satellite imageries. The map can also give information regarding the properties of rock, soil, underground potentials of water reserves, etc.

2. A detailed study of various aspects of land should be done. A programme of land use can be worked out on the basis of such information.

3. Changes resulting from land use have to be monitored. This can be done by remote sensing.

4. Investigation and estimation of anticipated intensity of natural hazards likely to threaten a particular area or region should be carried out.

5. A comprehensive study of the programme and plan of land management with a view to preserve the land by reducing or checking the intensity of erosion or soil sickness should be undertaken.

Waste Land Development

To meet the needs of the increasing population, the demand on land for agriculture, industry and settlement is increasing. On the other hand, good land is shrinking due to degradation. As explained above, a large part of our country's land is considered as waste land. Waste lands can be broadly classified into two types, (i) culturable waste land, (ii) unculturable waste lands.

Culturable waste lands include ravenous and gullied lands, surface water logged and marsh, saline lands and lands with lateritic soils, shifting cultivation areas, degraded forest lands, strip lands, mining and industrial waste lands. Unculturable waste lands include barren rocky areas, steep slopes, snow-capped mountains and glaciers. Waste lands are those which for one reason or the other do not fulfill their life sustaining potential. Increasing misuse of land resources through short sighted development policies has resulted into waste lands. About half of the land area of the country is lying as waste land of varying intensity of degradation.

Development and reclamation of culturable waste lands can increase the availability of land for productivity. Reclamation of waste land involves high expenditure, expertise and manpower. But waste land that is reclaimable within the financial means and known techniques should be immediately undertaken.

Agencies involved in Waste Land Development: There are different Government and non-government agencies involved in waste land management programmes.

1. **The National Waste lands Development Board (NWDB): NWDB** was set up in 1985 with the main objective of preventing cultivable land from becoming waste land. Besides this, NWDB is also involved in regeneration of degraded forest areas and reclamation of ravines, user land arid tracts, mine spoils, etc.

2. **Eco-task forces:** Similar activities are also being carried out by ECO-TASK forces of ex-servicemen, a joint venture of the Ministry of Environment and Forests, Ministry of Defense and concerned State Governments.

3. **Co-operative agencies:** There are some other co-operative agencies which are collaborating with NWDB in waste land management programme. For instance, the Indian Farmers Fertilizer Co-operative Ltd. (IFFCO) is providing funds for schemes of waste land development in Rajasthan. Under this project, thousands of hectares of waste land have been brought under plantation.

4. **Social-forestry:** To augment fuel wood production in rural areas, social forestry programmes are useful for waste land development.

4.3 Population Explosion

The term 'population explosion' refers to the sudden and drastic increase in the number of people which has been observed in the recent years. The following facts justified the use of the term.

Man appeared in his present form (*Homo sapiens*) not more than 50,000 years ago, somewhere in Africa. For most of the human history, the total human population remained small. Human population was less than 300 millions at the time of Christ, about 2,000 years ago. By 1850 it had reached 1 billion (1,000 millions) and since then it has grown very rapidly and has already exceeded 5 billions, in just about 135 years. Table 4.1 gives an idea of how population has increased. Though it took tens of thousands of years to reach the first billion, human population today is set to increase by 4 billions (from 4 to 8 billions) in just 42 years.

Table 4.1: Growth of World Population

It took from	For world population to reach	Time taken
Beginning of man to Birth of Christ	300 millions	All of human history
0 – 1500 A.D.	300 millions	1500 years
1500 – 1850	1 billions	350 years
1850 – 1925	2 billions	75 years
1925 – 1960	3 billions	35 years
1960 – 1975	4 billions	15 years
1975 – 1985	5 billions	10 years

Fig. 4.1 clearly indicates two things. First, the slow growth of human population till about the 17th century, and second, its rapid 'explosion' since then. This clearly indicates that the population situation today is very different from that in all of human history.

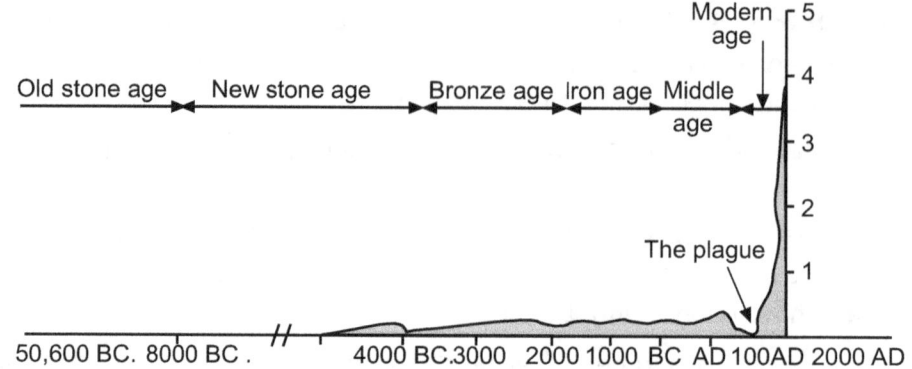

Fig. 4.1: Growth Curve showing World Population

Note the rapid increase in population in the last 2000 years.

Historical Overview

There are different factors for the slow growth of human population for thousands of years and its sudden increase in recent times. These are:

1. Throughout most of human history, the human population remained small, so that births and deaths were roughly equal.

2. Many died due to disease, famine and war.

3. Man had average life expectancy of only 17 years in the stone age. While ancient Romans and Egyptians had life expectancy 30 years. (In contrast, the average life expectancy in many countries of the world today is over 70 years).

4. Many died as a result of large scale epidemics which swept across continents from time to time e.g. In 14th century a quarter of population died in Europe due to bubonic plague.

5. Other killer diseases like cholera, yellow fever, typhus, malaria and small pox also controlled the population.

6. Wars were also responsible for killing large number of people, including civilians i.e. during second world war 100 millions people were killed. The recent Afghan war also killed about a million lives.

7. War created famine and caused diseases.

Despite the above checks on the growth of human population, remarkable changes were being brought about by man himself, particularly in the past few centuries which favoured the growth of human population. From the time when man began to fashion tools, to use energy other than his muscle power, to make machines, to grow crops and protect them, his productivity has increased enormously. Man has been able to increase his food and shelter resources beyond imagination and to subdue all other living organisms of this earth. Due to advances in sanitation and modern medicine, particularly from the

17th century onward the major killer diseases have been practically wiped out – at least in the more developed countries. One has only to think of the role of immunisations and antibiotics like penicillin in saving life. As a result, life expectancy in most countries has risen remarkably, and death rates have dropped sharply. The advances in modern times have more than outweighed the natural checks and are to a great extent responsible for the population explosion, especially in the less developed countries.

Variations among Nations

Population growth rate varies from nation to nation. On one hand some nations show very high growth rates, above 3 per cent (doubling time about 23 years); on the other, some are not growing at all, and a few even have declining populations. It is important to know under what conditions this occurs and how.

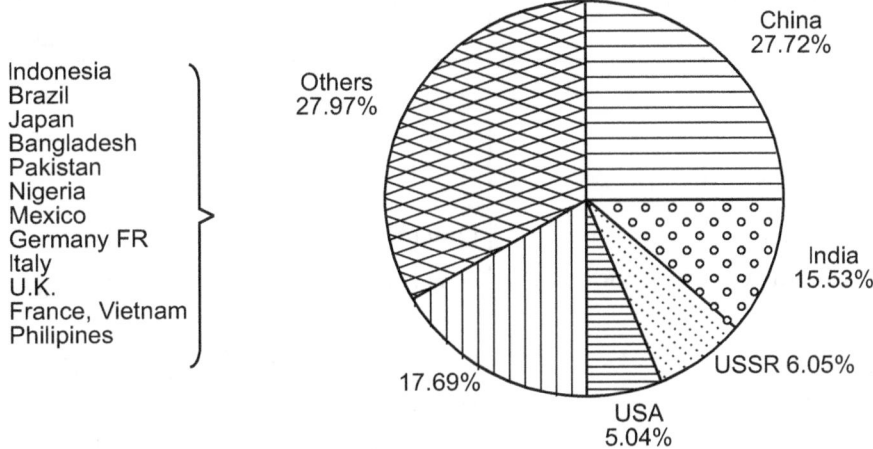

Fig. 4.2: Distribution of World's Population

Fig. 4.2 shows that about 75% of world's population is in the developing countries of Asia, Africa and Latin America, where the growth rate is around 2.5% as compared to 1% in the developing countries.

The population in this century was 1.6 billion, by 1960, it has become 3 billions and by 1987, 5 billions. Currently, the world population is 6 billions. It would reach to 7.8 billions by 2025 and 9 billions by 2050. The world population will increase till equilibrium is achieved, i.e. number of births becomes equal to the number of deaths. Currently 80 millions people are being added every year to the world's population. This indicates that after every 12 or 13 years a billions people will be added. Moreover, the addition in the world's population will be more in developing countries than in developed countries. India's contribution alone amounts to 17 millions every year.

In case of developed nations, they show a long history of very slow growth over thousands of years during which birth and death rates must have been roughly equal. Secondly, in 17th and 18th centuries, their death rates were reduced due to better sanitation and health care. Moreover, it was observed that within a few decades, their birth rates also began to decline, resulting in a decrease in a population growth rate. Such a decrease, first in the death rates, resulting in increased growth rates, then in the birth rates, so that birth and death rates are once again roughly equal, results in very low or zero growth rates. This phenomenon is called demographic transition.

On the other hand up to the 20th century, people in developing countries, did not benefit from better health care and sanitation. Since then, their death rates have declined sharply, but there was no sufficient decrease in birth rates. Therefore, their growth rates have been increased to above 2%, in some case 3% with doubling times of 24-35 years.

Table 4.2: Characteristics of Developed and Developing Countries

Characteristics	Developing Countries	Developed Countries
1. Growth	High (2.1%)	Low (0.6%)
2. Infant mortality	High (50-100)	Low (5-25)
(0-1 years per 1000 live births)		
3. Life expectancy in years	Low (40-50)	High (69-75)
4. Daily food intake in calories per person	Low (1500-2700)	High (3100-3500)
5. Literacy	Low to moderate (25-75%)	High (above 95%)
6. Income in U.S. $	Low to moderate	High
per capita	(200-3000)	High
7. Energy use per capita	Low	High
8. Industrialisation	Low	High
9. Standard of living	Low	High
10. Population	Rural (66%)	(Urban 72%)

From Table 4.2, it is evident that developed countries progressed due to improved nutrition, health, education, higher income and industrialisation which have raised the socio-economic standard of these countries. But in case of developing countries the situation is the opposite because of no population control.

Population Explosion in India

In the Indian context, population explosion is one of the most important problems which India is facing. With 2-4 per cent of land mass, India supports 16% of the world population. India is in the midst of a population explosion. The population is growing at the rate of 17 millions annually which means a staggering 45,000 births per day and 31 births per minute. If this situation continues, by the year 2050 India would have crossed 162 crores, which may be more than any other country of the world.

Table 4.3: Population of Selected Populous Countries (mid-2000)

Country	Population (in millions)
China	1,364
India	1,296
U.S.A.	318
Indonesia	251
Brazil	203
Pakistan	194
Nigeria	177
Bangladesh	158
Russia	144
Japan	127

Source: World population data sheet 2014

The term 'population' refers the whole number of people or inhabitants in a country or region and the meaning of term 'population explosion' is a geometric expansion of numbers of a biological population. As the number of people in a pyramid increases, so do the problems related to the increased population. The main factors affecting the population change are the birth rate, death rate and migration. Over population is not the population density but the number of people in an area relative to its resources and the capacity of the environment to sustain human activities; that is to the area's carrying capacity. Moreover, if the long-term carrying capacity of an area is degraded by its current human occupants, that area is then considered to be over populated. Considering this aspect, now the entire planet and every country is vastly over populated. Africa is over populated because soil and forests are rapidly being depleted. Thus, in future its carrying capacity will be very low. U.S.A. is also over populated because it is also depleting its soil and water resources and also destroying global environment. The advanced countries like Europe, Japan, and the Soviet Union are also over populated as they are releasing large quantities of CO_2 in atmosphere. The rich nations are also rapidly exploiting the natural resources around the world and hence they are also considered to be over populated.

Man is indiscriminately exploiting the natural resources of our planet. More the number of people, more the impact on Earth's life support system. At the same time the impact depends on how the people utilise their natural resources. With this consideration it is obvious that rich or wealthy countries have population problem. People from developed countries consume more natural resources than is necessary and follow the use and throw policy rather than reuse and recycle. As a result the populations of poor countries lack even basic facilities like clean drinking water and electricity whereas there is indiscriminate wastage of these facilities in the developed countries. The world population is ever expanding because of:

(i) The increase in birth rates due to medical improvements and

(ii) Decrease in death rates due to better medical facilities and advancements in the field of medicine.

Table 4.4: Population of India (1901-2011)

Censuses of India, 1901-2011

Census Years	Population	Change in Population Between Censuses	Per cent Change Between Censuses	Annual Growth Rate (per cent)
1901	238,396,327	—	—	—
1911	252,093,390	13,697,063	5.8	0.6
1921	251,321,213	−772,177	−0.03	0
1931	278,977,238	27,656,025	11.0	1.0
1941	318,660,580	39,683,342	14.2	1.3
1951	361,088,090	42,427,510	13.3	1.3
1961	439,234,771	78,146,681	21.6	2.0
1971	548,159,652	108,924,881	24.8	2.2
1981	683,329,097	135,169,445	24.7	2.2
1991	846,421,039	163,091,942	23.9	2.2
2001	1,028,737,436	182,316,397	21.5	2.0
2011	1,210,193,422	181,455,986	17.6	1.6

Source: Registrar General of India, Census 2011, Provisional Population Totals.

There is vital relationship between population and growth and many aspects of development, such as education, health care, urbanisation, social status of women, social awareness, etc. India is a developing country and there exists many misconceptions like the excessive preference for a male child. As a result people continue to have children till the birth of a male child and leads to more children than the family can afford. Because of some social evils like dowry, people consider female child as a burden and thus female infanticide is common in some parts of our country. Even after 69 years of independence the status of women in India is not quite appealing. Low status for females means lower degree of female education, low age of marriage and more children.

Due to dramatic improvements in our capabilities to fight famines, epidemic, etc. average life expectancy has gone up sharply. On the other hand, there has been no decline in the birth rate which is responsible for the population increase. Kerala is the only state which has shown tremendous development of women with literacy. Thus, it is a shining example of success.

The need of the day is to chalk out a concrete plan of action regarding population control; otherwise it is estimated that by 2050, India will most likely overtake China to become the most populous country on the earth with 17.2% population living here. As compared to India, China has registered a much lower annual growth rate of population during 1990-2000. In fact the growth rate of China is now much comparable to that of USA. Therefore, this is the right time to think seriously and undertake measures to control population in India.

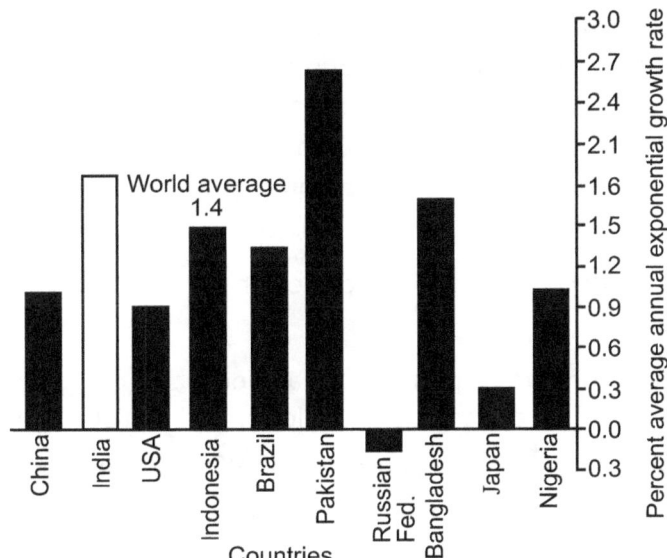

Fig. 4.3: Growth Rate of Population in India and Selected Countries, 1990-2000

Determinants of Population Explosion

The population explosion in India has created several problems such as poverty, unemployment, air and water pollution, shortage of food, health resources and educational resources. There are three main important determinants of population explosion

Birth Rate

The birth of new individuals in the population is also called natality and is usually expressed as the number of births per year per thousand persons in the population. Our country is currently facing 33 births a minute, 2000 an hour, 48000 a day, which reaches up to 12 millions a year. But there is no increase in the resources to feed the ever increasing population. Poverty is the main cause of population increase in India. Per capita income is very poor. About 130 millions people are unemployed. Many families produce more children this means more earning hands. In poor families infant mortality is higher due to lack of food and medical facilities. Hence, they produce more children so that some may survive. Such an attitude eventually results in population increase.

Death Rate

In a population, members die due to various causes such as malnutrition, disease and old age. In India, crude death rate was 12.5/1000 in 1981 and it decreased approximately to 8.7/1000 in 1999. Infant mortality rate in India decreased from 129/1000 in 1981 to approximately 72/1000 in 1999. These numbers indicate improvement in the medical field. The average life expectancy of people in India has increased from 52.9 years in 1975-80 to 62.4 years in 1995-2000. In some religions in India abortions are not allowed. Children are considered to be gift of God so more children are produced in these religions.

Migration

People from neighbouring countries like Bangladesh, Pakistan and Nepal migrate to India, which increases the population of our country. During the 1971 war between India and Pakistan over Bangladesh, the immigration rate increased tremendously. However, currently the migration in India is 0.08 migrants per 1000 population and it is decreasing further. This is good for India because more people may get job opportunities and further education.

Ill Effects of Population Explosion

Following are the ill effects of population explosion

(A) Environmental Pollution

(i)   Increase in factories are responsible for air and water pollution. Toxic gases, fumes, particulate matter are added due to vehicular and industrial emission.

(ii)   Deforestation results because of use of wood for fuel and houses.

(iii) Due to increased pollution, millions of people suffer from air borne diseases like asthma, chronic obstructive pulmonary disease, cardiovascular diseases and lung cancer, etc.

(iv)   Global warming is another problem due to overpopulation.

(v)   Water pollution is another problem due to overpopulation, agriculture, pesticidies, etc.

(B) Poverty

Over population results in shortage of food. According to the World Bank more than half of all children under the age of four are malnourished, 30% new borns are underweight and 60% of women are anaemic. India spends $ 10 billions each year on treating malnutrition.

(C) Unemployment

India is an overpopulated developing country with limited number of jobs available. Unemployment rates are only bound to rise. Several graduates and post-graduates are jobless. This situation leads to corruption and exploitation of the people by a few who own factories. Parents who cannot afford education for their children send them to work (child labour).

(D) Illiteracy

In India, nearly half of the population over 15 years old is illiterate. Basic education has become too expensive for common people. About 32 million primary school age children mostly girls or those from poorest families are not in school, more than half of rural students drop out before completing their primary education and only one third of females make it to the secondary level.

Control Measures

1.   India should follow strict birth control measures like China.

2.   Promote family planning programmes by using vasectomy, tubectomy, IUD (Intra Uterine Devices), conventional contraceptives and oral pills.

3.   In addition, induced abortion is available free of charge in institutions recognised by the Government for this purpose.

4.   Educate women about family planning.

5.   Advertise family planning and provide facilities in rural areas.

6.   Use of electronic media, mass media, audio-visual aids.

7.   Involvement of NGOs in motivation of people in family planning and welfare programmes.

8.   Political parties should consider this problem to be on top of the national agenda.

9.   Government should launch more and more literacy programmes.

4.4 Family Welfare Programmes

Family Welfare (formerly planning) Programme is perhaps the most effective policy to control fertility and stabilise population growth. There are different family planning methods provided by the Family Welfare Programme, namely vasectomy, tubectomy, the Intra Uterine Devices (IUD) like Copper T, abortion, and conventional contraceptives like condoms, diaphragms, jelly cream tubes, foam tablets and oral pills.

Family welfare is not only concerned with limiting the number of children through preventive measures, but it is related with aspects of health care of mother and child and better standard of living.

The effect of programme varies from state to state. After independence, family planning programme was stepped up. To reduce the rate of birth was the main aim of this programme. However, India could not succeed in the control of birth rate. Some communities do not adopt the family planning programme. There are other factors like illiteracy and poverty responsible for failure of family planning.

More emphasis was given on sterilisation method in India. In 1972-73 over 3 millions sterilisations were performed. During the period of emergency, almost 11 millions sterilisations were performed but later on this programme witnessed a virtual collapse. In very few states like Maharashtra, Andhra Pradesh, Gujarat, Kerala, Karnataka and Tamil Nadu, this programme is doing well.

In our country, contraceptive pills have a discouraging history. Only 1.2% of fertile couples currently rely on this method of family planning. It is primarily because of limited awareness of contraceptives methods and the myths and misconceptions about the method. Lack of easy, effective distribution of pills and condoms also contribute to ineffective family planning.

National Population Policy, 2000 (NPP, 2000)

The immediate objective of this policy is to address the unmet needs for contraception, health care infrastructure and health personnel, and to provide integrated service delivery for basic reproductive and child health care. The medium-term objective is to bring the Total Fertility Rate (TFR) to replacement levels by 2010, through vigorous implementation of strategies. The long-term objective is to achieve a stable population by 2045.

Thus, following goals are to be achieved

1. Address the unmet needs for basic reproductive and child health services, supplies and infrastructure.

2. Make school education up to 14 years free and compulsory and reduce dropouts at primary and secondary school level to below 20% for both boys and girls.

3. Reduce infant mortality rate.

4. Reduce maternal mortality ratio.

5. Achieve universal immunisation of children against all vaccine preventable diseases.

6. Promote delayed marriage not earlier than the age of 18 years for girls, and not earlier than 21 years of age in boys.

7. Achieve 80% institutional deliveries and 100% deliveries by trained personnels.

8. Achieve 100% registration of births, deaths, marriage and pregnancy.

9. Control AIDS and other Sexually Transmitted Diseases (STDs).

10. Prevent and control of communicable diseases.

11. Promote vigorously the small family norms to achieve replacement levels to the TFR.

12. Spacing and surgical family planning methods.

13. Mother and child health care.

14. Safe abortion (MTP, MR).

15. Advice and services for infertility.

16. Sterilisation camps in distant rural areas.

17. Distribution of condoms and pills by practitioners of modern and traditional medicine and trained volunteers in villages and industries.

4.5 Urbanisation and Industrialisation

4.5.1 Urbanisation

Urbanisation is the process by which a large number of people become permanently concentrated in small areas, forming cities. Large numbers of people from rural areas migrate to urban areas for jobs. Along with industrial growth there is tremendous increase in the slum areas in and around the industrial cities like Mumbai, Delhi, Kanpur and Kolkata. Human settlements have brought drastic change in the natural environment. The process of urbanisation is very complicated and has allowed many bacterial diseases to flourish in epidemic form. Air and water quality is such that it is harmful for human consumption. Due to acute shortage of housing in metropolitan cities, slum areas are increasing and they have no water, light, drainage, and sanitation facilities. These result into many social evils and ill health. According to a survey of National Building Organisation there are about 25 million people live in slum settlements of which 40% live in metropolitan cities like Mumbai, Bengaluru, Nagpur, Lucknow, Delhi, Kanpur, etc.

Due to lack of basic amenities they develop health hazards not only in slum dwellers but also in other people of the urban areas. The changed environment causes several problems in the people. Stress is a major problem in urban areas. The crowding results in problems such as stress, confusion and physiological problems. For example, it has been observed that mothers living in crowded conditions are unable to maintain proper emotional bonds with their children. This affects normal development of children. Crowding may also bring out violent instincts. Children develop violent behaviour. Even adults become more violent under crowded living conditions.

Changed environment is also responsible for stress. For example, people migrating from rural to urban areas face drastic changes and they find it very difficult to adapt to the new environment. They have to suffer from lots of stress and strain. There is high frequency of mental illness among city dwellers that have migrated from rural areas. They do get any emotional support and do not form any stable relationships. So people feel isolated and lonely leading to psychiatric problems like depression.

Urban Problems

Urbanisation is the process by which a large number of people become permanently concentrated in small areas forming cities. However, the definition of city or urban area changes from time to time and place to place. The UNO has recommended that member countries regard all places with more than 20,000 inhabitants living together as urban.

India has fourth largest urban population in the world next to U.S.A., USSR and China. There are a large number of cities like Mumbai, Kolkata, Delhi, Chennai, Kanpur, Pune which are over populated and people living in these cities are facing the following urban problems

(1) Housing Problems

There is continuous flow of people from rural areas to cities for jobs. Due to this migration, people face the problem of housing. The rents are higher as well as cost of land is also high. Hence, people cannot afford such heavy prices. Because of this situation, many family members live in a small house. This acute situation is seen in larger metropolitan cities like Mumbai, Kolkata. Many people live on the footpath. As per the estimate of UNO in developed countries there is scarcity of 6 crore houses and in developing countries this figure is rises up to 22 crores. Even in Mumbai every year more than 1 lakh houses are required. Therefore, Government of India is launching several schemes for poor people. According to one estimate in Mumbai 72% families are living in a small room of 10×10 sq ft. In Kolkata it is 71% and in Delhi it is 64%. This condition has created many health problems.

(2) Slums

Because of housing problem there is another severe problem of slums. Slums represent one of the worst types of environmental degradation which have become concomitant to urbanisation and industrialisation. About 18.75% of India's urban population lives in slums. Delhi records the highest of 47.50% of slum dwellers. Among the states, Bihar has 37.50% of its urban population as slum dwellers followed by Maharashtra (32.63%) and West Bengal (31.53%). Kerala with 8.81% and Karnataka with 14.43% are the two states with lowest percentage of urban population in slums.

The slum dwellers have with inadequate living space, water supply, sewerage facilities. This causes steady deterioration of surrounding region as well as human health. Slums do not have a healthy atmosphere hence, they become the centres of antisocial elements.

(3) Depletion of Water Resources

With the rapidly increasing urban population and limited resources water requirement is becoming increasingly difficult to meet the requirements of water supply. In Mumbai, as against the estimated 305 litres per capita, only 227.5 litres are being supplied. Delhi is no better with an average water supply of 267 litres per capita per day. Most of the 'A' Class cities are facing the problem of water scarcity. In smaller towns, the condition of water supply is much worse. Due to growth of cities, the demand for water has increased and people have to draw water from long distances. For example, Delhi is drawing water from Ramganga, 180 km away, Indore is drawing water from Narmada, 75 km away and Bangalore is drawing water from Cauvery at a distance of 100 km. There are towns where water is supplied on every alternate or sometimes after every 3-4 days.

(4) Pollution Problem

Industrial development goes almost hand in hand with urbanisation. Metropolitan cities like Mumbai, Kolkata, Chennai, Delhi are alarming examples. Due to heavy industrialisation and urbanisation air, water, and sound pollutions have become serious problems. Discharge of toxic gases like sulphur dioxide (SO_2), oxides of nitrogen (NO_2), hydrogen sulphide and suspended particles, such as fly ash, dust, etc. from industrial and auto vehicles cause the problem of air pollution. The polluted air injures plants, animals and human health.

Water pollution is another problem of urbanisation. About 90% of the drinking water in our country comes from rivers polluted by human activities. The cities pour nearly 286 thousand mm^3 of waste water into the natural water courses. Further Indian cities are either not fully sewered or have inadequate facilities. Thus, sewage either seeps in the soil or pollutes ground water or it flows through streams and rivers. Delhi alone pours over 500 million litres of untreated sewage into Yamuna every day. Ganga receives sewage and industrial wastes from 24 urban settlements affected by polluted water and spread of diseases among the community. Sirens, pneumatic horns of auto vehicles, whistles of locomotives, noise produced by aircrafts are all responsible for noise pollution which affects human health.

In addition to these problems, there is always a gap between rich and poor inhabitants in bigger cities. Poor people live in slums whereas rich people live in areas where all facilities are available.

(5) Larger cities face the following problems:

  (i)   Shortage of electricity.

  (ii) Inadequate or inefficient public transport system.

  (iii) Lack of adequate civic amenities and waste disposal facilities.

  (iv) Heavily burdened public health services.

  (v)   Food adulteration.

  (vi) Stress on educational institutes due to population.

4.5.2 Industrialisation

After industrial revolution, urbanisation and industrialization got push and large number of small scale and large scale industries were set up in our country. Though there was rapid growth of industrialization in developed countries but these was also fast development of industries in developing countries. No doubt industrialization is essential for economic development of the country but heavy industrialization has created several environmental problems due to toxic pollutants and effluents released in the environment. These pollutants are harmful not only to man but also to the plants and animals. Heavily industrialized areas, cities have created environmental problems. Need for energy has increased many folds. To generate electricity the fossil fuel like coal is used in a very large scale in thermal power plants. These plants produce huge quantities of toxic gases like SO_2, NO_2, CO and fly ash. These gases are responsible for air pollution, acid rain and ozone depletion. When these gases mix with water vapour are converted into sulphuric acid, nitric acid and carbonic acid and in the form of acid rain they damage vegetation, forests, building and historical monuments like Taj Mahal.

Every year millions of autovehicles are coming on road and they require huge quantity of fossil fuels like petroleum, diesel. They emit very large quantity of pollutants in the air which pollute air. Thus, these gases and particulate matter are harmful to the environment. Along with the toxic green house gases CO_2 is also released by these industries is responsible for greenhouse effect. Thus, the temperature of earth's surface is increasing. This is the global warming impact of industries. Smog is formed by the combination of fog and smoke and it is common phenomenon over the industrial and urban centres. The smog is poisonous and hazardous to human beings. Carbon monoxide is also dangerous gas which acts 200 times faster than O_2 and thus resulting in suffocation.

Bhopal gas tragedy was the worst incidence occurred in India 2nd and 3rd December, 1984 caused death of more than 5,000 people when methyl isocyanate gas leaked from the container of Union Carbide Factory of USA in Bhopal. Many people suffered from disabilities. New born babies suffered from various diseases and they lost their eye sight. Every year acid rains destroy thousands of hectare forest areas in world.

Industries are not only responsible for air pollution but also for water and soil pollution. Noise pollution is another problem of industries. Many industries do not take the efforts of effluent treatment and directly discharge the toxic effluents in streams, rivers and in sea. These water bodies are polluted due to industries. Our major rivers like Ganga, Yamuna, Kaveri, Periyar, Gomati and Godawari are heavily polluted. Yamuna river is polluted by the effluents of pesticide industries. Food processing industries, fertilizer factories, thermal power stations are harmful to our rivers and oceans. Effluents skill thousands of aquatic animals and plants. The polluted river water does not remain potable for human beings. Sugar factories along with air pollution are responsible for soil pollution.

Many industries require huge quantities of water. In leather industry for one ton leather require 0.7 million litres water. For the production of 1 ton rubber 2 million litres of water required.

Many industries produce noise due to machines, sirens. The intensity of noise is more than 110 decibels. This noise pollution is harmful to the workers and environment. Many workers become deaf. They suffer from various health problems. Therefore, such industries should take the precautionary measures for the welfare of their staff.

1. Many industries destroy natural resources.
2. Thermal pollution is caused due to discharge of hot water in the water bodies.
3. Some industries discharge toxic heavy metals in the soil or in the water.
4. Many times fertile land is used for industry.
5. Forests are also cleared for setup of the big industries. The industry becomes harmful to that forest ecosystem.
6. Due to industrialization there is reduction in agriculture yield. Also damage to the crops, vegetables and fruits.

Thus, industrialization has created several environmental problems all over the world.

Points to Remember

- Living organisms, plants or microorganisms indicate the status of environment.
- Biological indicators and biological accumulators (chemical monitoring species) are bioindicators.
- Dominant species in an area are most important indicators.
- Forests serves as indicators of productivity of land.
- Some plants are indicators of agriculture.
- Some plants are indicators of climate.
- Bioindicators also show soil type and minerals.
- There are also indicators of water condition and pollution.
- Soil or land is precious resources.
- There are different factors responsible for land degradation.
- Control measures are adopted for control of land degradation.
- There are different agencies for waste land development.
- Sudden and drastic increase in the number of people is called population explosion.
- There is variation in population growth rate in different nations.
- The birth of new individuals in population is called natality.
- Pollution, poverty, unemployment, illiteracy are some of the effects of population explosion.
- Several measures can be used to control population explosion.
- Family welfare programmes are important for stabilize population growth.
- Under National Population Policy 2000, the long-term objective is to achieve a stable population by 2045.
- Urbanisation is the process in which large number of people become permanently concentrated in small areas forming cities.
- Urban problems are housing, slums, depletion of water resources and pollution.
- There is shortage of electricity, public transport, waste disposal facilities, public health services and education facilities.
- After industrial revolution industrialization increased very rapidly in India.
- Heavy industrialization enhanced economic development but at the same time created several environmental problems.
- Air, water, soil, noise pollution are the gift of industrialization.

Questions

1. What do you know about bioindicators. Describe bioindicators with suitable examples.

2. What is land degradation? Give an account of factors responsible for land degradation and add note on control measures.

3. What is population explosion? Give an account of determinants of population explosion.

4. Give an account of effects of population explosion.

5. Describe family welfare programme and National Population Policy 2000.

6. What is urbanization? Give an account of urban problems.

7. What is industrialization? Comment on impact of industrialization on environment.

8. Write short notes on:

   (a) Industrialization and pollution

   (b) Urbanization

   (c) Urban problems

   (d) National Population Policy 2000

   (e) Family welfare programme

   (f) Determinants of population explosion

   (g) Population explosion in India

   (h) Land management

   (i) Land degradation factors

   (j) Control of land degradation

   (k) Examples of bioindicators and biological indicators

   (l) Classification of bioindicators.

Chapter 5...

Natural Resources and Conservation

Contents ...

5.1 Natural Resources

The word resource means *a source of supply or support generally held in reserve. Natural resources are the components of the atmosphere, hydrosphere and lithosphere which can be drawn upon for supporting life.* There are both living and non-living resources. The living resources include forests, wild life and organisms living in water or on land. The non-living resources are light energy, atmosphere (air), water, soil and mineral deposits. For humans, *resources are those materials and sources of energy which are needed for their survival and prosperity.* Some of these resources are found in abundance, while others are found in limited quantities and that too in some restricted parts of our land or the ocean.

The natural resources are essential for civilised living, prosperity and welfare, therefore they are being used indiscriminately. This is partly because of the tremendous increase in population and partly because there is insufficient realisation that these resources will be exhausted one day. Industrial and technological progress is also responsible for the over use of these resources. We should, therefore know what our natural resources are, what are their uses and how judiciously we can make use of these resources and conserve them. Careful and planned use will no doubt preserve these natural resources for our future generations. For this, it is necessary that we are able to explore our natural resources and estimate their reserve. Modern technology has made scientific exploration of natural resources possible.

5.2 Renewable and Non-renewable Resources

Natural resources are principally of two kinds, i.e. renewable and non-renewable. *Resources that have the inherent capacity to reappear or replenish themselves by quick recycling, reproduction and replacement within a reasonable time and maintain themselves are called renewable resources.* Water, forests, wild life are renewable resources. The rate at which their renewal occurs varies. *Resources which once used are lost forever and cannot be regenerated are called non-renewable resources.* For example, fossils fuels like coal, petroleum and minerals (Table 5.1) are non-renewable resources. These resources can be classified in different ways depending on the needs.

Table 5.1: Some important minerals and some of their uses

Minerals	Uses
1. Metallic Minerals	
Uranium	Nuclear bombs, electricity, tinting glass.
Thorium	Nuclear bombs, electricity, gas mantles.
Manganese	Alloy steels, disinfectants.
Cobalt	Alloys, catalysts, radiography, therapeutics.
Chromium	Metallurgy, refractory, chemicals.
Nickel	Over 3000 alloys.
Tungsten	Alloys and chemicals.
Copper	Electrical products and alloys.
Lead	Batteries, gasoline, paints, alloys.
Tin	Tin plate, solder, die-casting.
Aluminium	Aircraft, rockets, building materials, electrical wiring, utensils.
Gold	Monetary purposes, jewellery, dentistry.
Radium	Medical and industrial uses, radiography.
2. Non-metallic Minerals	
Asbestos	Insulation, textiles, roofings, glass ceramics, gasoline, solid propellants.
Feldspar	Ceramic flux, artificial teeth.
Fluorospar	Flux, acid, refrigerants, propellants.
Sulphur	Fertilisers, acid, iron and steel industries.

As stated earlier, renewable resources are in principle inexhaustible, because they get regenerated naturally. However, through misuse, we can interfere in this natural process and cause irrepairable damage to these resources. Resources such as underground water, forests and wild life are renewable resources but can become non-renewable if used rapidly and are overexploited. Water is required for various purposes like irrigation, navigation, generation of hydro-electricity, domestic and industrial needs. But, due to misuse or over-use of surface and underground water, we are facing scarcity of water and it has now become non-renewable resource. Forests are our treasures, which provide us with fuel, wood, fodder, fibre, fruit, timber, herbal drugs, cosmetics, etc. A variety of wild life gets shelter and food from the forests. Moreover, they maintain oxygen supply in the air that we breathe. But increased use of wood and other forest products, without putting adequate efforts to regenerate them, will result in their depletion. This has caused environmental imbalance. Thus, forests are now becoming a non-renewable resource.

5.3 Soil Conservation

Land Resource and Management

Land is the most precious resource which supports human population and other living beings on land. India is predominantly an agricultural country and nearly 44 per cent of land in India is used for agricultural purposes. Out of this land, 11-14 per cent is covered with forests and 4 per cent of land is used as pastures and grazing fields. The remaining 8 per cent is used for various other purposes such as housing, agro-forestry, establishment of industries, development of roads and reservation, etc.

About 14 per cent of our land is barren i.e. it cannot be used for the cultivation of crops. Nearly $1/3^{rd}$ of the barren land has lost its productivity due to alkalinity or salinity of the soil and water logging. Soil erosion causes great harm to productivity of the soil, because in this process, the top soil which supports plant growth is washed away by water or swept away by wind. Depletion of the nutrient rich top soil affects plant growth and also results in desertification. The soil that is blown away blocks waterways, reducing the water carrying capacity of dams and rivers and adversely affects aquatic life. A large number of our industries also depend on agriculture. A survey of the present status of land in India has shown that most of our crop lands, wood lands and grass lands have already deteriorated owing to faulty agricultural practices. Soil erosion, deforestation, water logging, salination and urban enchroachment have considerably affected our productive lands.

The man to land ratio is very low in India. Due to high population pressure, the per capita available land in our country is only 0.48 hectares. We must learn to survive with this serious limitation. This requires understanding, planning and management of land.

Land Degradation: There are several factors responsible for land degradation. They are:

1. **Soil pollution:** Soil pollution occurs due to dumping and disposal of wastes, application of agro-chemicals. The soil pollutants include pesticides, fertilisers, industrial wastes, salts, heavy metals, excretory products of people and livestock.

2. **Salination of soil:** Increase in the concentration of soluble salts adversely affects the soil productivity and degrades the quality of land. Salts dissolved in irrigation water accumulate on the soil surface. Additionally, salts from the lower layers move up by capillary action during summer season and are deposited as white crusts on the surface. Intensive farming with poor drainage is causing serious salination damage in large areas of India.

3. **Soil erosion:** Soil erosion occurs by water, wind, ocean waves and glaciers. Human activities such as felling of trees, over grazing, over cropping and improper tilling accelerate soil erosion.

4. **Shifting cultivation:** This consists of cutting down trees and setting them on fire and raising crops on the resulting ash. It is also called jhuming in north-eastern India. This is an unhealthy method of cultivation which degrades forest and disturbs soil stability.

5. **Desertification:** It results because of erosion of top soil, shifting of sand-dunes by wind and overgrazing in lands sparsely covered by grass.

Control of Land Degradation and Land Management: Land degradation can be controlled with the help of the following measures:

1. Prevention and control of soil erosion: It is attempted through restoring forest and grass cover to check erosion and floods. Construction of drainage system can prevent free, uncontrolled flow of water and control deep soil erosion. Formation of a broad wall of stone along coasts is also effective in controlling erosion by sea waves and currents.

In the mountain and hilly areas, planting of stems and branches of self propagating trees and shrubs, not only strengthens the slope of the terrace but also provides fuel, wood and fodder to the farmers. Alternation of beds of crops with strips of erosion resistant vegetation like grasses, shrubs, trees, maize, sugarcane, cotton, etc. brings about stabilisation of terraced fields on mountainous and hilly areas.

The most effective step in controlling erosion and mass movement, such as landslides in the hills, is the construction of a network of the drainage ditches, which are filled, with fragments of stones or bricks so that water flows out through them. Netting is another method to check the erosion, which holds the soil material together and adds nutrients.

2. Change in farming practices: Shifting cultivation can be replaced by crop rotation, mixed cropping or developing plantation crops which would improve soil fertility and support large population.

3. Use of biofertilisers: No doubt chemical fertilisers like urea, superphosphates, NPK mixtures are important for increasing yield, but their overuse causes the problem of soil pollution. Soil microflora is lost due to these chemicals. Therefore, cow dung, poultry excreta, compost manure and biofertilisers like algae, *Azotobacter* should be used to increase the fertility of soil. Use of pesticides for crop protection should be minimised to avoid soil pollution.

4. Rotation of crops: Due to over use, soil becomes deficient in the requisite nutrients and loses its fertility. Rotation of crops and vegetables, such as peas and beans, helps to remove the deficiency of nutrients. Plants such as peas add nitrogen to the soil and thus increase its binding property as well as productivity. The roots and off shoots of the crops are left in the field for a certain period of time to protect the soil from erosion.

5. Prevention of salinity: Excessive irrigation causes complete saturation or water logging of the soil which consequently loses its productivity. As a result of over irrigation in some areas, salinity and alkalinity of the soil increases, making it sick. This kind of soil sickness can be controlled by sealing off all points of leakages from canals, reservoirs, tanks and ponds and by use of only required amount of water. Alkalinity and salinity of the soil can also be reduced by application of some chemicals like gypsum (a chalk like substance, from which plaster of paris is made), phosphogypsum (gypsum with phosphates), pyrites (sulphides of copper, iron, etc.) in addition to organic manures and fertilisers. Planting of salt resistant plants such as barley, millets, soya, cotton, spinach, date palm is another way of overcoming the problem of salination of the soil.

6. Use of mulching: Shifting sand can be controlled by mulching (use of artificial protective covering) or covering the area with appropriate plant species and by growing trees as wind breaks.

7. Proper use of land: The encroachment of fertile agricultural lands for non-agricultural purposes like construction of roads and buildings should be reduced to the minimum. Extreme care should be taken in selecting sites for development of industries, construction of dams and water reservoirs, etc. In locating sites for the development of urban centres, the need for housing, water supply, disposal of waste and garbage, etc. should be taken into consideration.

Essential Components of Land Management

1. Drawing up of a land capability map indicating soil productivity and ability to support various human activities in rural and urban areas. This kind of map is prepared with the help of photos and satellite imageries. The map can also give information regarding the properties of rock, soil, underground potentials of water reserves, etc.

2. A detailed study of various aspects of land should be done. A programme of land use can be worked out on the basis of such information.

3. Changes resulting from land use have to be monitored. This can be done by remote sensing.

4. Investigation and estimation of anticipated intensity of natural hazards likely to threaten a particular area or region should be carried out.

5. A comprehensive study of the programme and plan of land management with a view to preserve the land by reducing or checking the intensity of erosion or soil sickness should be undertaken.

Waste Land Development

To meet the needs of the increasing population, the demand on land for agriculture, industry and settlement is increasing. On the other hand, good land is shrinking due to degradation. As explained above, a large part of our country's land is considered as waste land. Waste lands can be broadly classified into two types, (i) culturable waste land, (ii) unculturable waste lands.

Culturable waste lands include ravenous and gullied lands, surface water logged and marsh, saline lands and lands with lateritic soils, shifting cultivation areas, degraded forest lands, strip lands, mining and industrial waste lands. Unculturable waste lands include barren rocky areas, steep slopes, snow-capped mountains and glaciers. Waste lands are those which for one reason or the other do not fulfill their life sustaining potential. Increasing misuse of land resources through short sighted development policies has resulted into waste lands. About half of the land area of the country is lying as waste land of varying intensity of degradation.

Development and reclamation of culturable waste lands can increase the availability of land for productivity. Reclamation of waste land involves high expenditure, expertise and manpower. But waste land that is reclaimable within the financial means and known techniques should be immediately undertaken.

Agencies involved in Waste Land Development: There are different Government and non-government agencies involved in waste land management programmes.

1. **The National Waste lands Development Board (NWDB): NWDB** was set up in 1985 with the main objective of preventing cultivable land from becoming waste land. Besides this, NWDB is also involved in regeneration of degraded forest areas and reclamation of ravines, user land arid tracts, mine spoils, etc.

2. **Eco-task forces:** Similar activities are also being carried out by ECO-TASK forces of ex-servicemen, a joint venture of the Ministry of Environment and Forests, Ministry of Defense and concerned State Governments.

3. **Co-operative agencies:** There are some other co-operative agencies which are collaborating with NWDB in waste land management programme. For instance, the Indian Farmers Fertiliser Co-operative Ltd. (IFFCO) is providing funds for schemes of waste land development in Rajasthan. Under this project, thousands of hectares of waste land have been brought under plantation.

4. **Social-forestry:** To augment fuel wood production in rural areas, social forestry programmes are useful for waste land development.

5.4 Forest Conservation

Forest is defined as a biotic community mainly comprising of trees, shrubs and animals. These plants grow close to each other, so that a closed canopy is formed. In forests, light does not penetrate to the ground through such canopy. Forests therefore, appear dark even during the day time. Forests vary in their composition of plants and in their density. Type of forest depends on several climatic factors like water supply, humidity, temperature, altitude etc. India in its forest composition represents a miniature world as India has varied climatic factors from Himalayan region to the penninsular end in the South. All kinds of forest compositions occur in India from alpine, temperate to the tropical and subtropical types. The economy of any country depends on the wealth of forests. These forests play different roles.

Roles of Forests: Forests are large biotic communities. They include and support several types of plants, animals and micro-organisms. Forests protect the environment. Forests regulate the level of rainfall necessary for the existence of vegetation. Forests also help in recycling moisture back into the atmosphere. Forests prevent erosion of soil by wind and water. In the forests due to canopy, soil is not exposed to atmosphere directly and hence water is retained in the soil. The soil remains moist even in summer. A forest checks the velocity of raindrops or wind striking the ground and reduces dislodging of the soil particles. The root system of plants in forests firmly binds the soil. In the forests, leaves and branches of trees fall down and form a cover on the ground. This cover supports micro-organisms. These microbes bring about the decomposition of dead bodies of plants and animals and form organic matter called humus. The humus increases the moisture and nutrient retaining capacity of the soil thus improving soil fertility. Such soil covered by humus retains water and does not allow water to flow quickly. This prevents floods. The level of water gradually increases in streams, ponds and lakes. Thus, there is constant supply of water. The humidity is quite high in forests due to transpiration through plants. It keeps temperature low and constant. Under such conditions, other plants grow well in forests. The animals dependent on such plants sustain well and a balance in ecosystem is achieved.

The forests are ecologically important because they reduce atmospheric pollution. The particulate matter settles on trees. The trees absorb carbon dioxide and release oxygen.

The forests are important to man. Man is dependent on forests for his many requirements. Wood is the main product of forests. It is primarily used in construction of houses, bridges, in making doors, railway sleepers, carts, ploughs, sport goods and so on. Wood is a raw material for the manufacture of paper, rayon and film in industries.

Forests supply fuel wood. Man is still dependent on wood for energy requirement. In rural areas, about 80% of forest product is used as fuel.

There is large number of minor products of forests. Bamboos are used for construction of houses, for making baskets, and other articles, as a raw material in paper and rayon.

Another important forest product is the essential oil. Many forest plants like Sandalwood, Khus produce oil which is used in the manufacture of soaps, cosmetics, pharmaceuticals, confectionery, pipe tobacco and perfumes. Many forest plants produce tanning materials, dyes, gums and resins. They also produce camphor, drugs, spices, poisons and insecticides. The leaves of many plants are used as wrappers for bidis e.g. leaves of Tendu. Some products like ritha and shikakai are important commercial products. The other products of forests are lac, honey, wax. Horns, hides and ivory obtained from forests are also economically important.

The forests are very important in the life of tribals. They are completely dependent on forests for their food, medicines and shelter. Forests have a great aesthetic value and can generate revenue through ecotourism

Indian Forests

Forests of India have been classified into different types depending on climatic factors and composition of species.

1. Tropical wet evergreen forests: These forests are the most luxuriant and remain green throughout the year. These are found in regions where there is 250 cm (100") of rainfall and average temperature is 27°C. They extend up to an altitude 1370 m. The common trees are *Dipterocarpus, Hopea, Mesua Aini, Artocarpus, Mangifera, Michelia* etc. They are found in the Western Ghats, Upper Assam, Eastern Himalaya, Andaman and Nicobar islands.

2. Tropical moist deciduous forests: These forests are very common and flourish along the foothills of the Himalayas, Western Ghats, Chhota Nagpur, in parts of Vindhyas and Satpuras, and in the hills of Assam. An annual rainfall here ranges from 1500 to 2500 mm, the weather may be dry for a period of up to 6 months. They are further sub-divided into two distinct types:

(a) Southern type: Growing on hilly ground with an average temperature of 24°C (75°F), the trees attain a height of 30 m (100) or more. Although deciduous i.e. in some season they appear dry, they tend to give an evergreen appearance, as the evergreens are mixed partially in the lower storey. Some of them shed their leaves as early as April, while others like Teak do so with the advent of autumn or cold season. Toon and Shisham come into new leaf in spring and carry full canopy during summers. The common species besides the above are *Bombax ceiba, Cassia fistula, Terminalias, Pterocarpus, Adina cordifolia* and Bamboo.

(b) Northern type: This type is seen on the Indo-Gangetic plain with Sal restricted to higher levels. It prefers an average annual temperature of about 27°C (80°F) and a rainfall ranging from 1000 to 2000 mm. Sal *(Shorea robusta)* grows to the height of about 30 m (100'). It has a brief leafless period of week or so, just at the beginning of the hot season. Shrubs and grasses grow underneath. Other prominent species of the region are *Terminalia* (Hirda, Baheda), *Lagerstroemia, Jamun (Syzygium cumini).*

3. Tropical dry deciduous forests: This extends from foothills of the Himalayas to the Southern tip of Kanyakumari. These are Sal and Teak forests. The rainfall ranges from 750 to 1250 mm. The average height of plants is 18 m. The trees shed their leaves during summer. *Teak, Axlewood (Anogeissus latifolia), Terminalia, and* Bamboo are the common species.

4. Tropical thorn forests: An average temperature is about 27°C and the average rainfall ranges from 250 to 750 mm. The height of trees is up to 9 m (30). The spiny shrubs grow under these trees. These forests occur in South Punjab, Rajputana, Deccan plateau, Hyderabad, Mysore and Tamil Nadu States. The *Babul* and other *Acacias*, fleshy *Euphorbias* and *Capparis* etc. are the common representatives.

5. Sub-tropical pine forests: These forests are found in the Himalayas, central and western portions are in Khasi Hills of Assam. These are found at an altitude of 900 to 1800 m. The average temperature requirement is 16°C. There is no undergrowth. The pine plants (*Pinus*) are the major trees formed in these forests.

6. Moist-temperate forests: These types of forests are found at an altitude of 1500 to 3000 m in the central and western Himalayas. The rainfall is more than 1000 mm. The main species are deodar, blue pine, spruce and silver fir. Oaks grow as undergrowth. Some species of bamboos also grow in this area.

7. Alpine forests: These forests grow at the highest altitude 2900 to 3000 m. The temperature is very low. High level silver fir (*Abies spectabilis*) and blue pine grow in these forests but are stunted and have denser foliage. Birch (*Betula utilis*), a broad leaved tree with clear tall stem grows in this region. In these forests, shrubs like Rhododendrons, Roses, *Lonicera* and *Primula* species are also common.

Area under Forests

Forests cover 7.53 lakh sq. km that which is about 23 per cent of the total geographical area of India. Forest area is unevenly distributed. National Forest Policy Resolution of 1952 proposed that the area be increased to 33.3 per cent. The following figures show where we stand in comparison to other countries

Japan - 63%,	USA - 34%,	Europe - 30%,
World - 33%,	USSR - 51%,	UK - 7%

The forest cover in India is dwindling rapidly. The forest trees are cut down on large scale due to high demand for wood used in construction and for fuel. Forest lands are cleared for agriculture, for building dams, railroads and highways. Rapid urbanisation is one of the major reasons for forests being cleared.

Hazards of Deforestation: Deforestation is the permanent destruction of forests to make land available for other uses.

The forests are cut mainly because there is increasing demand for forest trees as fuel. In rural areas people have to depend on forest trees as wood from these trees is the only source of energy for cooking and other activities. As there is food shortage in India, forests are cut down excessively for agricultural purpose, to make way for rapidly expanding cities. Forests are also cut for industrial establishments. Forest trees are cut for their economic value, e.g. Bamboos are cut for paper industry. According to an estimate, forests in India have dwindled from about 7000 million hectares in 1900 to 2890 million hectares in 1975. By the year 2013 only 72.92 million hectares land is left with forest.

The excessive deforestation has adverse effects on environment, fauna and man.

The forests support the life of many animals. But habitats which protect wildlife, are being converted to human settlements, harbours, dams, mining sites, etc. These activities destroy the habitats of the animals resulting in man-animal conflict and the subsequently many species of wildlife face the threat of extinction. Migratory birds are very much affected whenever their natural habitats as breeding spots are disturbed. People living on the edges of forests kill wild animals like cheetas and lions to protect their livestock.

Deforestation causes reduction in rainfall. Loss of green cover exposes the top soil to the elements of nature resulting in soil erosion. Every year an estimated 6,000 million tonnes of top soil, containing 2.5 million tonnes of nitrogen, 3.8 million tonnes of phosphorus and 2.6 million tonnes of potassium is lost. Deforestation also affects the atmospheric temperature. The trees in forests keep the atmospheric temperature low. The trees form a shade which retains water in soil. The trees give out water vapour in the process of transpiration. The humidity increases and it reduces the temperature. But deforestation causes the increase in temperature.

Afforestation

It is found that for sustaining agriculture and maintaining the quality of environment at least one-third of 33.3% of country's land should be under forests. In India, forest cover is only 23% and it is reducing every year. The Union and State Governments have launched several afforestation programmes as part of forest conservation. The Social Forestry Programme started in 1976. It seeks the use of public and common land to produce firewood, fodder and small timber. This would relieve pressure on existing forests needed for soil and water conservation. The programme includes raising, planting and protecting trees with multiple uses. In afforestation programmes, trees which grow fast are selected e.g. Subabul *(Leucaena leucocephala)*. The trees are selected which can provide fuel wood e.g. *Acacia* species. The trees like Teak, Shisham are cultivated for their wood to be used for making furniture. Many fruit plants like Tamarind, Artocarpus or Jackfruit plant, custard apple etc. are cultivated. *Acacia, Glircidia* is cultivated as fodder plants.

The existing forests are protected and conserved by the Government. There are many restrictions in cutting the forest trees. Tree felling is matched by tree planting programmes. In afforestation programmes modern techniques are used to raise the seedlings of forest trees. In this programme, waste lands are used for afforestation. Afforestation requires action at all level, the individuals, the community and the government. These have been several people's movements in recent times in India, such as the chipko movement (Tehri Garhwal area of Uttar Pradesh) and public agitation for preventing the construction of a hydro-electric project in the Silent Valley region.

5.5 Energy Resources

Man is only a part of the energy flow in nature. With the passage of time, human energy needs are rapidly increasing. Presently, the major energy sources are fuel wood, fossil fuels such as coal, petroleum and natural gas. In several developing countries of Asia and Africa, the energy of drought animals (such as bullocks, camels and buffaloes) constitutes an important energy input. Other direct sources of energy are sunlight, hydroelectric and wind power, tidal energy, and nuclear and geothermal energy.

During the hunter-gatherer stage of civilisation, the total energy required by one man was 2000-4000 kilocalories per day. This was obtained entirely through the food chain, and man used his own muscular energy for work. Later, he discovered fire and used wood as fuel for cooking and keeping himself warm. Agricultural societies used domestic animals for work. The per capita fuel consumption gradually increased. The 19th century industrial societies used fossil fuels, and the daily per capita energy utilisation jumped to 70,000 kcal. Today, we require energy for agriculture, industry, transport, communication, comfort and defense. The energy consumption per capita per day in U.S.A. is about 2,50,000 kcal. But people in other countries use far less energy. It is as low as 10,000 kcal in several developing countries. However, it is increasing fast with rapid industrialisation and increased use of automobiles.

Today, the world's energy resources have reached a critical stage. The reasons are many. First, the world's almost total dependence on the fossil fuels – coal, petroleum and natural gas has caused such depletion that these fuels may last for only another few centuries.

The availability and distribution of energy sources among different countries and among economic groups within a country are grossly unequal. Thirty per cent of the world's population, living in industrialised countries, consumes about 80 per cent of the global energy. Privileged nations and affluent groups use energy lavishly while in the developing countries majority of people cannot even meet their minimum energy needs. Moreover, the developed nations bank on the fossil fuels to meet their energy requirements. On the other hand, the poorer nations rely more on firewood for cooking and heating and animal power for transport. Lack of capacity for proper harnessing of resources in developing countries often adds to their critical energy position. For example, in India about 24 per cent of precious natural gas is wasted owing to inadequate infrastructure and dearth of gas based industries. The weaker sections in many countries find it difficult to collect enough firewood for their daily needs. Deforestation is leading to soil erosion and floods. The compelling need is to use the cow dung as domestic fuel is resulting in the wastage of valuable organic manure.

The recently harnessed source of energy i.e. nuclear energy has its attendant problems. Nuclear power plants release a tremendous amount of waste heat and require cooling. Thermal pollution in local rivers, lakes and estuaries is causing serious ecological concern. Emission of trace amounts of radionuclides is hazardous. The storage of radioactive wastes for hundreds and thousands of years is a stupendous problem.

The present critical energy position demands an organised effort at all levels from individual practices to international action. Considerable amount of energy can be saved by reducing wastage and using energy efficient devices.

Following are some of the important measures:

(1) Reduction in man's dependence on fossil fuels and development of newer alternative sources of energy such as solar energy, wind energy, geothermal energy, biogas, etc.

(2) Preparation of smokeless and efficient chulhas (wood stoves).

(3) Improvement and expansion of sources of solar energy, solar photovoltic panels, cookers, heaters and solar battery driven cars need to be improved technically and made cost-effective.

(4) The use of biogas plants must be encouraged so that agricultural and animal wastes can be used to produce both energy and fertilisers.

(5) Improvement in design, manufacture and maintenance of biogas plants, engines and pumps. Generation of hydroelectric, wind and tidal power has to be explored more extensively.

(6) Programmes for growing fuel wood trees and shrubs under the control and maintenance of local communities have to be implemented in the rural areas of the developing countries.

5.6 Conventional and Non-conventional Energy Sources

5.6.1 Non-conventional Energy Sources

Renewable energy resources or non-conventional energy sources which are quickly renewed and recycled in nature and hence constitute sustainable energy sources. The techniques for their exploitation have been developed comparatively recently. They include solar energy, wind energy, ocean (tidal) energy, geothermal energy and biomass based energy.

1. Solar Energy: It is an inexhaustible non-conventional energy source. It is perennial, non-polluting and cheap and unlimited source of energy. Japan is prime country in utilizing solar energy. Domestic heating and water supply can be met by this. In Israel, such systems of heating homes and water supply are already in operation. In USA, commercial solar heaters are available. India receives abundant sunshine with about 1648-2108 kwh/m^2/year with nearly 250-300 days of useful sunshine in a year. The daily solar energy incidence is between 5 to 7 kwh/m^2 at different parts of the country. This enormous solar energy resource may be converted into other form of energy through thermal or photovoltaic conversion routes. The solar thermal route uses radiation in the form of heat that in turn may be converted to mechanical, electrical or chemical energy.

The solar energy is trapped by various ways:

(i) Direct heating: Plate collectors, solar panels, reflectors, concentrators etc. are used to collect and concentrate solar energy. Solar energy increases the temperature. This technology is being used in solar cookers, solar ovens, solar dryers, solar water heaters, solar distillation etc.

(ii) **Solar Photovoltaic Cells (SPVC):** This technology is used for direct conversion of solar radiation into electricity using solar cells. Each cell has thin wafers of silicon (semi-conductor material) with traces of gallium and cadmium. When light falls over silicon, electrons flow out of the wafer as an electric current which may be used to operate solar batteries or transmitted along transmission lines. The solar cells may be connected both in parallel and in series to form PV module. These modules are combined to form PV array systems generating electricity of required potential. Such systems are used for community lighting, radio and TV sets, light houses, street lighting, domestic lighting, small power plans and operation of railway signals. They are installed in remote village known as Urjagrams, far from power lines. In many States of India portable SPV lanterns are in use. Solar energy is now used all over the world and India for various purposes. However, the technology is still not cheaper.

2.   Wind Energy: Wind energy is also a best source of energy. High speed winds have a great source of energy. It is inexhaustible source of energy available all over the day and night. Wind energy may be converted into mechanical and electrical energies. About 20,000 mW electricity can be generated in India from wind. Wind energy is utilized for power generation, pumping water and other domestic purposes, particularly in rural areas. It is also useful for pumping water for irrigation and drinking water requirements, battery charging to run generators. It is an ideal source of energy for the small farmers cottage, micro and small industries. It is also useful source of energy for those living in isolated, hilly coastal and other regions which are far away from electric transmission network. Wind power is cost effective, ecofriendly, unlimited, non-polluting and freely available.

Wind mill is the instrument for harnessing wind power. It can have vertical or horizontal axis with straight or savonium single to multibladded wheels. Wind mills are used locally in the Netherlands and Denmark for supply of electricity in homes and small flour mills. To generate electricity, the speed of the wind should be from 10-20 km/h, which is available on coast, mountain, certain valleys and plains. The force of wind rotates the wheel, which is connected to a generator or turbine for generation of electricity. There are large number of wind farms have been set up in different states of India such as Gujarat, Maharashtra, Tamil Nadu, Orissa, M.P., Kerala and Karnataka.

Currently, the wind power installed capacity of the country has reached to 1175 MW. World Watch Institute USA ranked India as a wind superpower Muppanda (Tamil Nadu) has the highest concentration (400 MW) of wind farms in Asia and third highest in the world.

There are also some disadvantages of wind generators like they are large in size with unattractive outlook to the landscapes and extremely noisy and disturb residues of the area. Sometimes, their blades may interfere with television reception or with microwave communication used by telephone companies. The installer has to face nature's problems, because wind does not blow all the time, therefore, back up systems are required and the electricity should be stored until it is used.

3.   Ocean (Tidal) Energy: The tides are daily movement of large bodies of water driven by gravitation attractions between the sun, earth and moon. Twice a day, large volumes of water flow in and out of bays and rivers opening on the coast to produce high and low tides. The principle of tidal power generation is the same as that employed in hydroelectric plant.

The tidal movement of water has vast potential of energy. It is estimated by the National Oceanographic Atmospheric Administration (US), the tidal potential at global level is 30,00,000 MW.

Tidal power generation depends on harnessing of rise and fall of sea level due to tidal action. The most important application of tidal power is in electricity generation. In 1966, France constructed first major tidal electric plant. In India, perspective sites for exploitation of tidal energy are Gulfs of Kutch, Cambay and Sunderbans. In Kutch, French assistance has been received. Other suitable sites are Lakshadweep Islands and Andaman and Nicobar Islands. In India tidal power potential of the order of 9,000 mW has been identified of which 800-1000 mW in Gulf of Kutch, 7000-8000 mW in Gulf of Cambay and rest is in Sunderbans.

India could intensify work on Ocean Thermal Energy Conversion (OTEC) and wave energy, that can fulfill the power requirements in remote oceanic islands and coastal towns. India has an excellent OTEC potential and the best sites are Lakshadweep and Andaman and Nicobar. Total OTEC potential around India is nearly 50,000 mW. In case of OTEC, we may utilize the temperature difference existing between warn surface sea water (20-30°C) and cold deep sea water (5-7°C) which is available at a depth of about 800 to 1000 m in tropical waters. The advantage is that the power is continuous, renewable and pollution free. A floating OTEC plant can generate power even at mid-sea and can be used to provide for operations like off-shore mining and processing of manganese nodules.

4.   Wind Wave Energy: Waves move across the surface of the sea in the form of wind waves constitute a source of energy. This energy is used to generate electricity. There are also some plants, which produce electricity from both the rise and fall of individual waves. In 1986, Norway brought the world's first wave power plant of 500 kWe capacity on line. It provides electricity for Norwegian National Grid. The plant consists a reservoir, connected to the sea by a channel that narrows as it approaches the reservoir. As waves approach the top of the channel, they spill over the sides of the channel, keeping the reservoir 3 metres above the seal level. As they return to the ocean, the water passes through a turbine, generating electricity. India has wave power potential of 60,000 MW. About 1.5% of the incoming energy from sun is converted to wind energy. Part of this is transferred to the sea surface resulting in the generation of waves. This then carried to coastal lines where it is dissipated as the waves break. Extract of energy from waves is more efficient than direct collection of power from wind, since wave energy is concentrated through the interaction of the wind and the free ocean surface. India has 6000 km coastal line. There are many other benefits in extraction of wave energy line the calm pool can be used as a harbour, space for aquculture, space for coastal transportation with lighter and faster crafts and share protection against the erosion by sea. Gujarat may become the first state of the country to make use of tidal power.

5.   Geothermal Energy: The earth contains large amounts of geothermal energy with temperature as high as 4400°C. The heat in the interior of earth can be utilized for power generation. This is possible in volcanic regions or where hot springs and geysers occur. This energy comes from magma, molten rock material beneath the surface of the earth. In some regions, this molten material breaks through the earth's crust and produces volcanoes. Geysers and hot springs are natural areas where hot water and steam come to the surface. In such areas geothermal energy is tapped by drilling wells to obtain steam. The major geothermal belts are in Pacific areas. There are 80 countries which have geothermal resources. This source is cheaper than thermal and nuclear power. This source was exploited earlier by USA, Italy, Japan, New Zealand, Iceland etc. These plants are small and serve local needs. It is also used in space heating and power generation, in small cottage industries drying and processing of conventional and cash crops, animal husbandry, dairy, poultry, silviculture, spinning, weaving, painting and garment industry. In India, there are about 300 hot springs widely distributed in Peninsular and extra Peninsular India. Of these, Puga valley (Ladakh) is the only potent, economical and viable source of geothermal energy. Geothermal energy is helpful to uplift the socio-economic status and the life style of the people, particularly those living in far remote areas of the country and where this source of energy is in abundance.

6. Biomass Based Energy: Biomass is nothing but the materials originating from photosynthesis. Thus, biomass includes, all new plant growth, residues and wastes, herbaceous plants, freshwater and marine algae, aquatic plants, agricultural and forest residues (straw husks, bagasse, corn cobs, bark, saw dust, roots, wood shaving, animal dropping), wastes (garbage, night soil, sewage, industrial refuse etc. Biodegradable organic effluents from industries like cannaries sugar mills, sloughter houses, meat packing breweries, distilleries etc. are also included in this category. Hydrocarbon plants also produce biomass, oil etc. Biomass systems are renewable and a sink for CO_2 helps to conserve soil and water and helps also in water run-off and in halting desertification march.

(a) Petroplants: There are number of plant species which are sources of liquid hydrocarbons a substitute for liquid fuels. The hydrocarbons of these plants are converted into liquid. The Indian Institute of Petroleum, Deharadun has done excellent work on this area. The products obtained from their latex processes biocrude were gases, kerosene, naphtha, gas oil, coke etc.

(b) Biogas: It consists mainly of methane gas. It is produced when organic matter decays under unaerobic conditions. The cow dung, faecal matter and other biodegradable wastes are allowed to decay under anaerobic conditions in digesters equipped with device to collect methane thus formed. The residue is reach in plant nutrients which can be used as fertilisers. The biogas is used as a fuel which is pollution free, clean and cheap source of energy.

(c) Dendrothermal energy: Denuded waste land can be used to produce fast growing shrubs and trees with high calorific value. The trees can be used to provide fuel wood, charcoal, fodder and similarly baggase, the pulp and waste discarded after expulsion of juice from sugarcane during the manufacture of sugar can be used to generate energy for local use.

(d) Hydrogen as the future fuel: Like natural gas and oil, hydrogen can also provide energy for domestic purpose, factories and motor vehicles. Hydrogen when burned produces 284 kilo-joules per mole of energy and the products of combustion are water vapours only.

$$H_2 + O \longrightarrow H_2O + 284 \text{ kilo-joules per mole}$$

It is better than methane. Methane produces 55.6 kilo-joules per gm of energy as compared to hydrogen which yields 142 kilo-joules per gm of gas burnt. For hydrogen storage is the problem because of its low density. For pressurised hydrogen large containers are required which are heavy to carry. Research is joining on and future fuel will be hydrogen.

5.6.2 Conventional Energy Sources

These are the energy sources which are once utilized they are not appear again or not renewable. Major sources of energy in this type are coal, mineral oil and natural gas, fire wood and nuclear power.

1.   Coal: About 6000 billion tons of coal lies under the earth. Out of this 200 billion tons had been used. All over the world this fossil fuel is used on large scale. Coal is prime source of industrial energy. In developed countries, there is a trend of shift from coal to oil or gas. In India, many states are good source of coal. But Indian coal is poor in terms of heat capacity. The coal is used to generate electricity, gas and even oil. Therefore, thermal power stations are located on the coal fields to produce electric power to feed regional greeds per capita coal consumption is neary 225 kg. Lignite (brown coal) is low quality coal. More than 600 mW thermal power is produced from coal.

2.   Oil and natural gas: Plant and animal fossils in sedimentary rocks are about 10 to 20 crores years old and they are the source of mineral oil. It is unevenly distributed. USA, Mexico, USSR and West Asian region (like Iraq, Kuwait, Iran, UAE, Qatar etc.) are major oil producing countries in the world. Oil is used on large scale all over the world. It is drawn from its underground deposits but it is in crude form. It has to be refined by fractional distillation. Petrol, kerosene, diesel, lubricating oils, naphtha etc. are produced. We have about 356.2 billion metric tons of oil reserves, more than half of which about 55% occurs in Middle East countries alone. About 40% of the total energy consumed in the entire world is now contributed by oil.

3.   Natural gas: Oil and gas usually occur together. Gas consists mainly of methane (CH_4) the simplest of hydrocarbon and it is accompanied by varying amounts of oxides of carbon, as well as other inflammable gases like ethane and propane. It is used as cooking as (LPG) which is very common domestic fuel.

4.   Thermal power: Thermal power plants use coal, petroleum and natural gas to produce thermal electricity. These energy sources are also called fossil fuels. They are exhaustible and polluting. Electricity whether thermal, nuclear or hydro is the most convenient and versatile form of energy. It has great demand in industry, agriculture, transport and domestic sectors. Thermal power plants use huge amount of coal and they are scattered all over the country. Electricity produced by them is fed into regional grids.

5.   Fire wood (fuel wood): Nearly 70% of firewood demand pertains to the rural areas. For firewood the source is the forests, present day chullahs have very low 2-10% efficiency. This results into waste of wood, forest and environment degradation and health problems.

Department of non-conventional energy sources could design the improved stoves with thermal efficiency about 15-25%. These stoves besides wood can also use coal cakes, cow dung, pallets etc.

6.   Hydropower: It is an economical, renewable and non-polluting source of energy, which includes construction of dams to produce water falls than power turbines. Hydel power has several advantages such as:

(i)   It is clean source of the energy.

(ii) It provides irrigation facilities.

(iii) It provides drinking water to people living in Rajasthan and Gujarat.

For hydropower generation, hilly and highland areas are suitable for this purpose where there is continuous flow of water in large amounts falling from high slopes. The energy can be transmitted to long distance through wires and cables. But this form of the energy cannot be stored for future. Number of dams are constructed in India like Nagarjun, Bhakra Nangal, Hirakud and Koyana for generation of hydro electric power. In many Western countries about 75% of total electricity consumption comes from water.

7.   Nuclear power: The energy generated from radioactive material is called nuclear power. A small quantity of radio active material can produce an enormous amount of energy and therefore this is the main source of energy. One ton of Uranium^{235} would provide as much energy as by three million tons of coal or 12 million barrels of oil. Besides electricity, atomic power is also used as fuel for marine vessels, heat generation for chemical and food processing plants and for space crafts.

Nuclear reactors are required for atomic energy. The decay of fissionable matter produces enormous heat. This is used to make steam and channeled through a turbine connected to an electric generator. Light water reactors and heavy water reactors, liquid metal fast breeder reactors are used for nuclear energy. Nuclear power corporation has established nuclear power plants in Tarapur (M.S.), Rajasthan (Kota), Tamil Nadu (Kalpakkam), Kakrapar (Gujarat), Narora (U.P.), Karwar (Karnataka) are the units generating nuclear power.

Points to Remember

- Renewable resources of energy are quickly renewed.
- Solar energy, ocean (tidal) energy, wind energy, biomass based energy are the renewable sources of energy.
- Coal, oil and natural gas, thermal power, firewood, nuclear power, hydropower are the conventional or non-renewable energy sources.
- Hydrogen gas may be future energy source.
- Natural resources are essential for survival and prosperity.
- Natural resources are of two types like renewable and non-renewable resources.
- They are again classified into metallic and non-metallic.
- Soil is precious natural resource.
- Several factors are responsible for soil degradation.
- Forests are large biotic communities and play an important role for protection of our environment.

- Forests cover 23% area in India.
- There are different types of forests found in India.
- Forests are cut for various purposes.
- In afforestation modern techniques are used.
- Energy sources are of two types: renewable and non-renewable.
- Renewable sources are non-renewable resources which are quickly renewed and recycled in nature and they are sustainable energy sources.
- Solar energy, wind, energy, tidal energy, geothermal energy, biomass based energy, biogas, hydrogen etc. are non-conventional energy sources.
- Coal, oil and natural gas, thermal power, firewood, hydropower, nuclear power are conventional energy sources.

Questions

1. Comment and discuss the alternative energy source.
2. Give an account of recently developed biomass based energy sources.
3. Give an account of chief conventional energy source.
4. What are natural resources? Give an account of soil as a natural resource.
5. What is forest resource? Give an account of role of forests.
6. Describe deforestation and afforestation.
7. What is energy resource? Give an account of renewable and non-renewable energy sources.
8. Write short notes on:
   (i) Wind power
   (ii) Solar energy
   (iii) Tidal energy
   (iv) Biogas
   (v) Petro plants
   (vi) Biomass based energy
   (vii) Geothermal energy
   (viii) Nuclear power
   (ix) Hydropower
   (x) Firewood
   (xi) Thermal power
   (xii) Oil and natural gas
   (xiii) Soil as a natural resource
   (xiv) Forest as a natural resource
   (xv) Indian forests
   (xvi) Deforestation
   (xvii) Afforestation
   (xviii) Energy resource
   (xix) Renewable energy resources
   (xx) Non-renewable energy resources

***

Chapter 6...

Wild Life Management

Contents ...

6.1 Introduction

Wild life management refers to the protection, preservation, perpetuation and judicious control of populations of rare species of plants and animals in their natural habitat. Due to rapid industrialisation, urbanisation and over population, man has disrupted the delicate balance existing in the natural ecosystems of the world. Due to human interference in the nature, several animals and plants have became extinct and there is continuous increase in the number of endangered species of flora and fauna of wild life. Therefore, steps have been taken to protect and manage the wild life of the country. Non-governmental voluntary organisations as well as governmental organisations both at central and state levels have been set up to protect the wild life.

6.2 Aims of Wild Life Management

1. To protect and preserve the rare species of plants and animals from extinction.
2. To preserve the breeding stock.
3. To prevent deforestation.
4. To maintain the balance of nature.
5. Maintenance of viable number of species in protected areas like national park, sanctuary, biosphere reserve etc.
6. Protection through legislation.
7. Imposing restrictions on export of rare plant and animal species and their products.
8. Educating public for environmental protection at all levels of education.

Need for Wild Life Conservation

Following are the important advantages in wild life conservation:

(1) Balance of Nature: Wild life conservation helps in maintaining a balance of nature. Due to destruction of herbivorous animals from forest, the predator animals like lions and tiger attack human beings and domesticated animals. Rat population has increase due to killing of snakes for their skin.

(2) Genetic Resource: The wild flora and fauna are rich resource of genes which can be used in breeding new forms of plants and animals with desired characters like disease resistance, high productivity etc.

(3) Economic Value: Wild life is a wealth of the country and it is good source of income. Wild life yields timber, firewood, medicines, gums and resins, hides, ivory, horns, fur etc. Live and dead animals can be stored in zoos and museums for exhibition.

(4) Recreation: Wild life forms a source of enjoyment and recreation to human beings.

(5) Education: Visits to sanctuaries give education to the students of schools and colleges.

6.3 Causes of the Depletion of Biodiversity or Wild Life

There are several causes of the loss of biodiversity. Threat to biodiversity can be represented by the acronym. HIPPO which was preferred by Edward O. Wilson.

H   -   **Habitat** destruction or loss.

I   -   **Introduced species:** Introduction of exotic species can be detrimental to biodiversity.

P   -   **Population:** Over population of human being initiates and contributes to biodiversity loss, e.g. hunting, poaching.

P   -   **Pollution:** Air, water and sound pollution and pollutants are harmful to biodiversity.

O   -   **Over consumption:** Increased demands and advanced technologies lead to over consumption and over exploitation of natural resources which are the great threats to biodiversity. The evaluation of the conservation status of species and subspecies was initiated by International Union for Conservation of Nature and Natural Resources in 1963. The organisation complies and updates the Red Data Book to provide information about threatened species. Animals and plants have been categorized into the following:

1.   **Extinct:** A taxon is extinct when last individual has also died.

2.   **Endangered:** A taxon is endangered, when number have been reduced to a critical level and are at immediate danger of extinction.

3. **Critically endangered:** A taxon critically endangered, when it is facing an extremely high risk of extinction in the near future.

4. **Vulnerable:** Taxon, which is likely to move into the endangered category in the near future e.g. Golden Lungur.

5. **Rare:** The taxon with small populations in the world.

6. **Threatened:** Taxa which are in one of the categories of endangered, vulnerable or rare.

The main cause of the loss of biodiversity can be attributed to the influence of human begins on the world's ecosystem, infact, human beings have deeply altered the environment and have modified the territory, exploiting the species directly, for example: by fishing and hunting, changing the biogeochemical cycles and transferring species from one area to another of the planet.

1.   Habitat loss: Alteration or transformation of the habitat or the natural areas determines not only the loss of the vegetable species, but also a decrease in the animal species, associated them. One of the greatest threats for survival of the species are the change, loss and fragmentation of their habitat. The natural habitats are being destroyed by man for his settlement, industrial development, the expansion of transportation networks and agriculture and fishing on an industrial scale. Man is also responsible for habitat destruction because of his activities like construction of dams, roads, railway tracks, deforestation, urbanization, excessive use of agrochemicals, spread of epidemics, overgrazing, and forest fires.

Sometimes habitat is broken into smaller fragmented areas. Islands become far apart and animals are not able to meet for the purpose of reproduction. Thus, remaining areas of habitat become isolated. This is also an important region, why species become endangered.

Human settlements: Settlements for the most part have been on flat areas along the coastlines. These areas are no longer available in abundance. This had led to increased and indiscriminate construction of homes on the slopes and ghats and some encroachment on the forest areas by squatters. Most recently, residential settlements are being established on sugar lands. These practices result in deforestation and soil erosion as well as the loss of habitat and wild life.

Sand Mining: The mining of sand for construction purposes is another threat to bio-diversity. The houses are built from blocks and concrete. There is legislation in force that forbids large scale sand removal from beaches and rivers. However, illegal sand removal has led to severe beach or river erosion in some areas and loss of recreational areas in others. Indiscriminate removal of sand from beaches increases the level of exposure of the coastal low lands to flooding from sea surges and hurricanes.

Introduction to Exotic Species and Genetically Modified Organisms

Exotic or invasive species are those whose origin is in other geographic areas and that therefore have not adapted, through the long natural selection processes, the new environment in which they are introduced. It has been calculated that approximately 20% of the cases of extinction of birds and mammals is due to the direct action of animals introduced by man. The reason for this extinction can be attributed to various causes: to competition for limited resources, to predation by the 'new' species, to the diffusion of new diseases and to the damages that the species that have been introduced can cause to the natural vegetation, to the cultivations and to zootechnies. e.g. in Europe the grey squirrel imported from North America, that is replacing the red European squirrels. The exotic species have been transported by human and these are responsible for many recorded species extinction. Water hyacyth, parthenium, some exotic species of fishes are creating problems for native species in our country.

Another problem that causes the loss of biodiversity is to be attributed to the introduction in the environment of Genetically Modified Organisms (GMO) that are also known as transgenic organisms. A GMO is an organism, in whose chromosomes a foreign gene, taken from an organisation of a different species, is inserted with genetic engineering techniques. In this way, it is possible to create a new organism with particular desired characteristics. e.g. some organisms of the vegetable kingdom may become more resistant to herbicides or harmful insects. Some livestock animals become more productive or more resistant to infections. Some people believe that due to this genetic pollution there is impact on environment whereas some believe that the advantages for medicine and society are greater than the possible effects on the environment. Endemic species can be threatened with extinction through the process of genetic pollution, i.e. uncontrolled hybridization, introgression and genetic swamping. These phenomena can be detrimental to rare species that come into contact with more abundant ones.

Over exploitation: Over exploitation occurs when a resource is consumed at an unsustainable rate. This occurs on land in the form of overhunting, excessive logging, poor soil conservation in agriculture and the illegal wild-life trade. When the activities connected with capturing and harvesting (hunting, fishing, farming) a renewable natural resources in a particular area is excessively intense, the resource itself may become exhausted, as for example, is the case of sardines, herrings, cod, tuna and many other species that man captures without leaving enough time for the organisms to reproduce.

Use of wood and charcoal for cooking come under socio economic practices. To some extent wood and charcoal is still used as fuel for cooking.

Hunting: Marine turtles, native birds and deer are the species most threatened by this practice. Turtles have been indiscriminately hunted for their eggs and meat. The deer, where introduced as pets in 19th century, are now listed as a protected species. Man has hunted animals for their products such as skin, meat, tusks, antlers, perfumes, cosmetics, medicine, decorative purpose, dress material and jewellery, pharmaceuticals. In Africa, in recent years 95% of the black rhinoceros populations have been exterminated by poachers for their horns. Today, the rhino horn costs more than 15,000 dollars in the pharmaceutical market. In our country tigers are hunted for bones and skin, musk deer for musk, elephant for ivory, gharial and crocodiles for their skin and jackal for fur. Hunting for sport is also a factor for loss of animal diversity.

Pollution: Pollution is a global problem created by human activities. Air, water and sound pollution alter the natural habitats. Water pollution is especially injurious to the plants and animals species of estuary and coastal ecoystems. Oil spills, sewage, toxic effluents which are discharged in river or sea are harmful to the variety of species. Pesticides, toxic gases, chemicals, acid rain, sound, ozone depletion and global warming affect adversely the chemical and plant species.

Climate change: Global warming or heating of earth's surface affects biodiversity because it endangers all the species that adapted to the cold due latitude (the polar species) or the altitude (mountain species). Many land and aquatic species are very sensitive to climate change. Excessive heat due to global warming is not tolerated by the species which may lead to extinction.

Population Size and Distribution: The growth of population has the potential to adversely affect the environment, since a growing population creates pressure on the existing resources. In our country, the increasing population has created tremendous pressure on our environment and natural resources. Therefore, many species are in danger. Space for homes, land for agriculture, such demands are increasing and ultimately there is deforestation.

Tourism: Tourism like other sectors, uses resources, generates wastes and creates environmental problems. Areas that are particularly appealing to tourists are often places with high biodiversity. There is always threat of tourism to the species of that area as well as to the environment. Elements of the environment that were found to be moist susceptible to tourism impacts included. The coastal and marine resources, terrestrial vegetation and freshwater biodiversity. Tourists dump the refuse in sea which damage coral reefs, destruction of marine life as a result of water sports activities that the tourists enjoy.

Natural Hazards: Natural hazards are generally unavoidable and potentially very destructive. They are: (i) Hurricanes, (ii) Flooding, (iii) Drought, (iv) Bush fires, (v) Volcanic eruptions etc.

Following factors are responsible for the decline and depletion of wild life:

(1) Deforestation.

(2) Hunting.

(3) Poaching.

(4) Conversion of wild life habitats into house sites, into transport routes, agricultural land, industrial sites etc. for our increasing population.

(5) Establishment of hydroelectric projects. e.g. The silent valley in Kerala.

(6) Air and Water pollution.

(7) Poor breeding potential in wild animals.

(8) The breeding of wild animals near human dwellings. For example, marine turtles breed on the sea shore and their eggs are stolen for eating purpose by human beings.

(9) Natural calamities, such as floods, droughts, fires, epidemics etc.

6.4 Endangered Species

Some species of plants and animals have already become extinct and there are many facing danger of extinctions. During the last 2000 years, about 106 species of animals and 139 species of birds have become extinct. Now it is estimated that about 600 species of birds and animals are going to become extinct, if proper protective measures are not taken. These species are called *endangered species*. Most of the endangered species are mammals and birds. Some of them are listed below:

1.	Rhinoceros	-	*Rhinoceros unicornis*
2.	Lion	-	*Panthera leo*
3.	Tiger	-	*Panthera paradus*
4.	Musk deer	-	*Moschus moschiferus*
5.	Spotted deer	-	*Axis axis*
6.	Wild buffalo	-	*Bibalus bibalis*
7.	Indian Gazella	-	*Gazella benetti*
8.	Crocodiles	-	*Crocodilus porosus*
9.	Python	-	*Python molums*
10.	Pangolin	-	*Manis crassicaudata*
11.	Peacock	-	*Pavp cristatus*
12.	Pheasants	-	*Tragopan satyra*
13.	Indian bison	-	*Bos gaurus*
14.	Lion tailed monkey	-	*Macaca silenus*
15.	Giant squirrel	-	*Ratufa indica*

Methods for Conservation

(1) **Knowledge of Wild Life:** For proper wild life management, a thorough knowledge of ecology of wild life is essential.

(2) **Appointment of Officials:** The wild life management programme can be made effective by appointing suitable officials. These officials should have inherent love and keen interest for wild life and they should be trained in this field.

(3) **Protective Laws:** Restrictive laws should be framed at the Government level to prevent exploitation of endangered species. Following acts have been framed for the protection of wild life:

    (i)   Madras Wild Elephant Preservation Act, 1873,

    (ii)   All India Elephant Preservation Act, 1879,

    (iii)   The wild Birds and Animals Protection Act, 1912,

    (iv)   Bengal Rhinoceros Preservation Act, 1954,

    (v)   Indian Board for Wild Life, l952,

    (vi)   Wild life Protection Act, 1972.

(4) Restriction of Hunting: Hunting should be prohibited, when hunting licence is given, clear instruction should be given to hunters not to hunt the endangered species.

(5) Poaching: It is the illegal exploitation of wild species for fur, ivory, skin, feathers etc. The offenders should be severely punished.

(6) Habitat Improvement: Habitats of wild life should be improved by constructing water holes and salt licks and by raising plantations of better and nourishing fodder, grasses and trees.

(7) Restoration of Habitats: Disturbances caused to wild life must be removed. Forest that have been denuded earlier can be restored by reforestation. Polluted rivers can be made clean by treating the effluents.

(8) Clonal Bank: The cells of the rare species of plants are collected, preserved and stored safely. In case, these plants become extinct the preserved cells can be cultured and grown into plants. This is called clonal bank and the technique is useful to preserve the rare species.

(9) Provision for Shelter and Cover: The survival of wild animals can be encouraged by providing natural shelter and cover. This can be achieved by rearing herbs and shrubs.

(10) Artificial Stocking: Certain species can be introduced into a new area by importing them from another area.

(11) Game Farming: The rare or endangered species can be reared in protected areas and then they can be released in their natural habitat. For example, the marine turtles lay their eggs on the sea shore. The eggs can be collected and hatched in the laboratories and the young ones are released into the sea.

(12) Epidemic Control: Veterinary experts should be appointed to take care of wild life.

(13) Census: Effective census operations should be adopted to measure the population sizes of various wild animals.

(14) Educating the Public: Common men should be properly educated about the advantages and disadvantages of wild life.

(15) Establishment of Sanctuaries and National Parks: Wild animals can be well protected by establishing sanctuaries and national parks provide protection and optimum living conditions to wild animals.

6.5 National Parks and Sanctuaries

In India, there are 67 national parks and 394 sanctuaries with a total area of about 1,41,298, sq. km representing roughly 4% of the country's geographic area. In year 1981, there were only 19 national parks and 202 sanctuaries in our country. National parks are set up for preserving the flora, landscapes of an area. Sanctuaries are forest areas where the killing and capturing of any animals is prohibited except under orders of the authorities concerned.

Following are the important National Parks and Sanctuaries of India:

State		National Parks/Sanctuaries
Andhra Pradesh	-	Neelapattu, Pakhal, Rawal, Pocharam
Arunachal Pradesh	-	Namidapha
Assam	-	Kaziranga, Manas
Bihar	-	Betla, Hazaribarh
Goa	-	Mollen
Gujarat	-	Gir, Nal Sarovar
Haryana	-	Sultanpur Lake
Himachal Pradesh	-	Govind Sagar
Jammu and Kashmir	-	Dachigam
Karnataka	-	Bandipur, Nagarhole
Kerala	-	Periyar, Waynrd, Neyyar,
Madhya Pradesh	-	Kanha, Shivpuri
Maharashtra	-	Pench, Taboba, Navegaon, Karnala
Manipur	-	Keibul Lamjao,
Meghalaya	-	Balpakram,
Mizoram	-	Dampa
Nagaland	-	Intangki
Orissa	-	Simlipal, Salkasia, Chilka lake
Punjab	-	Abohar
Rajasthan	-	Ghana, Sariska, Ranthambore
Sikkim	-	Kanchengunga
Tamil Nadu	-	Annamalai, Mundumalai
Uttar Pradesh	-	Corbett, Dudwa
West Bengal	-	Mahanandi, Sunderban, Jaldapara

Government of India has also undertaken special projects for endangered species like Bengal Tiger, Gir Lion, Rhinoceros, Crocodile and Snow Leopard.

(1) Project Tiger: About 40 thousand Royal Bengal tigers were there in l909-1910. Because of hunting, poaching, the tiger population declined and only 2500 tigers remained in the year 1982. To protect this animal, Task Force of the IBWL recommended the project Tiger Reserves in different kinds of habitats in nine states. Later on few more Reserves were added and now the number is 17, covering an area of 26,643 sq.km. Sundarban (W. Bengal), Melghat (Maharashtra), Manas (Assam), Bandipur (Karnataka), Corbett, Dudwa (UP), Periyar (Kerla) are some of the important Tiger Reserves of India. This project has helped in increase of number of tiger.

(2) Gir Lion Project: The Gir Lion is found only in Gir forest of Gujarat. Destruction of forest for agriculture, excessive cattle grazing and other factors led to decline in the lion population. The total area of Gir sanctuary is now 1412.12 sq. km and it was declared as National Park in 1978. Because of this project, the population of Gir Lion has been considerably increased. In the year 1968, there was 177 lions in the Gir. This number increased to 180 in 1974.

(3) Crocodile Breeding Project: This project was initiated in 1975 for increasing the crocodile population by the consultation of FAO expert Dr. H. R. Busard. There are three species of crocodiles in India. Salt water crocodile, freshwater crocodile (mugger) and gharial. This project started first in Orissa, where Gharial eggs were hatched for the first time in captivity anywhere in the world. Kukrail is another Crocodile park near Lucknow, where also a small batch of Gharial also hatched. Now there are eleven crocodile sanctuaries declared under this project. Krishna sanctuary (A.P.) and Chambal sanctuary are the largest sancturies in the country.

(4) Rhinoceros Conservation: This project is undertaken to conserve the Indian rhinoceros in Assam, since 1987.

(5) Snow-leopard Project: This project is being taken to create 12 snow leopard Reserves throughout the Himalayas.

6.6 Conservation of Wild Life

When man was in the hunter gatherer stage of civilisation, he was entirely dependent on biodiversity for his survival. But now in the age of science and technology, he is mostly dependent on agriculture and industrialisation. Therefore, the emphasis on biodiversity has decreased. No doubt, biodiversity is the very basis of life, either in wild or domesticated forms; biodiversity is the source of food, medicine, clothing and housing. Moreover, it is also the source of much of the cultural diversity and most of the intellectual and spiritual inspiration. But unfortunately this precious biodiversity of the earth is at serious risk of extinction over the next 2-3 decades. Now, man has realised the importance of biodiversity, because loss of biodiversity may threaten his very existence. Therefore, man has started to initiate steps to conserve biodiversity.

Organisations like World Resources Institute (WRI) and International Union for Conservation of Nature and Natural Resources (IUCN) have been developing plans for biodiversity conservation with support from the World Bank and other organisations. The conservation plan is based on holistic approach and covers the whole spectrum of biota ranging from ecosystems at the macro level (*in-situ* conservation) to DNA libraries at the molecular level (*ex-situ* conservation).

For the conservation of biodiversity, the immediate action will be to devise and enforce time bound programme for saving the fauna and flora as well as habitats of biological resource.

Action plan for conservation should include the following aspects:

1. To make a list of biological resources in different parts of the country including the island ecosystem.

2. Biodiversity conservation can be undertaken through a network of protected areas including National Parks, Sanctuaries, Biosphere Reserves, Marine Reserves, Gene Banks, Wetlands, Coral reefs, etc.

3. Rehabilitation of tribals displaced due to creation of protected areas.

4. Control of over exploitation through various organisations.

5. Protection of domesticated plant and animal species to conserve indigenous genetic diversity.

6. There should be protection and sustainable use of genetic resources or germplasm through appropriate laws and practices.

7. There should be corridors between different nature reserves for the purpose of migration.

8. There should be emphasis on traditional skills and knowledge of conservation.

9. Avoid monoculture plantation.

10. Avoid introduction of exotic species without enough investigations.

Conservation Methods

There are two basic approaches for conservation of biodiversity namely ***in-situ*** and ***ex-situ*** conservation.

1. *In-situ* Conservation

This method is applied for conservation of ecosystems and natural habitats, and domesticated or cultivated species like crop plants, forest and pasture species. This approach refers to protection zones and areas of high biological diversity. These areas are nothing but natural ecosystems which protect species with minimum human interference. For the protection of endangered species of plants and animals there should be strict protection against poaching. This is essential for threatened organisms which occur in biotic communities in open sites. For *in-situ* conservation, the biosphere reserves offer the best site of natural conservation of threatened flora. There are 75 national parks and 421 wild life sancturies which cover an area about 1.4 lakh km^2. The protected area includes 23 tiger reserves as well as 14 biosphere reserves. Our country is doing its best for *in-situ* conservation. There is significant increase in the population of some important species like the great Indian bustard, tiger, elephant, hangul, crocodile, etc. It is the result of proper measures adopted for conservation of biodiversity.

The Wild Life Institute of India has also emphasised the need to identify the new protected areas in different parts of the country to ensure the representation of maximum wild life habitats. The institute has suggested increasing national parks up to 147 and wild life sanctuaries up to 519, so that total land area covered will be 5.06%.

Considerable efforts should be made towards conservation of plants which are of potential, economic and scientific value. Measures should be undertaken for rehabilitative strategies for rare, threatened and endangered plant and animal species. In order to derive maximum benefit from *in-situ* conservation, incentives to grow domesticated economically important biota and develop herbal drug industry by providing waste lands of the country. For *in-situ* conservation, there is need of comprehensive National Biological Inventory and it should focus on the following important aspects:

1. Setup applied research laboratories for conservation of living resources.
2. Establish inter relations between plant and animal species.
3. Quantitative assessment of conservation status of the species.
4. Use of biotechnology for multiplication and restoration of endangered, rare and endemic species.
5. Ecological restoration of degraded micro and macro habitats.
6. Assessment of the impact of exotic species on ecosystem.
7. Determination of impact on ecosystem of various activities in protected areas.
8. Impact of climate change on biodiversity.
9. Hydrological changes and their impact on protected areas.
10. Primary production and cycling of nutrients in the soil.

Thus, the important aspect in *in-situ* conservation is that the forest trees, wild plants, wild animals and micro-organisms all occur together in an ecosystem. Therefore, if more emphasis is given to conserve and enrich the ecosystem we can achieve this goal in a single step. At the same time local communities should be involved in the management of biological resources and to benefit from their sustenance. This can be achieved by integrating rural development with ecosystem conservation.

2. *Ex-situ* Conservation

This type of conservation includes the use of botanical garden and arboreta on one hand and gene bank on the other. It is the oldest form of conservation which was reported from Europe in the 15th and 16th centuries. Our country has contributed commendably well in *ex-situ* conservation of crop genetic resources. Thus, *ex-situ* conservation is nothing but the conservation of components of biological diversity outside their natural habitats. In India, *ex-situ* conservation work is being undertaken on livestock, poultry and fish genetic resources. However, there is a need to develop facilities for long term conservation. This can be achieved by:

   (i) Establishing Genetic Enhancement Centres for the production of good quality of seeds.

   (ii) Enhancement in the existing zoos and botanical garden network.

   (iii) Seed-gene banks.

   (iv) Tissue culture gene banks.

   (v) Pollen and spores banks.

   (vi) Captive breeding in zoological gardens and

   (vii) *In-vivo* and *in-vitro* preservation.

However, both ex-situ and in-situ conservation of forest trees and micro-organisms have not received much attention. For both conservation types equal importance should be given. Release of genetically modified organisms should be regulated at national and international level and adequate information about such release should be given by respective countries.

Points to Remember

- Wild life management is nothing but the protection, preservation, perpetuation and judicious control of population of rare species of plants and animals.
- Balance of nature, genetic resource, economic value, recreation, education are necessary for wild life conservation.
- There are several causes for wild life depletion.
- There are endangered, rare, critically endangered, threatened and vulnerable animal species.
- Habitat loss, over exploitation, hunting, pollution, climate change, tourism are the factors responsible for depletion of wild life.
- There are different methods of conservation.
- National parks and sanctuaries are important for wild life conservation.
- There are also two methods for conservation of wild life namely *in-situ* and *ex-situ* conservation.

Questions

1. Define wild life management. Comment upon need for wild life conservation.
2. Give an account of factors responsible for depletion of wild life.
3. Describe different methods of conservation of wild life.
4. Write short notes on:
   (a) Need for wild life conservation
   (b) Causes of wild life depletion
   (c) Methods for conservation
   (d) National parks and sanctuaries
   (e) *In-situ* conservation
   (f) *Ex-situ* conservation.

 ✷✷✷

Chapter 7...

Toxicants and Toxicity

Contents ...

7.1 Definition of Toxicology, Scope and Branches

The word toxicology is derived from 'Toxicon' which was used as poison on arrow heads. Toxicology (from the ancient Greek words *toxikos* 'Poisonous' and logos) is a branch of biology, chemistry and medicine (more specifically pharmacology) concerned with the study of the adverse effects of chemicals on living organism. It also studies the harmful effects of chemical, biological and physical agents in biological systems that establishes the extent of damage in living organisms.

In brief, the toxicology is defined as the branch of Science which deals with the study of poisons in reference to their sources, characters, properties, mechanism of action, signs and symptoms, lethal dose, causes of death, treatment, detection, estimation and postmortem findings. Mathew Joseph Orfila is father of toxicology.

Relationship between dose and its effects on the exposed organism is of high significance in toxicology. Factors that influence chemical toxicity include the dosage (whether it is acute or chronic); the route of exposure, the species, age, sex and environment.

Basic Toxicology: The goal of toxicity assessment is to identify adverse effects of a substance. Adverse effects depend on two main factors. (i) route of exposure (oral, inhalation or dermal) and (ii) dose (duration and concentration of exposure). To explore dose, substances are tested in both acute and chronic models.

Factors that Influence Chemical Toxicity

(1) **Dosage:** Both large single exposures (acute) and continuous small exposures (chronic) are studied.

(2) **Route of exposure:** Ingestion, inhalation or skin absorption.

(3) **Other factors:** Species, Age, Sex, Health, Environment and individual characteristics.

(7.1)

Testing Methods

Toxicity experiments may be conducted *in-vivo* (using the whole animal) or in *in-vitro* (Testing on isolated cells or tissues) or *in-silico* (in a computer simulation).

Animal Testing Methods: The classic experimental tool of toxicology is animal testing.

While testing in animal models remains the best method of estimating human effects, there are both ethical and technical concerns with animal testing. Since, the late 1950s, the field of toxicology has sought to reduce or eliminate animal testing under the rubric of 'Three Rs.' (i) reduce the number of experiments with animals to the minimum necessary, (ii) refine experiments to cause less suffering and (iii) replace *in-vivo* experiment with other types, or use more simple forms of life when possible. Now there is ban on animal use in toxicology experiments. European Union prohibited use of animal testing for cosmetics in 2013. Computer modeling in an example of alternative testing methods.

Branches of Toxicology

(1) **Forensic Toxicology:** It deals with medical and legal aspects of the harmful effects of poisons on the human body, including causes and circumstances of death.

(2) **Clinical Toxicology:** It deals with mechanism of action, manifestations, diagnosis and method of treatment of a poison.

(3) **Pharmacological Toxicology:** It is assessing toxicity of therapeutic agents while toxicity in occupational environment and its prevention is occupational toxicology.

(4) **Toxinology:** It is the study of toxins produced by living organisms plants or animals which are harmful to man.

(5) **Computational Toxicology:** It is a discipline that develops mathematical and computer based models to better understand and predict adverse health effects caused by chemicals such as environmental pollutants and pharmaceuticals. Within the Toxicology in 21st century project, the best predictive models were identified to be Deep Neural Networks, Random Forests and Support vector Machines which can reach the performance of *in-vitro* experiments.

Toxicology as a Profession: A toxicologist is a scientist or medical personnel who specializes in the study of symptoms, mechanisms, treatments and detection venoms and toxins, especially the poisoning of people. To work as a toxicologist one should obtain a degree in toxicology or related degree like biology, chemistry or biochemistry. Toxicologists perform many different duties including research in the academic, non-profit and industrial fields, products safety evaluation, consulting, public service and legal regulation. In order to research and assess the effects of chemicals, toxicologists perform carefully designed studies and experiments. These experiments help to identify the specific amount of a chemical that may cause harm and potential risks of being near or using products that contain certain chemicals.

Research projects may range from assessing the effects of toxic pollutants on the environment to evaluating how the human immune system responds to chemical compounds within pharmaceutical drugs. While the basic duties of toxicologists are to determine the effects of chemicals on organisms and their surroundings. Specific job duties many vary based on industry and employment. For example, forensic toxicologists may look for toxic substances in a crime scene, whereas aquatic toxicologists may analyse the toxicity level of waste water.

7.2 Types of Toxicants

A toxicant is any toxic substance. In popular usage the term is often used to denote substances made by humans or introduced into the environment by human activity; in contrast to toxins, which are toxicants produced naturally by a living organism. Toxicants are poisonous. They come in all shapes and sizes and they create their effects on human and environmental health.

Types: There are wide variety of toxicants in the environment. They can be classified based on the types of problems they cause.

(1) **Carcinogens:** These are probably the best known toxicants because they are cancer causing chemicals. There are large number of chemicals which are used as biocides. Variety of pesticides are used to control the pest in agriculture. Organo-phosphate pesticides like Malathion, Sumithion are highly toxic. Organo-chlorine pesticides like DDT, BHC, Endrin etc. are highly toxic and they remain in the environment for long period. Carbamate pesticides like carbaryl are also toxic. These chemicals are Neurotoxins which attack the nervous system. There are also chemicals like herbicides, insecticides, fertilisers, fungicides, rodenticides, molluscicides.

(2) **Mutagens:** These are mutation causing chemicals. When organisms are exposed to a mutagen, it literally mutates their DNA, leading to cancer and other disorders.

(3) **Teratogens:** These are chemicals that cause harm to unborn babies. These chemicals cause birth defects during development in the womb. Many pesticides are known teratogens. For example, organo-phosphate insecticides are potent teratogens in the fishes. They cause variety of birth defects in the hatching embryos. Thalidomide was used in 1950s as a sleeping pill and to prevent nausea during pregnancy, but turned out to be a very harmful teratogen. Even a single dose is powerful enough to cause severe birth defects in children.

(4) **Allergens:** These are chemicals that stimulate overactivity in immune system. When you are exposed to allergens, your body goes into overdrive, triggering an immune response to try and get rid of the allergens. This is why pollen and dust cause symptoms, that are similar to being sick.

(5) **Neurotoxins:** These are chemicals that attack the nervous system. These include heavy metals, like lead and mercury, copper, zinc as well as pesticides and chemical

weapons. Neurotoxins can lead to symptoms like slurred speech, loss of muscle control and even death.

(6) Endocrine disrupters: These are the chemicals that disrupt the endocrine system in organisms and most often come from prescription drugs and chemicals in plastics. The endocrine system is also known as the hormone system, and this part of your body is what regulates growth, development, sexual maturity, brain function and even appetite. These chemicals lead to some serious problems because they so closely resemble real hormones in your body. Reptiles and amphibian are sensitive to endocrine disrupters and they lead to feminization of male animals.

Sources of Toxicants

We are surrounded by synthetic chemicals and encounter them countless times on a daily basis. Plastics, household cleaners, solvents, detergents, cosmetics and perfumes are all toxicant. Antibiotics, drugs, steroids, food additives, preservatives and other things which we ingest are also toxicants. Pesticides, herbicides, fungicides, biocide micro-organisms, fertilisers are also toxicants. Toxicants are circulated in the environment. They may find their way into aquatic systems as they get carried away by runoff from large areas of land. They get concentrated in the water. They leak in drinking water, ground water. Many are water soluble.

7.3 Factors Influencing Toxicity

Following factors of the environment affects toxicity: pH, Temperature, Reproductive Status, Age, Physiological State.

There are many abiotic and biotic factors of the environment that may modify the toxicity of the chemicals. The environmental factors affecting the toxicity of chemicals have been studied extensively for the aquatic medium and aquatic toxicology is now considered an important branch of science.

The environment factor of aquatic medium like pH and temperature affect toxicity of the chemicals.

1.   pH: The pH of water may have greater effects on the toxicity of chemicals that can ionise under the influence of pH. Generally, an undissociated form of a chemical is more toxic to organisms because it can penetrate the cell membrane. The unionized form of ammonia (NH_3) is highly toxic to fish and quite low concentration, 0.2 mg/l to 0.7 mg/l adversely affect Salmonids. However, the ionized form of ammonia, ammonium ion (NH_4^+) is little or no toxic. An increase of pH by one unit within the usual middle ranges increases the proportion of NH_3 by about six folds hence six folds increase the toxicity of the chemical. The pH has profound effect on metal toxicity, as metal ionize under the influence of pH. The salinity and hardness of water also toxicity.

2.   Temperature: Of all the environmental factors of the aquatic medium, the water temperature greatly affects the toxicity of xerobiotic chemicals. An increase in water temperature increases the solubility of many substances, alters the chemical structure of some toxicant and also lowers the dissolved oxygen contents of water. However, some pesticides have been reported to be more toxic at higher temperatures while some others show stronger lethal action at low temperatures. It was observed that DDT was three times more toxic at 10°C than at 27°C. Omkar (1983) in has toxicity studies of pesticides, using freshwater prawns as test organisms, observed that increase in water temperature increases the toxicity of pesticides.

Toxicity of a chemical is generally evaluated against a particular organism or a group of organism. It is experimentally proved that the toxicity of a chemical varies according to the size, life history stage, age, sex and health and nutritional status of the organism.

Juveniles of a particular species are more sensitive to a particular chemical than the adult individuals. In care of fishes fingerlings are more sensitive than the adult fishes.

7.4 Dose, LD_{50} and LC_{50}

Dose or Concentration: A toxic substance products its toxic effects after its interaction with appropriate receptors of the organism. The effect is directly dependent on the concentration of the chemical at the target site and concentration at the target site is related to the amount (dose) of the chemical administered.

Paracelsus stated 'No substance is a poision by itself. It is the dose i.e. the amount of exposure that makes a substance a poison and the right dose differentiates a poison and remedy'. This statement becomes the basis for 'dose response relation'. The lower doses of the chemical cause mild effects whereas high doses may cause serious and long lasting effects. If dose is administered through mouth, or applied on the skin, or into the respiratory tract, transport across the membranes may be identical with the dose administered. In environmental exposures, an estimate of the dose can be made from the measurement of environmental and food concentrations as a function of time, and involves the assessments of food intake rate of inhalation and, the deposition and retention factors.

The doses in the tissues and organs may be estimated from:

(a)   intake or administered dose,

(b)   assessment of concentrations in samples of tissues and organs and

(c)   measurement of concentration in excreta or exhaled air.

However, estimation of dose by these methods depends on time taken for transport, absorption, distribution, retention, biotransformation and excretion of the chemical or it metabolites when the site of action is very near to the site of application, then the time concentration estimate may be quite reliable. But when the site of action is located away, as the liver cells, then the estimates of dose may not be reliable. The presence of a chemical in low or high concentration in the blood indicates absorption. However, the blood concentration of a toxic chemical depends on several other factors such as rate of absorption, distribution, tissue storage, metabolic transformation and excretion.

Toxicity Test (LC_{50} / LD_{50})

White evaluating the safety of the chemical substances it is essential to know a precise of expressing the toxicity and quantitative method of measuring it.

Toxicity tests are experiments designed to evaluate dose/concentrations of toxicants and the dilution of exposure required to produce a criterion effect. Usually, the criterion of effect may be death of the exposed animals. The effects produced by a chemical in laboratory animals can be used to predict the possible effects on human beings.

Bioassays: The aquatic tests are frequently referred to as bioassays. Bioassays may be defined as a 'test in which the quantity or strength of the material is determined by the reaction of a living organism to it.

The effects produced by a chemical in laboratory animals can be used to predict the possible effects on human beings. The toxicity tests may be used to evaluate relatively safe doses for human beings.

Terminology: Some terms used in toxicity are given below:

(i) **Acute:** Involving a stimulus, severe enough to bring about a response, usually within four days (96 hours) for fish.

(ii) **Cronic:** Involving a stimulus, which is lingering or continuous for a long time, after covering considerable part of the life (e.g. 30 days).

(iii) **Lethal:** Causing death by direct action.

(iv) **Sublethal:** Below the level which directly death.

(v) **Cumulative:** Increased in strength, by successive addition at different times or in different ways.

(vi) **Lethal Concentration (LC):** LC is used to express the results of toxicity tests having leathality as the criterion of toxicity. A numerical is used with it, for example, LC_0, LC_{10}. LC_{50}, LC_{100}, to indicate the percentage of test animals killed at a given concentration of the test material. The time of exposure is also indicated, for example, 24 hrs., LC_{50} 96 hrs., LC_{50}, 10 day LC_{50}.

(vii) **Median Lethal Concentration (LC_{50}):** The median lethal concentration is the usual method of reporting results. The current trend is to use the symbol LC_{50}. For example, the 90 hrs. LC_{50} is the concentration of a substance that is lethal to 50% of the test animals in 96 hours.

(viii) **Median Lethal Dose (LD_{50}):** It means the amount of drug or toxicant, which is actually received inside the body, for example, by injection or by eating; and which is lethal to 50% animals.

(ix) **Median Tolerance Limit (TLm):** In early times of acute toxicity tests, data was expressed as the median tolerance limit (TLm or TL_{50}). The test material concentration at which 50% of the test organisms survive for a specified exposure times (usually 24 to 96 hours). This term has now been replaced by median lethal concentration (LC_{50}) and median effective concentration (EC_{50}). In other words TL_{50} is the same as LC_{50}, but TL_{10} is equivalent to LC_{90} and TL_{90} to LC_{10}.

(x) NOEC: Its full form is No Observed Effect Concentration or no effect concentration. This is maximum concentration of the test material that produces no statistically significant harmful effect on test organisms as compared to control in a specific test.

(xi) LOEC: Its full form is Lowest Observed Effect Concentration or MTC (Minimum Threshold Concentration), which is the lowest that has a statistically significant deleterious effects on test organisms compared to control in a specific test.

Types of Toxicity Tests: These test are performed at three levels.

Single species test, multi-species tests and ecosystem tests can be conducted in laboratory.

Acute Toxicity Test: 'Severe effects experienced by the organisms during short-term exposure to toxicants' is called acute toxicity. It provides rapid estimates of dose/concentration of test chemicals producing deleterious effects on a group of test organisms during short tern exposure under controlled laboratory conditions.

Test Animals and Chemicals: This test can be conducted in aquatic and terrestrial animals.

(a) Exposure system: Different exposure systems are used like (i) static system, (ii) Renewal system and (iii) flow through system.

(b) Diluent water: Aquatic toxicity tests are conducted by dissolving chemicals in water.

(c) Conducting tests: Following steps are used:

(i) Determination of physico-chemical characteristics of water like pH, DO, hardness, temperature etc.

(ii) Use glass aquaria or troughs for tests. Transfer the test animals to the test and control solutions usually after 1 hour of addition of test chemicals. Select dose range.

(d) Feeding: The feeding of test organisms are usually avoided during test. If test period is long then feeding is required.

(e) Duration: Acute toxicity test is normally conducted upto 96 hours.

(g) Biological data: Usually death is the criterion of effect considered for acute toxicity test, in such cases, the toxicity is conventionally represented in terms of LC_{50}.

In case of acute toxicity tests in terrestrial animals, rats and mice selected for the study. Toxicant generally administered in the form of injection. Volatile chemicals are exposed in vapour form to evaluate inhalation toxicity. Some chemicals are applied on the certain parts of the body of organisms. In some cases, animals may be dipped in the test solution. The toxicants is mixed with the feed and fed to the animals.

(h) Doses and number of animals: For evaluation of acute toxicity (LD_{50}) four or five doses of test chemical are exposed to test animals. Generally, 10 test animals are used for each concentration. If chemical is highly toxic then doses can be given in ppm (parts per million) or ppb (parts per billion) or mg/l, μg/l.

Observations: During the period of toxicity testing the behaviour of the organisms should be recorded. Mortality is recorded after every 24 hours until the end of the test.

The results of acute toxicity tests are represented in terms of LC_{50} or LD_{50}. But in case of some invertebrates (e.g. Daphnia, midge larva etc.) death is not easily determined and criterion of effect is immobilization which is defined as lack of movement. In this case, the results of toxicity test is determined in terms of EC_{50} (median effective concentration). Acute toxicity tests provide rapid estimates of dose/concentration of test chemicals that cause direct irreversible damage to the organisms.

Calculation of LC_{50} or LD_{50}

LC_{50} values calculated by two methods.

1. Graphic Interpolation Method

A graph is plotted between the doses/concentrations of toxicant and per cent mortality of organisms observed at each dose. The obtained curve is known as dose mortality curve. The exact dose or concentration is read as 50% morality and this is reported as LD_{50} or LC_{50} for the particular exposure duration under certain set of laboratory conditions. For the initial test measurement in toxicological evaluation it is in practice to use mortality/lethality as an index for LC_{50} or LD_{50} determination. It is useful for finding the potency of a chemical.

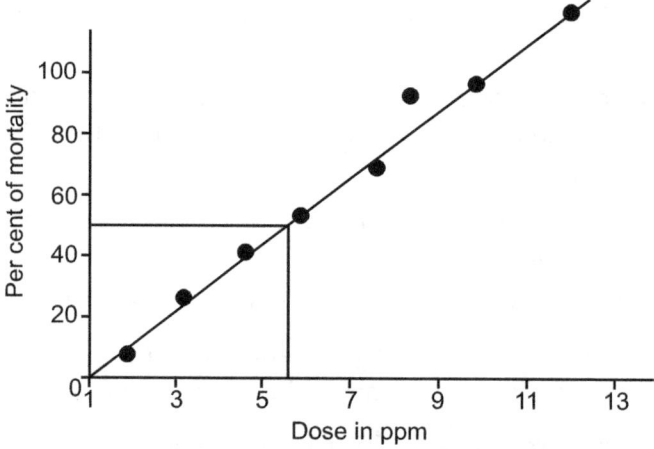

Fig. 7.1: Dose Mortality Curve

2. Probit Mortality Curve

It is another method for calculation of LC_{50}. In this method, the logarithmic values are read for each concentration/dose exposed and probit values are read for the per cent of mortality. Then the graph is plotted between logarithmic dose/concentration and the probit mortality. The curve so obtained is called probit mortality curve.

From this curve the values of expected probits are read and then corrected probits are calculated by the formula given by Finney (1971) to finally calculate LC_{50} or LD_{50} values.

In chronic toxicity test, the effects of chemical are observed over prolong periods either to entire life cycle or to a particular stage. In this test, sensitive stage in the life cycle is assessed. This test can give idea about safe level of toxicants.

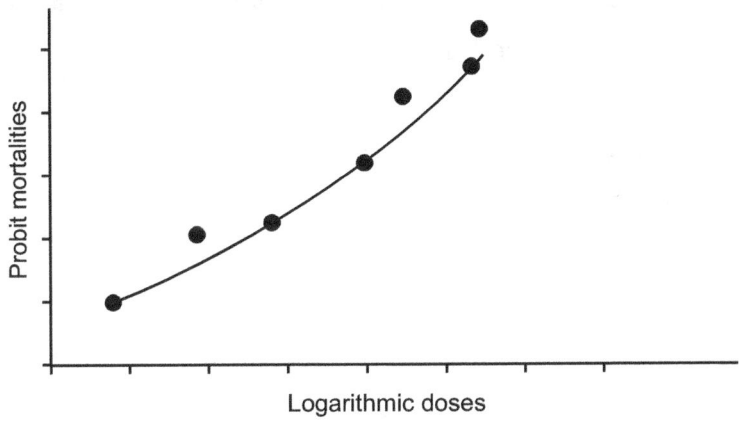

Fig. 7.2: Probit Mortality Curve

Points to Remember

- Toxicology is study of adverse effects of chemicals on living organisms.

- In toxicology, we can study the poisons, their sources, characteristics, properties, mechanism of action, signs and symptoms, lethal dose, causes of death, treatment etc.

- Doses are acute or chronic.

- Adverse effects depend on two main factors namely route of exposure and dose.

- Testing methods are of two types namely *in-vivo* and *in-vitro*.

- Forensic toxicology, clinical toxicology, pharmacological toxicology, toxinology, computational toxicology are the different branches of toxicology.

- One can select toxicology as a profession.

- There are different types of toxicants; namely, carcinogens, mutagens, teratogens, allergens, neurotoxins and endocrine disrupters.

- Factors which influencing toxicity are pH, temperature, reproductive status, age, physiological state.

- Bioassay tests are carried out for determination of lethal dose.
- Bioassay test are conducted by static system or by renewal system.
- LC_{50} values can be calculated by graphic interpolation method or by probit mortality curve.

Questions

1. Define the term toxicology, comment upon factors that influence chemical toxicity, testing methods.

2. Define toxicant and give an account of different types of toxicants.

3. Describe the factors which influence the toxicity.

4. What is dose? Give an account of LD_{50} and LC_{50}.

5. What is toxicity test? Describe the methods used in/different types of toxicity test.

6. How LC_{50} values are calculated?

Chapter 8...

Toxicants of Public Health and Hazards

Contents ...

8.1 Pesticides

In modern days, a large number of pesticides and insecticides are used. Many pesticides persist in the environment for long time and remain accumulated in the vital tissues of animals. Which ultimately go into the body of human.

Following are the important types of pesticides and cause toxicity to non-target organisms including man:

(1) Organophosphate insecticides: There are esters of phosphoric acid (Dichlorvos) and theophosphoric acid (Parathion). There are many organophosphorus insecticides like malathion, Sumithion, Diazinon, Dimethoate etc. Their toxic effects vary over a wide range. They act by inhibiting acetylcholinesterase (AchE). As a result, the accumulated acetylcholine (Ach) includes tremor, in co-ordination and convulsion. Muscle contraction, loss of reflexes and paralysis are symptoms. These toxicants may cause delayed neurotoxicity.

(2) Organochlorine Insecticides: There are chlorinated ethane derivations, such as DDT, methoxychlor, cyclodines such as endrin, aldrin, dieldrine, heptachlor, mirex, BHC, lindane. These are highly toxic chemicals. They stimulate nervous system and induce irritability, tremor, loss of equilibrium and convulsions. Some affect neurotransmitter activity. These chemicals are stored in fatty tissues.

(8.1)

(3) **Carbamate Insecticides:** This includes Carbaryl, (Sevin), Aldicarb, Carbofuran, Methomyl etc. They also inhibit AchE, but it is readily reversible.

(4) **Herbicides:** 2, 4-D. (2, 4-dichlorophenoxy-acetic acid), Paraquat, Diaquat are commonly used herbicides. They retard growth of weeds by inhibiting photosynthesis, respiration and cell division. Their toxicity in animals is relatively low. Some causes lung damage after inhalation. Also cause hemorrhage fibrosis.

(5) **Rodenticides:** Thioureas, Warfarin, Sodium fluoroacetate are commonly used rodenticides. They are highly toxic to rats.

(6) **Fungicides:** The effective fungicides are methyl and ethyl mercury. They cause permanent neurologic damage and deaths. They are widely used in agriculture and some of them are reported to have carcinogenic effects.

8.2 Heavy Metals

There are number of toxic heavy metals present in the environment. Metals of major toxicological concern are Lead, Mercury and Cadmium.

Lead (Pb): It is found in soil (5–25 mg/kg), ground water (1–60 µg/l), and in air below 1 µg/m^3. In most people, the lead intake from food is 100–300 µg/day. In some countries, average lead levels in the blood of children have been found 4–6 µg/100 ml. It is deposited in bones and released from mothers bones to the blood reaching fetus. It inhibits synthesis of heme. It causes anemia, induces fragality of erythrocyte membrane. Lead poisoning of children is a matter of serious concern. Lead acts on nervous system and encephalopathy may occur. Children may show hyperactivity, low attention span and decreased IQ. It also cause renal failure after long term exposure.

Mercury: It affects nervous system and small babies are more sensitive to its adverse effects. Through food chain there is accumulation of mercury in fishes (200–1000 µg/kg). Mercury poisoning occurs due to fungicide or fish contaminated with methyl mercury and causes effects on nervous system. Symptoms are ataxia, deafness, dysarthria and eventually death may occur. Mercury is also used in filling dental cavities. That may also cause mercury poisoning. The amalgam is linked to arthritis, multiple sclerosis and mental disorders.

Cadmium: Its level is raised by smelting and industrial uses. Food grains and cereal products are the main sources of cadmium. Cigarette smoking is leads to exposure of cadmium. It is accumulated in liver and kidney. Cadmium poisoning in Japan has once resulted in *itai itai* disease, which was due to eating of rice produced from soil containing very high levels of cadmium.

Hypertension and prostate cancer are common in occupational workers.

Other Metals: Arsenic, Beryllium, Nickel and Selenium are also toxic cause serious problems, such as skin and lung cancers. Nasal cancer and cancers of kidney, lung and stomach are due to Nikel. Selenium causes hair loss, nail pathology and teeth decay. It also induces liver necrosis, anemia, disorders of reproductive function of erythrocytes.

8.3 Fertilisers

Several artificial fertilisers are used in modern agriculture for the purpose of getting more yield. Fertilisers containing nitrates and phosphates are more in use in agriculture. Some of these are washed off the agricultural fields through irrigation, rainfall and drainage into nearby rivers and ponds where they affect aquatic ecosystem.

Excessive use of fertilisers often leads to accumulation of nitrates in water. If such contaminated water is used by the animals, these nitrates are reduced to toxic nitrates by their intestinal bacteria. Nitrates are responsible for serious disease called methaemoglobinameia or blue baby disease in rural areas. The nitrates, which are soluble in water, tricle down through layers of soil into deeper layers of earth and ultimately contaminate underground water. Babies are very sensitive to this pollutant. These nitrates damage respiratory and vascular system even cause suffocation.

Artificial fertilisers or plant nutrient are water pollutants. Nitrogen, phosphorus and potassium are essential elements for plants and animals for growth and metabolism. Nitrate make water unfit for drinking and cause diseases. Several children died due to nitrate poisoning. They also cause gastric cancer. Plant nutrients also contribute to eutrophication, which leads to depletion of oxygen due to excessive algal growth. It leads to death of fish and aquatic organisms.

8.4 Food Additives

Food additives are the substances which are added to food to preserve flavour or enhance its taste and appearance. Some additives have been used for centuries, for example, preserving food by pickling (with vinegar), salting, as with bacon, preserving sweets or using sulfur dioxide as with wines. With the advent of processed foods in the second half of the 20th century, many more additives have been introduced of both natural and artificial origin.

To regulate these additives, and inform consumers, each additive is assigned a unique number, termed as 'E numbers' which is used in Europe for all approved additives. E numbers are all prefixed by 'E', but countries outside the Europe use only the number, whether the additive is approved in Europe or not. For example, acetic acid is written as E 260 on products sold in Europe, but is simply known as additive 260 in some countries. There are large number of additives used in the world, such as acids (vinegar, citric acid, tartaric acid, malic acid, fumaric acid and lactic acid). Some are acidity regulators, anti-craking agents, antifoaming agents, antioxidants (Vitamin C), bulking agents, food colouring, colour retention agents, emulsifiers, flavours, flavour enhancers, glazing agents, humectants, Tracer gas, preservatives, stabilizers, sweeteners, thickeners etc.

With the increasing use of processed foods since the 19th century there has been a great increase in the used food additives of varying levels of safety. This has led to legislation in many countries regulating their use. For example, boric acid was widely used as a food preservative from 1870s to the 1920s but was banned after World War I due to its toxicity, as demonstrated in animal and human studies. In America, Carcinogenic substances are not allowed to use as food additives. Some mix additives commonly found in children's food increase level of hyperactivity. The artificial colours and sodium benzoate preservatives are also problematic for children. Some artificial food additives have been linked with cancer, digestive problems, neurological conditions, heart disease or obesity. Natural additives may be similarly harmful or be the cause of allergic reactions in certain individuals. For example, safrole was used to flavour rootbeer until it was shown to be carcinogenic.

Blue 1, 2, Red 3 and yellow 6 are food colouring that have been linked to various health risks in animal models. Blue 1 cause cancer in mice, Blue 2 cause brain tumor in mice and Red 3 cause thyroid tumours in mice.

There are many food additives which are hazardous to human health and it is better to avoid them.

(1) **Artificial sweetners:** Aspartame (E 951) is found in foods labeled diet or sugar free. It is believed to be carcinogenic neurotoxic. It affects short term memory, also causes brain tumour, diseases like lymphoma, diabetes multiple sclerosis, Parkinson's, Alzheimer's, emotional disorders like depression and anxiety attacks dizziness, headaches, mental confusion.

(2) **High Fructose Corn Syrup:** It is found in almost all processed foods. It is the good source of calories in America. It increases LDL (bad) colesterol levels and also contributes to the development of diabetes. Found in bread, candy, flavoured yogurt, canned vegetables cereals.

(3) **Monosodium Glutamate (MSG / E 621):** It is an amino acid used as a flavour enhancer in soups, salad, dressing, chips, etc. It is known as an excitotoxin, a substance which overexcites cells to the point of damage or death. Regular consumption results in adverse side effects like depression, disorientation, eye damage, fatigue, headache and obesity. It is found in Chinese food, manl, snaks, chips, frozen dinners and lunch meats.

(4) **Trans Fat:** It enhance and extend the life of food. But it is very dangerous. It increases bad cholesterol and decreases good cholesterol (HDL), increases the risk of heart attacks, heart diseases and other health problems.

(5) **Common food dys:** Blue 1, Blue 2 are banned in Norway, Finland and France. They may cause chromosomal damage. Found in candy, cereals, soft drinks, sports drink and pet food.

   Red dye 3 cause thyroid cancer and chromosomal damage in laboratory animals. Found in fruit cocktail, ice-cream, candy, bakery products.

(6) **Potassium Bromate:** Additive used in bread, rolls. It is known to cause cancer in animals.

(7) **Sulfur Dioxide (E 220):** Sulfur additives are toxic and are banned in USA for their use in fruits and vegetables. They cause branchial problems, hypotension, destroys vitamins B_1 and E. It is found in beer, soft drinks, dried fruit, juices, wine, vinegar and potato products.

(8) **Sodium nitrate/nitrite:** Used as preservatives, colouring and flavouring in bacon, hain, hot dogs, lunch meats, corned beef, smoked fish. It is highly carcinogenic toxic. It is colour fixer. Dead meat appears fresh.

8.5 Radiation Pollution

Radiation is a part of man's environment. In its broadest sense, radiation is energy being propagated from one place to another place. The radiation that is of concern as pollution is ionising radiation, radiation of sufficiently great energy to ionize atoms and molecules. The sources of radiation to which man is exposed are dived into two groups: natural and man made.

(A) Natural Sources: Man is constantly exposed to natural radiation from time immemorial. Following are the natural sources of radiation.

(a) **Cosmic rays:** These originate in outer space but they become weak while travelling through the atmosphere. At ordinary living altitudes, their impact is about 35 m rads a year. At altitudes above 20 km cosmic radiation becomes important. It has been calculated that a commercial jet pilot receives about 300 m rad per year from cosmic radiation.

(b) **Environmental sources**

1. **Terrestrial radiation:** Radioactive element such as thorium, uranium, radium and an isotope of potassium (K^{40}) are present in man's environment, e.g. soil, rocks and buildings. Man receives about 50 m rads per year from terrestrial radiation. Kerala beach sand has thorium and rock contains uranium.

2. **Atmospheric radiation:** Radioactive gases radon and thoron also cause radiation.

Table 8.1: Sources of Radiation Exposure

Natural	Man-made
1. **Cosmic Rays**	1. Medical and dental: X-rays, Radioisotopes.
2. **Environmental:** (a) **Terrestrial** (b) **Atmospheric**	2. Occupational Exposure
	3. Nuclear: Radioactive falls out
3. **Internal** Potassium^{-40} Carbon^{-14}	4. Miscellaneous: Television Sets Radioactive Dial Watches, Isotope Tagged Products Luminous Markers

(c) **Internal radiation:** The radioactive matter stored in the body tissue causes internal radiation. Uranium, thorium and related substances and isotopes of potassium (K^{40}), strontium (Sr^{90}) and carbon (C^{14}) cause the internal radiation about 25 to 80 m rads.

(B) Man Made Sources: In addition to natural radiation, man is exposed to artificial or man-made sources. They are:

(a) **X-rays:** Medical procedures are the major source of artificial radiation, exposure. Medical and dental X-ray examinations in which both patients and radiologists are exposed to this radiation. It gives about 300 rems exposure over part of the body.

(b) **Radioactive fallout:** Nuclear explosions release a tremendous amount of energy in the form of heat, light and ionising radiations.

The important isotopes being those of Carbon (C^{14}), Iodine (I^{131}), Cesium (Cs^{137}) and Strontium (Sr^{90}). Cs^{137} and Sr^{90} are very important as they are liberated in large amounts and remain radioactive for many years. The *'half life'* of Sr^{90} is about 28 years and that of Cs^{37} is 30 years. These radioactive particles released into the atmosphere float down to earth for some years afterwards. Because, of air currents, the particles are distributed fairly over a large area.

(c) **Miscellaneous:** There are a number of other everyday sources of artificial radiation. Some everyday appliances such as T. V. sets, luminous wrist watch, etc. are radioactive. But radiation from these sources at present is negligible.

8.5.1 Types of Radiation

The term 'ionizing radiation' is applied to radiation which has the ability to penetrate tissues and deposit its energy within them. Ionizing radiation may be divided into two main groups:

(i) **Electromagnetic radiation:** X-rays, and gamma rays.

(ii) **Corpuscular radiations:** Alpha particles, beta particles, electrons and protons. Alpha particles are 10 times as harmful as X-rays, beta particles or gamma rays. Alpha particles have little penetrating power. However, if the radioactive substance has entered in the body by inhalation or through a wound the alpha particles can be very dangerous.

Radiation Units: The potency of radiation is measured in three ways:

1. **Rad:** Rad is the unit of absorbed dose. It is the amount of radioactive energy absorbed per gram of the tissue or any material.

1 mini rad = 0.001 rad.

2. **Rontgen:** It is the unit of exposure. It is the amount of radiation absorbed at a given point, i.e. number of ions produced in 1 ml of air.

3. **Rem:** Rem is the product of the absorbed dose of the modifying factors. It indicates the degree of potential danger to health.

8.5.2 Biological Effects of Radiation

The effects of ionizing radiation can be grouped into two types: Somatic effects and Genetic effects.

1. **Somatic Effects:** A dose of 400 to 500 rontgens on the whole body is fatal in about 50% of cases, and high dose of 600 to 700 rontgens is fatal in every case. While blood corpuscles are affected by a dose of 25 to 50 rontgens, the dose also produce mild lassitude and softening of the muscles. The delayed effects takes time to develop and the time required is a few weeks to years. Leukaemia, foetal developmental abnormalities, malignant tumours and shortening of life and the delayed effects of ionizing radiation.

2. **Genetic protection:** Radiation also causes genetic effects which are manifested in the offspring. Radiation causes damage to chromosomes, resulting into chromosome mutation and point mutations. Chromosome mutation is associated with sterility. Point mutation affects the genes.

Radiation Protection

(1)   Man made radiation should not exceed 5 rads a year.

(2)   Unnecessary X-ray examinations should be avoided, particularly in case of pregnant women and children.

(3)   Radiologists, X-rays technicians should use lead shields and lead rubber aprons.

(4)   Workers must wear a film badge or dosimeter which shows accumulated exposure to radiation.

(5)   Periodical medical examinations.

8.5.3 Nuclear Accidents

The radioactive substances are hazardous and injurious to human beings. These substances in the forms of waste are released in the environment either as gases, liquids or solids. Generally, nuclear power plants are designed in such a way that there is no leakage of radioactive substances. However, no nuclear plant is hundred per cent safe as many nuclear disasters have occurred in different places in the world. The best known examples of nuclear accidents are Three Mile Island nuclear power plant leakage in U.S.A. in 1979 and Chernobyl nuclear power plant in USSR in 1986. These accidents caused escape of radionuclides in atmosphere.

The Chernobyl Disaster: This disaster occurred in Ukraine (USSR) and has significantly highlighted the dangers of nuclear radiation. It was one of the largest power plants in USSR. On April 26th 1986, one of the clusters of four power reactors got overheated and is reported to have melted. As a result, radioactive material from this reactor evaporated and spread into the atmosphere. Places as far as Eastern Europe were soon showered with radioactive dust. It is the biggest disaster in the history of nuclear power generation resulting in the death of 31 persons in the vicinity and affecting a large population which was exposed to radiation. According to some estimates, over 6000 additional deaths are likely from cancer, over the next 70 years. Large areas of USSR were contaminated and this accident compelled to evacuate and resettlement of about 2,00,000 people. Moreover, many countries of USSR have to pay the substantial costs for decontamination and health care due to this serious accident. Because of wind currents the clouds of radioactive nuclides have spread in Belorussia, Poland and Sweden where maximum radiation was detected. After explosion of reactor, fire fighters bombarded 5000 tonnes of shielding material containing lead, boron, sand and clay. After this horrifying accident the remaining reactors 1, 2 and 3 were restarted in November 86 and December 87.

Nagasaki and Hiroshima (Japan): During the Second World War on August 6, and August 9, 1945, United States Army Air Force plane released an Atomic bomb on Hiroshima and Nagasaki. It was a deliberate attack on Japan, almost both the cities were ruined and millions of people died and injured. The world had experienced the destructive power of atom bomb during the Second World War. Thus, manufacturing of nuclear bombs is nothing but the grave yards, dug out by man for himself. In future, there is fear of III World War and it will be nuclear war in which whole world and the entire biological community including human beings will be destroyed within no time. Therefore, it is high time for human beings to think seriously about the use of nuclear power for peace and not for war.

Points to Remember

- There are different types of toxicants present in the environment.
- They are pesticides, Heavy metals, fertilisers, food additives and radioactive substances.
- Pesticides are of three types namely, organophosphates, organochlorine pesticides, carbamate pesticides.
- Lead, Mercury, Cadmium, Arsenic, Nickel, Selenium are toxic metals cause different diseases in man and animals.
- Nitrates are responsible for methaemoglobinameia or blue baby disease in rural areas.
- Food additives are substance which are added to food to preserve flavour or enhance its taste and appearance.
- Food additives are used in a large scale due to increasing use of processed food.
- Artificial Sweetners, High fructose corn syrup, monosodium glutamate, trans fat, food dyes, Potassium bromate, sulfur dioxide, sodium nitrate etc are the important food additives.
- Radioactive substance such as Carbon (C^{14}), Iodine (I^{13}), Cesium (Cs^{137}) and strontium (Sr^{90}) are important.
- X-rays, gamma rays, alpha particles, beta particles, electrons and protons are also harmful.
- Red, Rontgen, Rem are the radiation units.
- Biological effects of radiation are Somatic effects and Genetic effects.

Questions

1. Which are the toxicants of public health and hazards? Describe in brief with their effects.
2. What are pesticides? Describe different types of pesticides with their harmful effects.
3. What are heavy metals? Describe their ill effects on human beings.
4. Describe fertilisers as a toxicant of public health.
5. What are food additives? Give an account of the food additives used in the processed food.
6. What are radioactive substances? Comment upon their harmful effects on human beings.
7. Write short notes on:
   (i) Biological effects of radioactive substances.
   (ii) Radioactive substances
   (iii) Nuclear accidents
   (iv) Pesticides
   (v) Heavy metals
   (vi) Fertilisers
   (vii) Food additives.

✱✱✱

www.ingramcontent.com/pod-product-compliance
Lightning Source LLC
Chambersburg PA
CBHW080906020726

47502CB00008B/2369